# JOSQUIN

## THE HEALER OF CASSICA

### BOOK I
### THE CASSICAN CHRONICLES

# MARTHA J. VAUGHT

Cassican Press, LLC

United States of America

Cassican Press, LLC
USA


Josquin: The Healer of Cassica
Book I
The Cassican Chronicles

Cover illustration by Danny O'Leary, www.Illustrationweb.com
Interior design by Anne Thompson, www.ebookannie.com

First printing 2018

Printed in the United States of America


Josquin: The Healer of Cassica/Martha J. Vaught
Library of Congress Control Number: 2018902924

ISBN  978-1-7321107-0-0 (pbk)
ISBN  978-1-7321107-1-7 (ebook)


Contact:
www.Cassicanpress.com
email: Martha@cassicanpress.com
Martha J. Vaught, Facebook

The use of paragraph dialogue format is intentional. – The Author

*For the One Who Heals me,*
*You have set my heart free....*

*The Edict of Byzanthia*

*...and as for the rebellious land, Heaven, itself, will mark your subjugation.*

*A daughter of Cassica will be born on the same date as the last son of Byzanthia. Before her seventeenth birthday, Cassica must surrender her daughter, as tribute, to Byzanthia's son, presented as the prisoner of war she is. And the son may ransom or kill The Tribute as he desires.*

*And so shall the terms of The Edict be, forever, satisfied....*

I

She had the look of someone expecting company. Company which, after five centuries in coming, was now four hours late. There was nothing more to do. So she sat, contemplating Soren, her mittens, her fear. It was her fear particularly that occupied her. It was late, much too late in the day. Her owner had made it clear: he would gather the woman this morning, deliver her to the guards, receive her and bring her to the chamber. They should arrive at lunch. Prepare a bath, he'd told her. Prepare food. Prepare herself. All she had attended. But there was no woman. Clarece fretted the shiny clasps on her new mittens: something was terribly wrong.

Afternoon faded and in its absence, the room assumed a familiar shade of cold. The slave shivered. Respectfully, she dismissed her purring companion to add coal to the fire. She must have the room warm for the princess. After a few minutes, she smiled, pleased, into the buttressed flame. She was always good with a fire. Clarece turned from the flame to the curtains. She should close them against the chill. She stood and took five steps. And stopped.

From outside, distantly as in the city, rose a cry that sounded all the world like a jousting match, cheers rising and falling as a wave. The woman turned cold: it was the princess; it must be. It must be the crowd responding to her - but why now? Why so late in the day? She went to the windows and gazed. She could see nothing, of course, except the lowering sun and the brownish, golden hues of winter coming. But in her imagination, she saw.

Anticipation is the hallmark of every good slave and Clarece was a good slave. She closed the curtains. She returned to her mittens and determinedly, shod her claws with them. Their new copper fasteners fitted well and worked cooperatively with her teeth. She turned next to the bed her mastra had made specially for the princess. It was positioned to face the sitting area - and the doorway of the pen. A heavy burgundy comforter graced it as did new linen sheets. Clarece paused only a moment then acted. She pulled back cover and sheets, placed the pillow and lit a candle. The candle she set on the princess' nightstand. She thought quickly. Warm room. Warm water. Readied bed. Drink. She should warm some wine.

She sensed his approach before she heard. "Slave!" The woman ran toward the voice that ascended the garden stairs. She unlatched the heavy brass lever and stepped aside as her mastra burst into the room. "*Crispus!*" she cried silently. In her owner's arms was borne a bludgeoned and broken form, dark and bloodied. Frantically, Bastien scanned the room. "The bed, mastra," someone told him.

Tenderly the prince lay the lifeless body into her bed, careful to position her upon her stomach, away from the gashes in her back, away from the blood. But it did no good. Blood was everywhere. It soaked his cape, it soaked her body, it soaked the air. He backed away and gazed at his hands. They ran with red. He assessed the sight. Never in life, even in battle, had he seen so much blood.

Bastien spun to his property. Her eyes dropped to the floor. "I'm going for the physicians. Help her." *Help her?* Clarece thought as her owner raced from the room. His door slammed behind him. *Help her?*

She looked fearfully at the girl. A slave does not approach a royal but she must. There was little royal about the princess now, however. Gently, she removed the prince's mantle. A wave of nausea rose threateningly. As a slave, Clarece had seen floggings beyond number, but never one of such deadly intent. They had flogged her clothed. What remained of her blouse clung to her body, the color of her flesh: red.

It was an easy thing, even for the handless woman, to remove the remnants of cloth. There was no place to put the bloodied pieces except her clean floor. Clarece shook her head. Clearly, the princess died. She could not help her, but perhaps she might comfort her. Many slaves had she comforted on their deathbeds. Quickly, she took the warmed water and began bathing the dark face, aware as she did of the girl's ragged, labored breaths. Black hair fell from a neat braid into wisps. These Clarece swept cautiously from cheek, nose, and mouth and carefully wiped the eyes of salt and the lips of dirt and blood. She sang softly, as she worked, a slavish song of comfort.

Once, when she was a little girl, Clarece had come upon a fox, newly dead. She'd always admired these foxes with red tails and faces, and now she was able to touch one and study it closely. As she wondered at its thick fur and smart nose, she smiled and wept together, saddened by the knowledge that the beautiful creature must be dead for her to enjoy it so. She imagined, as she examined him, a place where live foxes and little girls would play together.

Such was her feeling now, examining the foreign face and features as she washed. But what most truly held her interest was the jewelry around the girl's throat. It was the necklace about which all Byzanthia speculated and, indeed, it was as nothing she'd ever seen. Light poured from what looked to be stones but not light only. Color - blues and reds and golds pulsated with energy. It was somewhat frightening. They lived, these stones - they lived and died in their color. Even as she watched, light faded from one like a leaf falling from a tree, turning the stone into a blackened rock. All slaves knew what it was like to wear something about the throat. Clarece reached, mesmerized, for the light.

The brown eyes opened. They penetrated her own. Clarece fell to her knees. Slavishly she looked down. "Forgive me, your highness," she stammered, guilty. "Who are you?" a voice asked. Cassican. Clarece knew nothing of Cassican. Cautiously, she shook her head. "I don't speak..." The eyes closed in realization.

"Who are you?" the princess asked again, this time in Byzanthian. The slave bowed humbly. "I am Prince Bastien's slave - Clarece." She glanced towards his room. "He's gone for help, Princess." "'Clarece'," the Cassican smiled, weakly, "'The Morning Light.' What a beautiful name." Clarece stared, amazed at the princess' interpretation of her name; amazed even more at her bothering with it at such a time. "I am Casica," the girl continued. Her breath rattled deep within her chest.

Tears fell silently from the dark eyes. Clarece reached haltingly for a dark hand. Instinctively, the foreign woman grasp it, filling the slave, at once, with warmth. She looked vaguely at the one called Clarece. Her vision was fading. She must tell her, tell her before it was too late. "Clarece." "My lady?" "I must sleep...." She coughed. The slave winced as blood splattered the white pillow. "I'll look to die - but I'm not - not yet." Her voice turned desperate. It was a healer's greatest fear. "Don't let them bury me alive - I beg you. Not alive. My stones - they'll grow dark... fall from my neck. Then I'm dead. Please - my mother - she must have it. The necklace...." She fought for breath. Something horrific gurgled in her throat.

Clarece placed her other mitten on the hand. This was no fallen creature. This was a child - years younger than she, frightened and crying for her mother. The princess wept openly now - but not in pain. It was sorrow that filled her tears. She was dying. *She.* Life was dying, drowning in her own blood. "Lady?"

Casica couldn't see anymore. It was coming. Sleep flowed from the remaining stones. "Maman," she whispered. "Baba... tell them I tried...I...." And she was gone.

Clarece stared, breathless. The body that pain had wracked so pitilessly quieted in death's embrace. Thoughtlessly, a mitten wiped her running nose. "Princess?" she whispered. She caressed the still face. "Princess?" she asked again, panicking. *Dear, God,* she thought. This never was supposed to have happened. The prince had ransomed her. She touched the necklace again. Immediately, the haze that shrouded her thoughts cleared. She wasn't dead. She said - *Scads, what had she said?* The stones - that's what she'd said! As long as there was light in the stones, she lived.

The slave's mind raced. So the Cassican was bleeding to death. Clarece had often treated floggings - they were a slave's regular allotment. She spun from her knees for the pen stairs. She must get her bag. She found what she needed and raced up to the chamber in time to see a face she knew well. He was kneeling, speaking softly to the foreigner.

"Sergeant Poul...." The man jumped up. "Clarece," he choked, rubbing his eyes, "where's Bastien?" The slave offered a half-kneel. "He's gone for the physicians."

As in reply, Bastien's door slammed. Clarece went to her knees. "Cursed physicians!" a voice bellowed. The prince appeared, flushed and raging. He stared into his friend.

"The physicians - they refuse to come!" Bastien explained to no one particularly. "They say they're forbidden - ." He dropped his head, spent. He had left the physicians treating one of their own, lying unconscious on the floor from his anger. "Those sons of - ." "Bastien - ," the sergeant interrupted, "she's beyond the physicians. We need greater help." Bastien studied his hands. Her blood had dried. "Who?" he asked defeated. "The city monks? They can't possibly - ."

"A healer," a voice interrupted meekly. The prince looked down at the kneeling form. "A healer, mastra. Surely there must be more like her in her country - tis not far...." *What?!* thought the distraught man. *Was the slave suggesting - .* "Exactly!" interjected his friend. "I know the port - there's a healer there! We can go - tis almost night - ." Bastien stared dumbly at Poul but already his friend had him by the arm. Somewhere in the sergeant, a plan was developing.

The prince's traveling cloak materialized on his shoulders. Bastien blinked. It was his property speaking. "Go, mastra - I'll be with her." He nodded. "Don't let anyone in - ," he instructed. "And don't let her die." *As if I've power to prevent the one more than the other,* the slave thought. "Yes, my lord," is what she said, kneeling. She listened as the garden door closed. Steps raced down the stone stairway.

Clarece bowed her head to the floor. The tapestried rug felt stiff to her brow. *This must be a dream,* she thought. The rhythm of the clock; the smell of petals boiling on the brazier, the silence - it must all be a dream. She lifted her eyes. The silent form of Cassica's daughter lay in the bed. It wasn't a dream.

Slowly, Clarece rose from her knees. *"Don't let her die."* She looked from the lifeless body that somehow possessed life. "Don't let her die," she prayed softly. "Please." She reached for the canvas bag. It was time to work.

## II

The scent of mesinet leaves drenched the room so, it almost sickened her. Clarece studied her mittens, nervously. Gone was all their newness. Dark splotches stained them through and through. Darkness. All that lit the room was a single candle and the covered light of the brazier. She wanted it that way - wanted the room to appear as if all inside slept. She looked quickly about. God, she was afraid, so very afraid. Every door she had locked. *This is madness,* she thought. As if a locked door could conceal this ruse should someone knock. She chewed her thumb, anxiously watching the necklace. Every few minutes, it seemed, another stone would turn black. What took them so long? Most the night was gone.

Her head pounded, her hands hurt, her stomach growled. Earlier, someone had knocked on the slave's door - that she hadn't answered. It was Asla, probably; still, the less her stallmate knew of all this, the better. She examined, again, her handiwork. A layer of mesinet a good stite thick covered the bludgeoned back and shoulders of the girl. It seemed to have stanched the blood - either that or the Cassican had none left to lose. Scads! What a fearsome thing! The body never moved. The girl did not breathe - of that the slave was certain; still the stones - what was left of them, glowed. She lived. What kind of foreign power was this? In her nervousness, Clarece stood and prowled the room. Let the guards find her! she decided. Let them torture the truth from her body! Nothing - *nothing* could possibly undo her more than she already was undone.

She froze.

The brass handle of the garden door was moving. The woman watched as, silently, the locked door opened of its own volition. She would have screamed except to do so required breath and for the moment, that had abandoned her. Her eyes widened in terror. Bastien's cloak floated in from the night. It stopped, turned and stared at her. Two orbs of blue blazed from within the empty hood. The slave collapsed to her knees. Had she seen her own expression, she would have understood the question.

"Which one of you needs me more?" the cloak asked. Clarece swallowed. Numbly, she pointed towards the bed. The cloak removed and draped itself on a chair. Silently, the specter inside it went beside the still form. "M'Yat...."

Clarece blinked. She'd heard that word before. Her eyes adjusted to the scene. It was a woman who knelt in the candle's light. A woman whose head time had crowned with silver and girded about with a regal presence. *The queen!* she realized. Instantly, she lowered her head to the floor, cowering before the royal person. With her head down, she didn't see the woman kiss the girl's cheek. She heard her speak, though, quietly as a prayer, but the words were Cassican.

"Clarece." The slave started. How could she possibly know her name? "My... my lady?" "Get me a drink." The blond head rose slightly. She must have misunderstood. "A drink," the voice repeated. The queen wanted a drink? "What would Your Majesty like?" "Look at me, girl." Cautiously, the kneeling woman looked at the queen's throat. She would never dare meet a sovereign's eyes. Light burned beneath her blouse. The face grinned.

"I'm no majesty and I'm no lady. I'm a Berea. Get me anything with a bite - get me the bottle." The slave bowed and obeyed. She returned from Bastien's room with his bottle of scotch. Aberea still kneeled beside Casica. One hand she had placed upon the girl's head, the other she had under her body, placed over the stilled heart. She motioned for the mittened woman. With the head hand, she took the decanter and drank directly from it. Clarece's brows rose with surprise. She was handed the bottle. Aberea emitted a slight burp.

"You did this?" she asked, referring to the leaves. The slave nodded, embarrassed. "Mesinet... what an ingenious idea."

Silence. Aberea frowned at the kneeling woman. Slavery. What a disgusting practice. Would Byzanthia never outgrow this barbaric institution? Her frown lifted to a smile. The slave was reddening from her attention.

"Have a drink, child," she ordered. The blond head jerked. Never in her life had she tasted scotch. *Well*, Clarece reconsidered, *there was that one time in the north wing....* It was with difficulty she lifted the bottle to her lips. The drink filled her with a fiery jolt. "Thank you, great lady, Aberea," she coughed. The great lady reached again for the libation, laughing to herself. "Just Berea, great Clarece."

Berea took another draft. Casica's colors drained dangerously. The necklace couldn't maintain its hold. Perhaps if she had more color - but that wouldn't come for decades. The ancient healer considered the situation. There was only one thing to be done. To do so would be to violate the greatest trust. She took another drink. Life mattered more than honor.

"You're not going to like this," she murmured. Thoughtfully, she reached into her blouse and drew out her own shalonn. Clarece risked a look. This necklace was filled with color - not a single stone shone white, like a mosaic of stained glass. Instinctively, Berea scanned the room. Surely, there were no bees in this place. She broke her stones' connection and lay the necklace on her knee. "Alright, M'Yat," she whispered, "Now, I'm doing this for your own good - don't hurt me."

It was no small thing to remove another's life. Taking a deep breath, Berea reached for the princess' shalonn. Her own blazed upon her knee as she closed her eyes in concentration and pulled gingerly at the dying stones. She strained only a breath before the stones surrendered with a slightest pop. Casica's hand moved. Inside, her spirit tried frantically to rescue her necklace but couldn't.

Swift as light, the healer exchanged Casica's necklace for her own. The stones met and locked in a blazing white. Colors, much fewer in variation, filled the pebbles, and in response, the girl breathed one single, unlabored breath. The slave turned her eyes from the sight. "Would you wash this?" the healer asked, reverently handing Clarece the princess' necklace.

Clarece received the offering as she would the girl's soul. At once, the stones turned dark. She stared, amazed. In her claws was a pile of connected rocks. Simple pebbles. So much for the necklace's purported value. She went to the water basin and there worked at her task. Her mittens made for effective scouring cloths, and with effort and time, she successfully cleansed the stones of blood. She knelt before the great lady and returned the offering.

At Berea's touch, the stones flared into a collage of color. The woman sealed the necklace about her throat, smiling. She felt much better. This called for a drink. "What made you think of mesinet -," she asked swallowing, "floggings?" A nod. The healer snorted. "And your mittens?" she inquired casually. "What's inside them?"

Clarece winced. She clutched her claws protectively against her chest, shamed. "Want," she whispered, answering. A hand rested tenderly on her head. Suddenly, all the ache in her body dissolved. "Well," Berea observed kindly, "there's nothing wanting in your mind. You saved M'Yat's life. I thank you." The slave-woman said nothing so lost in the blessedness of relief was she. Berea frowned at what she felt. Much more than a metal collar burdened this bound woman.

"You're exhausted, child," she said. "'Tis time for rest." Clarece bowed her head, first at the order and then in drowsiness. Something was happening inside her. Slowly, her head lowered to the floor and in that posture of submission, she slept, cuddled in the grace of peace.

It was the smell of smoke that first roused her. Her owner's pipe filled her dreams, pleasantly, as it did the chamber. The scent flowed into her the realization he was home. Clarece's eyes jerked open, panicked - she must serve him. But the thought ended as abruptly as it came. Something was amiss. It was the legs of a chair she saw - not Asla's cot.

"Good afternoon, girl," a voice chirped. It was the great lady. "Good sleep, yes?" The slave looked up. The woman sat in a chair and used another as a footstool. Bastien's favorite ivory pipe hung seductively in her mouth. Her left hand rested on the princess' forehead; the right held a glass of something. It wasn't scotch: that flask was empty.

Clarece glanced down at herself. It was the floor on which she slept. A pillow - her owner's - lay where her head was, and a cloak - his - covered her heavily. *Scads!* she thought, surveying the scene. His pillow, his cloak. She'd be flogged! She glanced round again. *What are you thinking?!* she berated herself. As if this woman's smoking the prince's pipe and drinking his drink and her sleeping on his belongings were the worst things happening here. There was a *Cassican* sitting in her wing, for pony's sake - *two* Cassicans, but at least the one had permission. The other - *scads!* This was treason! Panicked she glanced to the closed curtains. Either the day was late or cloudy.

"Want a puff?" the Cassican asked. "Lady?" Berea grinned playfully to herself. "How 'bout a drink?" "*Lady?*" Berea laughed. "How 'bout some bread?" Clarece glanced up. "Tis on the table," Berea motioned. "There was knock at your door. I opened it and, behold, was there food. Quite the room service. You slaves must be coming up in the world."

Clarece shook her head. What did it matter. She'd be gutted anyway. She might as well have her belly filled for the taking. "Yes, my lady," she answered, dumbly, rising. She lay her owner's cloak over a chair. The pillow she didn't know what to do with so she placed it at the foot of the princess' bed. Berea had been busy during her sleep. A pile of mesinet leaves joined the bloody cloths. Casica's body was washed as best it could be.

Her trousers hung at the end of the bed. A burgundy belt of some sort was coiled on the nightstand. Clean, white cloth lay lightly on the beaten back. Patches of red stained it. The comforter covered the girl's lower body. "Bring your bread here," the great woman invited. "Have a seat." The slave offered a half-kneel and complied.

From the former footstool she studied Berea curiously. She was a tall woman, with a little black mixed in her silver hair. Her eyes seemed to laugh with themselves and, strikingly, shone in blue. A Cassican with blue eyes, how strange. Clarece had the impression that the clothes she wore - a black cotton shirt and brown simple vest - weren't her own. Her trousers were black. A dark belt with curious designs peeped from under her vest. In all

Berea would have appeared a commoner except for two things: her boots - high riding boots, richly made of expensive leather, and secondly, her demeanor. Confidence and majesty emanated from her. She was beautiful in her age and something about her sensuality reminded Clarece of someone else.

Berea let out a slow breath of tobacco. Three circles floated by her companion. "Kerkun blend," she observed to herself. "You may tell your prince he has excellent taste in tobacco." "Yes, lady," the slave answered. She would never tell him that.

"'Like my boots?" Clarece glanced up, surprised. "You can't have too comfortable a pair of boots," Berea was saying. "Hundred twenty-nine years I've been wearing boots - best I've ever owned." *One hundred twenty-nine?!* Clarece gaped. *Water the well,* she decided. Berea wished for conversation. She might as well humor the Cassican. This was all a dream anyway, and if it weren't, she'd be dead soon.

"You age beautifully, my lady," she announced. The dark face laughed. Finally, the girl was speaking. "Clean living, great Clarece," she declared, grinning mischievously, "clean living." The slave grinned now. Clearly, much of this woman's living hadn't been clean.

"Go ahead and ask." "Ask what, my lady?" "Anything." Clarece studied the silent form of the princess. "Will she live?" All playfulness left the healer's face. Tenderly, she caressed the black hair. "Ah, M'Yat," she cooed, "They beat the life from you, didn't they?" Clarece watched as silently, the woman wept. She said something more in Cassican. "She's strong, this one. She'll live," she answered, softly. "'Twill take time, but she'll recover - won't you M'Yat?"

Berea lowered her face to the girl's and kissed her. She whispered something that may have been a prayer. At no time did she remove her hand from the head. "You worry about your master," she said, returning her attention to Clarece. "He's well. He's filling my place at an inn in Port o'Hau." *Port o'Hau,* considered the slave. It was the nearest port in Cassica. "Your Sergeant Poul is well also." The slave's interest peaked. "He'll come for me this evening." "You're leaving?" Berea drew deeply of the pipe. "We think it best. Old man Ars wouldn't take it too kindly - finding an old Cassican crone like me here."

Clarece slumped. There was about Berea something refresh-
ingly comforting. Even the manner with which she responded
to the princess' injury calmed her. Clearly, Berea loved the girl;
yet, nothing about her manner spoke of resentment or anger
over what had happened. Perhaps having lived so long, she recognized the brevity of life and held it lightly in her hands. The
slave glanced at the lines about her blue eyes. Here was a woman
who laughed often. Clarece had read about women who laugh at
the future, so confident are they in life. This must be that kind
of woman. Her hand went to her collar. What would it be like to
live in confidence, in assurance. The word for which she sought
was 'joy'.

Clarece didn't realize that as she studied Berea, Berea studied
her. The slave bore the features of her kind: thin, powerful body
- straight as a tree and quiet as its shade. The tip of a scar crept up
her breastbone towards her neck. Silver bound her throat. Her
blond eye lashes and brows were sprinkled with sand as was her
hair, beautifully plaited in four strands. It must be long, decided
Cassica's healer: even with such complex braiding it hung below
her shoulders. But it was the girl's eyes that intrigued Berea most.
Though averted they shone sapphire blue. The black rings encir-
cling them deepened and faded with their owner's shifting mood.
Slowly, the great healer shook her head. There was something familiar about this woman. *Ridiculous*, she thought. Still, she rarely
forgot a face. It seemed she should remember this one.

"Have we ever met, child?" The slave looked up and away.
What a ridiculous question. "No, my lady. I would remember
you." Berea snorted. "And I *think* I'd remember you. Oh, well,
'guess I'm getting senile." Clarece made no response though she
doubted this woman ever would become senile. She fretted with
her mittens. She wasn't used to sitting for so long. Her mind assumed the activity lacking in body. It spun with questions.

Was the princess anything like this Berea? Was she kind or
would she wish vengeance for her torture? And if so, would she
take it out on a Byzanthian slave? Clarece drew in her hands protectively. Fear ruled every slavish heart; for people who had so
much to fear, it was the greatest master, the most pitiless owner.
Clarece often had reckoned that truest freedom had nothing to

do with a collarless neck and everything to do with release from dread. A single tear escaped her thoughts.

"Clarece." The voice was the same Berea had used when addressing Casica. The blond head dropped, blushing at her weakness. "You have nothing to fear, child," Berea continued softly. "You're safe. You won't be found out. And Casica won't harm you." She leaned forward now and took into her hands the mittens stained with the blood of Pelana's child. The slave started. Warmth and something she couldn't identify filled her. Berea's voice dropped to a whisper. "M'Yat is the most gifted of healers. She can provide what's wanting in these mittens. When she regains herself and when you trust her, ask. You can be whole again."

Perhaps it was the kindness; perhaps her fatigue; perhaps a dozen things, but at this statement, the bound woman surrendered slavish composure and wept. Her sobs labored as for one not used to crying. "I've never been whole," Clarece whispered. The healer sighed, certain this slave spoke truthfully. How could anyone stripped and flogged and collared know what it meant to be whole? Ironic, thought she, that this enslaved woman knew about herself what so many freemen in her own land didn't: we are, all of us, born shattered and bound.

Berea rose. She bid Clarece stand and held her in a warm, protective embrace. "Neither have I ever been whole," she ventured, "but God has a way of restoring what's missing, Morning Light. Yes? We're like pobbles - dead as dirt till He touches us." And then she began to speak over the young woman; the words were Cassican but comforted the slave, nonetheless. For a long time the slave and healer stood. Clarece couldn't remember the last time she'd rested in the presence of an older woman. The Cassican felt almost maternal. She *did* keep calling her child. Clarece sighed. One hundred twenty-nine years. Surely everyone was "child" compared to this timeless woman.

With time, the room darkened. Evening fell. Berea released her young friend and smiled into the sapphire eyes. Her hand was warm on Clarece's face. "I'm happy M'Yat will share your world, child," she winked. "You'll make quite the pair, I think. For *you* are a piece of work." She looked at the curtains and then to Casica. "Now to finish *my* work."

The slave watched as Berea unfastened (if that's what one could call it) the princess' necklace. Again she lay it on her knee. "If you'll permit me once more, your highness," she asked. This time there was no resistance; it wasn't *her* shalonn Berea removed. Swiftly, the healer replaced Casica's light upon her. The stones locked into place. The necklace resumed its normal colors but now with increased intensity. Berea smiled at the return of her own shalonn. They'd been together a very long time.

"Your necklace has many more colors than the princess'," Clarece observed. The healer took a dram of drink. "When you're old as I, there aren't many blanks left to fill," she answered playfully. She looked to the door. "He's coming." Berea gazed into the fair face; she wouldn't forget it. "Great Clarece, you've been grand company." She motioned to the princess. "Now, she'll sleep for days - she's not dead, so don't let anyone bury her. When she wakes, she'll be weak as a lie and hungry as a whore. And she'll be disoriented. She won't be thinking rightly, she might be reckless - so watch her. Yes?" The blond head bowed. "Yes, great lady." A soft knock sounded on the garden door. It was time to go. Reluctantly, Clarece gathered Bastien's cloak and placed it on the lady's shoulders.

Berea turned and smiled knowingly. Memory was sometimes premonition. "As for you, Clarece, remember what I said - once she regains herself and you trust her, ask." With this she pulled out from her strange belt a bronze piece. It was a Cassican kobo. "Your dash. It only spends in Cassica," she grinned, placing the small coin in a mittened claw. "Buy a drink in my house someday." Berea turned to Casica's bed and kissed the dark face. She lingered only a moment. Timing was critical for this venture to end successfully.

Clarece bowed as she opened the door, hoping to God it was Poul and not some guard who stood without. The great lady offered a final smile. "Remember...." She slipped into the darkness and disappeared as she had come: like a dream.

Clarece stood, waiting for the dream to waken. She held in her hand a Cassican coin. A Cassican princess slept not ten cubits from her. She breathed of the night air. Familiar Byzanthian scents filled her lungs as did reality, her mind.

Slowly, Clarece d'Bastien closed the garden door. It secured with a comforting click. She had read once that to close a door was to end a story. Something within her stirred restlessly. This one, she suspected, had only begun.

# III

Casica stood at her windows. Their view tugged invitingly, beckoning her visit the garden and its sleeping life. How she wished to run down the stone steps at her garden door. Wished to run upon the earth and nature of a land she did not know. Wished to run past it to a waiting ship and be ferried to her home mere leagues away. But she couldn't; even if she had the freedom to escape, she hadn't the strength. All her body ached - her tortured back and shoulders. Her lungs. Her heart. Her mind. The simple act of standing was an accomplishment attained only through the immense power of Berea. Most of what flowed in her veins wasn't blood at all, Casica knew. Though her body quickly would replenish her supply, it was Berea, her pure healing, that kept her alive.

She considered her bare feet. She wasn't yet supple enough this morning to reach her boots and the slave Clarece hadn't hands to shod her. Her feet were cold. She was never cold. *God, I'm a mess*, she thought. It wouldn't take long to recover, but for now that knowledge did nothing to fortify her. She was lonely and desperately confused. Berea must have bound her memory, for she could remember neither coming to the city nor the days in bed recovering. Bed. The ailing girl closed her eyes against a wave of vertigo. She should return to bed. She turned carefully and noticed, in the doorway of the staircase, the silent form of the slave. The blond head gazed to the floor, as always, awaiting permission to enter her superior's world. "Clarece," a tired voice invited. "Come."

The slave offered a slight kneel and approached. Absently, Casica wondered how she saw to get around with her eyes riveted as they were below. She allowed a wide berth for the princess to pass on her way to bed. "May I get you something to eat, Lady, or drink?" The Cassican shook her head. "You may tell me where Bastien is. I haven't heard him this morning." "He's with the king, I believe, Princess." Casica nodded again, sighing. Bastien was the only person she felt any connection with in this place. Of him, she had glimpses in her mind. She sat on her bed and closed her eyes. Strangely, Berea had left her these memories:

His touch she remembered best. How quickly he had come to her in the meadow. There she had kneeled, alone - except for Rigel, packed with the few possessions allowed her - and tried to assess her situation. It had been a hectic, exhausting week. First, there were the goodbye's, the endless goodbye's. At the end, she felt numb to them, so spent was she with the emotional strain. Then there was leaving Elespoir, her beloved home at the palace. For a night, she prayed alone in the palace chapel releasing all that was left in her - including hope of rescue. The past was coming for her and she must pack. That she did the next day, choosing carefully what she would bring with her - and leave behind.

For a long time she debated over a certain possession. For months she'd considered her beloved armill. Fashioned from the same pobbles as her shalonn, the bracelet was as much a part of her as the glowing stones about her neck. Yet no amount of arguing with herself could dissuade the irrational conviction within: leave it, it said. But why? Her entire life was being taken from her. Why not keep this piece of her heart? Time for debating had expired. She must decide and she did.

Resolutely, Casica broke the seal of light and took the jewelry from her wrist. She laid it in its box and paused for just a moment - memorizing the feel and sight of the pobbles. She removed her hands and watched as, instantly, the light blackened into a collection of lifeless stones. The box she closed and propped lovingly against her dresser mirror. She looked now at her own reflection. The girl in the mirror wept with her and reflected perfectly the anguish she felt. It would be the last time she saw herself as she was: after the morrow, she would be forever changed.

When next she wore a bracelet, she was kneeling in a Byzanthian meadow. The bracelet was made of leather, by her own father's hands formed. Instinctively, she fretted with her bound wrists behind her back. Baba had tied them loosely, for it wasn't the leather that held them in place. It was the edict. That ancient pact was what brought her to this land and held her now. She was no longer the princess of Casica, but the slave of Byzanthia. Soon she would be surrendered to the king's guard as the prisoner of war she represented. The edict required a woman, for a country was feminine. It required a prisoner, for Cassica, Byzanthia had conquered hundreds of years before. It required the king's youngest son to receive her, for a captive as inferior as a Cassican didn't merit the attention of a crowned prince.

So she knelt, feeling as excruciatingly vulnerable in spirit as she was in body: bound, gagged, blindfolded, and hooded. She listened for any sound at all but could hear only her heart, pounding wildly. She tried to comfort herself, again, with what little knowledge she had of Byzanthia's prince, Bastien. He was kind, she was told. He had arranged for her "ransom" from abuse. Yet, how could she know? How could she know anything about the man who would have her? She knelt on enemy soil. Who could know what this son of a conquering king might do upon her defenseless estate?

She flexed her toes in nervousness, feeling the cool earth beneath her bare feet. A hawk shrilled above; she lifted her face to the call and with her breath, captured the rich scent of autumn come. It smelled like home. She smiled into her gag and breathed of hope. It was then she heard it, to her left: an approaching horse. He was coming, the fifth son of Ars, King of Byzanthia. The cadence of hooves stole her breath. Baba had relinquished her to a greater Father, and it was to Him she now prayed frantically.

"Whoa," a deep voice ordered quietly. He leapt from the saddle and tentatively approached. He could see her chest move with quick breaths; of course she would be frightened. The man squatted beside her and spoke before ever touching her. "Princess Casica," he said kindly. It was the kindness in his tone that calmed her.

"I'm Bastien. I'll more properly introduce myself later, but until then, I want you to know, you're safe. I won't hurt you in any way. Do... do you understand?" She nodded. It seemed her prayers were answered. "Good!" the man replied, scanning the meadow around them. He was smiling, she could tell.

And he was.

Though Bastien hated his role in this barbaric ritual, the truth was, after so many months of preparation, he thrilled at her arrival. For years he'd been anticipating knowing this woman fate destined for him and hoped, desperately, for a mutual interest. He looked again at her. It was almost done. All was arranged. He need only deliver her, receive her and strive with heaven for the best. He noticed her dark feet. She must be cold, unvested and barefoot as she was. Quickly, he removed his cloak and draped it around her. "Can you stand?" he asked. Another nod. He helped her rise, and as he fastened his mantel about her, shook his head in surprise. She was *tall*, this Cassican woman, almost as tall as he.

Bastien paused to gaze into the hood but could see nothing. *What do you look like?* he wondered. The one on the hood's other side wondered the same thing and wished, at the moment, she'd disobeyed and kept her eyes open under her father's kerchief that blindfolded her. Their shrouded observance he ended with a question, touching in its forthrightness. "Are you very afraid, Casica?" The hood turned away; in pride she almost shook her head but something of his tone allowed her vulnerability. He nodded with her.

"I am too," he confessed. "This isn't the way I would choose - anymore than you. Tis frightening not to be in control of one's life." He placed a hand on her shoulder. His touch was awkward but safe. Bastien had rehearsed this meeting a thousand times, but now all his practiced words abandoned him. He spoke more comfortably with action.

"Curse this edict," his heart voiced, "This is no way to treat you." He looked about at the meadow and glanced at the clouding sky. "Well," he thought aloud, "the sooner we start this, the sooner it'll end. You must be tired. There's a warm bed and good food awaiting you, Princess. You have your own room - I made it for you, myself." The hood cocked, surprised. Her own room? Perhaps there was nothing to fear after all.

"Well, alright," Bastien announced. "Let's play our part, shall we? I'll tell you everything so you'll know exactly what's happening. First, by your leave, I'll help you to my horse." Carefully he led Casica to his mount. It was awkward, to say the least, the delicate matter of helping the bound woman into his saddle but they managed it. The prince jumped to his place behind her and, taking the reins, turned to gather her horse. He needn't bother. Already Rigel was at his rear waiting to follow his lady. "Will your horse come?" A nod. Bastien grinned, impressed, then tapped his heels. The couple continued their drama.

Neither noticed another player on set. Cassica's King K'eran crouched a mere thirty cubits distant, hidden in the brush. A crossbow lowered in his arms. During this entire time, the son of Ars made a deadly target, more imperiled than ever the woman had been. For the king of Cassica had determined with himself, regardless of the consequences for his nation, to kill the boy if he lay an ignoble hand upon his beloved child. He watched as the two rode off. She was beyond his protection now. He must surrender more than his daughter. Powerless, he knelt to the ground and wept, praying.

Casica studied the room, her memory now leaving her. How thoughtful of Bastien to prepare this place for her. She glanced to the right. The doorway, there, led to his chamber. If she felt better, she would invite herself in and investigate it. Perhaps later in the day she would have strength; then he could show her, himself. She glanced at the clock on the wall. She hoped he would return soon.

A movement to her left startled her thoughts. The slave knelt silently near her sitting area. What on earth could she be thinking? the princess wondered. And why did she kneel? She hadn't been told to kneel. Casica opened her mouth to ask one of these questions when, from the other room, was the heavy sound of a door. It slammed - hard. The clock chimed slightly at the force. The slave didn't flinch.

"Slave!" an angry voice bellowed. The slavewoman rose. The fluidity of her motion intrigued the healer. "By your leave," she asked. Casica nodded. She could hear him clearly. "Clothing for Valdera!" Bastien ordered, chasing his words with the sound of glass. He was pouring himself a drink. The glass returned violently to the table.

The fifth son of Ars prowled his room in silence. *Curse, it all!* Sent to Valdera to work on the failing dam. *Failing dam, my arse,* he thought. When horses dance - that's why he's being sent there! His father wanted him away from her. He knew that was the reason and voiced as much to his immovable sire. She'd almost died coming here, he argued, and only God knew what would happen to her in his absence. Nothing would happen, his father countered. She had survived the transfer and now lived under his protection. His sending him away had nothing to do with the Cassican wench. Besides, she was in no condition to lay him anyway.

"You will leave this hour," Ars commanded him. "You will go as I tell you go. You will work as you are needed. I will send for you in time, and you may bed your Cassican vessel till you run dry." Bastien stewed, still, at this insult, familiar rage boiling towards his father. Ars never understood. Never accepted his son's decision to court Casica - not bed her. He wanted love, not power. He wanted a wife, not a captive.

The young man looked up into his thoughts and shook his head. It wasn't enough that all his arrangements had fallen apart; wasn't bad enough she'd been torn and abused like an enemy. Now, as she only yesterday gained strength enough to wake for a few hours, he was leaving her. What would she think? He was abandoning her, that's what she'd think. Would appear as cowardice or contempt. Curse, being a prince! If his father were a mere man, he would defy this order. But Ars was king. So he must leave within the hour. He must see her and try to explain.

Bastien stopped at the doorway before taking a deep breath. Calmly, he knocked on the frame. "Come in," came the voice so unlike any other he knew. He took a step into the room and looked. She sat quietly on the bed he'd made last year, praying as he fashioned it that her time in it would be short. So much for that prayer. She was dressed, today, except for a vest and boots. That was an improvement. Her face seemed pale in its alien manner, however, and while the dark eyes revealed nothing behind them, black lines beneath spoke of her ailing health.

"How do you feel this day?" he asked softly. "Weak." A moist sheen came over her gaze. "You're leaving," she said simply. The blond man dropped his head, biting his tongue against a barrage of arguments. "Yes. My father needs me in Valdera to repair a dam before the rains." "Your country hasn't engineers?" she asked, knowing this had nothing to do with some dam. "Many," he replied shortly. "I am but one. It appears my skills work more effectively with stone and wood than they do with life."

The builder caressed the maple paneling he'd set for her. Bastien smiled despite himself; even he couldn't detect the seams. The smile melted as he thought of what he must do. And when he turned again to her, his look was stern. The hard expression wasn't for her, but Casica couldn't know that.

"Princess, I'm sorry. Nothing has worked as I planned. I'll be leaving immediately." He watched, anxiously, as a dam within her threatened to burst. "When do you return?" she managed. The look on her face made him cringe. *Scads,* he needed to leave this place. Nothing unnerved him like helplessness and, pony, if he weren't anything but helpless to fix this breach. "I don't know when I'll return, Princess," he answered curtly. "I don't know. I'll return as soon as my father sends for me."

Her disappointment filled the room with an intensity of touch. Bastien's mind reeled. He must do something. He couldn't just leave her alone, questioning everything about him. He must leave something in his place. A gift. Behind him was the sound of his satchel being closed. *There* was his gift.

"Bring me my wallet," he ordered. Within seconds his wallet appeared, borne in the mittened hands of the slave. Clarece backed away and kneeled. Bastien flipped through his papers, found the parchment he wanted, and stepped to the table he'd made. He reached for a quill. Forcefully, his signature filled a lined space as did the name of another. There, it was done. Smiling, he approached the puzzled woman and offered the papers.

"For you," he announced. "A wedding gift. Tis not what I planned, but she will slave you well." "'Slave me'?" Casica countered, confused. She glanced at the parchment. The aged leather was soft to her touch. At the top was declared in bold indigo: *The property, Slavewoman called Clarece, forthwith purchased - .* Her mind exploded. "Clarece?! You're giving me your slave?" She stared at him incredulous. Her expression was utterly misinterpreted. "You're pleased!" he beamed, thinking, *Finally,* something

he did was right. "Yes!" he continued, "she now belongs to you."
The dark head shook.

"But I don't want her," Casica objected. "I don't want a slave."
"It's alright," he explained. "You don't have to do anything. Tis
done with my signature. Clarece is a good slave. She's a hard
worker." "You don't understand, my prince," Casica interrupted,
frantic. She looked at the kneeling form beside him. She needed
to be diplomatic. "I thank you for your consideration," she said,
controlled, "but I'll not own a human being the thought repulses
me." Bastien presented his hands to stop her.

"Princess Casica. This slave is my gift. She's maimed, tis true
but still, she's an excellent property. She's the chief slaveswoman.
However, if she fails to please you, we'll get shed of her when
I return or you can replace her while I'm gone. Just ask for the
broker. He'll arrange everything. You can get a servant, instead.
But there's nothing to owning a slave; they're no responsibility
at all." He motioned to the chair beside the silent form. "Tis like
owning that chair except you tell it move and it does. They're one
and the same."

So Bastien said, but there were distinct differences between
the two. For one, the fleshly furniture breathed, and at the moment, her breath came in quick and fearful draws. How suddenly
life changed. In an instant, fourteen years of security was stripped
from her. In a word, her world transferred from the familiar
ownership of her prince to this foreign creature who already had
voiced her displeasure. The collared woman fought, desperately,
to contain her tears. All her struggle was lost on the free man and
woman.

"I don't want her," the princess was saying. Had she felt better, had she strength, Casica could have made him to understand
but she hadn't and couldn't. Bastien shook his head, frustrated.
Arguing over a slave was senseless. "I haven't time to visit," he
said, dismissing the issue. "I must leave at once." He strained
to memorize the dark visage. "I'm sorry, Princess, but you'll be
alright. Clarece knows everything about the palace. She'll help
you." He didn't turn when he addressed her. "Clarece." Silence.
"You are property of the princess now. Obey and watch for her."
"My lord," a voice answered meekly.

Gazing at Casica, Bastien tried to smile. He worried for her. She was so weak. "Rest, please," he asked. "I'll return as soon as possible. This is your home now. You'll not be harmed." She looked at him with the same skepticism as with his statement concerning the slave. She didn't believe him. "I'll miss you," he was saying, and for these words, his expression bore witness of truth.

He paused. He wanted to touch her. To kiss her. He couldn't. He offered, instead, one final confused look then stepped quickly from the room. The princess of Cassica listened as Bastien exited his chamber. A door closed heavily behind him. He was gone.

For how long she didn't know, but the woman closed her eyes, fighting a metallic taste in her mouth. She was alone. Alone in a land that hated her, a land she now hated with growing intensity. All hope of being embraced by the man who so kindly had received her evaporated. She was abandoned. Lost. Casica sat as the pain in her tensing shoulders receded. She focused on the rhythm of her chamber clock then, with a deep breath, opened her eyes. There knelt her wedding gift.

*Wonderful,* she thought sarcastically. *Just wonderful. He couldn't give me jewelry or clothing - no. He had to give me a maimed slave.* She studied the worn parchment. Four names signified ownership of the kneeling woman. A fifth - her own - still dried in Bastien's hand. For a moment she desired to treat the wedding gift as she was presented: a piece of furniture. She wished only to sleep, to end this day and awaken to find she lived, presently, in a dream. She could ignore the "chair," slip under her covers and escape this incomprehensible situation. The mittened claws trembled slightly. The healer saw it and repented of her selfishness. "Please stand," she requested, kindly. "I prefer you stand."

Like a question, the woman rose. Her gaze remained riveted to the floor. Casica found herself imitating the posture. "So...'Clarece.' Tis a beautiful name. You were named for the queen?" The blond woman waited, ascertaining the question as a slave did. Often questions weren't meant to be answered. The free woman didn't continue, so she must desire a reply.

"Almost certainly not, my - mistra. To place upon a slave a queen's mantle would be insulting - for the queen. Queen Clarece was greatly honored. A slave wouldn't have stained her in such a way." "Oh, I see," replied Casica. *So much for that line of conversation.* She would try another. "Well, I see you've had several... people (she couldn't bear to say 'owners') in your life. How long must *I...* keep you?"

A stream of shame flooded the bowed neck. Instantly, the princess realized her mistake. *Idiot!* she chided herself but before she could explain, Clarece responded. "You mustn't keep me at all, my lady," she managed. "You may sell me. You may transfer me. You may give me - as did my master - or you may kill me, as it pleases you." *Kill you?* "Forgive me, Clarece," Casica hastened, "I misspoke. I merely referred to your papers. It seems you've had several people. I only wondered if there was a time limit to *my ...* having you." The slave paused, unconvinced. It was clear what the foreigner had meant. The mittens fretted with one another.

"There is no limit, mistra," came the quiet reply. "You may keep me a day or a lifetime - I am your possession to do upon as you wish."

Casica didn't have to be a healer to know she'd greatly harmed the woman. She fretted with her own fingers, desperately trying to redeem the situation. "And how long have you served the prince?" she asked. "Fourteen years." "Fourteen *years?* You must have come to Bastien as a young child." No reply. The statement didn't require one.

Casica stared at Clarece's papers. She ran her thumb over her own name. Empty lines waited below. "Well, Clarece - are you only addressed by 'Clarece'?" "My property name is now 'Clarece d'Casica.'" Casica winced. Never in her life could she have imagined her name attached to a slave's. What would her people think? She looked again at the empty lines. Fourteen years with Bastien. How abandoned Clarece must feel, she considered. She knew that feeling well. The slave waited wordlessly. Only God knew what Clarece thought, but perhaps there was something she could do to assure the woman.

"Well, Clarece d'Casica," the princess announced, "you have met your last... me. That is, unless you tire of me, which you may very well do. In which case," she tried to jest, "feel free to trade or sell me. All I ask is for a warning, which is more than you've had,

I believe." No response. So much for assurance. Casica looked around herself, lost.

"Is there anything I need to know about having you? I mean - do I need to do anything for you?" The head shook. "No, my lady, unless you wish to alter my food and clothing allotments." Food and clothing. So that was her responsibility. "Are they sufficient?" "Yes." Casica nodded. "And what about me? Is there anything I need to know about myself as your - owner?" (There. She had said it.)

The slavewoman's head cocked, quizzically, as she interpreted the question. "This doorway leads to the east slaves' pen," she ventured. "Your room was a storage chamber before the prince's renovations." (She needed to explain this, for to live above slaves was shameful.) "I sleep beneath you. A pull hangs at your bed. Ring and I will come forthwith." The slave paused as she considered what else might be important. Food. Food was always important.

"I will deliver your meals at six and every six hours till evening, mistra - unless you prefer otherwise. I rise at half past three if you need me earlier." "Three in the *morning*?" her owner interjected. "Yes, my lady."

"No wonder you're the morning light," Casica thought aloud. "I am *not* the morning light. Six is fine." "Yes, my lady." Clarece's mind spun with scenario's. Calling. Food. Attendance. "If you come into my presence, Princess, I will kneel. If you want me, receive me by placing your hand on my head. If you do not want me, don't receive me and I will continue with my duties."

Casica nodded. Slavish etiquette. She had no training for this. She wondered if Clarece knew she nodded. "I'm sure I've much to learn," she ventured aloud. No response. With a sigh, she gazed out the windows. It was clouding outside. Bastien's journey would be a wet one. A cramp knotted in her shoulder. She turned back to the woman.

"Clarece, I'm tired. If you will please, excuse me. I wish to sleep." "Of course, mistra," her slave quickly replied. "May I get you anything?" *Yes*, thought Casica. *You may get me the Hades out of here.* "No. Thank you." She watched the slave kneel before rising to leave. What a bizarre ritual.

On her way, Clarece paused at the cabinet Bastien had made for her owner's clothing. "My former mastra wished for you to have this," she said, kneeling, as she offered a wrapped object.

Curious, the princess unfolded the burgundy cloth. She smiled. A dagger. How could Bastien possibly have known? It would be a strange gift for a woman except that Casica collected knives, an enjoyment fostered by another man in her life; how her heart missed him. "My lord made this for you himself, my lady," the slave explained. "Tis for your boot." The princess swallowed a sob; the other man had given her blades for her boot. "The prince is a fine sword smith," she voiced. "Thank you, Clarece."

The slave bowed, rose, and offered a half kneel. She hastened toward her pen, anxious to flee this alien woman for her dark, familiar world below. Still, she thought, stepping quickly down the slave stairway, there was something strangely kind about the Cassican. Rarely had anyone free thanked her. The kindness flowed into her like warmth. In her stall, Clarece pondered this fact, as above, the woman who was her owner pondered the cool blade in her hand.

The world was growing dark.

# IV

Casica sat on her bed, exhausted. Her shalonn glowed with sustained vitality, filled as it was with Berea's power. But her body, her body hadn't regained even a measure of its energy. All her resources, it seemed, fought against the unyielding torment in her back. She leaned against the burning ache and moaned. Never in all her life had she known pain as this. She felt violated as if someone had torn into her vessel and ripped out her health. Health and her hope. She was alone. God, she was so alone.

She glanced to her dresser where Bastien's dagger lay. Her protection had abandoned her to a woman who eluded all understanding. Living with Clarece was as comforting as living with a machine. The slave was useful, yes. But she kept her heart far from her owner, hiding behind her collar and propriety. Casica had wanted so much to ask the quiet woman to stay with her this evening. To talk. To warm her with human interaction. But she hadn't the strength to span the distance between them. She hadn't the will.

For days now, Casica fought another enemy more debilitating than pain. Despair. With Bastien's parting, a deep sense of darkness had taken root. She was isolated. She who had known nothing but friendship and love and honor for sixteen years, now found herself in a cold world of hate and rejection. She could die in her bed tonight, and no one would care. More likely, the Byzanthian nation would rejoice at the death of their Cassican enemy. The darkness breeding these and many other such thoughts filled her mind as had blood her lungs. But this time, no Berea was here to heal. Casica thought of her family: Maman. Baba. K'ardan. What she wouldn't give to speak with them. To be a moment in their presence would feel like life.

Desire inspired her. Writing. Perhaps she could write away some of her loneliness. She stood and straightened her back, her muscles protesting as the deep wounds in her flesh tore at her. Heaven, she hurt. She forced herself to search for paper. She had a canvas and paints but no writing supplies, at least none she could find. Perhaps the slave Clarece could be of help. Casica considered ringing the service bell but thought against it. From her open door, she could hear the slaves at their supper; it would be good exercise to walk the short distance below.

She maneuvered slowly along the narrow stairway, noticing how it cooled with each step. No wonder she could hear the slaves; the passage was like a chute of air. She arrived at the bottom of the stairs, breathless. Regaining herself, she studied the supper scene. The slaves were a hive of activity, talking and laughing and eating. Colorful vests surrounded the large table as did much, much vitality. She smiled at the camaraderie. The familiarity of these fellows warmed her.

Suddenly all activity ceased. The men who faced her from the far side of the table noted Casica's presence and immediately silenced. She winced as a wave of hate and suspicion surged upon her. Her coming was a terrible mistake, she realized, a terrible mistake. The girl stepped back. In this moment, she wasn't a princess. She was prey.

A familiar form rose from the table. Clarece. The slave, with her unfastened vest and loose shirt, looked somewhat a stranger, especially in the unfamiliar setting. In fact everything around the princess seemed alien, ominous.

"What in Hades is this Cassican pig doing here?!" an angry male voice demanded. Casica stared, frightened at the man rising from his place. "I - forgive me for disturbing your meal," she spoke, confused. Her slave walked quickly towards her. "I... I'm sorry," Casica apologized. The angry man pounded the table, his face red with rage. "You bet you're sorry, you piece of Cassican filth!" he yelled. "Why didn't you die?! I lost a crown on you!"

The chief slaveswoman spun on her heel. "Jonas!" she commanded, cutting him short. "Sit!" The man obeyed, his eyes glaring at the Cassican woman. "Forgive him, my lady," Clarece begged, kneeling before her mistra. "Jonas hates all the world today. How may I help you?" Casica blinked. Why had she come down here? Her thoughts reeled. *Paper*, her mind said. Paper.

"I - I was wondering if you knew where I might find writing paper. But I'm sorry, I shouldn't have come here." "No - no, my lady," the slave answered, rising. "Tis well. I'll get paper for you." "No," the princess refused. "I've disturbed you. Only tell me where it is." "The steward, my lady. He will have it. I'll go at once and fetch some for you."

Here in her pen, Clarece felt freedom to study her owner openly. Her mistra frightened her; her face had paled and her breathing labored. She trembled in the cold and her eyes brimmed with suffering. The slave knew what she saw. She must get Casica back to her chamber, into her bed. "Come, Princess," she beckoned kindly. "Come. I will walk you to your chamber."

A burning wave swept over Casica's shoulders. Tears flowed down her face and dropped to the pen floor. She closed her eyes against the fire. When she opened them, she met Clarece's troubled expression. "Please, my lady," the slave prodded. "Let us go." "No," Casica ordered. "You stay for your meal." She looked at the confused group around the table. "Again," she addressed them, "please forgive my disturbing you." She caught the eyes of the angry man. "Die, Cassican!" he spat.

Casica winced. Jonas' curse took flight. It gripped her heart and began feeding. *Die*. Something in her spirit surrendered. "I believe I may," she breathed. Then turning, she retreated up the stairs.

The room filled with stunned silence. Clarece waited until the princess left her view. She spun and looked threateningly at Jonas, tears welling in her eyes. "Blast, your hate, Jonas! Twill be your death someday!" She glanced at the startled faces of her fellow slaves, then turning on her heel as a slave does, ran quickly up the stairs.

She found the princess propped beside her garden door, breathing in the cool night air from a slight opening. Clarece froze at the landing, waiting permission to enter. From her viewpoint she could see a growing spot of bright red on her mistra's back. She was bleeding again.

"My lady?" she asked finally. The face that turned to her greeting was haunted. All Casica saw was a bowed blond head. "Please," her slave was saying, "come to bed. I'll fetch you paper." Casica looked out the door into the darkness, shaking her head. "No. Tis time to leave." "You're bleeding, my lady," the slave observed. Casica laughed weakly. "That won't matter." She reached for the door lever.

Clarece broke etiquette and stepped into the room. Her owner's tone frightened her. "Where are you going my lady?" she asked quietly. "Away...."

*Please, please don't, Casica!* Clarece cried inside, wanting desperately to take the young woman and lead her to bed. "You'll be needing your cloak," she said instead, and reached for the rich blue garment near her. "No, I won't," Casica replied calmly.

In her fear, the slave looked up. Casica smiled weakly at the sight of her eyes. "Thank you for your kindnesses, Clarece. Goodbye." *Goodbye?* What could she mean? Some voice inside her screamed, *Stop her! Stop her!* But she couldn't. She was this woman's property. She could not touch nor even question the retreating figure. Clarece stood helplessly as the Cassican princess stepped into the night. The door closed quietly.

The slavewoman waited until she no longer heard her mistra's retreating steps. She slammed her fists into the air. "Fool!" she yelled to the empty room.

The pen was deathly quiet, with only the sounds of eating daring to breach the silence. Clarece stared into her bowl. She could feel Asla's gaze upon her. A wave of nausea rose within. What had she done? Curse her proper self! She hadn't done anything! Hadn't even tried to stop her. *Goodbye,* she had said. "Watch her," Berea had warned, "She won't be thinking rightly...." Panic gripped Clarece as she thought the unthinkable. *Dear God!*

Clarece sprang from the table and raced up the palace stairway. Perhaps the princess was simply going to find the steward, she argued with herself, running. Surely, that must be what she was intending.

She reached the main floor and slowed to a fast walk. The evening traffic impeded her progress, having to kneel as she did to every superior, and for a slave, everyone except another slave was superior. It took longer than she wished to reach the steward. She knocked as loudly as she could with her maimed hands. The sound of steps approached her; the slave greeted the opening door with a kneel.

"Clarece," the steward asked surprised. The chief slaveswoman never came to him at night. "How may I help you?" "Forgive me, Lord Steward," Clarece replied, "but my lady - has she been to see you?" The steward considered the question, though he didn't know why. Of course she hadn't come. "The Cassican? No. Why do you ask?" The slave bowed her head. "An error, my lord. Forgive my disturbing you." She turned before he could ask anything more and halfway down the hall, paused to think. Her prince was gone. To whom could she turn for help? *Poul*, the answer came. Poul would help her. He would know what to do.

Clarece glanced toward the clock at the end of the hall. Less than half an hour before curfew. Poul would be at the guard's house this time of night. She must hurry. After having to stop for a fifth kneel, the desperate woman decided to abandon the more direct route of the palace for the slaves' passageways.

She ran twenty cubits down the main hall and disappeared into a darkened stairway. During the day, reflected sunlight would light it from above. Now, however, small lamps illuminated the stairs. Thank God someone had done their job, the chief slave thought. She knew every step of every passage in the Byzanthian palace and at this moment, her knowledge served her well. She flowed down the stairway into a recess that ran to her right. She ducked through the tilted doorway and sprinted towards an opening forty cubits ahead. It was a maze, to be sure, but still she should make better time, running, as she could.

Clarece burst through this doorway and headed again to the right, skidding into a dark passage that should take her to the next floor. *Go, go, go!* her mind charged. She raced down the hall and leaped, landing gracefully eight stairs below. This was a strange passage, twisting in a series of senseless corners. Scads! At times like this, she could swear whoever designed the hidden passages did so to torment their slavish users. She reached a short drop-off and slid down a rickety railing only to run up five steps to regain the distance.

Finally, there she was, the main floor - on the wrong side of the castle but still the right level. She spun to her right into a span of darkness - and collided headlong into a burst of light. The light was in her brain; it was a closed door she struck. Clarece teetered. The collision nearly rendered her unconscious.

"What the deuce?!" she exclaimed, confused. She held her pounding head as her eyes adjusted to the soft light. She couldn't believe what she saw. "Well, this is just pony!" The door to this hallway was closed. It was *never* closed, but for some reason, it was closed. And unlike other doors that operated with levers, this newer one possessed a smooth, rounded knob. *Crispus!* Clarece stared, bewildered, at the small brassy piece. It seemed to smirk.

An internal clock chimed her to action. She dropped to her knees and, as quickly as possible, unfastened her cloth mittens and yanked them off with her teeth. Cautiously, she slid her bare forearms against the knob. Her wrists ached with the struggle. She pressed harder, moaning against the pain. Finally, a click. The door gave.

Clarece grabbed her mittens and stuffed them into her vest. She ran through this door to the last. A lever, thank God. One downward push and she was outside. She sped upon the covered sidewalk that followed the castle wall, sliding at the end to make a sharp turn left.

There it was, the path leading to the guards' quarters. *Run! Run!* she ordered herself. She could see it, could see the light from the guardhouse windows. Another three minutes and she'd be there.

A mighty hollow sound pierced the night. The slave froze in her tracks, skidding shortly through the gravel at her feet. *Oh, God!* she thought, *not now!* She gazed down the path to the guards' light. Two figures headed towards her. The night watchmen. She could never reach Poul without being arrested. And if she were arrested, it might be tomorrow night before anyone found her. A third chime pealed. For a single chime more, Clarece stood panting, helplessly facing the distant light. She had come so close. An oath escaped her clinched teeth and she spun and raced, again, against the clock - but this time to reach the palace.

"Run, slave, run!" she heard the guards yell, laughing. She did run. Ran until her chest ached and throat burned raw. At the eighth chime she slid from the sidewalk and fell into the nearest door. Nine. And she was safely inside.

The spent woman propped against the cool stone. Her heart beat her chest, filling her head with noise. Hot tears coursed her face. She slid down the wall and crouched, covering her shame with her claws. Her hands throbbed painfully as blood forced its way into her arms. Clarece sobbed; she had failed. Failed. *Dear, God*, she wept, *mercy. Please, have mercy.*

Hours later, Clarece trudged to the princess' room. Wanting to avoid her pen, she entered through Bastien's dark chamber, hoping against hope to see Casica lying in her bed. She didn't. She collapsed into a chair. She would send Asla to find Poul, but her friend was gone for the evening, servicing several men. She would ask a guard, except no guard on this shift would help a slave - even with a matter concerning a royal. There was nothing to be done now except wait.

Clarece looked about the quiet room. Little signs of the princess were everywhere. Her exquisite cloak draped over the couch by the garden door; her nightgown folded neatly on her bed, anticipating a sleeper who would not come. Her leather satchel propped near the sofa. A book. Her bright vest hanging from the chair in which she now sat. Everything pointed to the absent occupant.

The slave felt, suddenly, alone. Here she had been, avoiding the strange woman at every turn, and now that Casica was gone, she missed her. Why hadn't she stopped her? she asked herself again. It would have been so easy. A touch would have held the hurting girl.

"Why do I let fear rule me so?" Clarece asked aloud. She had yielded, yet again, to fear's tyranny and now her gentle mistra's life may have been lost. Only the day before, a slave from the north wing asked her to describe the peculiar new resident. "She is kindness," Clarece replied. Kindness....

Thunder awakened her. Clarece jolted her head from the table and looked uncertainly about. She glanced quickly to the bed. No

Casica. It was raining. She imagined her owner outside: no cloak, not even a vest for warmth. She glanced at the clock. Two hours till morning light. Two hours before she could get help.

She rose from her seat and walked to the sitting area, next to Casica's satchel. The leather bag was smooth with age yet polished and kept. This was a beloved possession, clearly. Clarece thought of herself; she certainly didn't qualify for such status.

She went to the windows and kneeled. Lightning lit the space. She was desperate. God, she knew, never answered prayers for herself, but perhaps He would those offered for the Cassican. She prayed until shortly before sunrise then left for the kitchen. There she begged a few items. Next, she returned to her pen and retrieved from her stall a plain woolen cloak. Asla had not yet returned.

Slowly, the slave walked up her owner's stairs. She wrapped herself in her garment and waited by the door, cradling the princess' cloak. There would be no sunlight this morning. A fine drizzle, what slaves called a zanzan, masked the garden below. Clarece glanced at the clock. As it wound to strike five, she opened the door and stepped quickly down the stairs, heading back to the guardhouse she had tried so desperately to reach a lifetime before. It was cold. Her breath steamed as she ran through the fog.

Upon entering the guardhouse, Clarece paused. She'd never been in the building this time of day. The sound of male voices told her where to go. She approached the main hall and stopped, standing quietly in the doorway. The men ceased their conversation, surprised at the sight of a woman. It was the chief slaveswoman, appearing very unchiefly in her disheveled person. Her face warmed with their attention.

Then she saw him. Poul had risen and now walked quickly to meet her. He led her away from the hall. "Clarece," he asked frightened, "what's wrong?" She didn't realize she was trembling. "She's gone, Poul. She's gone." "Casica?!" "Yes," she nodded. "She was hurting - and Jonas said something and I didn't stop her. I didn't stop her, Poul. She was so distraught - I'm afraid. Afraid for her life - ." "When did she leave?" he interrupted. "Last night.

Hours ago. I tried to tell you - but curfew caught me." The ser-geant stood, thinking frantically. "Come!" he ordered.

The two jogged to the livery. Casica's saddle hung on the rack. Poul ran through the quiet stable to Rigel's stall. The white horse was gone. "Dear, God," he heard a voice utter from behind. Clarece gaped into the empty space. "I've failed. I've killed her."

"No, Clarece," Poul whispered urgently. "I'll find the princess." "How can you begin to know where to look?" she asked. "I'll find her," he repeated. She watched him saddle and mount his horse. There was no time to lose.

"Here," she said, handing him the blue cloak and a cloth bag. Poul gently received the offering. Her face haunted him. Darkness lined her eyes and her body trembled with cold. Her maimed hands she clutched close to her chest.

Poul tried to sound confident. "Clarece, you've done all you can. Now go rest. I'm certain she's alright," he lied. The woman nodded, grateful to have this burden shared. She walked out with him and watched as his form vanished into the foggy mist.

Poul prayed the path he took was Rigel's. It disappeared into a wooded meadow. He stopped and studied the landscape. Where would she go? Where would she run if she had no place to turn? *Cassica*, he thought. That's where she would go. The nearest point to Cassica lay ahead a good two hours away. "Yah!" he yelled, spurring his horse into a dead run.

# V

The waves raged below, spitting a cold and salty mist into the woman's face. From the edge of the cliff, she watched, mesmerized by the sea's endless motion. Casica had stood here for hours, oblivious to the cold, oblivious to the rain soaking her within and without. Her hair hung limp and dripping. Rain ran off her nose and into her open mouth. She couldn't feel her shoulders anymore. There was no more pain.

*It should be here,* she thought, time and time again. Cassica should be out in the distance, on the horizon. She should see it. Was it gone? Was her land swallowed into the sea? *I should join you,* she thought. *I should fall from this place and join you forever.*

The darkness yawned as something darker than any night bid her jump. One move and, josquin or no, she would rest forever. No more pain. No more loneliness. No more. The thunder in the sky had ended hours ago. She missed the lightning and its company. But the thunder below continued, heedless of the sky above.

"Die, Cassican!" the surf ordered. "Die!" "I think I may," Casica answered dozens of times. To die was her destiny after all, was it not? She was the edict's sacrifice. The payment of her ancestors. Death was what she was born for. Life was to die. Who was she to disobey? The numb woman closed her eyes. It was calling her. The ocean called her name.

"Casica! Casica!" Poul yelled into the mist. He'd found Rigel standing forlornly in a low meadow. The ocean thundered ahead and all around him. Poul stroked the horse's neck. His owner must be near. *Curse, this mist,* he thought. She could be thirty cubits away and he wouldn't see her. The anxious man scampered up a knoll. He wasn't one to stand and wait. "Casica!" the sea called. "I'm here," the woman whispered. "I'm here."

"Casica?" The sea was closer now. It stood behind and to her left. Reality breathed into her thoughts. What was the ocean doing over there? "Casica!" She stood dangerously near the edge of the cliff. He mustn't frighten her.

"Your Highness!" Poul called in Cassican. The woman never turned. *Kai,* she thought. The Byzanthians had found her again. "Go away," she said. "I'm just leaving." "I hope you don't," the man said. "I need to apologize."

*Apologize?* she thought. "For what?" she asked dreamily. "I'm sorry. I'm sorry I broke your arm. I lied. I loosened your saddle on purpose." As he spoke, Poul moved cautiously towards the woman. He must get within arm's reach. But he must be careful lest she jump with fear - or throw him over. The josquin could easily overpower him.

*Saddle... broken arm....* Casica wondered absently. How on earth could anyone in this country know that? Was nothing about her secret? The man was getting too close.

She spun, startling the sergeant. "Who are you?" Casica asked dangerously. The man froze. "I'm K'net," he replied in Cassican. *K'net?* She cocked her head and studied him, looking all the world as though she examined a sculpture, then broke into a bitter laugh. "You lying son of Byzanthia. You're the wrong color for my cousin."

"Casica," K'net plead carefully. "Listen, please. Come away from the edge. Please, come talk with me. Look," he said, lifting her cloak. "'Tis the cloak Pelana made for you. Your mother, your father. Think of them." Her expression chilled him.

"I don't know who you are, but my parents are too far to think of." "No, they're not," he answered, cautiously gauging her distance. "They're right here, Casica. They sent me ahead of you so you wouldn't be alone in this place." The man stepped closer. She didn't move to stop him. To overpower the Byzanthian would be easy. He would join her in the ocean.

"Touch me," he now begged. "Only touch me and then I'll leave you." The princess looked into the sergeant's face. There *was* something familiar about him. He kneeled and, tentatively, reached out his hand, palm down. The gesture, too, looked vaguely familiar. "My queen," he whispered. Casica reached for the outstretched hand. It would feel good to touch even Byzanthian warmth. Her fingers brushed his flesh.

Instantly the wave of a beloved presence overwhelmed her. "K'net," she managed. Her knees buckled and she fell toward the emptiness below.

K'net caught her. He lifted his cousin into his arms and carried her to the woods, away from the ocean and its wind and cold. When Casica woke, she lay against him, warm in her mother's cloak. Her cousin's arms tightened about her drawing her closer to himself. "K'net?" she asked weakly. "Shhh..." he whispered comfortingly. "You're alright, M'Yat. You're safe." Casica smiled at the nickname. Rain patted against their canopy of leaves. The cold mist filled their lungs. *I must be dreaming,* she thought sleepily.

When next she awoke, much of the day had passed. She was now not so weak, only very, very hungry. "Hungry?" a male voice asked. Casica stirred from his embrace, moving slowly under his watchful gaze. The sergeant produced a stein filled with wine and a parcel of bread and cheese. "Here, my queen. Drink." Casica obeyed, relishing the warm sensation. "Eat." She took the bread and cheese and ate hungrily, studying her cousin as she did. It was fortunate for her that touch revealed more to a josquin than did sight. Looking at him was almost nightmarish. It was as if someone put K'net in another's body.

"K'net," she asked suspiciously, "when did you go white?" The man laughed. What she said was funnier in Cassican. "Berea's magic," he explained. "Your father wanted me to guardian you. I agreed. I've been here over two years." "*This* was your secret mission?" she asked remembering the day he'd left her. They were standing in the south field. Tears filled his blue eyes. "I'll see you again, M'Yat," he had told her.

"Yes. *You* are my secret mission." Baba had sent an altage, she realized.

"I'm utterly undone," she confessed shaking her head. "I'm not surprised," K'net grinned. "I can't tell you how long it took for me to recover from the change. I think Berea did something to my mind to help me with it. The only thing that could have made matters worse would to have been made a woman, too." His cousin smiled. "You'd make an ugly woman, cousin. But I must admit, if this weren't so queer, I'd think you a handsome Byzanthian." It was K'net's turn to smile. It was so good to be with her.

"How are you here?" she asked.

"The story is that I came as a transfer from the royal garrison. I grew up in Cassica as the charge of my uncle. Once here, I befriended your future husband. It wasn't hard to do. Bastien's a good man, Cousin. Kind and honorable."

She glanced down at the stein. "I wouldn't know," she observed, bitter. "He's gone." K'net nodded. "I know, but that's his father's doing - not his. And your being hurt -," his voice grew tender, "that wasn't his doing either. He had paid the guard to leave you untouched. He failed," he added, remembering that terrible day.

"You were there?" she asked. "Yes. How do you think Berea came to be with you?" Casica shook her head in amazement. "I had no idea." K'net reached for her hands. They were wonderfully familiar. "Bastien - Clarece, they risked their lives for you." Casica gazed at her cousin who wasn't her cousin. She hadn't been so alone after all.

"How did you know to look for me?" she asked finally. "Clarece," he grinned. "She's worried sick about you, Casica. She cares for you." "I wouldn't know," the princess repeated. "She hovers about like a sprite."

K'net glanced at the wet grass. "The cloak, the food, they're her doing," he defended gently. "Clarece... she is slave, Cass - she doesn't understand, but she's a treasure. Please, don't dismiss her so easily." Casica looked down and nodded. K'net looked into the sky. It was growing dark. There was so much to talk about but they hadn't time. They may never have time.

"We must go," he observed, reluctantly. "It'll be night when we return." He stood and reached for her. She rose unsteadily. "Can you ride?" he asked, concerned. "Yes. I'm just tired." Lord K'net took his queen into his arms and held her closely. She rested in the familiar embrace. "Thank God you're safe," he whispered. "You'll be alright, Casica. You'll be alright." He led her to Rigel and helped her mount. Taking his own horse, he rode beside her to the Byzanthian castle.

Casica had experienced more than her mind could digest. She rode silently. Outside the palace grounds, K'net dismounted. He went to Rigel and helped her to the ground. "I love you, M'Yat," he said smiling into his young cousin's face. "From here on, we don't know each other." "So we've never met?" she asked. "Not until today, no." The princess nodded in understanding. K'net gently kissed her brow and then her cheek in a Cassican ritual. He kneeled and bowed low before her. "My queen," he acknowledged.

Casica touched his head. A familiar warmth flooded him; he smiled at the sensation. He felt better already. Hers was the touch of Cassica. She bid him stand and looked in the eyes that, comfortingly, had not changed. "Thank you," she said simply.

They remounted and trotted to the garden stairway. A light shown in her room above. "Clarece is waiting," Poul observed. He took Rigel and waited until his cousin had safely ascended her stairs. He smiled in the darkness then returned to his guard.

The slave kneeled in the sitting area as she had all day. She had brought lunch and sent it away with Asla. Now, dinner awaited her mistra. For the hundredth time, she heard what she thought were footsteps. For the hundredth time, she stood. A shadow crossed the window. Clarece jumped to the door and opened it. It was the princess, alive and whole! Her face lit with gratitude. Some prayers could be answered!

In her excitement, Clarece kept her owner out in the damp longer than she knew but finally came to herself. "Welcome, my lady!" she bowed, inviting her mistra within. She closed the door then dropped humbly to her knees, awaiting receivership. Casica smiled wanly, resigned to the alien etiquette. She touched the slave's head; the blond woman started at the warmth that filled her. She rose and helped her mistra with her cloak. The princess was soaked and exhausted.

"Are you hungry, mistra? Dinner awaits you." "Yes. Clarece," Casica began, "I thank you for - ." "Do not spend your strength on me, my lady. Please, sit and eat," the slave urged. Casica obeyed. She was utterly famished. "I'll draw you a hot bath - by your leave." Casica nodded and listened as the anxious woman retreated to Bastien's chamber.

She ate thankfully. Thankful for K'net. Thankful for her parents' care. Thankful for food and for her warm, safe chamber. Thankful for life. She had completed her meal when Clarece returned. "Are you finished?" she asked quietly. Her owner nodded. She was exhausted. "Then, please, come with me...."

Clarece led the princess to a small room in Bastien's chamber. It was a bath room. A brazier warmed it from the corner and pipe fed hot water into a large tub. Fragrances, beautiful and bright filled the air. The place reminded Casica of home. Clarece was speaking. She gazed down at hands that could never manage a bath. "I've asked the slave Asla, my sala, to bathe you, princess. With your permission...." Casica nodded. She watched as Clarece disappeared.

In her place stepped a figure which literally stole the princess' breath. A young woman, not more than fifteen years, silhouetted the doorway. She stood easily as one relaxed in her own body, like a dancer. Her flawless form looked as though she'd stepped out of some divine imagination, a sacred sculpture come to life. Clearly, this woman did not belong to earth: her Maker had poured the heavens into her eyes. Mouth. Nose. Streaks of light that served as lashes and eyebrows. Everything of her was perfect. A long mane, more truly white than blond, glowed in the candle light. And against all this was set a complexion of which the Cassican had only heard. It was golden, creating the effect of a palomino - blending all into the characteristic features of one born on the Isle of g'Helderlend. No wonder the land was legendary: the woman stunned reality.

"I am Asla," the voice said quietly. *Yes, you are,* thought Casica, interpreting the woman's name: *The Beauty of God.* "I am insulit. May I touch you?" *Insulit?* wondered the princess. She'd heard of insulit; they, too, were legendary. Who would ever place upon one the name of God?

"I am Casica," Josquin replied in the woman's native g'Helderleicht. "I am Cassican. Yes, you may."

The young woman grinned at the use of her language and at the subtle humor. With a bow she approached the foreigner and began silently to disrobe her. At the sight of Casica's back, she winced. Never had she seen anyone, slave or free, so brutally beaten. Blood oozed from the left shoulder. Gently she helped the woman into the steaming bath. Casica breathed in the exquisite moment.

In the realm of baths, insulit reign, skilled in washing away much more than dirt and blood. Asla took special care with the tortured flesh, cleansing it tenderly as she massaged the wounded muscles. Her touch soothed the Cassican's spirit. Casica drifted to sleep in the tub.

Asla awakened her but not fully. She guided the princess to her bed and tucked her in. Casica never heard her wished goodnight. She slept before her eyes closed.

# VI

The morning sun had come and gone, leaving the afternoon shadows to dance about the garden below. Clarece maintained her silent vigil, waiting for her owner to wake. It was as that first sleep after the great lady came to her. So much sleep. Casica's shalonn glowed brightly, though, its colors undiminished; that was a good sign, Clarece now knew. The princess wasn't dying; she simply recovered. The slave knelt perfectly still. In penance, she did not allow herself even a book for company. She would wait. Wait and contemplate her actions of two days before.

Evening now crept along the chamber floor. With the shadows came a deep breath that filled the healer's lungs, massaging her body like a hand rubbing a cold foot. "Time to wake!" her body said. Casica's eyes opened and slowly took in her surroundings. She knew this place. She was still in Byzanthia; the other place had been a dream.

"My lady?" a familiar voice greeted her. "Are you well?" It was the slave, Clarece, kneeling beside her bed, a look of concern contorting her gaze. Her eyes met her owner's and instantly fell to the floor. She didn't wait for a response. "You'll be hungry," she observed remembering the other sleep. "I will procure your meal." She bowed then left the room.

She was afraid. The more Clarece had thought through the days before, the more certain she was she had failed her mistra miserably. A royal would not keep a slave who had so little voice in the presence of danger. She should have said something, at least; but she had feared more greatly, lashing and condemnation, than for her mistra's life. She was an utter failure. Certainly, a terrible blow had come against her worth in the princess' eyes.

Casica lay in bed for a little while longer. Apart from hunger, she felt very well indeed - in body and spirit. Awareness of K'net's presence rejuvenated her. She wasn't alone. She remembered her mother telling her, "You have not been sent out alone." Now she understood. K'net had been sent ahead of her; her parents had sent her dearest friend as her altage. She would not dishonor their love, nor K'net's great risk.

She got from her bed to dress and girded herself with her karosh as with a weapon. The belt felt heavy around her waist, reminding her who she was. She went to the window and stood, caressing the royal seal on her buckle thoughtfully. And in her heart she determined to battle for life, here, as best she could. Little did she know, it would be for many others' lives beside her own she would battle.

Clarece returned more quickly than Casica expected. She offered a half-kneel before entering the chamber. Quickly she placed Casica's dinner setting and, with a bow of her head, invited her mistra dine. Casica sat, uncomfortably aware of the presence behind her. Well, at least this time she waited on her feet, mindful of her owner's instruction.

"How long have I slept, Clarece?" Casica asked between bites. "Two days and this day," the slave answered, pouring her a second cup of warm wine. Casica drank it in one tilt. She needed courage to speak as she must to the slave. Filled, she pushed her plate away, prompting the slave to reach for its removal.

"Hold, Clarece," Casica ordered quietly, placing her hand before the leather mitten. "Please, sit." Clarece stared, confused; a slave would never sit at the table of a freewoman, much less an owner, but she obeyed, choosing the chair across from the princess. There she waited with her head bowed, her claws hidden in the pockets of her vest. Casica studied the woman tenderly. Clarece looked all the world like she expected to be beaten.

"Clarece, I wish to speak with you about the other night," Casica began. At these words the slave cringed, shoving her hands more deeply into her vest. This would not be easy. "What I did to you was cruel and inexcusable. Only God knows what I put you through. I ask your forgiveness. And I want you to know that you will *never* need search for me again. I promise."

The slave sat, deaf to the import of Casica's words. Anxiously she awaited the other shoe to drop. Surely there was more the princess had to say. Surely she would beret her for meddling with her affairs or for not interfering when she should. Surely it was coming, her owner's announcement that she had proven herself unacceptable and would be sold. The princess drew breath to speak again. Now it would come.

"Would you like some wine, Clarece?" The slave glanced up startled. "Milady?" she asked cautiously. "Wine." Her mistra was pouring wine into a glass. "I thought you might need some. Heaven knows I do."

Clarece dropped her head in confusion as she watched in the corner of her eye (in her "slave's line" as slaves called their line of adverted vision), a glass placed before her. Panic flooded her: wine was forbidden to slaves - mead alone was allowed them. But to refuse would be insulting, she decided. "Thank you," she spoke meekly, uncomfortably taking a single sip before setting the glass away from her.

It was the princess' turn for confusion. Nothing she did pleased this woman.

Clarece listened as her owner issued a deep sigh. *Nothing I do pleases this woman,* she thought. A voice, the same as spoke that night when she stood at the door voiceless, urged her. *Ask,* it said. *Ask what she wants from you.* Clarece had spent much of the past two days repenting of silence. God now put her to the test.

"My - my lady," she began nervously. "Yes?" a kind voice responded. Clarece swallowed hard. She felt somewhat sick. "My lady, what can I do to please you? To make you happier here?"

Casica focused on her wine glass. She spun it lightly with her fingers upon the table. "Clarece, no one can make another happy," she observed. "'Tis true, mistra," the slave agreed hesitatingly. "But one can offer a setting for happiness, as my Lord Bastien did in building this room for you." She bit her lip, struggling to continue her penance. "How may I furnish your life more to your taste?"

Casica sighed again. She leaned forward and propped her chin in her hand upon the table. *This woman, Clarece, may not speak often,* she thought, *but when she does, she certainly has a way with words.* The image of the chair came to her. "How may you furnish my life? What a provocative question," she said aloud. "Alright, Clarece," she announced leaning back into her chair. "I'll tell you. I long for you to treat me more as a person and less as a position. I'm a woman as you. I wish to be treated as one - that's all."

*A woman as you?* the slave thought, somewhat angry. How could Casica dare compare the two of them? In her world, Clarece didn't qualify as a woman at all. She was slave. A vessel. No more human than the glasses on the table. Of course, she knew the princess' meaning - it was the Cassican who didn't understand. Clarece needed the princess to address this question from *her* own perspective, to define her utility. "What must I do," she asked carefully, "to make you feel as though I treat you that way?"

Casica frowned. *She's doing it again,* she thought, frustrated - treating herself like a tool. No wonder she felt like an object in the slave's presence. How could an "it" relate to another without making them into an "it" as well? Something in the young woman chided her. Didn't her very response degrade Clarece into an object, also?

When Casica's answer came, it was considerate in its honesty. "Well, for one thing, you could look at me. I feel invisible in your presence, Clarece. I - I'm not even certain of the color of your eyes. I know they must be blue," she smiled, "because you're Byzanthian. But when you hide your face from me, I feel... rejected." The slave lowered her gaze even more. *Scads,* thought Casica. This was getting nowhere. But she would continue.

"And another thing. It would please me greatly for you to speak my name. I understand the propriety of titles, but kai, Clarece, we live together. I'm 'Casica' more truly than I'll ever be your 'Mistra' or 'Lady.'" She leaned forward. Clarece showed no indication of listening.

"What would also help - and I don't know your custom here, but I wish you would touch me. I miss human touch. Josquins – healers like me - don't do well without it. I'm not used to going days - weeks without feeling another's life. In my land," she explained, "I healed constantly, and healing almost always involves touch. I feel as though I'm shriveling like a dry leaf. But if it offends you to touch me, would you at least live in my general proximity? I'd like having you near me (*instead of twelve cubits away,*)" she concluded in thought.

Clarece sat, shrouded in an impenetrable silence. The princess shook her head. She had spoken too much. Clearly Clarece hadn't heard a word she'd said.

What Josquin couldn't know was that at the moment, the slave reeled at the impact of *every* word she'd spoken. In her silence, Clarece reviewed her owner's stipulations defining their relationship, and the more she thought, the more frustrated she became. Scads! The Cassican didn't know what she said! *How could anyone be so ignorant?* Her frustration doubled as courage.

"My lady," she said restlessly, her downward gaze hiding a frown, "you don't know of what you speak. All you mentioned is punishable by law." She fretted with her mittens. "You ask me to look at you. To meet your eyes would put me in stocks. A slave meets no one's eyes - not even a servant's. Only at each other do we look. And your name...." She uttered a short laugh. The thought was incomprehensible. "My lady. The punishment for speaking a free name is flogging."

"You mean you never use my name?" the princess interrupted, incredulous. "Of course I do - but only in reference to you. I would never address you as such." "As such as what?" Casica asked, maneuvering her. "As such as what is your name," Clarece replied, determined not to fall into the princess' ploy. Casica smiled despite herself. "And as for touching you...." The slave shook her head. *Tis suicide.* "To touch a noblewoman - is to attack the throne. Tis treason, punishable by death. By evisceration," she ended softly. Clarece shook her head - angered more by which she didn't know: that the princess spoke so lightly of these actions or that such innocent behavior was so perilous for her kind.

"But I would never press charges against you, Clarece," the princess was objecting. "You'd be in no harm." The blond woman squirmed in her seat, irritated. "You don't understand, mistra. You wouldn't need to. Anyone observing such behavior, another noble - or even a servant could report me. Especially me. A slave is less than nothing, but I'm a senior slave. I'm held as an example."

Casica looked sadly at the woman before her. So many, many rules bound her life. "I'm sorry, Clarece," she said. "I didn't understand." "Of course you wouldn't, Princess," Clarece acknowledged. "You're from a land free of slavery." She fretted with a fastener on her mitten. "People think we slaves are enslaved by Byzanthia. Sometimes, I think tis Byzanthia that's enslaved by slavery."

Casica leaned back into her chair, struck by the power of these words. "You do beat all, Clarece," she observed. "So we are at an impasse." "Perhaps not, my lady," the slave ventured quietly.

Clarece's inner world was in utter turmoil. She didn't know if she could do what she was considering. It would be a dreadful stretch for her, stepping outside her boundaries. Limitations were her safety. They told her who she was. On the other hand, Clarece wished, greatly, to please this woman, to help her be more at peace in her new land.

"These three things," she began, "they are public offenses. But in private, in our own company... I can try. I will endeavor to look at you, as you wish, and to touch you but to use your name - ," the thought made her wince. "*That*, I cannot do." She shook her head emphatically. "I cannot do that."

Casica smiled gratefully. Clarece's struggle wasn't lost on her. "Two out of three, that's more than generous. Thank you, Clarece." The slave nodded a response.

Josquin studied the woman across the table. She stood, and in an official voice introduced herself. "I am Casica Elespoir, Princess and Keeper of the Isle of Life." Clarece took a deep breath then followed suit. She stood herself up and forced her eyes to look into Casica's face. She couldn't fully, blinking and squinting as though staring into the sun. Her eyes *were* blue and now averted slightly down and to her right. This would take time.

"I am Clarece d'Casica," she offered, "Slave and Keeper of - well, you - my lady." Casica smiled broadly and with her hand, spanned the distance between them. "Tis my pleasure to meet you, Clarece d'Casica."

The slave took the dark, perfect hand into her own mittened one. Warmth filled her. "Likewise, my lady," she bowed. "I look forward to knowing you." "As do I you, Clarece," her owner nodded. "As do I you."

# VII

Asla slept like the dead. It was a skill she had developed to survive her life. It reminded her of a pearl diver she'd laid in g'Helderlend. He could hold his breath for nine minutes, the nameless man told her. He would fasten large rocks to his ankles and, jumping from his boat, sink like lead to the bottom of the cove. At the sea's floor, he'd release himself from his weights and harvest oysters. Surfacing was easy, he explained; staying below was the tricky part. His skill was evident in the fact that he could afford to fathom her for half the day.

What rocks were for the diver, sleep was for Asla. She'd learned to fasten sleep about her like so many rocks and dive into the darkness of oblivion. She loved that dark world where nothing lived. No men. No dreams. Nothing. If she could, she would stay below, forever. Clarece was amazed at Asla's ability to sleep through anything - the morning with its busy, noisy preparation and even dinner with all thirty slaves laughing and talking in celebration of another day's end.

Indeed only two things surfaced Asla from her dive: a small, brass bell and Clarece.

On the opposite side of Clarece's bed hung three small service bells: one connected to the prince's room, one for Casica's room and one for Edsner's room. In her four years at the palace, Asla had never heard Clarece's bells sound. Bastien was rarely in need of his slave, and it appeared the Cassican was unaware of her service pull's existence.

Edsner's bell did ring occasionally, rousing Asla from sleep, summoning her to rendezvous with her handler. Fortunately, Edsner preferred taking Asla in daylight, gambling as he did at night. As for the rest of the time, Clarece was Asla's alarm clock, waking her in the morning or during the day, as necessary, for her service schedule. But it was the other awakenings of Clarece that Asla dreaded.

Clarece was struggling with her new owner. The Cassican utterly confounded her as if Bastien had given her a book written in Cassican and now expected her to translate it into everyday life. Clarece spent her days puzzling over this strange woman, trying desperately to solve the riddle of her role as slave who acts as friend. Crispus, what a bizarre situation.

Another challenge for Clarece rested in the simple fact that Casica stayed in the palace. Bastien seldom was present in his chamber, using it primarily as sleeping quarters. On average, Clarece would see her master only during breakfast. Otherwise, she would go about her duties, living entirely to herself. But Casica was a woman (not to mention, a foreign woman finding her way in this new circumstance) and not having the social outlets of Bastien, was constantly underfoot. Clarece had never been houseslave to a woman; whereas all Bastien required was a clean room and clothing, a drawn bath and drawn sheets, Casica required attention. Clarece suddenly found herself a companion, and the adjustment wasn't coming easily. She was put upon in a way she hadn't known for a decade and the stress was eating away at her solitary composure.

Only today, she was looking back into her childhood, at her time in the kitchen, living under the barrage of her brutal mistra. Afterwards was the livery, with the men. Heaven, how she missed the comfort of her empty days.

It had been a difficult day learning this new language. Clarece's head hurt with practice at looking into the princess' face. Yet she desperately must please this new owner. If she didn't, it was clear the Cassican would sell her. Probably she was already contemplating it, Clarece thought. A younger slave could be trained to an owner's needs and desires. As for Clarece, well, she was the proverbial old dog and learning these new Cassican tricks might prove impossible. Or at least inconvenient. Yes, her lady likely was already planning her removal.

Fear of leaving the palace after so many years of familiarity stressed Clarece, further frustrating her performance. It felt good to finally leave Casica's chamber for the comfort of her own stall. Her wrists hurt from lifting her lady's dinner tray with its heavy pitcher of wine. She had anticipated Asla's ministration but returned to her stall to find her friend soundly asleep.

Clarece perched dejectedly on her cot and removed her vest, uniquely sewn with hooks in place of buttons. She studied her boots. Their laces looked to her like a maze of frustration. Even on good days, unlacing them was difficult; tonight, her aching hands hung from her arms like deadwood. This would take time. *This long day is not getting shorter*, she thought to herself. It took the better part of an hour's half before she finally lay herself down.

Somewhere in the night, Clarece's pain and stress took her deformed hands and led her down a frighteningly familiar corridor. Clarece knew its destination and the horror that awaited there, but despite years of frantic attempts, she'd never been able to break the nightmare's grip.

Asla woke as Clarece descended the dream's corridor, her steps sounding like sharp cries of pain to the frightened insulit. *Oh, scads, not tonight,* she thought. Asla hated her friend's torment. And hated her role in this too frequent ritual of fear. She turned in her bed to plead with the dreamer.

"Clarece! Clarece, wake up!" She watched as her friend trembled in her sleep, fighting against an unseen foe. Asla's heart sank. Trying to wake Clarece was useless; she was too deeply in her terror. The young woman stepped from her bed and cautiously approached her fretful friend. Experience had taught her to stay clear of Clarece's hands, resorting instead, to restraining her about the body and arms, until panicked woman regained reality. Asla hated the violent nature of overpowering her terrorized friend. But she knew the alternative, surrendering Clarece to whatever it was awaiting her, was the greater cruelty. Her terrified screams would wake the entire pen.

Asla made her move, feeling her friend lunge out of the corridor with a startled cry. With a desperate energy Clarece struggled against Asla's grasp, her panicked breathing filled with cries and growls. Asla gripped her tightly, her eyes closed against her part in Clarece's terror.

"Tis Asla, Asla!" she spoke into Clarece's darkness, thinking, *please, please wake up.* Clarece did, the horror fleeing at the opening of her eyes. The body in Asla's arms surrendered, collapsing in her embrace. Asla stroked Clarece's head, whispering soothingly, "Still, Rece. You're alright. Shhh... I've got you...." Asla felt her own pounding heart slowing; she sighed deeply and rested her face against Clarece's hair. It was over. "There you go...."

Clarece's breaths were deep and labored. "Oh, God...." she moaned. Her body trembled with exhausted crying. How long Asla held her sala, she didn't know. She would hold her until Clarece returned to sleep. She never returned to this nightmare in the same night, thank gods. Clarece was dozing now, breaths deep and steady. Asla held her a few minutes more, wishing the demons away.

Tenderly, she lay Clarece down and covered her with her sheet. In the morning, Clarece would have no memory of this frightening event, but she would feel it. These nightmares clung to her for days, like the scent of smoke in a burned field. Content that Clarece was resting, Asla returned to her own sleep, wondering how her friend would function in the morning after this blaze.

Morning came too quickly. The other slaves had been stirring for half an hour when Clarece woke from the noise. She sat up in bed slowly, reaching out to rouse Asla. God, she felt awful. It wasn't just her aching arms and nauseous stomach, it was her mind. Emotionally she felt raw with everything about her somewhat unreal, like in a dream.

"How are you this morning, Rece?" asked Asla. "I feel awful," Clarece replied putting her hand to her head. "You'd a rough night." "I don't remember," Clarece whispered, shaking her head exhaustedly.

"I didn't harm you, did I?" "No, but you need rest today." "I can't stay in, Asla." "Clarece," Asla tried to explain gently, "to put it politely, you look like rot. You're in no condition to serve. You have that look, you know? Your mind's not in a good place, sala. You stay here and rest. I'll cover you. I'll see the Cassican gets her meals."

Clarece looked into Asla's troubled face. She did feel like rot. Her feeling of disorientation frightened her, but there was no way she could not serve today. "Asla, I can't stay. What if - if I don't go up there, she might, you know, she might - sell me." Asla sighed. She was right of course. A new owner testing out her property? Yes, it could look bad. Scads, the specter of being sold off: it was like that sword hanging over that man's head in some story Clarece had told her.

"You're right," the junior slave conceded. "I'll help you get ready, but if you have any time today, come down and rest, yes? You know where to find me." Asla helped Clarece dress and did her morning chores for her around the pen. Then the two women joined the other slaves to procure breakfast for their owners.

For breakfast, the kitchen was serving porridge. *Why porridge? Why today?* thought Clarece gloomily. Usually, breakfast was a light tray but with porridge, the kitchen included a covered metal stein filled with boiling water to add to the concentrated meal. This culinary trick worked wonders for the food's flavor but it certainly added weight to her tray, forcing Clarece to walk carefully to her mistra's chamber.

The princess had been up for some time. She wasn't sleeping well in this unfamiliar place and last night there was a disturbance below her. She acquiesced to her sleeplessness and spent much of the night reading a book Clarece had given her on laws governing slaves in Byzanthia. Casica hoped these books would give her insight into her role as owner, explaining, as they did, this institution so alien to her. So far all they did was trouble her more.

"Good morning, mistra," greeted Clarece noticing that her owner had already opened the chamber curtains, something that she should be doing. Sunlight crept into the cool room. Casica returned Clarece's greeting. She glanced up from lacing her boots. Clarece looked unwell. "Are you alright this morning?" she asked finishing one last lace. "Yes, my lady."

*You certainly aren't,* the healer thought, *but you're not about to tell me that, are you? I'm an owner to you - not another woman.* Casica sat, frowning at the meal before her. Porridge. "I haven't had porridge since - I don't know when," she offered trying at conversation again. "Well, this is the best porridge in the kingdom, my lady," Clarece offered. "I can vouch for it; we slaves have it every night for supper."

*I must have misinterpreted that,* the princess thought. Pony! Even her language skill was off kilter today.

Casica was placing the napkin in her lap as Clarece reached to pour the steaming water into the porridge. Whether it was the weight of the stein in her awkward grasp or the steam rising to her eyes, Clarece never knew, but something in her troubled mind winced. In a moment, her aching hands failed, and the near-boiling water of the stein poured onto the princess' stomach.

Casica yelled - more startled than hurt - and sprang up, knocking her chair to the floor. The stein fell with a loud clang as Clarece stepped back in horror. Instantly, she was in a kitchen, with an enraged, tall woman looming over her. In her confusion, Clarece did what all slaves do when they don't  know what to do: she fell to her knees. "Sataka! Sataka!!" *Mercy! Mercy!* she cried, holding her trembling hands before her in protection. Casica stood, stunned in confusion.

What was happening? How could Clarece know that language? Why was she crying for mercy? Casica went to her knees before her charge. The eyes watching her were filled with a depth of terror she'd never seen. "Sataka! Please, mistra, don't hurt me!" Clarece repeated, blinking in anticipation of the coming blow.

Instinctively, Casica reached for Clarece's mittens. She gasped at the pain she felt. *My God! She's in agony! What's happening to this woman?!* Her mind raced frantically. "I won't hurt you! I won't hurt you," she quickly responded in the Sladish language Clarece spoke. "You're alright, Clarece," she continued, "you're safe."

The woman before her looked into the princess' face and blinked. She closed her eyes, trying frantically to match what she was seeing with the scene in her mind. Where was she? - where was the woman in the kitchen? She looked into darkness. There she was, the kitchen woman; she was fading away.

Clarece remained very still as, slowly, reality returned to her. It wasn't the kitchen woman, it was the pain in her arms fading away. She waited silently, waited as her arms returned to her. She waited as her breath returned to her bringing with it the ticking of the clock, the coolness of the room, the hardness of the floor and, lastly, the aroma of porridge.

Cautiously, Clarece studied the woman staring at her. She couldn't be certain. "Princess?" she asked quietly in Byzanthian. "Yes, Clarece," Casica replied, gently releasing the woman's mittens. Clarece shut her eyes in relief. She was here. Not in the kitchen. She was safe.

Casica reached tentatively and touched Clarece on the left side of her head. The slave winced, then surrendered to the sensation. Peace seemed to flow into her, quieting her mind. The hand moved and Clarece looked into the brown eyes of her lady. They were moist.

"Where are you, Clarece?" her mistress asked, searchingly. "Here, my lady." The princess nodded, seeing Clarece behind those saddened eyes. "And where were you?" "In hell." Casica breathed out slowly, resisting an urge to embrace the woman. Clarece needed a safe distance at this time. Instead, she placed her hands carefully on the kneeling woman's thighs, right above her knees. Her touch was comforting. "You were speaking Sladish," she offered.

"Sladish?" Clarece bowed her head, absently stroking her left temple as she tried so very hard to remember. Casica noticed, painfully, a scar above the temple, right at the hair line. "Sladish..." Clarece repeated. "But I don't know Sladish, my lady."

*You did at one time,* thought the healer. *Perhaps when you received that blow.* Clarece's wound had been deep. Casica wondered how she had survived.

Clarece looked at the hands resting on her knees. Between them rest her own crippled claws. She glanced to her left; there lay the stein. The water! She looked up suddenly.

"Did I hurt you?" "What? - No, no, Clarece. I'm fine." Clarece nodded, relieved, and returned her eyes to her hands. When she spoke again, her voice was resigned and focused. She knew what she had to do. Her secure life at the palace, her dread of being sold, none of this mattered anymore.

"This will not do," she announced softly. She looked up at Casica and made full eye contact. Strange that she found it so easily accomplished now. "My lady, I cannot serve you. A houseslave without hands is of no use to you. The truth is I can't dress you; I can't bathe you, feed you. Rigel with his hooves could serve you as well as I," she managed a defeated smile. "But it's not just my hands, my lady." Her eyes glanced away in shame. "My mind... I'm not well. I have endangered you. This can't be. Please, do not fault my Lord Bastien. He's seldom here and is unaware of how crippled I've become. He didn't know he was giving his lady such a broken vessel as her wedding gift." Clarece turned her gaze to the floor, analyzing.

"Still," she continued matter-of-factly, "you should receive a handsome price for me. I have been the property of royalty and that increases my value. My hands detract from my worth as a servant, but I am good stock for breeding. I think you could get three hundred pounds for me and with that -" she looked to the princess, "you can easily purchase a fine houseslave - or hire a servant - as you prefer."

Casica's mind went back to her reading, to the section guiding the purchase of slaves. Breeding potential. Physical condition. Strength. Skill. The four determinants of a slave's value. Clarece, a lifelong student of slavery, had assessed herself and set her value. Three hundred pounds. The going rate for this life before her. That Clarece could so easily assign a monetary value upon herself was sickening. Casica didn't know what she felt more, rage or despair. Didn't know what she wanted to do more, scream or cry. Good One, the evil of this institution was insidious.

Casica studied the vanquished woman. She'd never noticed how thin Clarece was nor how incredibly sea-blue were her eyes, glistening like sapphires. A dark ring framed them lucidly, hinting at the intelligence within. There was an elegance - regality - about her thin face. Casica had seen this face a hundred times in her palace at home. This is not the face of a slave, she thought; it is the face of a courtier.

Clarece misinterpreted Casica's stare and looked away ashamed. Surely, the princess was performing her own calculations; perhaps her assessment was not so optimistic.

Casica mulled Clarece's words. How could she possibly convince this woman of her security? "Clarece, please, look at me," She asked gently. The slave obeyed. "I want you to understand this and to never doubt me again. I am not selling you. Not today. Not ever. I have no need for a houseslave. I can dress myself. I can feed myself. But I cannot replace you. As for Rigel: he hasn't half your wit," she smiled. "Look, this isn't easy for either of us. I know I'm a poor owner and don't treat you as you wish. I have my limitations, too; but the truth is, you're not going anywhere. For better or worse, Clarece d'Casica, you're stuck with me for as long as I live."

The slave studied the young woman. She was telling the truth. But why? Why would a princess keep such a defective property? "Why do you care for me so, my lady? I am wholly unprofitable to you." "Why? Because you, Clarece, are the best thing that's happened to me in this country. You are God's great gift to me. There are thousands of slaves in this land, and of all the slaves He could have given me to, He chose you. I am so grateful for you."

*God's great gift to me*, Clarece thought, straining to receive Casica's meaning. "*You* belong to *me*? I don't know what you mean; you confuse me so much, my lady." Casica grinned at Clarece's confusion feeling very much a companion in it. "Don't feel alone. You, chief slaveswoman, you leave me utterly confounded. Only God knows the mind of a slave," she teased. A slight smile crossed Clarece's lips.

Casica looked at the crippled hands resting in Clarece's lap. Gently she took them into her own. "I *would* like to see your hands. I'm certain I can help them." Clarece tensed at the suggestion.

"This body is your own, my lady," she acknowledged. "You may do whatever you wish upon me. But the physicians examined me years ago and declared my hands unredeemable. They are horribly maimed. I would rather your highness not see them, but I do as you wish." Casica stroked her thumbs fondly over the mittens. Even through the leather, her touch was wonderfully warm.

"No," she was saying. "These precious friends are yours. But I am no physician, Clarece," she pronounced confidently. "I can do what no one you've ever met can. But there is a time for every healing. I'll wait until you're ready. In the meanwhile, will you please let me help your pain? The thought of someone living in my care with such... there's no need for your torment. I can help that without ever seeing your hands."

Clarece considered the two stumps connected to her arms. Freedom from pain - could that be? "Yes, my lady. I would like that very much." "Good. My guess is that they hurt most at night." Clarece was surprised. How could she know that? "How do you treat them now?" "Asla massages them with a heating ointment." "Tis good. Ointment is helpful, but it only goes so far and may eventually lose its effect." Again. How could she know that? "I want you to come to me day or night - wake me. It's not just the pain I'm concerned about. Tis the health of your hands. They have great potential, Clarece. I don't want you to lose that."

Clarece nodded. Casica was obviously operating from her strength. The slave began to wonder what all her mistra could do. It was becoming clear that her current position in Byzanthia did not even shadow what she'd known in her own land. Clarece began to suspect that in Cassica, this young woman must have been a person of great influence.

Casica assessed Clarece. She seemed fully recovered. "My legs are asleep," she grinned. "How do you live so easily upon your knees with these marble floors?" "Years of practice, my lady. Here, I'll help you up...."

The women stood, with Casica rubbing her knees and stretching her body. "I'll help you clean up, Clarece, and then, if you will, I think you should rest. Why don't you stay here? You can rest in the sunlight instead of below." Clarece winced at the inappropriateness of this suggestion. Rest where? The princess' bed?

"I can recommend the sofa," the mistra seemed to reply to her slave's thoughts. "It's just a suggestion. Do what you'd like." "Yes, my lady. I thank you." How this Cassican riddled her world with choices. Casica grabbed the stein and with it came an idea. "Clarece, I need to see the steward about something. I'll see you later. Make yourself at home."

"'*Make yourself at home...*,'" thought Clarece. A slave making herself at home in a princess' chamber. The Cassican had all sorts of queer ideas.

As Casica turned to leave through Bastien's room, Clarece called to her. "My lady? Thank you. I will never again doubt." The princess smiled broadly. A line had disappeared between them.

"Thank *you*, Clarece. Blessings upon you." "And upon you, Mistra," Clarece responded, adding a bow of her head. Casica's smile warmed with gratitude. So Byzanthians expressed this blessing too. "Rest well."

The princess walked quietly from the room, leaving Clarece to study the sofa, debating whether she'd dare opt for light or sleep in familiar darkness below.

# VIII

Casica strolled the east wing hall, contemplating the events of the morning. While she walked, she made a pointed effort to greet the guards stationed along the hall. As for the guards, they didn't know what to make of this foreigner. She was an enigma with her dark complexion and eyes and black hair that she kept long, like a slave, braided or pulled back. Then there was her height. The Cassican was as tall as almost any man in the palace.

Crowning her oddness was the alien's manner. Passing a guard she had not yet met, Casica stopped to introduce herself and learn his name. *What kind of royal gives a whiff about a guard's name?* he thought, informing the Cassican his name was Lancet. The princess smiled and complimented Lancet on his fine choice of a hand sword, noticing the ornamental counter balance of its hilt. It must handle beautifully, she surmised, and asked if she may see it.

Surprised, Lancet handed the large dagger of a sword to the woman. She inspected the handiwork approvingly then wielded it as one trained, commenting on its fine balance. Truly, it was magnificent, she declared presenting it, hilt first, to the astonished man.

Yes, my lady, it was, Lancet replied thinking how none of his colleagues had noticed his new acquisition. He had paid a handsome sum for this treasure and was pleased with the princess' attention. In fact, he thought, the Cassican was not unpleasant herself. Her keen eyes were warmly soft. And her skin, he'd never seen such color; it was as though her maker shaded it to blend into the hue of her eyes. Disappointment surprised Lancet when the dark woman dismissed herself and continued along.

Casica loved palace life with its ebb and flow of human activity contained, as it was, within a pool of political structure. Every castle had unique personality and the House of Ars was no exception. The Byzanthian palace was huge with five wings, three wings more than customary. The east wing steward, Clarece had explained, oversaw the library wing in addition to his residential one. Casica knew from experience that the best time to find a steward was in the morning, before the many problems and demands of the day called him into general palace life.

The princess located the steward's quarters. She was not disappointed. There he sat, steward of the east wing, planted at an oak desk, drink in hand, perusing his list of the day's requirements. He looked to be about fifty years, wrapped in the portly physique common to men of his profession. Casica liked stewards, in general. She found them to be a breed unto themselves, busy and efficient like worker bees in a chaotic colony; without them, no palatial hive could survive.

"May I interrupt, Lord Steward?" she asked respectfully. (Politeness goes a long way with these men.) The steward rose upon seeing the woman. Obviously, she was the Cassican princess living in his wing. "We have not yet met, Lord Steward. I am Casica, wife of Bastien," she greeted, surprised at how easily she referred to herself as "wife."

"Yes, my lady," he replied with a courteous bow. "And I am Silian, steward of the east and library wings. And how does the princess find her chambers in the east?" Silian took great pride in the accommodations of his wings.

"Very well, Lord Steward, thank you. Both service and appointments befit a palace of such distinction as this one. It is, no doubt, a reflection of Lord Steward's governance." Already Silian liked this woman. Unlike many in the palace, he held no prejudice against the Cassican. Stewards could ill-afford blind dislike: too many people to please. This woman seemed sensible; God knew he had his fill of demanding, petty female royalties.

"And how may I help you this morning, Princess?" "Just a small request, Lord Steward, but - first, may I inquire of your steward's health today? You seem to favor your right leg." A limp she noticed; one signaling an arthritic hip. "Oh, tis nothing, my lady. My hip gives me trouble. That cursed stiffening of old age."

"I see," replied Casica, thinking to herself, *Here is my door into this man's favor.* "In my own land, I am a kind of - physician, Lord Steward. May I the liberty to help you?" "Well ... of course, my lady, but my own physicians have already examined me and found - ." He stopped short. Casica touched his arm and, in response, the pain in his hip disappeared. Silian checked first at his hip and then at the dark woman before him. The Cassican smiled pleasantly as though this were merely the most natural occurrence in the world: she touches people and they stop hurting.

"Why, thank you, my lady," he said tentatively. He had heard rumors of josquins in the land of Cassica, but, gads, how'd she do that? "And how, may I ask, did you do that?" "Oh, tis nothing, Lord Steward. Just a trick I learned at home. Please feel free to contact me should your hip ever bother you again." Casica hadn't lived in a palace for nothing. She knew that to find favor with a castle's steward meant sharing a key to the king's store. For a mutually advantageous association, well, such was the language of stewards.

"Thank you, again, your highness," said a mystified Silian, swinging his leg with ease he hadn't known for years. "And what is this small request of yours?" "Very simple, Silian. I just wondered if your Lord Steward could provide a setting for serving tea. I don't seem to have one in my chambers." "No, my lady. That is because tea is to be served by your slave - Clarece, I believe." "Yes. Tis a fine slave; however, in my country, a hostess prepares and serves her own tea, a cultural tradition, you understand. I wish to continue this practice here as a comfort to my homesick heart."

"I see," nodded Silian. "Of course, my lady, I am pleased to provide you whatever you wish. We can visit the kitchen stores now, if you like, and choose a setting suitable for your lady's needs." *A healing touch invites marvelous effect,* thought Casica. Casica nodded in compliance and the two began their journey to the kitchen storage.

Along the way, Silian proved himself a spring of palatial information, identifying various chambers, pointing out servant and slave passageways and critiquing structural architecture. As he talked, Casica noticed the ownership and pride in the steward's voice. Satisfaction in his position flowed easily from his tone. The message was clear: this was his castle. As for her, Casica gathered information freely, asking, finally, something that had puzzled her since morning.

"My Lord Steward, am I correct in my understanding that slaves eat only porridge?" "Yes, my lady," the steward answered officially. "House slaves are provided porridge every evening at eight o'clock." "But, my lord, even horses eat a variety of foods - oats, barley....?" "Well, yes, Princess, but slaves aren't horses, now, are they?" He grinned at the absurdity of the comparison. "Besides, house slaves, such as yours, have scrap rights...." "Scrap rights?" Casica had never heard this phrase.

"Yes, my lady. As your slave, Clarece may eat whatever remains on your plate, a generous privilege of her position." *Generous if there's anything left on the plate,* thought Casica. It was clear she needed to change her eating habits. "You are fortunate to have the slave Clarece," Silian continued. "She is devoted and intelligent - pity about her hands. Nevertheless, she's certainly made my life easier." "And how is that?" Casica questioned.

"Her guild. It used to be that thirty slaves pestered me for their needs. Now only Clarece comes to me with their requests. A brilliant idea; efficient for all parties involved. Two other wings have followed her suit, the west wing excepting. Their egotism renders them unable to settle upon a leader. Pity the west wing steward, Princess," he concluded with a smile.

The couple arrived at their destination at which time the princess chose tea utensils fitting her taste. She included three place settings of silverware along with three silver plates. The steward noted her selection and ordered the attending servant to deliver them that afternoon. Quest complete, Casica excused herself from the steward. He had been more than kind, giving her, as he did, much of his morning. It was his pleasure, he assured her, thanking her, again, for her ministration to his hip. And please, feel free to come with any need, he invited. An important alliance had been forged, each thought to themselves.

Josquin left the steward for her chamber, wondering along the way, both how Clarece fared and where the esteemed slave had decided to rest.

She had passed the library wing when a striking form materialize via the servants' stairway. It was Asla. She had just completed a service with a prominent political official in town for the week. The man was drunk and crude in his ways, and Asla looked forward to pounding out the revolting hour on the gym floor. First, she wanted to check on Clarece. She was about to take a shortcut to the slaves' pen when she heard a familiar voice.

"Asla, hold please." The insulit turned and bowed in a single motion, a distinctly Aslatic movement, produced as it was from years of dance. The princess looked troubled, prompting Asla to greet her with a question. "How is she?" she asked quietly. Apparently, realized Casica, Clarece's episode of the morning was not unexpected to her stallmate.

"She had a bad morning. She's better now. Asla, did something happen last night to cause this?" "She had a... difficult night, Princess, but as to what causes these spells, it happened long ago. I don't know what it is."

"I see," the healer answered, but she didn't. Her mind couldn't imagine what could cause a mental break as Clarece experienced that morning. "Does this happen often?" Casica watched as the young woman debated within herself, fearing to betray the trust of her friend. "You don't have to answer, Asla." "No, my lady. Perhaps you can help her." Asla glanced around the hall. No one was nearby.

"Clarece has nightmares. I'm certain they're related to her hands, and they happen more frequently. Sometimes the morning after is not so bad. Sometimes, like today, she wakes without herself." *Wakes without herself,* thought the healer. What a poignant description.

Asla's mind raced. If she were going to speak for Clarece, now was the time. "My lady, forgive my speaking so freely, but Clarece is afraid you'll sell her off because of her hands - and her condition. I beg you, lady, do not do this. Rece is the best slave in the kingdom, and what she lacks in hand, she trumps in heart. She will slave you well. Just give her time. Please."

Asla wasn't accustomed to asking anything of anyone, and she knew the chief slaveswoman would angrily disapprove of what she just did, begging the princess on her behalf. But Clarece was her sala and the possibility of having her sold off was unthinkable. Perhaps the Cassican was more human than other mistras, being, as she was, from a country where there were no owners of human flesh. Regardless, she would not stand by and watch her friend drown, even if it meant looking like a fool or being stocked for her insolence.

Casica stood, moved by the g'Helderleit's words; certainly, there was no veiling Asla's love for the senior slave. "Asla, do not fear. I'm not selling your friend. I've told her as much this morning. I would rather a heart over hands any day," she smiled. "Clarece is blessed to have someone love her as you do."

Asla glanced away uncomfortably. "I am insulit, my lady. It is not within me to love." Casica frowned. "What do you mean?" "I am insulit," Asla responded, repeating the obvious. "I have no soul. The hollow cannot love. It is not within me." "Who told you this?" Casica asked, incredulous. Asla frowned, confused. *Who told her?* What a ridiculous question, like asking who told her she was a woman.

"My lady, I don't know that anyone has told me. Tis simply known. The clerics teach this - if that's what you mean." "The clerics?!" Josquin's mind exploded. *The clerics here teach that this beautiful woman has no soul? As if beauty could come some place other than God? Tis inhuman, enough, insulit exists at all, but to wrap this evil in such a lie - .*

Asla watched Casica's internal rant. She wasn't sure if the Cassican were angry at her or something she'd said, but decided that now might be a good time to distance herself.

"My lady," she hurried, "if you will, please, excuse me. I have a service to attend." *I'm quite certain you don't mean church service,* the angry princess thought. If the clergy teaches Asla she has no soul, what possible spiritual avenue were available to her? Maybe her books had a section on this.

"My lady?" Asla was waiting. "Yes, Asla. You are excused." "Thank you, princess," the relieved woman replied, "and thank you for your kindness to Clarece." Asla turned towards the pen. Once again the Cassican voice arrested her. "God's Beauty!" the princess called.

An angry shame spun the insulit around. The irony of her name was a frequent root of mockery, but how dare this princess taunt her on the heels of kindness! The face smiling at her bore no trace of ridicule, however. The Cassican seemed sincere.

"Don't believe everything you've heard. You not only have a soul, you are one." The insulit gaped at the foreign woman. *No wonder Clarece is going mad,* she thought, bowing as she continued on her way. Even so, the vial had been tipped. For as she made her way down the slaves' staircase, the princess' words clung to Asla like some exotic perfume, enticing her with the provocative scent of Truth.

The morning's errand took much longer than Casica had allowed. She entered her chamber to find lunch waiting, her place set, and no Clarece. She considered checking Clarece's stall but decided against it. Clarece needed freedom to be where she wanted without the interference of her mistra.

Casica inhaled. Ham. She loved ham. The kitchen of the Byzanthian palace certainly knew how to produce delectable fare. The young woman had a healthy appetite and easily could have cleaned her plate, but the steward's words haunted her. One meal a day for every slave. Casica had rarely missed a meal except for times of healing and during the week of her investment when she fasted seven days. Josquins were passionate eaters, but this needed to change.

Clarece needed food, nutritious food. Casica wondered how much the woman's fatigue was caused by her poor nutrition, wondered how the laborer slaves made it through the day at all. "Slaves aren't horses, now, are they?" the steward observed. No, they weren't. They were treated worse than horses. Twas a sadistic strategy, keeping a large segment of the kingdom's population starved and weakened. Starving people, kept alive just enough, have little room for dreaming and thoughts of rebellion. Survival keeps people contained, renders them more easily controlled. Casica decided to begin by eating three-fourths of her meal. After weeks of cleaning her plate, a sudden change of appetite would arouse suspicion in the ever-observant Clarece.

A quiet shadow entered Casica's chamber. Clarece approached her mistra with a slight kneel, one Casica was recognizing as a greeting kneel. "Welcome, mistra." "Thank you, Clarece. And how are you feeling?" She looked improved to the healer. More rested and centered.

"Much better, Princess. Your sofa is very comfortable," came the shy confession. *Good for you, Clarece*, thought her mistra, grinning. "And how was your meeting with Lord Steward?" the slave continued, concentrating on meeting the princess' eyes.

Casica indicated the chair opposite her. "Sit, Clarece. Very well. I like that man. In fact I don't think I've ever met a steward I didn't like. Their profession is peopled by the industrious and practical." "Yes, my lady, Silian is a fair man." "And he speaks highly of you, Clarece. He was telling me about your guild and how much easier your idea has made his life. It seems other wings have followed suit."

Clarece glanced down at the compliment. "It wasn't my idea, my lady. I read about it in a book on governing practices of the west sphere. It appears guilds have existed for millennia, starting, perhaps, with the Zinien kingdoms and progressing to the west only seven centuries ago...."

Casica ate as Clarece continued her lesson on guild development in the west sphere. The princess had never witnessed this kind of enthusiasm in the chief slaveswoman before. Clarece was positively enthralled by this information and swept Casica away with her. Who could have possibly thought guild development could be interesting, even fascinating; but in Clarece's tutorial it was. Clarece ended her presentation, catching herself with embarrassment. "I apologize, my lady. I was rambling."

"No, Clarece. You were fascinating! You, chief slaveswoman, are a teacher. Have you tutored before?" "No, my lady. Unless you count Asla. I taught her to read and write Byzanthian." "Language is no small subject," observed Casica. "You're very gifted, Chief."

"I believe language is one of your giftings, my lady," Clarece redirected. She wasn't comfortable with this attention on herself. "Poul, the sergeant, says that josquins can speak any language."

At this mention of her cousin, Josquin glowed. "He does, does he? Well, yes and no. Some truly can. Like my mother. Maman is a true linguist. She has studied every known language and masters them all. She tried to steer me that direction. But my interests lay elsewhere - art and riding. So instead," Casica grinned mischievously, "Maman taught me to cheat." "'Cheat,' my lady?"

"Yes," Casica explained. "I 'cheat' in that, while I myself may not know a language, I can - borrow - a speaker's knowledge. Like with -" she was going to use the morning's experience as an example but thought better of it - "Asla. She speaks g'Helderleicht, so in her presence I can speak g'Helderleicht. The advantage is that I can speak any language in the presence of a speaker, which is, of course, the only time I would want to speak that language. Another advantage is that I use their vocabulary. The disadvantage is that if they don't know a word, neither do I. And plus, I am learning here that speaking a common language is not the same as communicating."

"And what gives you the ability to do this?" asked an amazed Clarece. "My shalonn, my necklace." "Your necklace is magical?" "That's one way to describe it, but no josquin sees it that way. My shalonn is more akin to a tool. A tool... and a companion." Casica's hand reached for the pulsating stones at her neck. "We share with each other. Without me the stones are dead. Without them, I am not so nearly alive...." she concluded, quietly caressing her shalonn, lost in thought.

Clarece studied the princess, noticing a moist sheen on her dark eyes. She wished to ask what Casica were thinking, but to do so would be inappropriate. In fact, as much as she had enjoyed their conversation, she felt certain this, too, had been inappropriate. She had just spoken more with the Cassican than she had her entire fourteen years with Bastien - not counting the time he'd spent teaching her to read.

"Is your highness finished eating?" she asked returning to her proper role. "Yes, Clarece. I am. Compliments to the chef." Clarece frowned at the leftovers on the plate. Her mistra never left food. "It seems my recitation on guilds has ruined your appetite." "No, my teacher," Casica laughed, " I've simply had enough." Clarece bowed in response. Casica noticed a look in her eyes that, until now, had eluded her: hunger. Clarece was hungry. Casica had never met hunger. Now she lived under its roof.

"Clarece, I have a favor to ask of you." The slave listened attentively. "I would like for you to come for tea, tomorrow, at two." *Scads, another heavy utensil,* thought Clarece, imagining a silver tea pot. "Yes, my lady. I will have tea for you tomorrow at two." "No, no. That's not what I mean," the princess tried to clarify. "I want you to come for two." Clarece looked intently at her mistra, determined to understand her. "You are having tea for two and you wish me to come serve at two...."

Casica frowned at the confused woman, her own confusion rising. Why was this so difficult? *Oh,* it dawned upon her; *that's what I'm doing.* "Clarece am I speaking Cassican right now?" "Uh, no, my lady," Clarece answered suspiciously. "You are speaking Byzanthian." "Oh...." Well, that wasn't it. Why was this so hard? Could it be that the invitation itself was the language barrier?

"Let me say it like this. Tomorrow, you come here," she signaled with her hands, "at two o'clock. Bring nothing with you. Just come. Does that make sense?" *Yes and no,* thought Clarece. Yes, I understand what to do; no, I can't imagine why I'm to do this.

"I think I now understand, my lady. You wish for me to come here at two o'clock tomorrow and bring nothing but myself?" "Madala!" Casica lifted her hands in victory. The chief slaveswoman was profoundly befuddled, but at least she now understood her orders. "As you wish my lady," Clarece bowed, standing to remove her owner's lunch.

Five steps down the staircase was a nook consisting of a stone bench. Clarece sat there and contemplated the plate on her lap. Hurriedly, she took her mitten fasteners by her teeth and shed the leather from her right hand. She didn't even think to use her spoon, hidden away in her vest pocket. Instead, the hungry woman scooped up the food with her bare claw hand, shamelessly filling her mouth. She fed quickly, licking the juices from her maimed flesh.

Her small feast ended, Clarece sat back, satisfied. Sighing deeply she blessed it with a grateful smile. "Thank you, God, and thank you mistra." *From deepest hell to hog heaven,* she thought, allowing herself the poor jest. This had been perhaps the oddest day of her life. What would tomorrow bring?

## IX

Clarece paced her stall nervously. It was nearing two o'clock, and soon she'd ascend the stairs for only God knew what. Asla sat in her cot reading a book, watching her friend with an impish delight. She'd never seen Clarece so plain nervous before. This was fun.

"Rece," she asked, still studying her book, "what does 'trepidation' mean?" "It means nervousness or even terror," Clarece replied, fiddling with a fastener on her vest. "Oh, like in the sentence, 'The chief slaveswoman was trepidated at the thought of having tea'?" Asla looked up at her senior and smiled sweetly. Clarece's own facial expression was not so kind.

"Cursed insulit, you're mocking me." "No, I'm not." "Yes, you are." "Alright, maybe a little," Asla confessed mischievously. "But I can't help it, Rece. In all our years, I've never seen you nervous like this. It's like... you're going out with a man or something." "Asla, that's the point," the flustered slave explained. "I've never been "out" with a man. I've never even *served* tea, much less been to one. I mean, what do I do? What do I wear? You're the culturally experienced one - what's appropriate dress for this?"

Asla lay aside her book; this was more serious than she'd thought. "Well, in your case, the latest slave fashions would be appropriate." Her laugh was dispelled by the look that met it. "Seriously, Rece. You always look proper. I tell you what: why don't you wear your blue vest. It's royally becoming on you - 'twill boost your confidence." Clarece nodded, hurriedly unfastening her daily vest and replacing it with her birthday vest, the one Bastien had given her last year.

"There. What do you think?" she declared, presenting herself to the cultured one. Asla nodded approvingly. Clarece truly did glow in that color. "You look beautiful, Rece. Very nice." "You're not just saying that?" She didn't *feel* confident. "Not at all, my friend. You're just right for tea." Clarece sat on her cot, restlessly.

Asla studied Clarece's throat. One more thing needed done. "Come here," she instructed, "let me do something I haven't done in awhile." The chief slaveswoman moved to Asla's cot. Asla took a soft, oiled cloth and began polishing her friend's collar - carefully, for no slave liked having her collar touched. "You're all tarnished..." she observed smilingly.

Clarece closed her eyes, her voice filling with irritation. "This is insane; I'm not wearing a necklace, you know." "What are you talking about? I've done this lots of times." "That's not what I mean, Asla. Here you are polishing my *slave* collar so I'll look fit to have *tea* with a princess who is my *owner*. I'm a slave, for Crispus' sake! What am I doing acting like a freewoman? This is crazy!" Asla paused her work, her patience expired.

"You want to know crazy, Rece? I'll tell you crazy. Just listen to yourself. Scads, Clarece! You think too much. Look at the way I live. If I dissected my life the way you do, I'd have graced my neck with a noose years ago. When will you learn to take the pleasures offered you instead of analyzing your life away?" Clarece looked down at her hands, smarting from the rebuke.

"Look, this is just tea..." Asla added more quietly, regretting her anger. "All you do is go up there, sit down, drink some tea - it's appropriate to add milk - and visit. That's all teas are. An excuse to sit and talk with someone. And you're a talker, Rece, it's your forte. You know, some people actually *enjoy* teas. If you're not careful, you might even have fun. Now, may I finish?"

Clarece nodded, presenting the back of her collar. Asla cleaned gently, mindful of the scars on her friend's neck, formed as molten metal touched tender flesh. Collaring was a painful experience; it was clear whoever collared Clarece in the past had taken their time dousing the welded joint.

Clarece put her hand to her shiny silver collar. Taking a deep breath, she encouraged herself: "I can do this." "Yes!" grinned

Asla, teasingly, "That's the spirit, chief slaveswoman." Clarece glared playfully at the g'Helderleit.

"Really," Asla assured her warmly. "You'll do fine." "I'm so nervous. Asla, if you'd heard me yesterday; it took me a quarter hour to understand what she wanted me to do. I looked like a fool."

"I'm sure Casica is a little nervous, too." "What? Nervous about a slave coming to see her?" Clarece couldn't imagine that. "Of course. You'll be her first guest in her new home. I *know* you'll have a good time, Clarece. Trust me." "Oh, yeah. Trust you," Clarece smirked. "Weren't you the one who hung my camisole in the - ." "Scads!" Asla objected. "That was two years ago!"

Clarece laughed with her friend. The clock was winding to chime two. "I won't be here when you get back, but I wish hear all about it. Good luck!" Asla wished, offering one more nod of encouragement as Clarece began her ascent to the princess.

Casica had to smile at herself. "Kai, Cass, you'd think you've never served tea before... goodness." She was nervous. Tea was not a daily occurrence in Byzanthia as it was in Cassica. The kitchen woman was less than friendly with her attendance to the princess' requests for tea leaves. She had many varieties but couldn't understand a royal interrupting her day for such a need. Trying to explain proved useless, so Casica resorted to rank, assuring the maid this would be a common request on her part. Casica stopped short asking for refreshments to accompany her tea. She hadn't yet made the necessary arrangements for Clarece's unique needs.

The clock had just sounded two when a familiar presence filled her chamber. Clarece stood at the doorway, hands politely in front of her, waiting for whatever was to come. Casica paused at the sight of her charge. Clarece was positively beautiful in her royal vest. "Welcome, Clarece! Come in," she invited, watching as the slave offered her greeting kneel before taking a step. "You look lovely. I haven't seen that vest, have I?"

Clarece felt her face warm at the attention. "No, my lady. Tis my birthday present from last year. Prince Bastien gives me a vest each year for St. Crispus day." "So St. Crispus is your birthday? How fitting," her lady replied. "Actually, my lady, I don't know when I was born. For some reason, I haven't any original papers.

It was Prince Bastien who adopted St. Crispus for my birthday."
"Well, he shows good taste. Royal blue is your color."

Casica motioned for Clarece, inviting her to the table. Casica's chamber table was small but elegant, carved of quarter sawn cherry. The Cassican had set a place for Clarece at the head of the table, her own seat to Clarece's right. She'd found over the years she preferred this arrangement to sitting across from guests. The sense of less table between them seemed to enhance discussion.

Clarece sat quietly, bowing her head to the princess. She was careful to keep her hands in her lap and her back straight. This seemed the proper pose. As the slave looked over the setting, a panicked feeling swept into her. Silverware. Merry Crispus! She had completely overlooked having to use silverware. She closed her eyes, silently chastising herself. Clarece owned a single tin spoon, specially shaped to go around her thumb like a ring. Even if she'd thought to bring it, however, it certainly wasn't fit to grace this table.

"Clarece, thank you for coming today. I haven't served tea since doing so for my ladies-in-waiting, the week before I left home." "Thank you for having me, my lady," Clarece replied respectfully, thinking how bizarre it was the princess didn't realize that for a slave, an invitation and a command were one and the same - as if she had a choice to come today. *Clarece, stop it,* she scolded herself. *Don't take your anger out on the Cassican.*

"And how many chamber maids did you own?" she asked kindling the conversation. "Three. They all swaddled me," Casica smiled, remembering the kind women who surrounded her life. "But they weren't owned; they were servants." "They chose to serve you of their free will?" Casica considered the question. They did seem free in their service. "Yes, their families have served mine for generations, but never out of compulsion. They are free to leave but never choose to."

"I can imagine that," Clarece voiced honestly. "You are a kind mistra. To freely serve you would be an honorable employment." *I wonder if you feel any honor serving me as a slave,* Casica thought, noticing the brilliant silver band about Clarece's neck. How ironic, to use so precious a metal to devalue a human being.

The princess poured hot tea into Clarece's cup. As a pleasant, spicy aroma filled the air, Clarece's mind flashed to the day before. She quickly dismissed the memory. Better to stay here in the moment. Better to concentrate on not dropping the delicate china. "Would you like some milk?" the princess was asking. "Yes, please," the anxious woman responded, remembering Asla's words. Clarece watched as the princess took a spoon and slowly stirred the milk into her tea. She realized then there was no other silverware on the table. The guest smiled with relief.

"What are you smiling about?" her hostess asked curiously. "I'm thinking... I've never tasted tea." "You jest!" Casica was dumbfounded. "I thought you served in a kitchen." "I did, my lady, but as a scullery girl. I know much more about cleaning dishes than I do of their contents." "Well, then," Casica announced, as she poured tea for herself, "it's about time, chief slaveswoman." Casica lifted her cup to Clarece in a toast. Clarece joined her, carefully holding the delicate vessel with both hands. "To your first taste of tea, Clarece d'Casica, and to many more to come."

Clarece brought the cup to her lips. The hot liquid filled her mouth with a spicy pleasure and her body with a comforting warmth. "That is *delicious*, my lady," she said excitedly. "You like it?" the princess asked, pleased. "It's one of my favorite blends." "I've never imagined tea would be like this. I've read about it, but eyes haven't taste." The slave took another swallow, savoring the sensation. She'd no idea life held such a treasure. Casica watched her charge, enjoying her pleasure, enjoying the opportunity to share this simple gift with her.

Clarece carefully placed her cup upon its saucer. She turned to her mistra and bowed her head. "Tis very good, mistra. Thank you. Asla told me I would like tea." Casica smiled, still wondering how anyone could have lived in a palace as long as Clarece and not tasted tea. "How long have you known Asla, Clarece?" "Four years, my lady." The princess took a swallow. Clarece would be a good person to ask this question.

"I'm confused about something. I've been reading the books you recommended on slavery, but I haven't found a single reference to insulit." Clarece thought for a moment. "The only reference is in the work of Fr. Golane, page 117, I believe. He explains that insulit is a rather recent development in slavery structure, existing only about four hundred years."

Casica didn't know what to ask first: how Clarece knew the page was 117 or why the recent development. "Clarece, how do you know it's page 117 - there are hundreds of pages in that volume." "I know because I've read it my lady," she replied as if this were explanation enough. "You've *read* it," Casica repeated, clarifying. "Yes, my lady." "And do you always remember the page numbers of books you read?"

Clarece took another sip of tea, mentally reviewing the hundreds of books she'd read from the library. "Yes, my lady, I think so," she decided, "- when pages are assigned numbers." Casica gaped, amazed. It was obvious this accomplishment was unremarkable to Clarece.

"And just how do you do that?" "I don't know, my lady," replied the slave, admiring the fleur d'lis pattern of the tea pot. "I sometimes think I don't read as others do. It seems others read words; I read pages. It's like I see the page in my mind - like a picture? It stays there. I remember everything I read and most of what I see." Casica studied the woman sitting in the chair near her. Clarece took anther sip of tea, smiling to herself with the joy of discussing her passion.

"I've heard of people like you," the princess finally observed, thinking, *This woman possess a genius,* "but you're the first one I've ever met. In Cassica, we call your ability 'canvas memory.'" Clarece was unimpressed. "I call it a trick, my lady, like your 'cheating' in languages." Casica sat silent again, wondering who this woman was who served as slave.

"But to return to insulit," Clarece continued, uncomfortable with the princess' attention. "Fr. Golane believes insulit derived from the tradition of concubines. Apparently men decided the best use of their concubines was to rent them while they weren't laying their masters. You still see this in the way handlers treat their insulit. Edsner takes Asla regularly but rents her in between times. He's her primary service, however."

"I see," Casica nodded. "But what of the teaching of insulits' being the "souless," where does that come from?" "That, I don't know," Clarece conceded. She had mused the same question herself. "Sometimes I think it's based on expediency. How could a religious man justify sleeping with a whore? He can't unless the woman is not a whore, or - better yet - not a woman at all. If an insulit is soulless, she is inhuman; and if not human, then where is the quandary? This is only my opinion, however."

Casica sipped her own tea, considering Clarece's theory. It made sense. "Do you believe Asla is souless?" she asked quietly. Clarece held her cup thoughtfully. "No, my lady. Not now. But I confess, I did think so before I knew her. We slaves, we ostracize Asla; more truly, we fear her. Insulit are trained assassins. And it is said that they, being souless, possess the power to consign souls to hell. My guild does not recognize Asla's existence, and no slave ever touches an insulit."

Clarece lowered her head, grieved. "I guess every group, no matter how low a rung, wishes someone to step on. 'Tis cruel though. Slaves can attend church, practice confession, be buried even. Insulit cannot. Asla isn't allowed even in a cemetery. When insulit die, they are burned and their ashes thrown into the refuse pit.' Tis very cruel," she repeated, her eyes lost in her teacup. Casica watched as Clarece's mitten reached for her collar, stroking the smooth metal about her.

"You touch Asla, and you're a slave," she inquired gently. Clarece smiled to herself. "When Asla came to the palace, she was ten years old and had no one. My people wanted to harm her. I couldn't allow that, so I had her share my stall. Just living with Asla ruined my theology on insulit. There is *nothing* souless about that g'Helderleit, Princess; she shames me with her passion and pleasure in life. She is my sala." Casica turned her eyes to her guest. "You've used that word before. Is that like saying she's your best friend?"

"Yes and no, my lady," Clarece explained. "Asla is my dearest friend, but she is more: a sala is someone you share bread with." "You mean you share your food with each other?"

"No. Well, yes, we do, but to share bread is more. Slaves are less than nothing in this world - but we have two great rites. One is the mastras - or mistras, as in your case - this is a ritual a slave shares with their owner. I've never known of anyone performing this. The other is the sala'd, a ceremony between slaves. It involves sharing bread and wine with one another."

"Like communion?" Casica interjected. "Yes," smiled Clarece, "tis very much a communion between friends." "It sounds like a beautifully intimate ritual, Clarece." "It is, my lady," Clarece bowed in agreement. "Where did sharing bread begin?"

Clarece thought for a moment, touching her mitten to her mouth. "I don't know. But I tell Asla tis God's way of including insulit in His world - she hasn't decided whether to believe me or not," Clarece finished with a playful grin.

"Maybe the fact you include her in *your* world will help convince her," Casica suggested aloud. Clarece looked at the princess with heightened interest; her mistra was very insightful. *Is that what you're doing with me?* she wondered. *Are you including me in your world to convince me of something else?*

"Would you like another cup?" Clarece hesitated. Yes, she certainly wanted more of this nectar but was it right to ask for more? Casica alleviated her uncertainty by lifting the tea pot towards her guest. No one drinks only one cup of tea, at least not in Cassica. "Yes, my lady. Thank you." Clarece bowed.

"What about you, Clarece? In what state are you in God's world?" Casica asked, stirring a portion of milk into the slave's cup. "Sometimes I think I'm in a perpetual state of confusion, my lady," Clarece answered, quite seriously, prompting the princess to laugh. She, too, experienced this theology. "What do you mean?"

"My lady, you may laugh," the slave observed gravely. "You are royal and with that, divine. Your eternal soul is secure." "I disagree, but go on...," the princess invited.

"Well, I don't know what Cassicans believe, but we are taught that royals are born into heaven. Servants may go to heaven if they live righteously. As for us slaves, we are born damned - as God evidences in our class; only the cursed would be born enslaved; that His sign of our damnation." Clarece looked helplessly at her deformed hands. Another sign of His wrath. Casica was taken aback by her charge's forlorn expression. *She truly believes this,* she realized.

"We can hope to serve well," Clarece continued, humbly, "and live as best a slave can. Then perhaps, if God sees us and has mercy upon us, we can move out of damnation - if not into heaven itself. To be undamned is better if not heavenly." Casica watched her troubled guest fret with her mittened hands. "So we are taught, but I have little hope of this being true. God does not hear me;

He does not see me; how could He possibly know my actions? But even if He does, how could anyone serve that Sovereign well enough to enter *His* kingdom? It seems to me you must either be born into His realm or not at all."

The senior slave stared, frustrated, into her cup. She had exposed her whole life as meaningless. Nothing she could ever do would change her lot in life - not this present one or the next.

Casica contemplated Clarece's words. It was clear Byzanthian theology was designed to quell any hope from the enslaved. "You have given this matter much thought," she observed. Clarece glanced up at her owner, somewhat embarrassed.

"I ramble, my lady. But it's just that I don't know *why* I live - except to serve you, of course. Still, I want to live, to live well. Tis just I would that my life mattered." *And it doesn't. It never will.* "It is clear *your* life matters, my lady," Clarece pronounced, wanting to end this self-speculation. "You have life within you - I can see it, and I've felt it. Truly, you are a subject in His realm - Cassican or not," she added dryly, leaving Casica to wonder if she were jesting. It was impossible to tell. Only God knows the mind of a slave.

"I am a subject, Clarece," Casica began, "but not because I was born into it as you think. I was adopted  - as anyone, including you, can be. And I am certain God not only sees and hears you, but He is keenly interested in your life and where it is headed. You life does matter to Him," *and to me.* Casica felt a strong urge to continue her view, but thought against it. Clarece was a student, a questioner. She would ask for more when she was ready, as she would for help with her hands.

Clarece sipped her tea; if her cup were a pipe, she'd be puffing away. How the princess drew her out of herself, stretching her into a larger world. "You pour many deep things into my mind, mistra, like the milk you add to my tea."

The clock was chiming three. Clarece looked up surprised. The time had passed quickly. Though she never would have put words to it, Clarece was lonely for shared thought. No one could join her level of introspection, but in Casica, she had found a satisfying match. The slave finished her cup and placed it carefully upon the saucer. There. She had managed to live this afternoon without dropping anything. Turning to her mistra she bowed, respectfully.

"I must leave to prepare your dinner, my lady. May I be excused from your presence?" "Of course, Clarece," Casica replied thinking about the tea milk. The chief slaveswoman's smile was guarded but genuine.

"I thank you, my lady, for this experience. I'm sure my tongue is spoiled forever." "I'm happy you enjoyed it, Clarece. Tea is a daily - rite - in Cassica. You are wonderful company. Would you honor me with your presence again?"

*Honor you? Me honor you? She's doing it again,* thought Clarece. "I will do as you wish, my lady, but I must warn you, I have only one nice vest, and I need some afternoons to clean your linens and clothing." Again, Clarece spoke with absolute seriousness leaving the princess to wonder if she were teasing or speaking in earnest.

"Well, let us not wear out your vest before your next birthday," the hostess replied trying to match Clarece's tone. "How about the day after next. And come as you are." "Yes, my lady. I would like that very much. I wish to hear about your land - it is my hope to learn Cassican, if you think I could master it." "Clarece," said the princess looking directly into her sapphire eyes, "I think you can master anything you wish. We'll start with 'good-bye' as in the good-bye that means I will see you later: 'anastis'."

"'Anastis,' my lady," Clarece repeated with a bow of her head. Rising from her seat, she stood at attention. The princess joined her. "And how do I say 'thank you?'" the slave inquired. "Nai gode...."

"Nai gode, mistra." And with that and a kneel Clarece parted from her first tea, thinking to herself how, truly, it was milk that enriched the occasion.

# X

Clean sheets. Such a wonderful sensation to nose and skin, thought Clarece. Too bad the pleasure didn't extend to her hands. Washing all afternoon taxed her claws; the warm water did serve as a tradeoff but, unfortunately, that benefit expired about now. Still, it was satisfying, to know that the princess had clean linens tonight as did Asla and herself.

A neatly folded pile of clothing rested on Asla's shelf, matching the piles, above, in Casica's chamber and, here, with herself. The slave glanced at Asla's schedule. Tonight her friend serviced in the city, but no name was mentioned on the paper. Clarece drew back Asla's covers. Pony, it was going to be cold. A glance at the wall assured her that the insulit had taken her red cape, the warmer of her two cloaks.

The clock had already chimed one when Clarece heard her stallmate return. She turned in her cot to welcome Asla. The younger woman, who had not noticed her, sat quietly on her cot, her head cradled in her hands. Clarece recognized this posture; it had been a rough night.

"Welcome home, As," she whispered. Asla looked up at her friend and nodded exhaustedly. "Rough night?" In response Asla shook her head slowly. "I hate my life," she whispered. She reached behind her and pulled a large dagger from her belt. She only wore it when she went out into the city for service. The knife made a heavy thud on the night stand. Asla kept her eyes on it, watching the lamp light dance across its razor edge. *I should use that on myself,* she thought.

Clarece rose from her cot. Scads, it was cold. She sat next to the g'Helderleit and pulled her close. "Clarece, if you knew how I spent this evening, you wouldn't touch me. You might never touch me again." Clarece held her closer. Asla smelled of smoke and of something else she could not identify. "You are my sala. You're home now." She looked into the haunted face. "Are you hurt?" she asked gently.

The insulit's eyes welled with tears. Was she hurt? she wondered. Wouldn't she have to be living to hurt? She shook her head. "Not badly. I've been done worse. It's just that there were too many.... I'm so tired, Rece. I want to sleep forever."

Clarece sighed. She never knew how to help Asla in this situation, so she did what she could. "Here, Friend, let me help you with bed." She knelt before Asla and worked on her laces. The younger woman could have much more quickly untied her own boots, but she found Clarece's attendance comforting. Her sheets were clean too, she noticed. If only her mind could so easily be cleansed. Maybe it was a good thing insulit had no souls. Nothing could ever purify her.

Asla removed her belt. "You may want to remain clothed and wrapped in your cape," Clarece suggested, "it's cold." Asla nodded in agreement. She was so very cold. Clarece tucked the clean sheets around her sala. She took Asla's cloak from the wall and placed that over her too. "Thanks for washing my sheets," the insulit muttered sleepily. "You're welcome. Sleep well." Already Asla's deep breaths answered that she would indeed. She slept like the dead, this one.

Clarece took her own cloak and wrapped it about her. The pen was bitter. She stood and quietly checked on the other women, placing cloaks on beds that had none. When she reached Raina, she was surprised to find the young slave awake. "Raina, why are you up, little one?" Clarece asked gently, squatting beside the slave girl's cot.

"I'm so cold. My feet are freezing." Clarece reached for her feet; they were little blocks of ice. "Scads, girl, where are your socks?" "I haven't any. I lost them in the laundry, and I'm too afraid to ask my mistra for more." Clarece considered Raina's mistra. She would be afraid to ask, too.

"Well, here. You can wear mine; they're too big but they will keep you warm," she offered. "Let me see your feet." For a handless woman, putting socks on another, even large socks on small feet, was akin to putting socks on a rooster, but she succeeded. "Listen Raina," Clarece said, wanting to encourage the young slave, "Did you know this was my stall when I first came to the palace? Years before you were born." "Really?" the girl was amazed.

"Yes. I know it's hard to believe the palace is that old," Clarece smiled. "I lost things and broke things and failed in many ways. I would come here and cry and rest and try again the next day. This is a good stall. It was my faithful refuge. I made it and you will too. But you must tell me when you lose things or need help, alright? That's my job." "Yes, mistress," the tired voice said.

"Now try to sleep. You'll be warmer now." Clarece took the small cloak and lay it over the smaller form. She considered for a moment and then added her own cloak to the covers. Raina was too young for her position.

While she was up, Clarece decided she may as well check on the princess. She hadn't added extra coal to her brazier at bed time. The chamber may well need more heat. The slave went silently to the princess' room and squatted near the brazier. The room was unusually cool though certainly nothing like the one below. Quietly, she added more coal, blowing on it to stoke the flame. She didn't know she was being observed by the restless occupant.

Casica sat in her bed, finishing the last volume on slavery. She had found page 117 and continued beyond. Slavery made for provocative reading, but the material left her with as many questions as answers. The princess debated on whether it was better to startle Clarece intentionally or have her startled unintentionally. Her charge would almost certainly notice her shadowed form as she left.

"Clarece?" Casica closed her eyes. The slave jumped. "My lady?" was the cautious reply. "It's only me. I didn't want to frighten you. I'm going to open my eyes, alright?" Clarece watched as two little orbs of vacillating blue appear from the darkness.

"Scads, lady! That truly is unnerving," she said, approaching the princess' bed. "Unnerves me too, sometimes. When I catch myself in a mirror at night - kai! What are you doing up?" "I was with Asla. She just came in from the city. She had a rough night." "Oh," the eyes looked down. "Is she harmed?" "Not physically, it doesn't seem, but her heart...," she left the thought unfinished. "I'm sorry, Clarece. You must hurt so for your friend." "I do my lady. I wish she at least had someone to talk to - a confessor. I think that would help but she won't use me. Shame is an awful stock."

Casica agreed. She reached out to touch Clarece and was startled by the woman's chill. "Kai, Clarece, you're freezing." "'Tis very cold below, my lady." "Well, make sure you cover with lots of blankets." The slave shook her head. "We haven't any blankets, Mistra." "What? Why on earth not?"

"'Blankets,'" quoted the chief slaveswoman bitterly, "'are for horses.'" "I swear," the Cassican responded sarcastically, "if Byzanthian horses knew their prominence, they'd stage a coup d'etat - and don't repeat that." The slave smiled silently.

A sudden thought came to Casica. "Clarece, do you ride?" Clarece brightened. "Yes, my lady!" she answered excitedly. "I love to ride. I haven't in years, but I love to." "Good! I was thinking that we should go riding tomorrow, have our tea outside. What do you think?" "I would like that very much, Mistra."

Casica enjoyed Clarece's excitement. It would be so fun to spend an afternoon outside. Though the nights froze this time of year, days were quite pleasant.

"Excellent. Will you tell Sgt. Poul tomorrow morning that we'll need mounts for the afternoon. Rigel, of course, for me." "Yes, my lady. I will." Not only riding, Clarece thought, happily, but a chance to see Poul. She could feel herself warming already. "I will have finished my reading by then," the princess continued. "There are some issues I want to discuss with you."

"Is that what you're doing my lady? Reading in the dark?" "It's not dark to me...," Casica defended. "That may be, but to read in darkness - it is simply unnatural, mistra." Casica smiled at Clarece's outrage. "Would you prefer me to light a candle, chief slaveswoman?" "No, my lady. I would prefer to go below and freeze with the other mortals." "*I* am mortal, Clarece." "Not as mortal as I, my lady," the slave rejoined. "Rigel doesn't sprout wings, does he?" she asked flatly.

Casica couldn't tell if she were serious or not. "No. At least, not in Cassica he didn't." "Well. I leave you to your night, mistra."

Casica reached for the woman's hands. "Wait, senior slave." Clarece obeyed. She felt a slight warming stir in her hands. The warmth continued through her arms and into her body, taking with it not only the aching of her hands, but her chill as well. It was like warming on a sunny day, she thought, but from the inside out.

"There. You should be toasty all night." "Thank you, Princess," Clarece said gratefully. "It pays to know those who are not so mortal as I. Tis better than a blanket. It won't fall off."

Josquin grinned though the other woman couldn't see it. "Sleep well, dear Clarece. I'll see you in the morning - if I'm not spirited away." "If you are, Princess, may I have your cloak?" "Of course." "Then goodnight, my lady - or farewell as is appropriate." Casica shook her head as she watched the woman leave her quarters. Whoever had written these books, she thought, had never known Clarece d'Casica.

## XI

Clarece jogged down the stairs. Having delivered Casica's breakfast, she excitedly anticipated seeing Poul about the horses. She needed her cloak. "Asla!" she greeted, surprised to see her friend awake. She wasn't due for a service for several hours. "Why are you up, g'Helderleit?"

Asla sat on her cot, fingering her dagger. "Edsner rang," she explained, still focused on the knife. "What a morning for him to take me. Wretch. He knows what happened last night." The insulit took the knife and slid it into her belt, behind her.

"Are you going to the city later?" Clarece asked, taking her cloak and wrapping it around her. "Yes." "Do you know this man?" she inquired, hoping a kinder day for her friend. "Yes. It shouldn't be bad." "Good. While you're out, could you buy a pair of socks for small feet? We can pay you." Asla bent down to lace her boots. "What - for that scamp?" She was in no mood to play errand boy for the guild. "She won't survive the year, you know."

If her own heart hadn't convicted her, her friend's silence would. Asla stopped her lacing, regretful. "I'm sorry, Rece. That was cruel. I didn't mean it." She stood to face Clarece. "I feel like milk gone bad, today. Gods, I'm turning rancid. I don't know what's wrong with me."

The older slave sighed and took her friend into her arms. "You're exhausted among other things. Doesn't Edsner take you in soon?" The insulit nodded. "Next week, thank gods." "Well, in a few days, you'll be free," Clarece encouraged. She stepped back and smiled into Asla's face. "A few days is nothing for the Mighty g'Helderleit." Asla nodded. She could survive anything for a few days.

"Look, Asla, don't bother with the socks. My request was inappropriate." "No, it's alright. And keep your money. I'll get her two pairs. One to lose and one to wear. And what about you, chief slaveswoman? Where are *you* off to this morning?"

Clarece beamed. "To see Poul about mounts. Casica and I are riding this afternoon." "Riding?! Scads, Clarece. You haven't done that in forever!" "Fourteen years." "Well, they say you never forget, but hang on just in case. All you need is to break your neck – of course, you'll be with the right person if you do." "Thanks for the encouragement," Clarece replied wryly. "You're welcome," Asla teased, flashing her impish grin.

Clarece turned to leave but paused mid-step. "Sala, I wish you could join us."

Asla looked away. She was raw from mounting. "Thanks, Rece. Have a wonderful time. I'll see you tonight?" she asked hopefully. Clarece nodded, "Tonight - if I don't break my neck. Take care in the city." "I will." Asla watched as Clarece disappeared up the princess' stairway.

The morning was icy cold. Frost whitened the lawn and little drops of ice turned to water as the sun lit leafy tips. Turning to face the light, Clarece stopped and breathed deeply of the morning. She was so rarely out this time of day. The moist cold filled her lungs with an almost spicy sensation. She breathed out playfully and watched her air steam. It felt good to be alive today. A long frozen puddle ran before her, its glassy surface inviting her irresistibly. Clarece skated across the makeshift toy, skipping girlishly off its face and back onto the dirt. Slaves were nothing if not graceful of feet. Senior slave, Clarece d' Casica, arrived at the guardhouse red-faced and smiling.

"If you're looking for Poul, he's in blades," an impatient corporal answered before she spoke. Obviously, the whole world wasn't as happy as she, but that mattered not. She found the master swordsman bending over a group of training blades, sorting them by weight. She stood for a few minutes enjoying the sight of this man who filled the happiest of her dreams. Poul felt her gaze and turned to see the visitor. Yes!  He hadn't seen her in weeks. His heart swelled with pleasure. "Clarece!" he called excitedly as he and she walked to meet each other. "What are you doing here?"

"Sergeant," she addressed, offering a half kneel before him. "I've been sent by my mistra." "Well, that's my good fortune," Poul replied, happily. "I haven't seen you in so long. You look beautiful." Clarece bowed shyly. "Thank you. And how are you?" The sergeant crossed his arms and looked full into her face. "Better than a minute ago," he grinned.

Clarece felt the blood rise in her face. How this man undid her. She should get to the matter at hand. "The princess asks if you will prepare Rigel and a mount for me this afternoon. She wishes to ride." "Well, whatever the queen desires is my command - and I'll do it for the Cassican, too," he teased. "You, my lord sergeant," Clarece noted, "are in fine form this morning." "I am but a foil, Clarece," he said quietly, no jest in his voice now. "It is you who are the morning light."

These words drew the woman into Poul's eyes. *What would it be like to touch him?* she wondered, as she had so often. To be touched by him? Though her collar was only a quarter-stite thick, the chasm it cut between her and this freeman was immeasurable. The law of slavery would keep them apart forever.

"You are kind, my lord," she replied, bowing. "Your reply to the princess?" Poul studied the woman before him. For over two years, he had tried to win her familiarity; yet she persisted in treating him as her superior. He wondered if she would ever let him into her heart.

"You may tell Princess Casica it is my honor to serve her. I will see you both this afternoon." "Thank you, my lord." The slave glanced into the blue eyes that were so different from her own and smiled. Kneeling, she turned and walked hurriedly away, taking his light with her.

It took forever, but the afternoon finally arrived. Clarece had begun to fear a sudden change in weather, such as was common in Byzanthia, but the day that began so beautifully remained. As the women walked the garden path towards the stable, they admired the sun-filled, cloudless sky. It was a rare thing, this close to the ocean, to see a sky so empty of clouds. Clarece walked alongside her mistra; being as they were outside, she was not required the usual pace behind her owner. Casica enjoyed her company. The slave was tutoring her in the history of equestrian development of Byzanthian breeds. She knew much of horses, not only from her extensive readings but also from her years as a stable girl.

"So that is where you learned to ride, during those years," the princess assumed. "Yes, my lady. The men gamed and drank all night and slept into the morning. It was my duty to feed the horses and clean their stalls. Afterward I would choose a horse to ride. In those days, my hands were stronger. I didn't even need a saddle. I would race across the fields and wave to the morning sun. I used to think I was named after it - the sun," she smiled shyly. "Riding is the closest I've ever known of freedom...." her eyes turned soft with memory.

*Freedom*, thought Casica. What would it be like for a woman as Clarece to live in freedom? "Can slaves by freed?" she asked. "I noticed when you gave me options for what I could do with a slave, you didn't mention freeing you." Clarece shook her head. The possibility never occurred to her.

"Because you can't, my lady. Freeing is not your privilege. I am the king's property, ultimately. His permission is not required for you to do anything with me, but release is his prerogative, alone. A slave is only freed by the word of the king." "Does he ever free slaves?" "None in my lifetime. It is reputed the king's father freed a man once. The slave saved his life in battle. But to be freed, tis unimaginable."

"I see," said Casica, her heart downcast. She had hoped to re-lease this woman. The books she had read mentioned nothing of freedom; now she knew why. "But you must dream of freedom," the princess suggested.

"No, my lady, truly. I would lie if I said I did not wish to be free. But all dreams must contain an element of possibility - even if it hinges on the miraculous. There is none for me." Casica was about to inquire as to why this was so when a familiar voice reached them.

"Greetings, esteemed ladies!" Poul called. "Your humble sta-bleman salutes you this grand day." "Good afternoon, Sgt. Poul," Casica greeted, nodding her head to Poul's low bow. "And how are all the studs in this place," she teased, addressing him in

Cassican. "Rigel will never know," he murmured, receiving from his cousin a stern look. This was an old argument between them. The gelding had been her choice for a horse - not his.

"Rigel is a fine woman's horse," he observed in Byzanthian. "Rigel is the best of all horses, Sergeant," the princess countered. "Aren't you, Rigel?" she asked the white steed, approaching to scratch his ears. The horse nodded in agreement.

Behind the princess, another greeting was forming. "Hello, Clarece," Poul spoke quietly, his eyes filled with her. "Poul," she offered bowing slightly. "Thank you," he said, receiving her gift of his name.

Casica glanced over her shoulder. It was a feeling that made her turn, not their verbal exchange. The princess half-expected to see a third party standing with Clarece and K'net, so strong was the sensation. There was none visible. It was the two, themselves, who formed the third presence, Casica realized. She had experienced this awareness countless times in her life. She grew up with it in her parents' company and sensed it in a different form between friends and relatives. There was no denying what she could not see. *"My God,"* she thought, astonished, *"K'net and Clarece, they love each other."* When did this happen? Why did he not tell me?" The josquin glanced away, blushing at her intrusion upon their intimacy.

"I have chosen a special mount for you," Poul was telling Clarece, escorting her to a braided golden dun. "She's gentle and sure-hoofed - but not boring." "She's beautiful," Clarece observed, rubbing the mare. "What is her name?" "Leharen." "Leharen," Clarece repeated. "'A running brook.'" "Yes," said Poul, leading the tall horse from her stall. "A fitting name for her rider. Would you like the reins knotted, my lady?" he asked officially. "Please, my lord," the smiling slave nodded. "Let's see if I remember how to do this...."

In one smooth motion, Clarece slipped into the saddle. She ran her hand along Leharen's neck. Even without her mittens, she could not have felt the horse's hair. Her hands had lost all feeling long ago; but her mind could feel, allowing Clarece to smile at the smooth, hot neck. Poul handed the happy slave the reins and adjusted the length of her stirrups. Her legs were longer than he had guessed.

Casica was adjusting her thoughts - and her girth - as horse and rider and Poul came to her. She announced loudly, "I'll cinch the saddle - just in case. Someone saddled Rigel too loosely once - made for an ugly fall. I broke my arm." "Well, Princess," Poul assured her, "you can trust me not to make that mistake." *Not to make that mistake twice,* Casica thought, smiling at her cousin.

The Cassican hopped from the ground into her saddle and reined Rigel round to face Clarece. "Where to, chief slaveswoman?" she asked. Clarece was positively beaming. "It matters not, my lady." "Then let's go see Cassica." With a farewell to the sergeant livery boy, the women led their mounts behind the stable, down a path Casica knew from a night that seemed so long ago. Clarece rode easily. It must be true, that you don't forget how to ride. But she had forgotten the muscles riding required.

"I won't be able to walk the morrow," she announced to her owner. Casica laughed with her. "That may be true, but you cut a striking figure, Clarece d'Casica. You are a true horsewoman - of that there is no doubt!" "Thank you, my lady," she replied, "but it is you Cassicans, is it not, who are renowned for horsemanship." "True, friend Byzanthian. We Cassicans are the equestrians against whom all others compare."

With this prideful remark, the princess leapt from her stirrups into her saddle, balancing effortlessly on Rigel's back. Raising her hands with a flourish, the joyful woman yelled in Cassican, "I am Casica! Rider of the one who reigns with the night sky hunter. I live today, Byzanthia. I live!" She pirouetted and dropped into the saddle, riding backwards, her feet propped upon Rigel's rump.

Clarece clapped her maimed hands, laughing with pleasure. "I don't know what you said, but I'm sure I agree!" she announced. "And you're right: you Cassicans rule in the realm of riding. Pity, your island kingdom is so small." Casica's smile vanished. She tried in vain to judge the earnestness of Clarece's observation.

"That's the third time I've heard someone comment on Cassica's being small. Where do you get this information?" "Well, 'tis common knowledge my lady," replied the Byzanthian. "Everyone knows that yours is a little island" "'Everyone'? You mean every ignorant Byzanthian, I would think," Casica replied indignantly. "You would ride three months to see the breadth of Cassica - even longer for her length. She is a large, glorious isle - filled with green and life."

"If you say so, my lady," Clarece conceded - jesting or not, Casica still could not determine. "I only know what I am taught." Casica's snort made Rigel glance back. "I think you Byzanthians write history to suit your needs," the princess observed. Clarece's hidden smile was not lost on the Cassican. "Of course, my lady. It *is* the *victors* who write history," she bowed, and with a kick to Leheran's flanks, sprung ahead of the backwards rider. They had entered a meadow and the open place beckoned her irresistibly.

It was fortunate for Clarece that most of riding rests in the legs. She hadn't the courage to break into a dead run, knowing neither her mount nor her own retained skill, but to gallop was invigorating. The slave closed her eyes and felt the wind rush against her face and flow into her ears. Heaven, how she had missed this! For a moment she was young again, too young to imagine a lifetime in bondage.

A white blur passed to her left. Casica and Rigel flowed as one. Suddenly the two stopped in their tracks and spun dizzily to their right. Rigel lifted his fore legs and without so much as staining, leapt straight into the air, kicking his hinds legs, it seemed, in sheer joy of his strength. Casica's laughter filled the meadow as she and her steed hopped from side to side. Clarece had never seen such movements in a horse. Or anything else, for that matter, except perhaps Asla on the dance floor.

The princess was oblivious, herself lost in the joy of the moment. She hopped from the saddle and embraced Rigel's sweating neck. "I love you," she spoke in Cassican. "With you, I am home." Clarece whoaed Leheran.

"Crispus, my lady - were you born on a horse?" "Almost. Mother was riding when she came into labor with me. Her water broke in the saddle." Clarece gaped in amazement. "*That* is a lesser known fact of her Majesty's history," Casica confided. It was certain Maman would not appreciate her sharing this.

"Well," replied Clarece, somewhat taken aback, "*that* explains why you ride as though poured onto Rigel." The women laughed, and Clarece realized, suddenly, how natural it felt to look into her mistra's face. One of Casica's requests of her was not so difficult to fulfill after all.

Casica remounted and the two trotted through the meadow into a wood. The scent of pine was everywhere, and they commented on the beauty of the smell. At one point they stopped to rest in the moment. The wind flowed through the tops, bringing with it that exquisite sound of power. Casica noticed tears flowing from her charge's eyes.

"I haven't heard that sound in sixteen years," Clarece explained softly. "Not since I slaved in Kanasa. I used to lay in the grass and pretend I was at the ocean. I imagined that was how it must sound." Casica smiled at Clarece's memory. So, Clarece had gathered more than nightmares from that time of life, she thought.

An hour more and the forest left the women in the care of a grassy plain. An invisible hand caressed the tall grasses and brought with it a sound that seemed, all the world, like thunder. A light drizzle accompanied the sound. But this made no sense, thought Clarece. She looked above her. The sky remained cloudless. "What is this?" she wondered aloud. Casica grinned. "Wait and see...."

As the two riders ascended a hill, the thunder exchanged its voice for movement. The air, itself, seemed to shake with the impact of surf. "Great God!" Clarece exclaimed, topping the hill.

Before her was a cliff and beyond that, the living, breathing, embodiment of omnipotence, standing like an eternal canvas before her. She gaped, awed, her breaths coming quick and deep. *Oh, Heaven!* she thought. *Crispus! It's the ocean. Tis the end of Byzanthia!*

Clarece slid from her horse and walked, mesmerized, to the cliff. Pounding, surging waves broke over a lower rocky shelf, and christened her with their salty spray. She blinked, somewhat afraid. Never in her life had she been in the presence of such absolute power - at once frightening and inspiring.

"This must be something like standing in the presence of God," she said turning to the woman who now stood beside her. "I've read of the ocean," she continued, "but nothing prepared me for this... this – ," she tried vainly to describe what was before her. "This..." she surrendered, presenting her arms to the indescribable scene. Her poet's mouth failed her. That too must be something of God, being left speechless. "Tis astounding!" she declared.

"It is indeed," the Cassican thought but not about the ocean. And not about the realization that this woman had never seen the ocean until now. Casica scanned the horizon carefully. It should be right in front of them. On such a clear day, they should be able to see it. Suddenly, there flashed a light upon the line where the ocean seemed to end. Was it her imagination? She watched. There it was again.

"Clarece! Watch! Look at the horizon, right before you. Watch. You'll see a light." Casica waited for the next distant swell. "There! Did you see it? Did you see it?!" she exclaimed. "Yes!" Clarece shouted.

"There it is again! Cassica, Clarece! Tis the lighthouse at Pau d' Len. Tis Cassica! My home!" The princess' heart ached with desire. Oh, how she loved her land. How she missed her land. "Sol kana shea!" she shouted in Cassican, "sol kana shea!" The slave turned to her mistra. The princess glowed.

"What does that mean?" Clarece asked. "'I love you' - in the feminine. 'Sol kana shew' is masculine," Casica explained thinking, even at this moment, Clarece should know the proper form for K'net - if the occasion were to arise. The two women stood a long time, each seeing the spectacular display through her own dreams.

Clarece shuddered visibly. "Come, Clarece," Casica invited. "We should warm ourselves." The Cassican and Byzanthian walked down the knoll where wind and cold were somewhat blocked. From Rigel's saddlebag, Casica produced a stein and two small parcels. She removed her cloak and, draping it fully upon the moist ground, invited Clarece sit.

Clarece obeyed, smiling in anticipation of tea - and also at the curious work of the cloak. Its warmth began in her backside and continued its way into the rest of her body. "How does your cloak do this, my lady?" she asked in wonder.

"I don't know," Casica replied, shaking her head. "Something of my mother - passed down from her mother. She promises to share the secret with me. Comforting, is it not?" "Indeed. It warms like your touch, except in cloth." Casica considered the comparison as she opened the first parcel. "That may be her secret," she speculated.

The princess turned her attention to Clarece. "I raided the kitchen this morning," she confessed mischievously. From the first parcel, she presented a loaf of bread. From the other, thick roasted beef. The meat she had already sliced into Clarece-sized pieces. The slave looked upon the sliced beef. No knife was necessary. "Thank you," she said gratefully, more in reference to the princess' thoughtfulness than for the food. Casica broke the bread into pieces and placed it before her guest. The stein had done its work, rendering their tea warm to their chilled bodies.

"God's blessings upon you," the princess wished her charge. "And upon you," Clarece returned. Riding and water always enhance one's appetite, and this proved true for them. As they ate, the ocean provided a mighty symphony for their meal.

Clarece looked about her. The sun shone brightly, warming her from above even as the cloak did from below. The wind blew not so violently as on the cliff. Here, it brought with it the ocean in a measure she could contain. "I think this is the happiest day of my life, Princess," she observed. "Thank you for giving this to me."

"You're welcome, Clarece," Casica replied brightly. "I'm happy we can share it. Beauty is doubled in the company of another." *What a good quote*, thought the slave. She would remember it. Filled and content, the women rested in the sunlight. Casica finally broke their silence with a question.

"Clarece, I finished the slavery books." "In the dark, I assume," her charge interrupted. "Yes. And there they have left me, in some respect. The greatest of which is the origin of slavery. Its lack of discussion is conspicuous. Does no one know how slavery originated in Byzanthia?"

The slave sat for a moment, reviewing her readings. The princess was correct. She had read no explanation of slavery in Byzanthia - had heard no stories even. "My lady, I guess when an institution is as fundamental to a region as is slavery to Byzanthia, its existence is assumed. It would be as speculating on the origin of air."

The Cassican princess nodded in agreement. "Yes, but God originated air. I considered that possibility of slavery being native to Byzanthia. And that theory might hold if it were not for the existence of Cassica. Byzanthia and Cassica were once one nation, one people. Yet in Cassica there is no record - not even in song - of slavery existing. We haven't even a symbol in our language to represent it. Do you not find this strange?"

Clarece thought carefully. She imagined a slice of bread sprinkled with seeds. How could one tear the slice without having seeds on both pieces? For that to happen, the seeds must be in one place and not covering the entire slice. "Could it be that slavery existed in only a particular region of the ancient Byzanthian/Cassican land?" she speculated. Casica nodded in agreement.

"That's how I lean. But if this is true, why the absence of record? Rarely, was slavery discussed in my classes." "What of the root of the great battle between our lands? Was this mentioned in your studies?" Clarece asked.

"No," the princess decided. "It wasn't. Twas though the war were so distant, the reason for it is irrelevant." "Perhaps slavery falls into the same heap, my lady," the slave suggested. "Perhaps it has existed so long, its origin is considered irrelevant. Either that or - ," the slave hesitated. Her thought felt almost treasonous. "Or what?" Casica inquired. "Perhaps, it is as you said earlier. History is easily rewritten - or erased - as suits the needs of the writers. Truly, you can't trust man's written word any more than you may the spoken."

Casica's mind went to another subject, to the edict that brought her to this place. She had memorized the ancient document, reasoning that something which so mastered her life should be mastered as much as possible. Five centuries earlier, a compact had been made between her nation and its conqueror, Byzanthia. Cassica was allowed to exist on one condition: when Life had brought both a Byzanthian prince and Cassican princess to earth on the same date, the woman would be surrendered to the man in her sixteenth year. Byzanthia, in the person of the prince, could choose to accept or destroy the Cassican offering.

For centuries, the edict had terrorized the island nation, filling each queenly mother with dread at the coming of her child. The power of the edict fueled among her countrymen hate and suspicion of its founding fathers. And then she arrived, born on the birth date of Bastien, fifth sons of Ars. And five centuries of terror took on flesh.

But now as she sat in the sun, with the surf pounding behind her, Casica wondered if its designers had ever imagined this scene she shared with Clarece. What if the edict's creators had foreseen this day? What if, instead of being a curse of terror, they had meant it as a covenant of reconciliation? Long ago, her own heart was convinced the document must have a deeper purpose than merely humiliating one nation before the other. Whether her conviction was born from the womb of truth or simply from her desperate need to believe herself more than a pawn of evil men, she hadn't determined. But at this moment she did know: God had woven the blessing of Heaven into the curse of men. Clarece interrupted her musings.

"In Cassica, which are you taught, my lady: that the social division happened first or the geographical one?" Casica thought for a moment. "We are taught that the war came before the division of land. Why do you ask?" she asked curiously. "I'm not certain, mistra. It seems that fact is significant...." In Clarece's mind, thought raced over knowledge as the wind did the grass before her. The princess had sparked an entirely new area for investigation. "I have not considered this issue, Princess," the teacher announced. "It is worthy of greater study."

Casica smiled at the chief slaveswoman. She was certain this conversation would continue. "Clarece, you would love living in Cassica. And Cassica would love you." "My lady?" the slave asked, surprised. "Yes. In the royal city is a university. I see you attending it as a student - and a teacher." "To see that, my lady, your imagination must match the ocean in its depth," the slave replied, lowering her head. A university, she thought. What would it be like to be surrounded by knowledge and learning? "Besides, my lady," she continued, "Byzanthians are forbidden entry into your country."

"You mean except for politicians, spies, and the military of course," the princess countered sarcastically. "And the law to which you refer is Byzanthian - not Cassican." "I did not mean to offend, my lady," Clarece offered, backpedaling. Casica shook her head. "You did not offend me, Clarece. My anger is aimed at another target. I hate this ignorance that exists between former countrymen."

"Not all are ignorant, my lady. Sgt. Poul speaks highly of his years in Cassica. He was raised by his uncle in the garrison of your royal city. He speaks well of your father's throne - and your people. Though he is happy to be among his own now." Casica smiled at Clarece's words. To ask what she wished would be to skate closely on the edge of propriety in more ways than one. But she asked anyway.

"How long have you known Sgt. Poul, Clarece?" "More than two years, my lady." "And how did you meet?" Clarece blushed lightly. "He and the Prince Bastien are friends. I went one day to deliver a message from his highness." She shortened her story, uncomfortable sharing it at all. "We met feeding a horse, my lady," she explained abruptly. "A horse? How romantic," Casica smiled playfully. "And what do you think of Poul?" The slave fell silent for a time. "I think - what I think of him - I should not think," her face blushed over her quiet words. "He is free. I am slave." That settled all matters of her heart. Or it should.

"Can slaves not marry?" the princess asked gently. *What an absurd question,* Clarece thought. "No, my lady. For slave to even lay with free is considered treasonous." "What of one slave marrying another?" "No," the slave answered, bitterly. "We can breed, but it is as horses or some other beast. Nothing more." Casica sighed, thinking of what lay between this woman and the man she called Poul. "This is a travesty. What harm could come from slaves marrying?" Clarece looked down, her eyes hardening with anger. "To allow us that pleasure would be to assign us humanity."

Casica nodded. Clarece was right, of course. She looked up at the sky. The sun was setting on their conversation and the day. Darkness would accompany their return to the palace. "What say you to one last view of the ocean before we leave?" she asked. Clarece's face brightened. "Yes! I would that I had a hundred eyes to be filled with that sight."

The women left their tea and strolled together to the cliff. The ocean darkened with the sunset, but its waves glowed in a reddish light. Casica watched for the lighthouse. Soon every glimpse would be hidden in the evening fog. Glimpses of Cassica. Glimpses of Byzanthia. She would have neither had she not come to be in this place. Clarece broke their silence. "I do not question your honesty, my lady, but your land does appear to be very small indeed."

Casica laughed, thinking, *surely she is not serious*. Only God knew the mind of a slave, and even He, at times, must lose Himself in this one. "She trumps in heart," Asla had said of her friend. *Indeed*, thought Casica. She looked at the island she could not see. She often saw things she could not see. She would pray for Clarece's freedom, the princess decided, and strive for the impossible.

It was dark when the women reached the stable. Poul greeted them warmly and inquired of their day. "It was the best of my life," Clarece answered plainly. In her chambers, the princess handed Clarece the two parcels. "For you and Asla," she offered. "We thank you," the slave bowed. "And thank you again, for this day." The slave found it more difficult now to face her mistra. But she refused to do as she did that night when she remained silent. "Your Highness," Clarece began. She so rarely used that title that Casica focused more closely. "Yes?" "Thank you for keeping me as your slave. I am fortunate to slave for one as you." There. She had said it.

Casica smiled warmly. Apart from her life itself, this was the greatest gift Clarece had offered her. "The good fortune is mine, Clarece. Good night." The slave kneeled gracefully, and turned for her stairs. She might not be able to kneel so gracefully on the morrow, but for now she was filled with grace - grace, happiness, and roast beef.

Clarece paused in her nook before entering the slaves quarters. With her mouth, she removed her left mitten. She licked what would have been a finger, ran it across her cheek and tasted. Her flesh was salty. The ocean remained with her - at least for the time being. As she skipped down to Asla, Clarece smiled to herself. She would not wash her face this night. And even then, time would not wash this day from her heart.

# XII

The next morning, Raina greeted her senior slave with a smile and a kneel. Upon her legs, showing below trousers that had grown too short, she sported a green band, the cuff of her new socks. "Mistress Clarece! *Green*! Three pairs of green woolens! Thank you so much, my lady." The little slave's face beamed with joy. Clarece rose from her cot and kneeled, achingly, to examine Raina's socks. They were the finest of any she'd seen, made of rich, thick wool.

"Your socks are beautiful, Raina," she admired. "I've never seen their like. But you haven't me to thank for them." "Then I will thank the guild," the slave announced. "It wasn't their gift either. Asla gave these to you." The young girl looked confused. The insult? The insulit had bought these for her?

Asla was facing the nightstand braiding her hair. She didn't turn at the conversation. *Scads, Clarece. Why are you telling her this?* she wondered, embarrassed. She had done other things for the guild and Clarece had not told. Of course, she had told her not to, something she failed to mention this time. "Mistress Asla?" a soft voice asked. Asla sighed and turned to look down at the mouse of a slave. Raina kneeled humbly before this mysterious woman. She had been told by the other slaves to ignore the insulit, that to speak to her invoked the wrath of God. But surely, her young mind reasoned, surely no one who would give her green socks could make God angry.

"I thank you, so much, my lady. How may I earn them?" Asla propped against the stand and crossed her arms, studying the little slave before her. Raina was barely five years if that old. Her thin arms lost themselves in her blouse as did her small throat in an adult collar. She wasn't even old enough to wear a vest. *Young. You are so very young,* Asla thought. The insulit remembered herself at this age, playing on the shores of g'Helderlend between lessons with her handler. The ocean had been her secret joy in those years. Yesterday, the cloth vender at the city market couldn't understand her wanting colored socks for feet so small. Asla knew why she wanted the special socks. Raina needed an ocean in this cold place.

"You don't earn a gift, Raina," the insulit explained. "They are yours - just for being you." The smile she offered was genuine. "I'm happy you like them." "Like them?" the small girl declared. "They are the grandest socks in the kingdom. How did you know, mistress, that I like green?" "Well, I have ears, too, you know." Asla grinned. How could anyone in the pen not know the newest slave's favorite color?

Raina's face glowed with the beautiful woman's attention. "I thank you, mistress Asla. I will not lose them," she stated determinedly. "The laundry bucket is notorious for its thievery," the insulit divulged. "If it takes these, let me know and I'll replace them." "Yes, my lady," the slave bowed. "Thank you. Thank you so very much!" Asla nodded to the waif who then kneeled to the two women. She turned and skipped from the stall.

Clarece beamed at her friend. "What are you looking at Byzanthian?" the insulit asked with a playful glare. "*Green?* You've a heart of gold, Asla of g'Helderlend. And don't you deny it." The insulit snorted. "I haven't a heart at all, remember?" "As if you'd let me forget. But your socks betray you," Clarece said mysteriously. Asla smiled. She was feeling much better. Two more days, and she would be free for a week.

"Speaking of socks," she remembered. "One of your guild mentioned last night that he is in need of boots." "Who?" "The slave Donnel. His master is transferring him to outdoor service. He was going to ask to you last night. I thought you would want to know." "Thank you," Clarece nodded. *Well, this is just pony,* she thought. Their guild's budget hadn't the resources for boots. Winter was upon them. What could she do? Perhaps the steward had a used pair. She would try to see him today, she decided.

"Where are you off to this morning, As?" she asked. "Edsner. He wants to speak to me about something. I can't imagine what - unless someone is complaining about my service," *which certainly no one would.* She despised how gifted a whore she was. "And you?" "Nothing special today." Clarece rubbed her bum. "I must concentrate on walking. My legs and backside - the mind remembered how to ride. My body didn't," she smiled. "Well, try stretching," the gymnast advised. It was time to go. "I'll see you tonight?" the older slave asked. "Yes. Remember: stretch, old girl."

Clarece shook her head at the retreating insulit. "'Old girl,'" indeed. If she weren't so sore - . Then again, on her best day she could never catch her.

The day began pleasantly. About mid-morning, it began to rain, the kind of slow rain that often indicated the coming of winter. Clarece excused herself from the princess and went to see the steward. He was in his quarters. "Chief slaveswoman," the steward greeted, "and how may your humble servant help you?" *Good,* thought Clarece. She had found Silian was in a pleasant humor. "My lord steward," she replied, kneeling low before him. "I was wondering, my lord, if you might be able to help me with a pair of man's boots. One of our guild has been transferred outside and is in need." Silian thought but for a moment.

"I'm no use to you today, Chief. I've no boots at all. I rarely deal in leather." Of course he didn't, Clarece realized. Residents of the castle bought their own clothing and, usually, owners provided clothing for their property. Still, she had hoped. It was certain Donnel's owner had no intention of caring for his slave's need.

Clarece thanked the kind steward and made her way to Casica's quarters. On a whim she took a side passage. Sometimes she could meet slaves she had not seen in awhile. She enjoyed catching up with news from other wings.

Halfway down the passage, she saw someone she knew intimately. Asla was standing by a window, watching the weather change. "Asla!" Clarece greeted happily. Rarely did she see her friend during the day. The g'Helderleit turned, shocked at the voice. *Scads,* she thought. Clarece was the last person she wanted to see. The senior slave approached her friend. Asla avoided her gaze and acted as though to leave.

"Wait, Asla!" Clarece called. "Where are you going?" Asla turned toward the speaker. Clarece's smile disappeared immediately. Her friend was crying. "Asla," she asked reaching for the woman's arm. "What's wrong?" The insulit jerked away.

"Nothing is wrong," she retorted, glaring beneath her tears. "What do you mean? Something is terribly wrong. Are you harmed?" Clarece asked more quietly. "No, curse it! Tis none your frapping business," Asla spat. "Since when is your life none my business?" her senior asked, growing more angry or concerned; she didn't know which.

"As of now," the insulit announced turning to walk away. "Asla!" Clarece called after her. The blond woman continued down the passageway. Clarece knew better than to follow. *God, what's happened?* she wondered helplessly as she watched her sala disappear into the darkness.

Casica glanced up from her writing. Tea filled the air of her darkening chamber, tea and a dark tension resting somewhere within her charge. Clarece sat on the sofa acting like she read but she wasn't, that was clear. Her tea remained untouched and her attention, even now, went to the garden outside. Casica wanted to inquire, again, as she had yesterday about the trouble that weighed so heavily on Clarece's mind. Yesterday, her charge had avoided her question. It was almost certain she would do so again. Only God knew the mind of a slave. Despite all the progress that had been gained in their budding relationship, it was clear the line separating slave and owner remained as broad as ever.

"Clarece?" she asked breaking the silence. The slave turned her attention to her owner. "Have I done something to offend you? Is that what's wrong?" Clarece ducked her eyes. "No, my lady. I... I have much on my mind. But it does not concern you, Mistra."

Casica lowered her eyes. Would it always be this way? Would Clarece always feel her life did not concern her? The slave chafed under her owner's silence. How she wished she could talk with someone about Asla. Her friend had not spoken to her for days now. She stalked the pen and their stall like a stranger, wearing her anger as a rampart. Clarece considered countless times confiding in her mistra, but to do so would breech all propriety. It was not her place to bring Casica into her world. It was queer enough that the princess brought her into the world of the free, she mused, glancing at the cooling tea.

The slave took her cup and drank quickly. She needed to leave. Needed to focus on something else. Donnel's boots perhaps. "May I be excused, my lady? I should prepare for your dinner...." Casica looked up. "Of course, Clarece," she answered noting inwardly the time. Clarece was leaving much sooner than usual. The slave rose and thanked her owner. Then kneeling she stepped silently into her world below.

# XIII

C larece lay listlessly. Usually, this stall she had known for so many years served as her sanctuary. But now, with so many unspoken words between her and her stallmate filling the small compartment, it felt more like a cell. The chief slaveswoman didn't feel like dealing with Donnel's situation; she had little energy for it. She wanted to sleep, to surrender her body to the fatigue that plagued her thoughts. But winter was coming in full force and any bootless slave with outdoor duties, well, this was not going to just go away.

She recounted her visit with Silian. He didn't deal in leather but who would? The answer insinuated itself into the moment her eyes closed in sleep. *Of course!* she thought, waking herself. Every livery has a leather smith. The guard's livery smith was a solid soul with a kind face. Surely he could provide a used or refurbished pair of men's boots for a reasonable price. Clarece yawned at the solution. She would visit the smith as soon as she delivered Casica's dinner this evening. It wouldn't take long and she would be back for her own supper in plenty of time.

She considered sharing her plans with Asla; she rarely departed from her routine without telling her friend, but Asla's mood changed her mind. Clarece knew it was only a matter of time before the two came to blows. No, she didn't feel like hastening that event. This errand was simple; she would go without notice.

Clarece took her usual place among the house slaves' supper line. Tonight the princess would be pleased: vegetable stew. The princess loved stews and soups - she called them soul foods, comforting and nutritious. Casica was reading her history book as Clarece brought in the tray.

"Ah, Clarece. You bear good tidings tonight," she declared, breathing in the aroma. Clarece smiled at her excitement. It didn't take much to please this royal. She arranged the princess' tray, asking if she may be excused instead of remaining as she usually did. "Of course, Clarece. I'll see you this evening." "Thank you, my lady. May you be warmed and comforted," she grinned, trying out her limited Cassican. Casica smiled.

"And you. It looks like a storm. I think the night will be bitter." Clarece's hands told her that. She almost went down to her stall to retrieve her cloak but thought better of it. She would be out only a little while. Instead she exited though Casica's chamber and skipped smoothly down the stone stairs. After all these years, she still enjoyed the sound of stone. It was the same pleasure as sashaying through crisp, autumn leaves.

It *was* going to storm. To the northwest, ominous green clouds gathered. The wind was picking up and the air had that unmistakable smell of cold moisture. Clarece loved the prelude of a storm. All the scents seemed amplified and the electricity and windiness gave her a sense of being joined to a power, both playful and frightening.

She was happy, though, to enter the guard's quarters, with its warmth and cozy lighting. The guards were eating, filling the room with deep male laughter. Clarece wondered if Poul were there eating and laughing with his men. She hoped for a glimpse of him during this short mission.

Probably the leather smith was eating in his quarters as was common among craftsmen. Rarely did one see blacksmiths or armorers eating with the group. Though they joined the number of the guardsmen, they themselves were not guards, neither called nor trained to battle. Even in war they lived separately, keeping to their duties away from the men they served.

Clarece was right. The smith was sitting near his fireplace, a piece of chicken in one hand, a pipe in the other, gazing into the fire, visiting with his own thoughts. Clarece's presence was not unwelcome. He knew her, of course, as did all the guardsmen and palace servants. Her long history and hands made her conspicuous - as did her nebulous affair with Sgt. Poul. All the men knew

Poul was laying the quiet woman though none could figure out when nor where. As for Poul, well, instead of bragging as the men did, he was silent on his dealings with this mixture of beauty and brokenness.

"Glory! Tis the chief slaveswoman. To what do I owe this unexpected honor?" Smith's voice smirked but not unkindly. "Looking for a warm spot on this cold night," she smiled back. "Aye. Tis a bitter storm moving in. Twill be here within the hour, I'd gauge. "I'd wager you're right. I'll make my stay short." Clarece began to explain her need, a pair of men's boots, fitting for an outside laborer. Did Mr. Smith have any for sale, especially a used pair as money was of extreme shortage? Yes, he could arrange this; he had several pairs turned in for saddle and armor favors. The two bartered for a short time and settled on a half-pound, a price Clarece did not yet have but at least could conceive of paying somehow.

She visited awhile longer, listening to the leather smith's story of a guardsman's cheating him out of a magnificent belt. Her time was running out. With a nod and half kneel, the slave stepped back into the voices of men. No Poul. *Pony.* As she stepped into the weather, a cold blast of wind cut through her thoughts as easily as her cotton blouse. Scads!

Clarece decided to return by way of the south path. The trees may block some of the wind, she reasoned, and she could enter the palace by way of the west wing, hoping to catch Asla on her way to supper. The senior slave had been rethinking her avoidance of her friend; she needed to speak with Asla sooner, not later, and learn from where this stream of rage flowed.

The sky was dark now with the threatening thunderheads looming above. Clarece jogged along the trail and was rounding the gazebo curve when, suddenly, a voice arrested her tracks. She heard it so rarely; it was the unfamiliarity that struck her. Then she knew. She dropped to her knees, as though tripped, down into the appropriate stance of body upright, head down. It was the crown prince, Bastil, hailing her from within the gazebo.

"Clarece, hold! This, Earl, is the queen of slaves, Clarece d'Casica, who until recently was Clarece d'Bastien, my baby brother. She's served him fourteen years before being given over to the Cassican." The voice was moving towards her now.

She could not see the prince but realized he must be speaking to Earl Dakat, newly arrived from northern Byzanthia. She had heard rumors of him. Apparently his father tired of his exploits at home and decided palace housing may turn his questionable tide. If Prince Bastil served as his moral compass, Clarece thought to herself, this noble venture was doomed to founder. The men approached her, beer steins evident from her side view. *Be very still,* she hoped, and maybe, just maybe, he'll keep walking. He didn't.

"So anyway," Bastil informed the earl, "she's been here forever. I tried to buy her, once, from Bastien. Wouldn't do it. Tried to breed her, too. Wouldn't allow that either. She's like his favorite pet. Now she belongs to the Cassican who belongs to my brother. And how is your new owner, Clarece?" "Well, my lord." "How does she treat you?" "Well, my lord." The prince laughed drunkenly. His words slurred.

"She don't talk much but she's smart as a whip. Reads. Would write, too, except she hasn't any hands. Show the earl your claws." Obediently, Clarece drew her mittens from her vest and held them before her. "See? God gave her claws for hands. Still, she's a faithful slave." He was about to leave when the prince had a most hilarious idea, one that would impress the earl and humiliate this slave all at once.

"Hey, watch this, Dak. You can't do this with a servant but, scads, you can have alot of fun with a slave. Clarece," he said with mocked royal authority, "I forbid you move until... tomorrow. You can get up at midnight." Basil howled. "Now *that's* power, Dak. You see this wench? She'll be obedient as any your hunting bitches. Won't move a muscle till the morrow. Slaves - they can be alot of fun - can be a pain in the arse, too, but still you'll have some fun. It's like being a god or something...."

For his part, the earl said nothing, looking upon the woman with a strange sense of embarrassment. He almost questioned Basil's command, looking at the sky and the approaching of storm. But his liege was drunk and powerful and for himself, he was new to the palace and wanted desperately to gain favor. So he joined in the prince's laughter at the kneeling woman – no, not woman: slave, he must remember that - and took on more water in the hull of his heart. They were walking away now, their voices receding into the growing darkness behind her.

Clarece stared at the ground, head shaking at the absurdity of her situation. If only she'd gone the other way - she never took this route. If only she'd let Donnel's boots rest until tomorrow or had at least told Asla her whereabouts or at least, Crispus, worn her cloak! She lifted her head to the dark clouds. The bottom was about to drop.

"God," she prayed, "Casica says that you see me. You know me and hear the words of my slave heart. If this is true, I beg you: Your book says you make rain to fall upon the good and wicked. I am a wicked woman. Please, please let your rain fall not upon the wicked, at least the wicked located on the south lawn. Amen." (She added "amen" to enhance the effect, she hoped.)

Clarece bowed her head and waited for God's reply. Within seconds it came. The wind burst into the lawn and swept her breath away with its fierce cold. And then, plop. A single, huge rain drop fell at her bended knees. Another followed, this one landing with a singular strike on her head.

"Figures," she muttered, adding a decidedly unsacred oath. The clouds tore open and immediately, the slave was inundated by a multitude of icy messengers of Heaven.

Asla stewed. Joslin served tonight, and Clarece was not yet here to give her bowl to her. Where in Hades was she? The slaves had already mouthed their blessings over this slop. Sounds of hungry mouths eating filled her ears, reminding her belly how empty it was. With Edsner gone she had had no scraps, no drink, nothing. And now with Clarece absent she would be mealless again. She could smell the bowl next to her sitting before an empty chair. Curse it all! Clarece could get her own food when she did arrive, something Asla could not do.

She took Clarece's bowl and glared at the slaves around the table, daring them, just daring them to say anything. *You can't say anything to me without speaking to me,* she thought, *and you won't do that so curse you all, I'm doing this.* Heads returned to bowls and nothing was spoken, but she could feel it, feel their disdain. Insulit. How dare she take another's food. Asla ate quickly and retreated to her stall.

As she removed her boots and vest, she listened for Clarece's voice above her in the princess's quarters. She often listened as their quiet voices and laughter skipped down the stone corridor. At this distance, Asla couldn't understand what they were saying, but she found the sound comforting, like that of a fire. She sometimes struggled with envy at their intimacy. But no voices now. No sounds at all coming down the staircase.

Asla resorted to her journal for escape and comfort. She began filling her pages with rage and curses and tears. What was she to do? She felt so alone in this place, so unknown and unwanted. She hated this life, her life. She hated the men who forced themselves upon her and into her. Hated Edsner. Hated Clarece. Hated everyone. And hated herself for this hate within.

Asla wrote a good hour before realizing Clarece had not yet returned. She listened for movement above, but still, nothing. As the clock struck on the half-hour, she looked to her friend's bed. No slave misses a meal. And Clarece always told her when she'd be late. Perhaps the princess had her on an errand. Yes, that was it, though she couldn't imagine what. Certainly nothing requiring her to leave the palace. Even here, in the basement, the sound of wind and rain seeped through the walls. And the gutter tin, which sounded only with hail, occasionally uttered a plink. The young woman sat and steamed and worried.

"Curse it, I'm not your wet nurse, Clarece," she yelled under her breath. "I am not responsible for your safekeeping." Even as she said this, though, the young woman repented, somewhat shamed. For she knew it was a lie: she *was* responsible for her friend.

Every slave, no matter how old or what position, needed someone to watch out for them. It was as when she was very young, living near the ocean in g'Helderlend, learning to swim. You didn't swim without a partner, at least learning you didn't. Someone needed to watch you in the swells, needed to see if those sounds were you laughing with pleasure or crying out for help. And in this ocean of slavery, the swells never ceased.

A slave's life was in constant turmoil; you wouldn't know it by looking at the mundane tasks of cleaning, cooking, washing. But danger existed everywhere. Illness and abuse. Accusation and rumor. The female guards and drunken noblemen or a jealous slavemate. A misstep or forgotten kneel. Hundreds of little things, things that for a freeman or woman would have no consequence at all, could place a slave in jeopardy.

Fate had been kind to Asla, she knew. It wasn't kind in other ways, but in bringing her to Clarece's pen, it was most merciful. In Clarece, Asla had someone who not only spoke to her and acknowledged her existence, but also someone who cared for her and covered her with protection. Every evening, after all her years here, the insult was still ignored at serving time. She was invisible to the other slaves.

Asla remembered that first frightening night when she introduced herself to the pen. It was Clarece who kept her from being harmed. Clarece who invited her to share her stall. And Clarece whom, every evening, would take the bowl of food placed before her and give it to Asla, forcing the server to pour another bowl for herself. No one would do that for her except Clarece, and the slaves would accommodate no one like that except Clarece. Clarece covered Asla in many ways she did not know.

For her part, Asla covered her senior friend in turn. One disadvantage of being the chief slaveswoman was isolation. Slaves approached Clarece constantly with this problem or need and that frustration or concern. But it was issues that came to her; rarely the person bearing it. The pen considered themselves somewhat subjects to Clarece, and nothing she had tried changed this. Along with her status was the ever present barrier of Clarece's hands. Her mittens formed a veil shrouding the humanity of this simple woman.

With Asla none of these dynamics existed. Though a slave, she did not move in the circle of the other house slaves. Invisibility had its advantages: she could come and go as she pleased; she would never know the tip of the whip and was privy to the most secret parts and situations of noblemen beyond number. She walked within a world foreign to Clarece and the others, one made of opulent decadence.

Outside this world, however, Asla did not walk alone. Clarece was Asla's stallmate and, as such, each was known intimately. To Asla's eyes, Clarece was exposed as someone with great need to accompany her many gifts. Her hands, first and always, were her great adversaries.

During the almost four years Asla had known Clarece, she watched as her friend's condition worsened, at times belying her keen mind and rendering her helpless. It was Asla who acted as Clarece's personal servant, lacing her boots, braiding her hair, writing notes, lighting the lamp, fastening a shirt and a dozen other things a handless woman could not do. And then there was the pain, relentless and tormenting. It, too, had increased over the years. It was Asla who waked Clarece from her nightmares and held her until she slept again. It was Asla who knew what no one else did, the sight of Clarece's hands or what was left of them.

She remembered that night when Clarece woke her asking, "Asla, forgive me for waking you. You do not know me nor I you, and I would not ask if I could bear another hour. But my hands are torturing me. Will you please massage them?" Clarece's hands were shrouded with mittens as they always were even at night. Asla took them into her own and gently massaged them, trying to increase their flow of blood. They felt like wood to her touch, locked into their permanent curl. She watched as this woman she did not know, but felt so drawn to, bowed her head and quietly sobbed, trembling with pain. This would not do.

"Clarece, I have some ointment I use for my muscles when I hurt them in dance. It has a heating about it and soothes my pain. Would you like for me to rub some into your hands? I... I could put out the lamp if you would like." She waited patiently for a reply. She could see the fight going on in the aching woman, one pitted against need and shame. She, herself, was familiar with this battle.

Finally, Clarece nodded, closing her eyes against the silent tears that traced her face. Looking down, she whispered, "Asla, my hands are hideous. They are no hands at all. No one has seen them in years. I'm afraid I'll repulse you...." Asla sighed with understanding. "You aren't repulsive, Clarece. I know what it's like to hide. Twill be alright." After a moment, Clarece nodded again and presented her claws.

Asla gently removed the mittens and held a thin mass of scarred and stained flesh in her own flawless hands for a full minute before applying the ointment. Whether it was the ointment or the effect of human touch, Asla did not know, but Clarece's pain subsided and from that night on, this treatment became a regular part of their week together. But, oh, on those "bad nights" when the pain possessed Clarece as a devil, nothing helped. Nothing. And to the despair of the two friends, those nights grew more frequent.

Asla listened, pensive, to the storm outside. Gods, it was getting cold in the room. She stood and glanced at the wall clock. An hour before curfew. No sounds from upstairs. No Clarece below. Clarece should be preparing the princess' chamber for bed. She must be on an errand, she must. Still.... Asla returned to her cot and laced her boots. She assumed her vest and buttoned it, thinking how much she did not want to disturb the Cassican princess above. "Blast it, Asla, just do it. And blast you, too, Clarece, if I find you sitting up there sipping tea and quoting poetry."

Asla jogged up the stairs, startled to find the door slid fully back into the wall. Before Casica's arrival, this door separating the slaves quarters from this chamber was rarely unlocked much less open. The princess, Clarece had explained, wanted the doorway open. She had what she called an "open door" policy (whatever that was) in her own country and wanted to continue this tradition here in Byzanthia. For their part, Clarece and Asla couldn't understand why any noblewoman would wish for her world of light and warmth to remain accessible to the dark, cold world of the slaves below. It was certain she could hear the activities of the slaves from her bedroom. Only gods knew what the strange woman was thinking.

Asla stopped at the doorway and scanned the room. No Clarece, but there was Casica, sitting at the table, supper plate pushed away. She had her legs propped up on the table, thoroughly engrossed in some book.

Asla was about to move her hand to knock when, suddenly, the princess looked directly at her. The insulit thought absurdly that the princess had felt her presence more than heard it. Casica blinked.

"Asla!" she greeted, smiling, not a scent of disapproval in her look, "What a pleasant surprise. Come in...." Asla walked only a few steps into the room, bowing as she did so. "Forgive me, my lady, but Clarece was not at supper. I wondered if you knew where she might be." Casica lowered her legs and closed her book. "No,

Asla, I don't. She asked to be excused when she brought me dinner. I haven't seen her since. I'd assumed she was with you."

Asla looked toward the door. It sounded like sleet blowing against the glass. In her native tongue she muttered angrily,
"She's with her lover not doubt." In Byzanthian she turned to
the princess. "I think I know where she is; she's probably at the
guardhouse, waiting out this storm, but with your permission, my
lady, I would like to check just in case. It's not like Clarece to go
missing like this."

Casica still reeled with the thought, *"Clarece has a lover?"* when
she returned her attention to Asla. A wave of concern washed
in. Wasn't curfew nearing? Clarece must be in the palace somewhere. The only place she could imagine would be the library.

"By all means, Asla, check for her. Do you need a pass?" "No,
my lady, I come and go as I please. I am often out at night." Casica
nodded, chiding herself for not realizing this. "Alright, but here,
wear my cloak. It will keep you warm."

Casica took her cloak and placed it on the girl. It was much
too big, dragging the floor. Casica reached around Asla and pulled
two tassels on either side of the cloak. As she did so the hem
raised. Asla was intrigued. "How does that work?"

"I don't know," Casica mused. "My mother made this for me.
She did all sorts of little things like that to this garment. She's a
master seamstress, something I am not." Casica took a covered
lamp, lit it and handed it to Asla. "I hate for you to go out in that,"
she observed, considering doing it herself. "I'll be alright, Casica,"
*and I'm going to rake that slave over the coals when I find her,* she
thought. "I won't be gone long." Casica nodded. "The only place
I can think she might be is the library. I'll check there." "Yes, my
lady," Asla replied, thinking, she's not in the library; she's with
Poul.

Casica opened the door, inviting cold and bitter rain into her
room. Asla paused on the landing to adjust her hood. As she made
her way down the stairs her mind was a mix of cursing and fear.
It would be completely dark soon, and nothing good happened
to a slave in the dark. As she ran along the path, she marveled at
Casica's cloak. It did not so much keep her warm as it did make
her warm, like the cloak, itself, was producing heat. What kind
of Cassican magic was this? She didn't mind the sensation, how-

ever, and arrived at the guardhouse warm and dry. The house was filled with the sound of male voices at ease. Asla loved that sound and the scent of men, pipe smoke, that accompanied it. She went directly to the source of the voices, the open room.

Even when she wasn't trying, Asla made an entrance. The voices stopped as the guardsmen looked up from their card games to gaze upon the queen of hearts. Only God knew how many of them wished with all their might for the money to rent her for a time, if only an hour. Most of the men looked upon Asla with wonder and kindness. She was a regular visitor to their gym, and her ease with them was as pleasant as her form. She truly enjoyed them, they sensed, and her presence was always a blessed reminder of why they liked being men.

"Excuse me gentlemen," she said, smiling winsomely, "but I think I have lost a slave. Has anyone seen Clarece this evening?" She was speaking to the group but addressed one particular man near the fireplace, drink in hand. She now glanced at Poul as to say, "Has she been with you?" He slowly shook his head. Founder! she had come out in this stew for nothing. "I've seen Clarece," a voice answered. "She was with Smith. I saw her leave his shop but that was a good two hours ago." Asla glanced at  the guardsman and then gazed at the floor. Something was terribly wrong.

At the fireplace, Poul was rising from his chair. "I'll help you look for her, Asla." "Thank you, Sgt..." Poul walked with Asla to the door, taking a cloak from the wall as he did so. "I came by way of the west path, Poul." "Well, there are only two other paths to the palace. I'll take the slope path, it's longer. You take the south path. We'll start with that and go from there. Scads, it's cold," his voice was filled with concern. "I'll meet you back at the palace," she said walking back into the winter storm thinking, "Where on earth are you, Clarece?"

Clarece was precisely where Prince Bastil had left her almost three hours before, kneeling in the middle of the south path, head bowed in the sleet, trying desperately to breathe. Her whole body shook with cold, and her teeth chattered until her jaws locked. She was utterly drenched, wet as much within as without. With misery she thought of the gazebo not twenty feet away. Six steps and she would be out of the wet if not the cold.

The decision to rise and take those steps never occurred to her, any more than it would have occurred to a statue to leave its base. She had been commanded to kneel here until the morrow, and for now, this was her only purpose in life (though she had begun to wonder how long this life might be). At first she feared being found out by the guards; curfew was fast approaching. Now she feared not being found. Better the jail than this open place.

She had given up cursing an hour ago. She had given up the distinctly slave-like feeling of having been made a fool, the purpose for this entire scenario. She had given up her fear of arrest. All that was left was desperation.

"Dear, God," she gasped, watching her breath steam in the fading light, "even if you don't hear me, have mercy. Please help me...." She knew this prayer. She had uttered it often in the night when her hands and wrists rebelled against the rest of her body, burning with fire as though someone had poured molten lead into her veins. And the result now was as it always was then. Nothing.

Clarece didn't know why she prayed at all except that if she didn't, she would simply be talking to herself. And even though both actions produced the same results, the one was socially acceptable, even for slaves, the other, well, her hands were enough of a defect in her person. She finally broke her upright stance and kneeled fully to the ground, her head touching the earth, streams of water and ice flowing about her. Her arms ached beneath her. Would this never end? Thunder filled the air and washed her in a whitish light. She sobbed in her state of helplessness and wondered who, if anyone above, looked upon slaves. St. Crispus, clearly, was detained elsewhere at this time.

She never heard Asla's approach. "In the name of gods, Clarece! What the devils are you doing here? We've been looking everywhere!" Asla was bending over her wretched friend, virtually yelling over the din of rain and sleet. Clarece managed to look up into her face. "Praying, Asla. Vespers."

"Curse your wit, Clarece! This is no time to jest. Get up. You're freezing." "'Get up'. My, what a brilliant idea, As! I should have thought of that hours ago. I can't get up, you idiot! Prince Bastil ordered me here until the morrow. I can't leave without his or

Casica's permission - or the King's if you can find him." "I might be an idiot, but I'm not the one kneeling in a puddle of ice freezing my (thunder) off! Scads! Alright, then: I have been sent in Casica's name to give you leave to come home. Now get up and let's go."

"Asla, you know you can't do that. Only a peer can undo a prince's order. Casica must come here herself." "What the - curse them, Clarece. Knock the rules and come home! It's curfew. If the guards find you and arrest you as a runaway, then where will you be?" "In a drier place, I venture. Why don't you run and get my mistra, Asla. I promise to stay right here." "You sarcastic - scads, if you aren't the most pigheaded...." Asla began, continuing with several choice g'Helderleicht phrases best uninterpreted.

She ceased her tirade to look into Clarece's face. It was pale with cold and pain. Blast that prince. She knelt in the rivers cascading around her and embraced her friend. "Hold on, Rece. I'll be right back." With a kiss to the woman's cheek, Asla jumped up and ran down the path. Founder! What a night.

Casica was sitting at the table, musing over Clarece's whereabouts, when Asla burst through the door. As quickly as she could, she explained the situation. "How do I get to where she is?" Transferring the cloak to Casica, Asla explained how to reach Clarece. Casica reached for the door handle when Asla said, "Wait, Princess. You'll need the lamp." "No, I won't," and out Josquin ran, her eyes burning blue in the darkness.

Seeing at night is of great help. She saw the gazebo long before she reached it, but Casica could sight no Clarece. She stopped in the path, removing her hood and searching all about in the rain. No. Clarece was not here. Heaven, where could she be? The wet princess turned and jogged up the path. She ran up the stairs, careful of the ice and met Asla on the landing.

"She isn't there, Asla...." "Scads. She's been arrested, that's the only explanation." "Arrested?!" "Yes. The guards must have found her." "But she was ordered there by a prince." "Doesn't matter, my lady. Clarece is out past curfew, without a pass. It wouldn't matter if the king himself were the cause. She's a runaway." "Alright, Asla," Casica gave in. "Where do I find her?"

Casica's anger was growing great as Asla's. Asla described the location of the palace jail. It could be reached through the palace, but the more direct route would be back into the yard and around the north wing. Casica listened carefully. She was unfamiliar with the north yard of the palace and had no desire to get lost on this miserable night. Once she felt certain she understood, she stepped back into the rain and down the stairs.

As she jogged to the north yard, Casica wondered two things: she wondered, first, how Clarece was holding up, especially her hands, having been out in this ice for so long. Secondly, she wondered how she would hold up. She hated this sense of responsibility for another's life. Surely, she'd had such responsibility before, but that was in healing crises. Once the illness or injury was cured, her place in the person's life ended. Now she was feeling the weight of her new role as a slave owner: this woman's life, a woman she did not understand and was only beginning to know, this woman's life was her responsibility forever. Casica suddenly felt very heavy.

The guards discovered Clarece not ten minutes after Asla left her. "Great Scads, Clarece! Is that you? What the dickens are you doing here?" Clarece knew the guards well, as did they her. "Learning patience, my lord. And humility (*or at least humiliation*, she thought). Prince Bastil ordered me here until midnight." "Blast. Will he never outgrow these games of his?" the corporal wondered aloud. "Well, we have to arrest you. 'Sorry. I'd rather send you home for a hot drink. Scads, Clarece, you must be frozen! Here, let me help you up." Clarece was grateful for the guards' help. Feeling had long left her legs.

The guards escorted Clarece to a place she had not been in years. As a child, newly arrived to the palace, she had been sent to take food to a slave arrested for stealing a cup from his master. He swore he hadn't done  it, and all the house slaves believed him. Palace slaves wouldn't dare steal, and a cup is positively useless. This slave had no gambling debts and no use for money. Anyway, the slave lost a hand and was sold on the open market. Clarece still felt sorrow as she remembered him. To her child's eyes, he seemed very handsome and very frightened. That was over ten years ago. She wondered if he still lived.

Now she was the one being signed into custody of the jailer. Runaway. Having released her to the jailer, the guards left wondering between them what would become of Byzanthia when Bastil assumed the crown. God curse him - Bastil could cause alot of mischief. Clarece was known to the jailer but his sympathy for her was no help: she was a slave and as such must be stored in the dungeons, like property. He led her to a cell, low in the basement of the prison. A narrow, grated vent was fit into the corner at the ceiling. From it flowed a stream of cold water, running as it was from the yard into the grate. The cell floor was covered by a layer of water a good three stites deep.

In his kindness, the jailer let Clarece keep her boots. He made her kneel and locked her wrists into a small stock fastened to the floor. He left her ankles unchained, reluctant to chain her at all. It was required for all slaves to be chained kneeling, though. Clarece nodded in understanding. She watched as the jailer lifted his torch from the cell wall. He proceeded to leave her cell and with him went all light. The door closed with a rusted clang.

She was alone. Out of the sleet, but still planted in ice water, splashed in the face by the icy fountain from above. But it was not the cold that made her cry out and moan in fear: it was the room. For all around, the cell began to close about her. The weight of its walls pressed upon her psyche until her chest convulsed and left her fighting for precious, precious air. Air that the darkness stole and sucked from her, like innocence, on a cold, hard livery floor.

The rain was letting up. Casica couldn't remember many storms like this on Cassica. Cassica. As she wove her away round columns and steps, the weary woman thought, longingly, of home. It was the night, she knew, with its stress and confusion. And the cloak. She smiled at its familiar warmth and at the slight sense of her mother's presence. Funny. At home, living as she did with her parents and brother, she had never noticed this, but now so removed from all that was familiar, it was so evident. Maman had woven some of herself into this garment. It had with it the feeling of her mother, like she was present somehow in the cloth.

Maman had told her when she was little that all loved garments take on the feel of their owners, like a fragrance of perfume captured in a blouse or scarf. With a smile, Casica breathed deeply of her mother's fragrance. Maman would know exactly what to do. She glanced up at the night, wondering if her mother were in bed and if the rain that pelted her daughter fell on her roof now, lulling her to sleep.

Light. Pretend the water is light, Clarece told herself. You're a poet. You're a story teller. You specialize in taking reality and bending it to your will. So do it. Light. You kneel in a puddle of light, surrounded by it, splashed by it, soaked in it; light pours through the vent there; it fills your garments. It falls upon the ground and into your ears. You are not in a dark place; you are ensconced in light.

Try as she might, this imagery, while it comforted and pleased some part of her poet's heart, failed miserably at restraining the panic within. It was like a horse pulling harder and harder at the bit she held, ignoring the pain in its mouth, determined to run wild and to take her with it. And she thought of Asla. By now Asla would know where she was. Surely she would come. It never occurred to Clarece the princess would come, not here, not to a prison. That would be too shaming.

Even as she thought this, however, the princess was coming. She had located the prison and had spoken with the jailer. Though he knew, at once, who she was and why she was there, the jailer was utterly startled at her presence. What was a royal doing here? Clarece was only a slave. He was guiding her now, each with a torch in hand, down the narrow stairs into the dungeons. Casica had been to jails before, caring for prisoners in her own land. There were no dungeons, however, and the sense of descending more deeply into the earth was unnerving, like walking into your own grave. She shuddered more at this sensation than at the cold.

The horse was dragging Clarece with him. Then a sound, a movement of a key in the lock wrenched her back into the present. The door opened and light flooded the cell. Clarece closed her eyes and breathed deeply of the glow; she needed to regain her breath. "I'll leave you, my lady." The door closed.

"*Clarece?*" the incredulous voice was not Asla's. The soaked slave looked up and squinted against the torch light. *My God,* she thought, *it's Casica.* What's the princess doing here? Casica scanned the cell in horror. *This can't be real,* she thought. In the midst of this flooded ice chamber knelt her Clarece, who not four hours before stood smiling, safe and bright in her chamber. Clarece bowed her head, humiliated. To have Asla here would have been one thing, but the princess – kai! would this night never end? Shame warmed her face.

"My lady," she whispered, bowed, "I can explain." She didn't know what she expected but Clarece wasn't expecting Casica's move. She felt the princess kneel beside her and tenderly, take her into her arms. As she cradled Clarece's head, Josquin breathed quietly against her face. Warmth from her body penetrated Clarece's stiffened form, warming her from the inside. "Peace, Clarece. You're not alone. I'm here."

And then they came. Tears poured from Clarece's heart. The fear and exhaustion and pain of the night wracked her body, and all the while Casica stayed there, holding the dear woman against her. Casica waited while Clarece's breathing resumed to a slow, steady rate. She could feel the woman relaxing in her arms. Only then did she ask, "Clarece, what happened? I need to know everything." Clarece took one more deep breath and looked into Casica's face.

"My lady, after I left you this evening, I went to speak with the leather smith at the guards' livery about a pair of boots for one of my people. On my way back to the palace, I met Prince Bastil and the earl, Dakat is his name. The prince was drinking and in one of his moods; he wanted to impress Dakat. So he ordered me to remain kneeling until the morrow. I had no way to inform you and no way to leave. The guards found me there, in the path, after curfew, and arrested me. I swear to you, great lady, I would never think of running away - I swear."

"I know, Clarece. I know." Josquin looked around at the cell, watched the rivulet of water pouring down the wall. "Clarece, all this is unknown to me. What will happen to you now?"

"You need not concern yourself anymore for me, my lady. You should not be here now - you a princess. I will be brought before the slave magistrate - tomorrow, most likely. My life isn't in jeopardy, I don't think - everyone knows how the prince is with slaves. I'll stand before the magistrate and be grilled over how foolish I am and how stupid it was for me to be on the path in the first place and then he'll have my foolishness taken out of my flesh."

"You mean you'll be flogged?" Casica was appalled. "You'll be lashed for this? when it wasn't your fault?" "It's always the slave's fault, my lady. And no slave is brought before the court without sound lashing." Clarece lowered her eyes from her owner's troubled face. She couldn't bear to see her concern. "I haven't felt the whip since coming to the palace." She pulled at the stocks around her hands. "And I've never been in irons. They say there's a first for everything." Clarece attempted a smile but it was lost. She closed her eyes and slowly shook her head. She simply could not believe this was happening to her. Surely it was a dream... surely she would waken soon.

"Clarece," Casica said pulling away gently from her friend. "I won't see you beaten. I don't know what I can do, but I'm going to do something. I'll be back for you. How are your hands?" Clarece hadn't noticed until the question, but her hands were fine. Her whole body felt warmed and at rest, almost sleepy. In the midst of this peace, the specter of imminent darkness tore into her thoughts. She tensed at the image. "What's wrong?" Casica was looking into her eyes now, trying to read the unreadable. Only God knew the mind of a slave.

"Oh, Mistra, I – I'm afraid of dark rooms." There. She had confessed what until now only Asla knew. Her shame was complete. Casica nodded with understanding, very certain there were reasons for her fear. "Tis alright, Clarece. You'll be alright. I'll be back soon. Yes?" Clarece met her gaze and nodded. Casica embraced her for a long moment then rose to leave. She knocked on the door.

As he opened it, the jailer reached for the torch burning in the cell. "Leave it," Casica ordered. The jailer bowed in acquiesce and closed the door behind him. Clarece listened for their steps and breathed a long sigh of relief.

"What can I do to end this prank, jailer?" Casica asked at the front. "My lady?" "I won't be bothered with my slave standing before some magistrate. I have need of her. What do I do to stop this ridiculous game now?" A threatening anger filled the woman's face and voice. *Scads*, thought the jailer. *What have I gotten myself into?* "Well, my lady, there is nothing you *can* do until the morrow. You can speak to the magistrate, yourself, but until then there is nothing to be done."

"Absurd, jailer. You and I both know this is an utter waste of all our time." Casica's mind was racing. Then the thought occurred to her: what the blazes was she doing up when the prince, the flaggert who caused all this, was sleeping, warm in his bed?

"What if I present you a statement signed by the prince that this is all a mistake? Will that suffice for Clarece's release?" "Well, of course, my lady, it would. But tis late. The prince won't be disturbed." "We'll see who's disturbed," she replied fastening the top of her cloak. "Don't close shop. I'll be back shortly." Knock it all. She would meet this prince.

Asla met Casica at the door. Josquin bore an expression that at once put Asla on the defensive. Was the princess mad at her? Had Clarece told her of their fighting? Casica all but ignored the woman. She found what she wanted, parchment and pen. She began scratching out a letter, it seemed, and then remembered the g'Helderleit.

"Asla, I want you to get me Clarece's cloak and then prepare a hot bath." "Yes, my lady." Asla was already on her way down the stairs. By the time she had returned, Casica was waiting with the document. She took the cloak and asked where she could find Prince Bastil. Asla gaped. Surely Casica wasn't thinking of disturbing the prince at this hour. No one in their right mind would do that - certainly not for the sake of a slave.

"He's in the west wing, my lady. Go to the west and ask any guard; he will show you the prince's bed chamber. And you're frappin crazy if you think any guard is going to let a Cassican refugee woman disturb the sleep of the crown prince." That last part, Asla didn't say aloud but she certainly thought it. Who on earth would dare do anything like this - and for a slave? What could possibly motivate her? Pride? Was Casica feeling a pawn in a power game? Was she feeling made a fool through the treatment of her property and wanting to come out feeling the winner? *You fool woman,* Asla thought. You're playing a game you can't possibly win.

The thought of love never occurred to the insulit. And not only because she was insulit; no slave would naturally think that way. To be loved meant you had to be something other than an object, and slaves rarely felt themselves to be otherwise. Teamwork among slaves was of necessity as was camaraderie but friendship was a stretch. How do you become friends with someone who is not fully human? Perhaps you could know the companionship of two pets living together but, friendship, as two freemen or women enjoy?

Even with Clarece, Asla struggled with affection. She knew Clarece loved her. Clarece would tell her this. The two shared bread together. Still in all her years of knowing and caring for Clarece, Asla could not bring herself to openly embrace her affection. Clarece had a soul, at least; surely she could love. But Asla, she had no soul, a souless one could not love no matter what she felt. It was a strange fact of their relationship that Asla would, without thought, give her life for Clarece but never once had said she loved her.

Asla watched as Casica left through Bastien's door. "What a fool," she breathed to herself.

Casica was no fool; she knew what she was about was foolish. But enough was enough. God would not stand by and let someone be tortured. Then catching herself, she thought, yes, He would. He did with her, standing by watching as some man possessed with evil beat the life from her. But even then, He was merciful. Merciful in preparing her for that day and for providing her protectors afterwards, one of whom knelt shivering in a cell, dreading the dimming light of a torch.

God watched but never passively. His not intervening in no way reflected a heart without mercy or love. He reveled in bringing good, unspeakable good, from unspeakable evil. Redemption, more often than prevention, Casica thought, was His hallmark.

Casica learned this, not only from years of sitting at the feet of teachers but from her own experiences. Countless times she observed how healings rendered people stronger in the harmed places. Bones were her favorite. A bone is never so strong as in the place where a break has healed. But Casica was in no mood to sit by and watch as a man's foolishness harmed a defenseless woman. Plus, she was just plain angry.

By the time she reached her destination, Casica's plan was set. Princes were no mystery to her. Her brother was a prince. She would draw her cards from this hand and play with the face of an owner. Poker was always one of her favorite games.

The guard was incredulous. Firstly, the Cassican princess was present, at midnight, in his west wing. Secondly, she was asking him to take her to the crown prince's chamber. At midnight. Unannounced. Was she drunk? She couldn't possibly be serious, but she was demanding that he do so now. The guard escorted Casica to the prince's door. He would pass this predicament to the prince's private guard.

The prince's guard was respectful but stern: no, he would not wake the prince; the princess may return tomorrow with an appointment. No, you do not understand, she countered. I am seeing the prince now, and if you do not wake him, I will. For a long time they stood there, toe to toe, neither wavering. The guard entertained for a moment the possibility that this Cassican may be mad. She may be dangerous. Her stance and stare were certainly not that of a passive, submissive woman. They looked more like those of a warrior, calling him out.

She paused a little longer and made a move to the door. The guard reached for her arm. Instantly, Casica caught his wrist and held it as in a vise. The guard pulled back but to his astonishment, was unable to break her grip. She was glaring at him, unmoved by his struggle. *Scads!* he thought realizing this woman out muscled him. His anger turned to fear. What kind of Cassican devil was this?

"Again, I would prefer if you wake the prince. I would rather not invade his privacy or modesty but I will." The guard relaxed his arm and she released him. "One moment, my lady," he said bowing with suspicion. The guard entered the room, leaving the door slightly ajar.

Casica could hear all manner of oaths and threats; she almost pitied the guard but she needed to remain strong. "Throw her the devil in!" "The prince will see you, now my lady." Casica walked into the room. There, lighted by a candle and in a clear rage of confusion and insult stood Bastil, Crown Prince of Byzanthia,

Defender of the Faith, Humiliator of Slaves. The game had begun. But Casica immediately changed her strategy.

In an instant she measured her opponent and realized direct confrontation would get her, and Clarece, nowhere. This man had mastered conflict; he was no guard at the door, no kid brother. The best card Casica had to play was her womanhood bent in the most self-defacing manner. She would act the naive, mindless woman, a part she despised but would gladly play for Clarece's release.

"What the devil are you doing waking me at this hour Cassican? I ought to have you flogged!" "You already have, great prince," she acknowledged with a slight bow. Bastil looked very much Bastien's brother, Casica thought. Slightly shorter and heavier but with the same structure and eyes. A handsome man.

Bastil wasn't expecting any response from this woman, much less the one she gave. He was taken aback and began eyeing her as he might a shadow in the woods during a hunt. What was she? Shadow, prey, or predator? For that matter, what was any woman if not all three.

"Prince Bastil," Josquin continued, "it is such an honor to meet you at last though it never occurred to me to do so in this way. I would never think to disturb you and your wife if not for an emergency. A thousand apologies to your highnesses. However, it seems the guards have misunderstood the playful nature of the prince and have taken a - pawn - from the board of my life and placed her in chains. Their ignorance has left me bathless and wineless and, if the prince does not intervene, will deprive me of breakfast as well - if not lunch and dinner. I am new to the palace, tis true, my lord, but I have a prince as a brother and know that you would not wish for your play to be construed as foolishness...."

Bastil didn't know what the devil this woman was talking about. Gads, why do women talk so much? His head was pounding, his stomach hurt and here's this woman he had never so much as seen rattling on about pawns, brothers and dinner. What the blast was going on? and he asked her as much.

"Clarece, my lord. My slave has been detained in your dungeons for your prank misconstrued. I understand but the jailers don't. I have a statement explaining your intent. All it needs is your lord's stamp and you may return to your sleep and I to my comfort."

What? The prince glanced at the statement held before him. It was all coming back now. Bastien's slave girl. The prince stared at the princess. She was tall. As tall as he and seemed completely oblivious to his irritation. She stood before him, addressing him as she might a horse dealer settling on a mutually satisfactory deal. He was utterly befuddled. He didn't know whether to strike her or thank her for coming to his aid. She was saying something, What?

"Your seal, my lord," she was saying as she leaned the candle to the parchment, dripping wax upon the bottom. Bastil stared into her once more, but she returned his look as though asking, Could there possibly be a problem with this? He guessed there weren't. He had no idea. Scads, he was getting groggy. Dumbly, the prince pressed his signet ring into the wax. He never noticed Casica's hand on his back.

"Thank you my lord. I look forward to meeting your wife soon, I hope. Blessings upon your rest." And with that she left. No bowing, no curtsy. Nothing. Simply walked out of his presence, leaving the dazed prince to wonder if all this were only a drunken dream

Josquin fled before the prince awakened enough to realize what had happened. If she plied her work well, placing sleep upon him with her hand, he would not fully awake. Most likely he would not remember the encounter at all come morning. That would depend on the effect but to any extent she had what she wanted: Clarece's freedom.

She smiled thinking, *Maman would not have approved but Berea certainly would. She would toast me.* (Of course, Berea would toast anyone, anytime, but that was beside the point.) She gathered Clarece's cloak from the dumbfounded guard, thanked him, and made her way down the marble corridor. Amazing how silent a palace becomes at night, like the bricks themselves sleep. Outside Casica regained her bearings. It felt good to stop and breathe. What a night. "Thank you," she prayed. "Let's gather Clarece."

The jailer wasn't surprised to see her, but he was shocked to read the order explaining Prince Bastil's wish to free the slave. It was the prince's seal. The Cassican didn't seem to have any injury about her, only an impatient desire for him to bring Clarece out - which he did at once. The sooner this all ended, the better for him. What a bizarre night in an otherwise boring job.

Clarece arrived with the jailer and the torch, still lit. She looked upon her mistra, her face filled with gratitude, fatigue and numbness. She dropped to her knees before her owner and bowed to the floor waiting for her acceptance. Casica remembered the ritual and placed her hand gently on the woman's head. "Let's go home."

At the doorway, Casica removed her own cloak, and silently wrapped her shivering friend in its warmth. All the while, Clarece watched Casica's face wondering what kind of woman this was. Clarece's cloak she garbed herself in and led Clarece down the path by her arm. It was pitch black and the women didn't have a lantern.

"Thank you, my lady," Clarece said simply. She couldn't think of what more to say. She couldn't think at all. In reply Casica drew the exhausted woman to her, and sensing Clarece's unsteady gait, walked slowly, watching for pitfalls along the way. For her part, Clarece avoided Casica's eyes; she didn't think she could bear those eerily glowing orbs this night.

Asla was waiting for them on the landing. She had half-expected to see Casica return alone, bruised and bloody from a beating by the prince. But here she was, healthy and smiling, Clarece in tow. "She's all yours, Asla. I'll see about getting some food." "Yes, my lady," Asla replied, removing the cloak from wilted shoulders. "Come, Clarece, I have a hot bath for you." Clarece said nothing, only looked into her friend's eyes to see where she was. Kindness reflected to her.

In the bath room, Asla embraced her sala for a long time, holding her, feeling her breathe, washed with gratefulness at her being returned home, safely. Undressed and in the hot, soothing water, Clarece wept silently in relief, resting in her friend's gentle touch of cloth and soap. A bath never felt so good. Slave or king, homecoming was a blessed advent.

# XIV

Casica sat on her table, a glass of Bastien's best held against her forehead. Asla and Clarece, warmed and fed, had retired to their beds long ago. The room was dark except for the glowing of the brazier. It was silent, except for the howling storm outside; wind had replaced rain and its roar rattled the windows, slipping in through every crack. A cool draft flowed from the slaves' quarters rendering the stairway a flue.

Casica listened to the wind, listened to her breath and tried to sort out her racing thoughts. It felt good to be alone after such a stressful night. Did any of this really happen? She should be in bed, like Clarece and Asla. But sleep evaded her, caught as it was, in her vortex of thought. To Casica it seemed her mind was the wind outside, fed by a system of anxious, confused energy. As much as she drank, as much as she tried to surrender her confusion, the weight on her heart pounded more and more truly. *Weight of her heart.*

The healer smiled, remembering herself as a little girl, not more than five, sitting in her dear Baba's lap. His arms wrapped her in regal sleeves; he must have just left a meeting of the council. She couldn't know that the meeting centered on her. K'Eran looked down at his daughter, blue eyes misty with affection and concern: "Heavy is the heart that bears the crown, M'Yat. The crown is glorious, but the weight of that glory ...," gently he shook his head, smiling at his precious one. *Ah, Baba, heavy is the heart, indeed,* she thought now.

What in the world was she doing here? She didn't belong here. Nothing, nothing could have prepared her to live here. Preparation. All those years of preparation. Josquin had never really thought of her life as training until the end, that night on the ship when her mother dressed her in one final act of love. She was girding Casica about with her karosh, the one she had completed for her sixteenth birthday, kneeling before her daughter as was the custom, fastening the last hook in place.

Pelana placed her hands upon her daughter's waist, and read the symbols before her, caressing the fine burgundy leather she had lovingly fashioned for this belt. How she wished the woman wearing it were herself. How she longed to take her daughter's place in this awful transaction of fate. What would become of her, what would become of her Love in that enemy land? She could not know and she was powerless to help. How swiftly the years had passed. Pelana pulled Casica gently to herself, and rested her head against her daughter's stomach. She felt Casica's shallow, quickened breathing; she was afraid.

The tall queen stood and lay her hands upon Casica's head. Closing her eyes, she spoke a blessing upon her daughter, her face resting against the young brow, as she tried to store the scent of her baby's hair. She gathered Casica and held her close to her heart. "I'm afraid, Maman," came the whisper.

"I know, Life, I know." Pelana reached for Casica's hand and placed it upon her necklace. At Casica's touch, her mother's stones glowed with renewed brilliance and in turn Casica could feel her own necklace warm with recognition. "You feel it, Casica? You feel my heart for you? No matter what happens this day. No matter what happens to you in the future, remember M'Yat: you are not alone. You have not been sent out alone. Remember the colors of your shalonn, they share my own. My heart goes with you. I will pray unceasingly for you."

Pelana kissed her daughter tenderly; their time was short. She stepped back and looked at the young woman before her. Though Pelana was tall, even for a Cassican, her daughter was only a few stites shorter than she. She seemed a reflection of her mother: same dark hair and eyes, deep with thought and emotion. Her nose was K'Eran's, though, as were her dimples.

The seamstress inspected her handiwork; except for her riding boots, Casica's costume was sewn by her. The edict stipulated that Casica be dressed simply, as the captive she embodied. Pelana had dressed her plainly but extravagantly: the white blouse was pure silk with a lining added for warmth. Its high collar had embroidered, in burgundy, Casica's royal seal on either end with the symbols, "Beloved," joining the seals from its back. Customary blue pants were replaced with a plain brown pair made of finest wool. For neck irons, hung her shalonn, stones radiating beneath the silk.

The only unusual piece was her karosh, but Casica refused to be without it. Pelana smiled to herself sadly. Her child was simply lovely. Cassica may be forced to surrender their daughter as a prisoner of war, but it would do so having wrapped her in the fabrics of a queen. God, would she ever look upon her daughter again? Pelana gazed into her child's frightened eyes - even in memory the love and sorrow Casica saw there pained her heart. "We have done all we can to prepare you for this day, for this time, M'Yat," her mother said. "I know we have not done enough. The gaps must be filled by God. My heart aches with love for you. God be with you." "And with you, Maman...." A quiet knock came to the cabin door. It was time to leave. Time to release.

Josquin's eyes glistened in memory. *Oh, Maman, how I love you; how I miss you. If we'd only known.* Gaps? All that time - the study, the strict training and discipline of Berea, the counsel and work, all that was poured into sixteen years of life, all served now to expose the gaping lack in her education: how to own a human life. Forget books; they should have straddled her with human life.

The only life Casica had ever owned was that of Rigel and even then, he was more of a companion than property. No one could truly own Rigel; how could anyone own a person? But she did. This night was forcing Casica to own herself, too; she could no longer pretend that Clarece's slavery was theoretical, treating her more as a concept of slavery instead of the very real person living in slavery she was. A person enslaved to  powers which, though unable to collar Casica, (being contained as they were to the world of the not-human,) bound her up nonetheless.

No wonder, she reasoned, did people here do so much to convince themselves slaves were not human. That must be the only sane recourse in this mad, unnatural relationship of owner and owned. If Clarece were mere property, Casica could easily have refrained from involvement this night. Allowing, instead, the laws governing property do their work, returning her possession to her damaged but serviceable. Casica would be sleeping now instead of fretting the unsolvable. Breakfast would have appeared via Asla, probably. Clarece certainly never would have voiced any pain. Life would have gone on.

But Clarece wasn't property; she was human, as human as Casica, filled with the image of God. How does one do this? she wondered. How do I live my role of owner but relate to Clarece as sister? The empty glass felt solid in her hand, much more so than she did to herself. "The gaps must be filled...."

Casica studied the doorway to her left. Through it, was the slaves' quarters where beneath her restless mind, they slept in their dark world. She rose from the table and made her way down those stairs. Slaves weren't the only ones who could walk in silence when they wished.

All were fast asleep with the deepness that comes when rising is near. Casica looked. To her left were Clarece and Asla. Clarece, her hands folded safely near her. Asla with a few fingers grasping lightly her own blond mane. A tiny oil lamp, its light only as bright as a single match bathed their sleep in a kindly hush. Farther down, separated from this first stall by a large closet was Raina, a cloak draped over her still form. One by one, Casica visited each stall and looked briefly upon its occupant. Fourteen women. Fourteen women of different age, position and personality, each dreaming from her unique history, each joined by a common silver collar about her throat.

Casica walked to the fireplace and perched on its hearth. The fire's embers were few but offered her companionship. She considered the sleeping women before her, her fingers resting on her lips as they did whenever she lost herself in thought.

"Father, I know tis no accident I live above this place. I know you have a reason for introducing me to their world. But I hate their world. I hate this world that exists parallel to my own, a world whose sole purpose is to sustain my own. I hate slavery and what it makes of these people. I hate this world of bondage. All I want to do is - destroy it... and I can't. What am I to do when I can't change a world?" She waited for an answer. The clock ticked. *God, there are so many clocks in this land,* she thought. A slave's life was ruled by time. Casica struggled with time; she wanted everything to happen at once. Waiting: it made a woman's world. Again she asked herself, "What am I to do when I can't change this world?"

*Bless it,* came a voice she knew well. *Bless them. And for this, you have been well-prepared.*

The storm in her mind quieted as something more solid than any stone awakened, returned, as it were, within Casica's heart. Quietly she remembered who she was. She was Josquin. A daughter of a josquin and of many before her. Though groomed to become queen of her people, Casica never assumed that throne. She assumed another and wore its crown about her throat, much as the collar of these sleeping women. She caressed her glowing necklace, pobble stones alive to her touch, her alive to theirs. She was a healer, and what was a healer if not a blesser? That's all healing was, really, moving into a broken, hurting, or empty place and offering it blessing.

And in this, Casica was gifted, more gifted than any before her, so did all the other josquins say. Gifted in many ways, and with one peculiar gifting that no one, not even Berea, could yet identify. "You are a mystery, girl - among other things," Berea would tease.

"'Casica,'" she whispered her name to herself. "Life." She loved life, was filled with it. On her island, she was called the Queen of Life. That is who she is; she is a life. Josquin turned her attention to the lives sleeping before her. They were slaves, yes, but truth be known, everyone lived in some sort of bondage, herself included, forced to live in this land she did not know and did not want. But in the midst of this reality she could - would - *live,* live freely within her restraints. So could these slavewomen - could they not? - as much as they were able, live as the children of God they were. *The truth be known.* Truth seemed a rare commodity in this place.

The clock chimed three. In a half hour, these women would wake to begin another day in slavery. Casica looked upon them and whispered a promise. "This is what I offer you. I will give you my life and all that I have. Perhaps, I cannot free you *from* your world, but I can offer you tastes of freedom *within* your world, for I am a servant too."

In her former land, her title was "Queen" but her reality was servant, a "servant queen," Maman said, ministering to her people through healing. She did this because she, too, was subject to a King, the true King of Life itself.[1] Her call was to bless His people. These were His people. She would serve them.

"I will serve you blessing," continued Casica, smiling; she knew her calling now. "I will pray God's heart to come upon you, and in the meantime, I will offer you two of His hands...."

Standing from the hearth, Casica took one last look at the sleepers. Then stepping lightly up the stairs, surrendered to her bed. She was fast asleep as life stirred below.

# XV

Breakfast did arrive via Asla though Casica never saw this. She slept through the delivery as did Clarece below her. Clarece woke later that morning to find a note on the night stand: "Fed the Hen. Gone to three cocks this morning. A." *My, what a bright, cheerful greeting for one following such a difficult night,* Clarece thought sarcastically. Makes one question one's ever teaching one to read and write.

Clearly, Asla's fury remained unabated. Clarece hated conflict for as long as she could remember. The slaves thought of her as a peacemaker, but she knew her skill wasn't born of courage or wisdom: it was bred in fear, a survival mechanism truly. Anyone who lived as she, with her weakness displayed so nakedly, well, you became expert at avoiding fights. In a physical struggle, Clarece had always been the loser. Her opponent needed merely clutch her hand to render her helpless. The men in the livery had taught her this quickly.

In a verbal fight, she was much better equipped, but still she loathed this situation. Heaven knew she did not want to face whatever it was in Asla, but she had grown frightened for her friend. She had never seen Asla like this. Certainly, the girl had her moments, but they were brief and resolved on the gym floor or in heated discussion with Clarece. But this, whatever it was, filled Asla with such venom, it threatened to poison her entire world. If Asla's rage continued, it would leak into the freeworld and then, who could tell what consequences would flood? She could not let Asla's furious isolation continue another day.

Clarece dressed as best she could. No slaves remained in the quarters this late in the morning, so she was left alone with her hair. It was impermissible for slaves, insulit excluded, to go about with their hair unbound. There was nothing to do except ask for Casica's help.

The princess was awake and, having eaten her breakfast, sat by the window, writing. Clarece met her greeting with an embarrassed smile. She didn't know what embarrassed her more, her hair or the events of the previous night. Was it just last night?

"Sanu, dazua," greeted Clarece in Cassican. "My lady, I wonder if you could rescue me again by plaiting my hair?" "Gladly, and if it doesn't involve swimming in ice and waking princes, I'll lace your boots, too," Casica teased.

As Casica braided Clarece's hair, they discussed the night before. Clarece tried to express her gratitude; if it weren't for the princess, she'd be bleeding by now and perhaps still imprisoned. For her part, Casica did not want to entertain this subject to the point of subjecting her friend to further shame. She was deeply grateful for Clarece's safe return and voiced this; otherwise, the entire episode was a mistake set into motion by a fool and she let it go as this. She was thankful God intervened. Clarece didn't know what to say to this except, "yes," so the evening was ended at last.

It was Casica's suggestion for Clarece to spend the day at rest, an order to which Clarece readily complied. After delivering Casica's lunch, Clarece retired to her stall. The quarters were empty, of course, and Clarece had just begun to doze when she heard a familiar gait. It was Asla, muttering curses and pounding the table as she passed. As her friend rounded into the stall, Clarece saw that she had been crying.

Asla's surprise at seeing Clarece was evident; what the devils was she doing here at this hour? Gods, could she not go anywhere to be alone? The morning had been particularly distasteful to her; she felt empty and invaded and now here was Clarece with that look in her eyes that said avoidance was impossible. Maybe she could postpone this encounter. She had had enough encounters for the morning and simply wished to rest.

"And how are you feeling this afternoon, Clarece?" Asla asked trying to sound detached and composed. "Better than you, I think.

I thank you for helping me last night, Asla, and for delivering the princess' breakfast this morning. Now, let's get to the point. What in heaven's name is wrong? You are venom and barbs these days." Asla retreated from the stall, afraid of the tears rising in her eyes, angry at her friend's insistence. Clarece rose from her bed and moved to confront her.

Asla glared threateningly. "Keep clear of me, Clarece. Tis none your cursed business what's wrong with me. There's enough wrong with you, so keep your nose out of my crack." The young woman's voice was ominous, with all pretense of civility departed. She turned to walk away.

"Enough of this, g'Helderleit!" spat Clarece. "Don't you *dare* walk away! I'm sick of you pushing me away!"

Asla spun to face the senior slave. "'Don't you dare?' Who in blazes are you to order me about?! You're not Edsner - you're a frappin slave, a pile of dung just like me!"

Their voices were rising and Clarece became acutely aware of the doorway above. She didn't want Casica to witness this. She walked towards the closet next to their stall. "Come with me, Asla." "I'm not going anywhere with you, slave," Asla growled, defiant and livid.

Clarece was fast losing her own temper. She opened the closet door and motioned Asla in. "Yes, you are! Get in here, you - ," she stopped short. Asla glared at the taller woman. She had an impulsive desire to grab Clarece by her hands and force her away. Instead she stalked into the closet and waited, daring Clarece to approach her.

Clarece shut the door behind her and sized up the situation. Asla was a good six years younger than she and easily seven stites less her height. Absently, Clarece wondered how tall Asla would grow into adulthood - if she survived to adulthood. Asla was smaller, but at this moment, she presented a daunting figure. Every muscle in her sculpted body was tense with rage, and her eyes, characteristically dancing with a light, alpine blue tint, had grown dark, simultaneously guarding their owner and piercing their enemy with a fierce glare. She looked all the world like a sparrow with fangs.

Clarece didn't know what to do with this stranger and considered, for a moment, retreating. She fought her rising instinct to hide her hands. Instead she presented them to Asla, taking a deep breath and speaking softly. "Asla, I'm sorry for speaking to you like that. I'm - afraid. You're my sala, and I will take your blows, gladly. But, for God's sake, let me know why I'm being struck. Speak with me; I beg you, please. Let me in and tell me what's wrong."

Tears welled in the younger woman's eyes and their presence served to further fuel her fear and anger. She would not allow this weakness. She could not. Her own hands were clinched and she looked beyond Clarece to the door, to escape. "There's nothing you can do for me, Clarece," she answered darkly. "Now let me go or so help me - I'll hurt you."

Clarece had never seen her friend like this. It was as if Asla were speaking from another place within herself, a place far before Clarece had met her. Clarece knew what it was like to be in such places. She knew her friend was not in her right mind, but she didn't know how to get her back. For a moment, she was genuinely afraid.

"I won't, Asla. I won't let you go. I don't know where you are, but I'm not leaving you. You want to go? You come through me. I'm not letting you step out there and destroy yourself."

Asla stood, tense with rage, tears streaming down her face. "I'm already destroyed, nothing can change that. You stand there like you own me or something while all you care about is yourself and your blast queen image! Well, I'm not part of your frappin guild for you to order about. You won't let me go? Well, I'll tell you where *you* can go, slave, and what you can do...." A deadly force conjured within her even as another voice deep inside cried, *No, Asla! No!* But hate, hate that had little to do with this moment, ripped out of her desperate fear and into the form barring her escape.

"Here's what you can do, freak," a voice spoke that was not Asla. "You can *go... to... hell.* I consign your soul to hell!" The words filled the closet and crashed upon the woman at the door.

Clarece gasped as though Asla had plunged a knife into her chest. *Oh, God! my God!* she screamed inside. A deep sense of doom overwhelmed her. *Damned, the insulit had damned her.*

Clarece stood there, gaping at her friend, her mittens to her heart, her eyes filled with terror and betrayal. In her shock she could manage but a single word, *"Asla..."* Asla blinked. She stared into Clarece's horror-filled eyes. Slowly, the impact of what she had done flooded over her. The room was spinning. Asla took two uncertain steps, whispering in horror, "Oh, gods. Oh, gods, Clarece, I didn't mean it."

She fell to her knees, sobbing, "I recant! Gods! I recant, I recant...." The truth silenced her words. She couldn't recant. Insulit could curse, they were bred of hell, but to undo a curse required a soul - something she did not have. No wonder she did not have a soul, being filled with such evil as this. The broken woman sobbed uncontrollably. What had she done - what had she made of Clarece? "Have mercy, Clarece," she plead. "I'm sorry, I'm so sorry... I beg you, have mercy on me."

Clarece stood frozen at the door. Her mind reeled, trying to comprehend what had just been done to her. To be damned by an insulit. What would be the repercussions of that? Who could rescue her soul now?

Asla's sobs broke Clarece's musings. She looked upon the shattered heap that was her friend. Clarece abandoned herself. She went to her knees before Asla and gathered her destroyer into her arms. Asla balked at Clarece's gesture. Surely no one could love her now.

"Clarece, please, please forgive me. Have mercy on me, Rece...." Clarece held the broken woman tighter, feeling her body tremble with sorrow. "Shhh... shhh. Tis well, sala. You're alright. I forgive you...." Asla couldn't understand. How could she do this? How could Clarece comfort the one who had just resigned her to eternity in hell? Clarece should beat her, curse her, something - anything but offer this kindness. Part of the girl wanted to run for her life, to flee this mercy. But a greater part stayed. She had been so alone. She was exhausted with herself, and to whom could she turn if not Clarece? If Asla could not be souled, herself, she desperately longed to be joined with one.

So she rested in her sala's embrace. It was a long time before she regained herself. Finally, Asla lifted her head to face the one she had destroyed. The women met each other's eyes and Asla whispered, "I can't undo it, Rece. I can't change what I've done." Clarece smiled wanly. "Tis well. I... I'm quite certain I was headed that general direction anyway."

Of course, what had happened wasn't alright. Clarece knew it; Asla knew it. But there was nothing to be done about it. Asla's eyes had returned to their powder blue. Clarece's mitten wiped a tear from them. She waited for some of the destruction to settle before asking quietly, "Now, will you please share what is tormenting you?"

Asla studied the strange lighting in the closet. She had never fully understood how reflected light from windows upstairs was channeled into the basement. Her energy level matched the dimness. She was so very tired.

"I'm in gods' trouble," she began. "I don't know where to turn. No one can help me now." Clarece's growing suspicion seemed confirmed. Dear God. "Asla, are you with child?" Asla closed her eyes and shook her head. "No, not yet. But I will be. Edsner told me he's laying me out beginning next month. Completely laying me out, Rece. No more keeping me in during my fertile time. He's made a huge gambling debt and I'm going to pay it...."

"But, Asla, if you conceive," Clarece parried, "you're useless to him. Your kind of service won't lay a bred woman." "That's what I said. Edsner told me that if I do conceive that will only help him. As far as he knows, I'm the only insulit in the region. He can get a great deal of gold for an insulit baby bred through me - enough to make up for the rent he'll lose during my carry." She glanced down at her waist. Breeding among insulit was unheard of in her country. Insulit were rare and there was a reason for this. The few insulit she'd met had come like her, through violation. She never conceived of this – scads! she shouldn't even think that word.

"Clarece," she said, looking into her friend's troubled face, "I've been beside myself. I don't know what to do. But I can't do this, I can't birth anyone into my world. You don't know what is done to an infant to seal them as insulit." Her mind flashed to scenes of that ritual. Cringing, she pushed them away. "You don't know, but I do. And even then, how I live - tis no way to live. And to die an insulit is worse than hell, to do what I do here but with devils...." Her eyes filled with despair.

"I may have no soul, but even souless, I have a - ," blast, she didn't know what she had. "I can't do this - I *won't* do this, Clarece. I... I've thought of taking my life but I haven't the courage. So I've decided to try another escape."

Clarece was stunned; never could she have guessed this dilemma and now that she knew, she hadn't a clue what to do. But running away? That was insane.

"You mean run away? How? To where, Asla? They'll find you. They'll impale you. You can't do this." "I got to try, Rece. If I can make it to g'Helderlend, there's a convent that will grant me sanctuary. I know I'll likely be caught. But at least I'll die trying, and I would rather die than to bring another of me into this world."

Clarece pondered her friend thinking, *"I would have the whole world be filled with you."* But she knew what Asla meant. Having been given the choice, she never had bred and for the same reason: to birth a child into slavery was unthinkable. But still, Asla's plan couldn't succeed.

"Look at you, Asla. Even without a collar, you can't exactly blend in with the general Byzanthian population. Your features are striking. Why, it would be like - Casica trying - ." And then a most remarkable idea came to her. *Casica.* Clarece remembered back to that morning, the morning of her hands. "'I am no physician.'" A physician couldn't help but a healer? "Casica...."

"What?" "Casica. Asla, she's a healer. I bet she's helped women conceive and if she can do that, well, maybe she can do the opposite. 'Keep a woman *from* conceiving." "But that's impossible, Rece. How could she do that?" "I don't know. But I don't know how she does anything she does. I could ask her though. It wouldn't hurt to try. What do you think?"

Asla was exhausted of thinking, but the prospect of submitting herself to the strange Cassican for such an intimate matter – scads! On the other hand, she regularly submitted to people much stranger and for no benefit of her own. The princess was not dangerous. And it was clear she cared for anything concerning Clarece. Curse the gods. She was desperate and spent. Anything was worth a try. She nodded tiredly.

"Alright, then," Clarece replied. "I'll ask Mistra tonight during her supper, generally speaking - I won't mention your name. I'll let you know what she says at bedtime. Are you going to be here tonight?" "Yes." "Good.... Asla," Clarece asked, wondering, "you've carried this so long. Why wouldn't you tell me?" "Tell you that I'm going to run away and have you executed as an accomplice? I don't know, Clarece. I feel separate from you in my slavery. I just didn't know what to do." Clarece nodded in under-standing. "Well, we'll see what happens."

The two stood. It had been a long afternoon. The clock already had chimed four. It was nearing dinner but there was still some time to rest, though Clarece doubted she would sleep. Asla would, though, she knew. She would leave this closet and this incident and sleep like the dead.

Clarece looked at her friend. "I love you, As," she smiled, not waiting for a reply, *but if I never share an afternoon like this again with you, it will be too soon.* "Let's get some rest before supper," and with this Clarece reached for the door lever.

It didn't give. She tried again. Nothing. The women looked quizzically at each other and then peered into the keyhole: yes, there was the key, locked on the other side. Asla looked at her se-nior with an expression that said, "Nice going, chief slaveswom-an." They broke into laughter - goodness, what a relief to laugh!

Asla searched the closet for a wire, found one suitable for the task and began picking the lock. "Will you *never* tell me how you learned to do that?" "Trust me, Clarece, like I've told you, you *really* don't want to know." Asla shook her head playfully and laughed, despite her doubts. It was so good not to be alone.

Casica had rested well that afternoon but, obviously, Clarece had not. She looked fatigued as she cleared the table of his mistra's dinner. "Clarece are you not feeling well or just tired?" "Tired, my lady, and troubled. Princess, may I speak with you?" "Of course you may," Casica replied pulling out a chair.

"Thank you, my lady. Mistra, I have a question to ask you. As a healer, can you prevent a woman's body from conceiving?" That's the last thing Casica expected to hear. "I mean, well, one of my women is being bred but does not wish to bear. She is desper-ate in this. I thought that a woman as yourself, a josquin, perhaps you could treat this slave so that she can't conceive - ever. Is this possible?"

Casica sat wondering to herself, *How does Clarece do this, jug-gle all these problems? And how on earth am I to respond?* She opted for honesty. "Yes, Clarece, it's possible. I can prevent a woman's conceiving. I have done so for a woman whose life would have been endangered with childbirth. But that's a rare situation. Such a treatment is no light thing. I can't say that I would do it for any situation not involving endangerment of life." *So she can do this,* thought Clarece. Now the question was: would she?

"I understand, my lady. This woman, I think, her life *is* in danger, but that is something about which she should speak with you. I wonder, Princess, may I invite her to meet with you tomorrow, say, after lunch?" Casica began guessing who this woman may be. If she's one of Clarece's people, she must part of the guild. *No,* she bereted herself, *stop this speculation.* The woman may decide not to seek her help at all. "Yes. Tell her to come here after lunch tomorrow. I'll talk with her." Clarece bowed her head. "Thank you, mistra. I will tell her." Clarece remained burdened; Casica wondered if there were more.

"By the way, Clarece, did you ever get those boots?" "Boots? Oh, Donnel's boots. No, my lady. The leather smith wants more than we currently have in our guild's budget. Our treasury has suffered setbacks recently. Raina has had a string of bad luck. First, she broke her mistra's crystal vase, which we replaced to save her flesh. Then her cloak was stolen from the laundry room. Another expenditure. She's young and still learning her way but she'll grow into her collar. Now we're holding our breaths for number three."

"Number three?" "Yes, my lady. A slave's luck - good or bad - always runs in three's." "Hmm," Casica nodded with understanding. "The trials of running a kingdom. How much money are we talking about here?" "Half a pound, my lady." Another nod. "What would you think about my donating to your people's fund?" "Thank you, mistra, but that would be highly inappropriate."

"Of course." Josquin caressed her shalonn. "You know, Clarece, it has been my observation that while kings kill each other, queens tend to stick together, being as we are the ones who pick up the pieces after the fighting. What say you, your highness, of one queen loaning funds to another - as a royal courtesy?"

Clarece smiled broadly, something Casica had never witnessed. "And what might your queen's terms be?" "Let's see. Repayment - with interest as determined by your kingdom's economy. Repayment, by the conclusion of... the summer games. After your savvy subjects gamble your treasury back into health."

Clarece laughed good-naturedly. This was fun. Donnel's need would be met. "Upon consideration of your terms, your highness, we accept your offer. And on behalf of my people, we thank you. We shall not forget this kindness."

Casica nodded as the queens sealed their contract with a hand-shake. "Now, Clarece, where does the good prince Bastien hide his gold?"

# XVI

Asla sat on her cot waiting for her courage to arrive as it usually did: at the last minute. She was used to this feeling of dread. Anytime she went to service a new man, she struggled with resolve to knock on the unfamiliar door and enter whatever waited on the other side. Even in the castle she felt insecure; Edsner may rent her to someone known, only for her to discover the name had been a front. A stranger waited for her, creating an entirely unpredictable situation, one that often proved painful. Men would do to an insulit what they would never dare upon a lover, living out the darkest of fantasies. Even after all her years of facing uncertainty, Asla could not shed it, the sense that someday she would enter a room and whatever waited there would enter her and never let her out. In all her world, the only place Asla felt safe was in dreamless sleep.

Clarece had delivered Casica's lunch a half hour earlier. Surely, the princess must have finished her meal by now. Asla stepped onto the floor and looked at the stairway. What awaited her this time?

Casica relaxed with her feet in a chair, her eyes surveying the garden below. In was sunny and the shadows on the lawn chased each other with the swaying trees. *I should start painting again,* she thought. *That poplar would make a* - an approaching presence interrupted her thoughts. Asla. She was coming up the stairs. Now Casica saw her, reflected in the window. Casica watched as the blond woman stood at the doorway, looking first at the woman in the chair, then at her feet, waiting for what, Casica did not know. The reflection spoke.

"You know I'm standing here, don't you?" "Yes, Asla. I see your reflection in the window." Josquin turned and smiled reassuredly at the nervous woman. "But you didn't need a reflection to know I was here, did you?"

"No," Casica admitted. "You bear a strong sense of presence. Please, come in." The insulit walked to the chair offered her and looked about. Casica's room was bright and warm. The windows Bastien had installed filled the chamber with outdoor life. Huge trees stood level with her eyes. It was almost like being in a tree house, thought Asla. Not that she had ever been in one, but surely it would be something like this. Asla turned her focus to the woman beside her. Casica's eyes were kind and attentive. The younger woman struggled with how to begin this awkward situation. Men were so much easier to read.

"I'm the woman Clarece told you about last night, Princess. She said that," her eyes turned to the table, "Clarece said you may not choose to help me." "I told her it all depends on the situation; if life is at stake." Asla nodded. *I wonder if my life ever really matters,* she thought, but she continued with her case. "Edsner is going to lay me out to cover a gambling debt, my lady. He wants me to conceive so that he can sell my offspring as an insulit." She looked directly at the healer. "My life *is* at stake, Casica. I refuse to birth an innocent into my world. If you can't help me...," the insulit stopped short of sharing her plans. If she did, the princess might feel compelled to report her.

Casica studied the woman before her. Tears welled in her eyes as she considered Asla's plight. "Asla, how old are you?" "I have lived 14 years," came the quiet answer. Casica thought how the eyes meeting hers were those of a much older woman. At this time those exquisite eyes were filled with anxious resolve. They were pleading, *Will you help me?*

Fourteen years. Casica remembered herself at that age; she had only a couple years before given off playing with dolls. This young woman had lived her entire life as a doll, an object for play and pleasure in games that Casica would not even try to imagine. For a moment, she wondered what would happen if Edsner learned of this, but there was no debating Asla's situation.

"I will help you, Asla." Asla closed her eyes against the tears filling them. "Thank you, my lady," she whispered relieved, "thank you."

Casica sighed deeply. "All right then. When would you like this done?" "As soon as possible." "Well. When was your last flow?" "Two weeks." The timing was right. "Would you have time now?"

Asla blinked. She never imagined it would happen so quickly. "Yes, my lady. I have nowhere to be until tonight." "Good. But before we begin, I want you to understand what I'm going to do to you."

Casica explained the procedure. She described a woman's body and how it conceived. This information was foreign to Asla, as was Casica's experience with most women. The girl sat in wonder at what she heard. Either Casica had an extraordinary imagination or a woman's body must be most fascinating thing in the world. She had no idea her body was so complex.

"So you're going to block the paths leading to where my fertility lies?" Asla summarized. "Generally speaking, yes." "Will I look or feel different to men?" "No. No one can tell I've done this - except another josquin. And she or I can undo this, should you decide someday you want to have a baby."

"That'll be the day," Asla observed scornfully. "Life can have surprises - even for you...," Casica suggested. "When horses dance, my lady. No, it can't - at least not the good kind like that would be." Casica did not argue. Who was she to question this woman? Their lesson completed, the women moved to Casica's bed. Asla asked if she should undress, her usual assumption in such a situation. With a different woman, Casica might have said 'yes', facilitating, as it did, the examination. With Asla, however, she considered differently; she was keenly aware of Asla's sense of vulnerability and wished to provide her a measure of control.

"That's not necessary, Asla. Just remove your stockings and vest before you lay down." As Asla complied, Casica closed the sliding door and secured the rest of the room. She left the curtains open, thinking her patient would prefer the openness the windows provided. Casica washed her hands and sat on the bed near the nervous woman. "How do you feel?" she asked quietly.

Asla looked about uncertainly. "I'm not sure." "I'm not surprised...but you have nothing to fear. I won't harm you in any way. I *would* like to examine you first - if that's agreeable with you." *"If I agree?"* Asla wondered, confused. She had never been asked permission about anything concerning her body. She didn't know what to do. So she stretched out on the bed and nodded.

The princess reached out to touch Asla's head then hesitated. Something was very strange here. She continued the motion, this time smiling to herself. "Is something wrong?" asked her patient. "Not at all. Tis something delightful actually. Usually, I have to win a body's trust, kind of move through it to apply healing. Your body just reaches out and takes it. See?" She took her hand and held it near Asla's arm. "'You feel that?" Asla nodded. "Usually, I would have to touch your arm for you to sense that. You, God's Beauty, are a josquin's dream patient," she smiled. Asla smiled back, relieved. Only Casica could call her "God's Beauty" without her feeling mocked. Perhaps this side of the door was safe for once.

With Casica's first touch upon her, Asla's fear melted away. The healer's gentle hands were filled with a warm kindness that seemed to flow from her into Asla's mind. Asla watched as Casica studied her face, stopping upon her own eyes. The two smiled with the contact. "Look up for me, Asla. Alright...perfect eyes," Josquin declared wondering what colors she would mix to gain that ethereal tint. A pause at the throat and then a move to the chest.

Casica placed one hand upon Asla's heart and the other underneath. Asla's breath quickened at the touch, feeling a powerful energy flowing between the hands. *Amazing*, Casica thought. "You feel that? You've the strongest pulse I've ever met." "Gymnastics...." "Yes. But it takes more than physical conditioning for a force like this." Casica left the chest to feel thin arms, soft hands.

As she touched Asla's left hand, something swept over the princess. To a josquin, touch is as smell, opening doors to vivid memory. The touch of Asla's hand was overwhelmingly familiar. *Why?* she wondered and suddenly, Casica saw: that day. The woman who offered her water... it was Asla! Why had she never told her? Casica massaged the hand before her, addressing it silently: *thank you.* "You have very strong hands," she offered aloud to Asla's questioning look.

Josquin left Asla's arms to let her hands rest on the woman's midsection. *Soft but firm, firm but soft.* Here she could sense the true state of a person's heart. Asla, despite her appearance of calm, was a very frightened woman. She stored her anxiety here, in this part of her body. Casica wondered if she ever truly knew peace. What must it be like to live as Asla did, prey to every sort of sensual hunger? Legs, ankles - "How did you hurt your ankle?"

"You can feel that?" Asla replied. "A wicked landing from the beam." "You might use a brace. Your right ankle isn't nearly as strong as your left. It's trying too hard." Casica let her hand rest there, feeling the muscles relax and heal under her touch.

Asla could feel this too and wondered at what was being done. This entire experience was not as she imagined. Here she was, lying on this Cassican's bed, being touched in a way she'd never experienced, and all the while she felt completely safe. Safe and something else... known. That's what she was feeling. The princess was knowing her, accepting her in a manner no one had ever done.

Asla had been "examined" a thousand times in her fourteen years. But those experiences all involved her being consumed; in this, she was being filled. Everywhere the princess' hands touched, they left in their wake a deep sense of nourishment and - light. That was the only image Asla could conjure. It was as if Casica were infusing her with light somehow. It reached far beyond muscle to touch the very fabric of her person. Asla wondered if what she was feeling was what Casica called "blessed."

Casica arrived at two small feet. *Even your feet are beautiful,* except for one thing: the left had a brutal scar, as though something had impaled it. Her exam ended, Josquin announced, "You are in perfect health, Asla of g'Helderlend. I can only hope such a constitution for all Byzanthians. Now, are you ready for me to treat you?"

Her patient nodded, feeling wonderfully relaxed. "I'm going to put you to sleep so you won't feel anything." Asla glanced up to say something, but her eyes closed upon themselves as her body slipped into a deep, deep sleep.

"That is just too easy," Casica observed. She loosened Asla's belt and placed her hand low below the girl's waist, locating the correct organs in her body. There they were. Casica closed her eyes and concentrated, directing a particular energy to this particular task.

The pobble stones of her shalonn glowed in response, flooding her with a collage of memories. The body stores experiences - remembers as it were - just like the mind, and any trained josquin could extract the memories attached anywhere on a body. Casica could have known without asking what had happened to Asla's ankle. But harvesting memories was a sacred practice (best left to the "Seekers" of her kind) and she avoided it. Asla's memories were her own. But the healer had sensed enough. This young woman had been brutally used. No wonder healing was so effortless. Asla had long been stripped of the most holy boundaries given to soul and body.

"I wonder how you even know your name," Casica whispered. "May God, Himself, heal you, in these places I cannot touch." But there was something she could do. Her first task completed, Josquin moved to another....

Asla began waking within the hour. "Well, hello!" It was the voice of the princess calling her back to consciousness. Asla opened her eyes to the afternoon light, her senses stirred by the aroma of tea. She found Casica, sitting near her on the bed. "Welcome back," the princess smiled, "You're just in time for tea." Asla breathed deeply. She sat up. With the movement, the sleepiness embracing her fell away and the young woman immediately regained herself. She took silent inventory of her surroundings. Something was changed.

"How do you feel?" the princess inquired. How *did* she feel? "I feel... different." Now she could she could put words to it. "Quiet inside. I feel...," *clean. Peacefully clean,* she thought. It was as if something had washed her inside; her body felt...fresh. Asla looked to Casica whose eyes glowed with some secret joy.

"The treatment went well. You won't notice any changes in your time, but I can assure you, Asla, you won't conceive. Come, let's have some tea." The thought of food redirected Asla's attention. She was famished. "But this is Clarece's time, isn't it?" Casica grinned. "I'm sure she won't mind. Here. Let me serve you."

Asla went to the table, relishing the new feeling within her. She sat, somewhat bewildered as the princess poured tea into their cups. This was very unnatural, being the served. The strangeness seemed utterly lost on the princess as she offered milk and a large roll to her guest. Asla emptied her tea, emptied the milk and ate her roll - and Casica's - with abandonment. Satisfied, the young woman relaxed in her chair, drawing up her knees and wrapping her arms around them. The ticking clock lulled her as she viewed the garden below. *Scads, I feel so well,* she thought, so safe. 'Cozy' was the word she sought.

"What are you thinking?" The princess' voice was satisfied too, pleased with her afternoon's work. "I am thinking I wish I could spend the rest of my life in this moment...." *I wish this for you, also,* the healer thought. *I wish I could guard your precious life, nurture it and help it thrive.* "Where will your life take you this evening?"

Asla shook her head, still peering into the garden. There was a slight opening in the window to her left and through it a waft carried the scent of moist earth. How she longed to join that scent and dwell with it outside. "It will take me to Baron Caddish. I deliver him supper tonight and will remain as his dessert. He eats quickly; I won't be there long. Afterwards, I go to - ." She stopped. "I shouldn't tell you these things, Casica. You'll know all these men eventually. I don't care a whiff for them, but you'll know their wives, too. And what I do with their husbands isn't their fault. Let's just say I'll be busy this evening."

An object in the distance caught Asla's eye. A hawk. How she loved hawks. Oh, to know the freedom of flight. "Why are you smiling?" asked Casica. "A hawk, my lady. See? How I wish to become her and flee my world."

Casica glanced at the hawk outside and the would-be one before her. The young woman's eyes glistened in the late afternoon light. *What is like to be Asla?* she wondered. To ask would either harm her further or to open a cell door. The healer followed her heart. "Asla, what is your world like?"

The insulit jerked and stared incredibly at the princess. "What?" she asked. *Oh, God, what have I done?* thought Josquin. "Your life, I mean. What is like to be you?" Tears crept from the insulit's eyes, large warm tears; she openly wept. "No one, not even Clarece, has ever asked me that. No one wants to know that." Asla gazed beyond the hawk into her mind. Her g'Helderleitch flowed like a brook.

"What is like to be me? I feel so alone, you know? I'm always alone, even though I'm with so many people." She looked back into the garden. "No one understands, only an insulit could, I guess. People here, the slaves? - they think I have it good just because my body is unscarred. Just because I'm unbeaten. Because I sleep with the richest people in the kingdom. They're so wrong. In a heartbeat, I'd trade places with any slave I know. I wish I could go below tonight and eat that disgusting porridge and laugh and talk and vex with them and wake up tomorrow and begin it all over again." She stroked the table.

"Compared to theirs, my life is boring and empty. People look at me and I know what they're thinking: here's this insulit; she must have this erotic life, must be this incredible lover. Gods, if they only knew. You want to know the truth, Casica? I've never been a lover." Asla's eyes went to the table. "To be a lover, you have to connect – soulfully – to your beloved. I don't have a soul to connect with. A lover is a person. I'm nothing more than a depository." Her laugh was bitter. "Sometimes, though, sometimes I wonder if I was born souless or if it just got used up along the way."

Asla stared into her hands. Her right thumb rubbed into her left palm. "Oh, I'm good at what I do. That's sure. You know what makes a skillful insulit?" The princess shook her head. "Two things: intuition and acting. I can size up a man's game in a moment. That's all it ever is if anything; just a game. So I see they what they want and I give it to them. I'm a great actor, Princess. I leave my audience thinking they're the kings of the world, kings of me. But they're not." Her eyes grew hard. "No one rules me. They're such fools they never even notice I've left the stage long ago. I leave them to play the scenes by themselves."

Asla looked back into the garden and spoke her deepest heart. "Sometimes I'm afraid I'll look into a mirror one day only to see there's no reflection at all," she whispered. "Sometimes I really wonder if I exist at all. I become invisible even to myself. I wonder where I go – and who takes my place. I wonder what it would take to keep me where I am, like I feel now. I want to stay here but I know I can't; already I'm slipping away. I am so rarely at home with myself. Except on the gym floor or dancing." She was smiling now. "That's when I soar." She closed her eyes with delight. "That's when I'm really here...." The clock ticked soothingly, a lullaby in this strange dream.

She turned to her listener. Silent tears traced Casica's face. "Oh, don't cry! It's not all bad. There is a single saving grace to my life," her smile was sad but genuine. "Do you know insulit have shorter lives than even laborer slaves? We do. It always happens the same: your owner begins renting you as an insulit but then he wants more money. So he stops selecting his services until eventually you become nothing more than a whore. After that, it's all over. If disease doesn't kill you, then some man who loves violence will. I won't live long. This is my comfort and hope. Of course, the afterlife is a different matter...." Asla's smile dissolved. Best leave that subject alone.

"You've never been with a man, have you?" Casica shook her head. "In a way neither have I, even though," Asla leaned back in her chair and stretched voluptuously, "there is one man - gods, he's spectacular." "Who is this?" Casica asked surprised at her changed tone. Asla smiled knowingly.

"Prince Tartan of Hathen. You know, Hathens are related to g'Helderleits. Tartan, this man - ." Casica laughed at Asla's expression. "I know Tartan does not love me, and I cannot him, but I feel safe with him. That feels something of love." Asla sighed deeply. "I also like that he's unmarried so I feel no guilt.

"Plus," she grinned at the princess, "he's a generous service. And he never hands me my dash. He always hides it in my vest for me to find, so when I leave him, I don't feel so much the whore I am. Tartan's is the only dash I keep for myself - the rest go to Clarece's guild. This year I'm going to use his dash to purchase a special gift for her birthday. I found a dealer in the city with a beautiful collection of poetry. I'm going to buy Rece a book," she concluded. "She'll be so pleased...."

The princess' mind grappled with images from Asla's words. She felt saddened yet intrigued. *God, Cass,* she thought, *you are such the maiden.* And Asla's description of Tartan seemed to hold a lesson. "Your prince is kind and thoughtful. It sounds like that's what makes him such a fine...companion," she offered. "You may be right," Asla replied. She saw Casica's wonderings and couldn't resist stirring the pot.

154 Martha J. Vaught

"*Your* prince will be a wonderful - companion," she declared. "He cares for you, you know. A good man is a good student. Every woman is a unique landscape. I don't know from personal experience, mind you, but I would think Bastien a worthy artist for your canvas." Casica turned red in her dark complexion. Asla laughed at her embarrassment.

The clock was chiming five. Outside, the garden blended into the evening. Asla turned to Josquin, her face relaxed and happy. "Thank you, Casica. Thank you so much for this. Clarece is - blessed, as you say, to have you as her mistra. To be in your presence is... peace." At this Asla lowered her eyes. "I must go. The baron will be waiting." She stood to leave and Casica rose with her.

"Come, Asla," she invited, taking the young woman into her arms. Gently, Casica placed her hand on the head of the hauntingly lovely woman. Warmth flooded Asla's being. "Blessings upon you, Asla. You are truly the Beauty of God." The insulit looked into her healer's eyes. Emotion rendered her unable to reply, except to return Casica's blessing with a grateful smile.

Bowing her head, Asla spun gracefully on her heel as a slave does. She opened the sliding door to reenter her familiar world. But to herself, she was not so familiar. The woman who now descended the stairs was not the same as she who had climbed them. For this time, Asla left the world above a truer version of herself.

## XVII

Casica ambled along the gazebo trail to the livery, anxious to see about Clarece's silverware; it might be ready. Upon Silian's suggestion, the princess had taken a silver spoon, knife and fork to Apsterdan d'Caleb two weeks earlier. Apparently, this slave not only served as blacksmith but also was regarded among the palace as a fine silversmith. Had he been free or at least a servant, the man would certainly be gainfully employed in this area of gifting. As it was, his collar relegated him to a smith's billows; even so not a few noblemen and women acquiesced to his class in their desire for fine works of jewelry. Usually this was done through the mediation of Silian.

The princess, having learned that Apsterdan had connections to the east wing, wished to speak with the smith personally. He was well-acquainted with Clarece's spoon design, the slave said, and thought he could make improvements upon it. He was surprised, for sure, at finding real silver being spent upon a slave; still, he, as did everyone else in the wing, knew of Casica's teas with the senior slave. Any royal queer enough to have a slave to tea, well, why not serve with silver? The utensils would be completed within a month, he assured the princess. He would take special care in the workmanship. The guild's leader had assisted him on several occasions; it pleased the burly artist to return the favor.

The morning was cool with the ocean bringing tidings of fog. Still everything seemed crisp and fresh to the Cassican. How she longed to walk in the damp of her homeland, she thought, a wave of homesickness washing upon her heart. She missed her family; missed the sense of secure belonging. As she walked alone, Casica wondered if she would ever be accepted in this place.

"Hail, Mighty Cassican!" a voice called in g'Helderleicht. "Prowling for fresh Byzanthian prey this fine morning, are we?" Casica smiled at a blond form wrapped in red. "Not today, mighty g'Helderleit," she responded in the woman's native tongue. "I've my fill of fighting foe. And what of you? Why are out this dazzling morning?" she asked, approaching the woman in the gazebo. "Preparing myself to become prey. I've a meeting with a hunter in the city. Where is your escort? I'm not used to seeing you alone."

"The chief slaveswoman is cleaning my chamber. I felt it best to get from under foot," *especially considering Clarece's peculiar attitude of late,* Casica ended in thought. She sat beside Asla. The insulit played with her dagger. She was poking holes in the bench. "Nice weapon," the princess noted, "may I see it?" The g'Helderleit offered her knife, noticing how easily the Cassican handled it. "It has a fine weight," Casica observed and, with flick of her wrist, implanted the dagger into the far side of the gazebo. "Very fine balance. Where did you get it?"

Asla still watched the throw in her mind, wondering who had taught the princess to handle blades so deftly. "It was given me when I was four - by an insulit who looked to be ancient." She smiled in memory. Probably the woman was only her age now. "Twas a welcoming gift for my trade," the insulit explained. "Proves useful at times."

Casica looked intently upon the smiling insulit. Her smile fronted deep, deep fear. "Must you defend yourself often?" she asked. The familiar movement of thumb into palm accompanied Asla's answer. "Not so often as you may think. Attack comes in waves, it seems: if I must fight for life once, I must several times; then I'll enjoy a season of safety." *What a hellish existence,* thought Casica, sadly. The young woman's eyes were misty; she looked very tired. "Have you any fights recently?"

Asla faced the dark woman cautiously, feeling her way in the moment. If felt safe. "One very recently. I dealt a death blow." The princess winced. "The worst of it," the insulit continued, "it was to my dearest friend. Clarece and I had a terrible row about what I came to see you for? Gods, I was so angry. I did the worst thing I can do to the souled." Asla looked out at the gloomy day. "I damned her to hell. I damned the best person I know to hell," she said quietly. Tears crept down the sculpted face. "I've put her into the pit and I can't undo it - ." "What do you mean?" Casica asked softly. She was unfamiliar with this teaching. "An insult can damn but not recant. We aren't able to come into the holy to remove our curse."

"I see," the princess replied, but she didn't. This entire concept of souless ones eluded her, so wicked was it. "What if the holy comes into you?" she suggested. "Could you then recant?"

The insulit snorted. "The holy come into me quite frequently, Princess. I see no help in it." Casica lowered her head with a sigh. Did nothing reflect sacredness to this woman? "Surely, you do not think clergy who would use you are holy?" she questioned.

"I do not know what to think," Asla answered flatly. "Tis a practice I avoid. I only know that I've no use for anyone's god; but if I could, I would beg any one of them to release Rece from what I've done. She's in misery. She's forgiven me; tis her nature to forgive, but I know. I see the torment in her eyes. Has she not mentioned this to you?" Casica shook her head. "That's her way," Asla concluded. "She'll carry this inside until it eats her alive."

The insulit turned again to her friend's owner. "Please don't mention this, Princess, but if Rece does, will you talk to her?" "Of course, Asla. I'll tell her your concern." "My concern does her no good. Nothing I do is good. It is a gift to this earth I live so shortly," she confessed, turning away. God's Beauty covered her face. "I am so evil," she whispered, "so very evil. The demons will feed well upon me."

Casica placed her arm around the broken woman and pulled her close. "You are not evil, Asla," she said. "The evil do not give green socks to little slave girls. Your deeds betray this lie that you are incapable of good." Asla smiled despite herself. 'Exactly what Clarece had said.

"You don't understand, Casica. When I do good," she explained, "it's to get something. Nothing more. I give socks to feel good, to gain a sense of being human for a moment. I feed the illusion that I've something to offer, but the truth is, I'm a user; a whore through and through."

Casica took a deep breath. "The truth is, we all could say that. One reason I miss healing so much is because of the pleasure it gives me. I need to feel needed. That doesn't make me a whore." Casica looked at the thinning fog. A memory met her. She turned to the insulit and asked, "I'm curious: when you gave water to a tortured stranger from an enemy land, what did you think to gain?" Asla looked up, stunned. "How could you possibly know that?" she asked incredulous.

Casica smiled and reached for her left hand. "You told me," she began. "I will never forget your kindness to me." Casica looked up at the memory. "I was dying and I knew it. My body was broken and torn. I'd never known agony. I felt so completely abandoned - by God, my family - everyone...." The woman closed her eyes, remembering. "And then in the midst of all this darkness, some-one touches me. And then I feel them free me of my gag that I may breathe. And they bring water to my lips to quench my thirst and place water on my face to ease my pain. I didn't know who did this for me; I only knew I wasn't alone."

Casica turned and looked at the insulit. "Your kindness gave me courage to go on, Asla. To get up off my knees and to live for as long as I was deemed. Truly, you were the hand of God for me that day."

Asla stared unbelievingly but not in disbelief of Casica's knowl-edge. Rather, in disbelief that she, a souless one, worked such a thing of goodness; in disbelief that Casica could actually link her with God - and not in name only. Casica smiled at the silenced woman, her own eyes were moist with gratitude.

"I've never thanked you for saving me. I do so now. May God repay you for your goodness, Asla." The young woman did not know how to respond. She sat confused, flooded with feelings she could not recognize. Her instinct told her to run, run from this! - whatever it was. But her heart, her heart rested as it did that day in Casica's chamber. Something very alive moved within her.

"You've hurt your wrist, I see," Casica observed breaking the silence. The insulit smiled, relieved with the change in subject. "A wicked fall. I'm trying for a triple twist. 'Tis very difficult - 'tis impossible, really. But it's my goal to do one before I die. I can complete a double - even a double and a quarter - but..." she shook her head. "I'm running out of time."

How easily Asla spoke of impending death thought the healer. Not dramatically; not anxiously. Simply. Like someone commenting on their height. In response, Casica took the injured wrist and poured healing into it. It was too easy.

"I swear, Asla. I think I could heal you with thought alone," she observed aloud. "Are you calling me easy?" the insulit quipped. Casica smiled and shook her head. "I'm saying you're receptive." Asla watched her, intently, suspiciously.

"Why are you so kind to me?" she asked finally. "Tis because I'm Clarece's friend, isn't it?" The josquin looked up, finished. "Well, no, Asla. It's because you're *my* friend." Asla looked searchingly into the dark eyes; she could target falsehood like a hawk a field mouse. There was none. "I don't think your mother would approve of the friends you're making here, Princess."

Casica laughed. "On the contrary. My mother would adore you," she smiled, thinking about a particular former prostitute who possessed an unnatural affinity for wine. "Maman loves whores. So do I."

The insulit considered the enigma before her. Casica spoke "whore" so easily, so shamelessly. Yet she was a maiden. Nothing of this woman made sense. "You Cassicans are a strange lot," she concluded aloud. Casica nodded to herself. "That seems to be the prevailing opinion...."

The insulit looked at the grounds. It seemed the sun would win its battle with the morning fog, after all. "I need to go," she said, rising. "The games begin." She rose and then turned to the sitting healer. "Thank you, Princess. Thank you for being Cassican," she grinned. Casica's smile embraced her warmly.

"God's blessings upon you, Asla of g'Helderlend," she wished. "When horses dance, my lady," was the reply. "Then watch yourself." The insulit popped her dagger from its wooden scabbard and slid it into her belt. "I always do. Good-bye."

It was time for the hunt. With a bow and spin, the woman left her cover and stepped into the openness of life, keenly aware, as she did, of the shrill cry of a hawk above her.

# XVIII

Clarece walked slowly along the courtyard. A deep, green canopy of holly helped shield her from the pouring sky. It was cold. Yet even in the cold, the green scent of life filled her senses. Moisture had that dramatic affect upon living things, bringing, as it did, the earth and all that grew within it to the surface. How the slave wished for something to do the same for her, to somehow induce hope into her brittle, parched heart. Her trip to the slave chapel did nothing to alleviate her distress. It seemed no amount of confession could cleanse her of the deep sense of doom that plagued her since her fight with Asla.

Asla's curse clung to the woman, spreading like the mold that had grown for years in the northwest corner of the pen. For a season, Clarece worked to rid the slaves' quarters of the greenish growth but nothing she did prevailed. It seemed the brick, itself, spawned the spores that grew so tenaciously in the damp environment of the stall. She determined, finally, that the only cure for the condition would be to remove the bricks themselves. This she could not do, so the mold remained.

To the troubled slave, her own soul was similarly diseased. It was not so much that her friend had sown something within her as it was that Asla's curse had provided for it a favorable atmosphere in which to thrive. As with the mold, it seemed to Clarece the only remedy would be to remove the source of her guilt and replace it with something clean; but as with the bricks, this, too, she was powerless to do.

Compounding the torment of her aching heart were the slave's aching claws. They had kept her up in the night with their contentious spasms, and Asla's heating ointment offered little relief. It was as the princess had predicted: her tricks for cheating the hands at their painful game were failing. For the first time in years, the slave toyed with having the royal physicians relieve her of her opponents. Though these men refused all treatment for her suffering, with this grisly request, she was certain, they would happily comply.

Casica was reading a collection of Byzanthian ballads when she heard her friend's steps on the garden stairway. Clarece's saddened mood only intensified with the passing days, leaving the princess to question if any religious devotion could help. The door opened, revealing a damp and wilted Clarece. The slave kneeled humbly for permission to enter.

"Enter, my friend, and welcome!" the princess said watching as water dripped silently from Clarece's simple brown cloak. The distinct smell of wet wool filled the chamber, reminding Casica of sheep in her father's pastures. She loved that scent. "Forgive my dripping upon your floor, mistra," replied the embarrassed slave, removing her cloak. "I was running late to clear your lunch, and this is the fastest route from the chapel," she explained anxiously.

"No need for confession here, Clarece," Casica said assuringly. "Drip to your heart's content. Tis a relief to have you home. I worry about you in rains."

"I avoided all princes, my lady," her slave announced, remembering the same evening. "Only the priests attended chapel today. I think all but the most desperate of heart remained indoors." Casica motioned for her friend to sit. "And what of your heart? Is it still so desperate?" she asked softly.

Clarece lowered her head and nodded. *Confession hasn't born fruit,* thought the Cassican sadly. How tragic it was that something designed to free one's soul so seldom did. In confession was mercy offered, but to receive the gift, that required the truest work of grace.

"What confession has not done for your heart, perhaps tea can do for your body," the princess ventured. "Would you join me in an earthly rite?" "Yes. Thank you, mistra," the grateful woman replied. Clarece watched with interest as Casica stood from the table to heat water at her brazier. A Cassican intern had presided over her confession today.

When he learned whose slave she was, he smiled through the grate and said, "So you serve the Queen of Life. How is the Princess Casica?" Clarece told the young man that the princess seemed well enough, adjusting, as she was, to her new home. The intern was pleased. "I will inform Queen Pelana when I return home. Your news will bless her." How an intern could gain audience with a queen was beyond the slave. Certainly, no intern here had access to the throne. How differently must God behave in the Cassican land.

The princess returned to sit with her guest. (A watched kettle never boiled, even in Byzanthia.) The senior slave appeared unwell to the josquin. Darkness lined Clarece's eyes and she held her mittened hands more closely than usual against her body. She seemed to nurse them. Casica looked outside the large windows and considered the falling rain. It was certain this weather aggravated her friend's condition. "How are you today, Clarece?" she asked finally.

The slave glanced into her mistra's eyes, then quickly lowered them. Help sat stites from her; still the hurting woman struggled to answer truthfully. The guilty stain she felt convicted her of nameless crimes. It judged that she had no right to live painlessly this day. She thought back to her confession.

"If you confess your sin, Clarece," the intern assured her, "tis forgiven. Your stain is removed." "But what if you can't put words upon your sin?" she argued, troubled. "What if the stain is so intrinsically part of you, it cannot be named? What then?" The intern sat, stumped. It was not often confessors asked such questions. "God knows the stain's name as surely as He does your own," he decided. "He will cleanse it...."

Such was the intern's final proclamation of truth but Clarece could not believe it. A few weeks ago, possibly - she had placed some distance between herself and damnation, had stood where God could see her if He desired. But now, Asla's curse had consigned her back into the dark pit where no light and no holiness could dwell. Surely, she and her stain were invisible again. God could not cleanse what He could not see.

The fire in her arms reminded her of her continued judgment. Still, the thought came suddenly, were not even the condemned offered water? The slave turned cautiously to her mistra, afraid of committing spiritual mutiny. She was in enough trouble as it was.

"I am not well, today, my lady," she confessed finally. "'Twas a rough night." Casica leaned closer to her guest. "Dreams?" she asked quietly. Clarece shook her head. "No sleep a'tall, mistra. My hands... they did not wish me rest, and Asla's ointment did little good." Josquin resisted a strong urge to touch her friend's pain, reminding herself that she must respect Clarece's freedom of choice. The slave debated with herself only a moment more. Mutinous or not, Casica's water could quench this fire.

Eyes, blue and moist with salt like the sea, met Casica's brown as Clarece extended her hands to the healer. "Will you help me, mistra?" she asked softly. Casica's dark hands cradled the leather mittens. Instantly, Clarece felt her pain dissolve in the presence of warmth and healing. She sighed with relief. "Oh, God," she whispered, receiving His gift to the condemned, "Dear God, thank you...."

Casica watched patiently as her friend's body relaxed in the absence of pain. As she waited, the healer examined Clarece's hands as best she could through the leather barrier. It was certain their health degenerated. In a few minutes, Clarece met her mistra's gaze. "Thank you, my lady," she said, her voice filled with gratitude. Casica nodded understandingly.

"Have you no feeling at all in your hands, Clarece?" The slave shook her head. "None from without, my lady. Only the feeling trapped within. I feel only pain." "But it has not always been this way has it?" Casica's words were more statement than question.

"No. I once could feel - but that was long ago." Their water was ready. Casica rose and stood at the brazier. How she wanted to order the hurting woman to shed her leather and begin her healing. If she waited, Clarece may never have use of her hands. But the decision must be hers, Casica determined. More harm had come upon Clarece through the violation of her will than ever had come through physical injury. Josquin refused to add to that harm.

Clarece was examining her hands as the princess returned with their tea water. They always felt lighter after the Cassican's touch, almost emptier. "Thank you, Princess," she offered again. "You're very welcome, chief," Casica smiled adding milk to her charge's cup. Clarece waited politely for the princess before drinking her own tea. Its warmth filled her as it always did, with pleasure and comfort. She would never grow tired of this refreshment. Now that the fire in her hands was out, the slave's mind had room for other thought. She studied the dark woman near her. Casica was watching a waterfall flow from a seam in the roof. "My lady?" The princess turned. "What does your mother look like?"

*What on earth made her ask that?* Casica wondered, smiling at the question. In her mind's eye she saw the image that so often visited her dreams. "She is - well, wait!" she stopped, remembering the gold sphere in her karosh. The princess reached into a hidden pocket in her belt. Out she pulled a gold orb, slightly flattened by its maker. On it hung a gold chain. Clearly the locket was meant to be worn, but the princess preferred to keep it hidden in her belt. She took the piece and began to unscrew it, producing a single click for each twist. With each click the locket unfolded a single leaf of gold, until, finally, three slices of the sphere extended to reveal three pictures. Two more pictures hid within the orb, but these were for her eyes alone.

The princess offered the piece to the smiling slave. Clarece had read of these picture lockets but never had seen one. She looked, amazed, upon the three portraits. It was as though someone had captured their owners' images and sealed them within glassed frames. How could anyone paint so clearly upon so small a canvas?

"That's my family," Casica was saying. "My mother, Pelana, my father, K'eran, and my brother, K'ardan." Clarece glanced from Pelana's portrait to Casica and back. The two women were distant reflections of each other. "You are your mother's daughter," she observed, "except for the nose. That is your father in you."

"Yes," Casica smiled. "Nose and dimples, but you can't see them under his beard." Clarece nodded. She wondered what Pelana was like in person. Did she share Casica's voice, her mannerisms? And what of the princess' father? Was he stern or kind as the portrait suggested. Clarece's eyes returned to her owner's mother. "She is lovely, as is her daughter," she announced. Casica's eyes brightened at her compliment.

"Your brother is a boy," Clarece continued, examining the young man in the locket. "Yes," said Casica. "Such is often the case in my land - that brothers are boys...." Clarece simpered, shaking her head. She should have seen that coming. "I refer to his age," she clarified. "Oh," Casica replied with mocked seriousness. "Yes. Dan is six years my junior. We had a sister between us." The princess paused, remembering that dark time. "But she died in my mother's womb."

Clarece glanced up shocked. She had no idea death lived in Casica's history. "I'm so sorry, mistra. I did not know." Casica nodded, her eyes tearing with grief. "We didn't know if Maman would ever recover. Dan's arrival was a blessed event. His name means 'joy returned.' And indeed, with him, it did. He is a great comfort to my mother and father, especially with me here."

Clarece nodded, looking again into the boy's face. He had more of the king in him, it seemed. She returned the locket carefully to its keeper. "Thank you for sharing your family with me," she said, bowing her head. Casica closed the portraits and looked at the silent slave. Clarece's focus had turned to the rain outside, but she suddenly felt much farther away. "What are you thinking, Clarece?" the princess asked gently.

The slave's eyes had lost themselves in a single raindrop clinging to the glass outside; it tried desperately not to slip and be swallowed up into another. Tears flowed, unheeded, down her cheeks.

"I have no memory of my mother," she said quietly. "No face. No name. It is most probable she did not know even the name of the man who bred me into her." Her eyes lowered in grief. "Slave infants nurse upon their mother's breasts only eight weeks. If we live, we are sent far from where we are born to nurse upon another slave whose baby has been taken from her," she explained. "With this woman we stay until weaned. After that they collar us and we are sold."

Clarece watched. The drop crept along the glass, slipped into another, and it, pregnant as it was with this addition, fell from of her view. The slave dropped her eyes, trying to remember what she never could: the second woman's face. "I don't remember the woman who weaned me. I don't know why - I must have been very young when I was sold." Another drop slipped down the glass.

"My earliest memories are of a kitchen. You would think a kitchen would be a warm place, but this one - it was cold and dark. My mistra. She - hated me. I don't know why." Clarece closed her eyes. This face she could remember.

"She never called me by my name. She donned me 'Reclace.'" Casica winced. The word meant something defective that is thrown away. "This woman. She beat me so often, so brutally - I never knew why. Even when I did something well, she flogged me. I tried so desperately to please her, but it seemed it was my very existence that displeased her."

The slave's eyes saw nothing outside now. All her senses operated within. Clarece had reached a protective boundary in her story, one she had never crossed accompanied. It kept her safe from the knowledge of her hands. Kept her safe from exposure to others, like the leather that hid her shame. The lonely woman had never brought a guest into this place, fearful that if she did, they too would be destroyed, as she was. But for some reason, in this particular moment, Clarece wanted someone to join her there on the other side of safety. She needed for someone to stand with her and look upon this darkest chamber of her heart. And as fate ordained, that someone would be her mistra. Without realizing she did so, Clarece took hold of Casica and led her within.

"One morning," she continued, lost in herself "... one morning, this woman, my mistra, ordered me to move a bowl of batter from the counter to the table. Our master was having a feast that night and she prepared spiced bread. I took the bowl, but it was too heavy for me. And I dropped it. It didn't break, but I dropped it, and the batter spilled all over the floor. Everything in the kitchen stopped. And I knew, oh, God, I knew, I'd be torn. I tried to run, but she caught me by my collar. She flung me to the floor and kicked me until I couldn't breathe...."

Clarece winced with the memory, her mittened hand coming to her lips. As she closed her eyes, she saw the little girl who was herself, and wept. Wept for what had happened. For what would come.

"Then... then she stripped me of my shirt and grabbed a leather meat strap from the table - to beat the life from me, I thought.

But that wasn't her plan." Clarece paused as the scene unfolded within her. She stood with that little girl and witnessed again the delivery of her worst nightmares. The terror of that moment gripped her in the present in a deadly vice. The slave swallowed hard. Her words, spoken through a sea of anguish, seemed as distant as her sight.

"My mistra, she took the strap and bound my arms together." In memory and in present, her arms came together, her hands curling into two fists. "She bound me - for what I didn't know - but I screamed for mercy. Oh, God, I screamed. But there was no mercy. Never mercy for the cursed. She grabbed me by my throat. 'You worthless brute! I'll add you to the master's pot.' I tried to get away. But I was hurt and my hands, they were bound and I couldn't escape.

"She picked me up. And carried me to the stew pot where our master's meat cooked. And then I knew. I saw what she planned. I saw the boiling water, the boiling meat. But it was too late. I begged. Oh, God, I begged, *Help me! Dear, God, please help me!* But He didn't. I don't know why, but He doesn't." Clarece closed her eyes, trying desperately to erase this moment. She couldn't. Just as in her nightmares, she couldn't. She dreamt awake now. "Oh, God," she whispered, her breath ragged and anguished. "She took me - she took my hands and forced me into...."

The unimaginable silenced her words. From somewhere deep within her, issued a solitary moan of torture. The woman brought her destroyed hands, slowly, to her face and buried her eyes within their familiar scent of leather. Her hands caressed her brow as best they could. Then surrendered. They could not comfort her. They could not feel her; nor she them.

Clarece bent over. She sobbed helplessly, her body racked with grief. She was lost. In time and place lost; fallen into an event that swallowed her whole and rendered her shattered. For a long time, the broken woman rocked in her chair as to comfort herself, with what were once her hands cradled tenderly against her. At length, time found her and drew her unwittingly into the present. With the present came her breath and the awareness that she had, once more, survived. Clarece gazed unseeingly at the table.

"When I woke," she whispered, "I was lying on the kitchen floor. It didn't feel like the kitchen, but I knew it must be; I could smell cooked meat. It was the strangest thing, though: it was snowing in the kitchen. I remember laying there wondering why was it snowing in the kitchen. Then I realized I wasn't in the kitchen. I was outside. The snow was falling upon me, covering me - and the stars, oh my, the stars... they seemed a mere cubit from me. They were dazzling. But that makes no sense, does it? How could I see stars if it were snowing?

"I was freezing cold. I'm always cold. I kept telling myself, 'Get up, Clarece! Get up. Or you'll die.' But I couldn't get up. I tried. But I couldn't...." Clarece winced at the horror of this memory. "I couldn't find my hands to get up with. I looked and looked, but I couldn't find them. They weren't on my arms as they should be. They weren't in the snow. I didn't know where they were." She closed her eyes.

"And then... I heard my name. I looked up. There was an old man kneeling over me. I didn't know him. I'd never seen him. How could he know my name? But he did. He... he started to peel the straps from my arms. I don't remember after that. I have so many gaps. I don't know why. The next thing I remember was lying by a fireplace with an old woman nearby." With this, she smiled distantly.

"I don't remember her name, but I remember she was kind to me. She kept me by the fire. She kept me warm. And fed me and helped me with my pain. I don't know how long I stayed with her. I lived in and out of sleep - mercifully.

"All I remember was dreaming, dreaming of my hands. I kept losing them. I don't know why, except that I must be wicked. Only a very wicked girl would lose her hands. I dreamt about mittens, that I would lose my mittens and when I found them, my hands would be inside, but I hadn't any way to put them back on my arms, so I would lose them all over again. I was so frightened when the woman, she made a pair of leather mittens to cover me. I was afraid to take them off, afraid my hands wouldn't be there. And they weren't there - they couldn't be there because I had lost them. I was wicked. That's why I couldn't find my hands."

Her breath was quieter now. The unimaginable was fading into a place of memory she could more easily grasp. "Then one day, the traders came and bought me from the woman. They took me to the open market at Sonataa. Some slavemen there purchased me. Stable hands. I came cheap," Clarece smiled bitterly. "They bought me for a sack of leather scraps. My hands, I was worthless without them. But I soon learned they hadn't bought me for my hands." Her tears came silently.

"There was one man, he never took me. Some nights, he would wait until the others had done with me, then he would wrap me in a horse blanket and carry me to his bed and tell me stories. I don't remember his name, but I do remember his stories," she smiled. "They were happy tales. I used to pretend he was my father. I slaved there for two years and a season.

"Then one day, something amazing happened. The king's hunting party? it came to our village. Bears had come down from the mountains.... I never saw the king, but on the first day of the hunt, his young son fell from a horse and broke his arm. And for the remaining time, that thorn shadowed my every move. Pony! what a royal pest he was, bothering me about my hands and everything else - why did I wear mittens? why did horses do this? what was that? Scads!

"Finally, I told him to go to Hades, but he didn't. And then the day the king's party was to leave? This boy comes to me and says that his father told him he could take home a pet. So I walked from Sonataa to the royal city. They exchanged my iron collar for a silver one and made me the Prince Bastien's personal slave."

Clarece was smiling now. "I thought I had walked into Heaven. I was fed. Everyday. I was clothed and no one molested me. Usually, a boy.... Prince Bastien, he never touched me. He still pestered me - but he taught me to read - as a game. I will never forget that day. It was as if something in me awakened. The world changed from black and white to color; everything was so much more beautiful in word than it had ever been in sight." Clarece closed her eyes and smiled, her expression the same as when she tasted tea for the first time.

"Mastra ordered the physicians to look at my hands. They obeyed, being as he was the king's son. They examined me and declared me the most wretched, irredeemable creature they had ever seen and recommended I be put to death at once. Bastien kept me alive, but he soon tired of me. I couldn't play as he.

"The other slaves avoided the freak in the east wing, all except one; the only one who mattered: the chief slaveswoman. She took me in her care and made of me a fine slave. In all this time, I saw neither king nor queen. "Then one day, while I was returning from the library, I met King Ars in the hallway. I prostrated myself and thought he would pass, but he stopped and asked who was I. I told him I was his son's slave from Sonataa.

"'Look at me!' he ordered. I did. And in that instant, I saw my death in his eyes. The king gaped at me as unto a ghost. It was my hands that frightened him. He didn't know that his son's pet was deformed. He drew his sword to take my head, all the while yelling, 'Who are you?! What are you?!' I finally remembered my name. 'Clarece!' I cried.

"And then he stopped. The king stood there with his sword over me and simply stared. Finally, he told me that the next time we met, my name would not save me - I had no idea the queen's name was Clarece.

"That was twelve years ago. I have not seen him since. It is a fearful thing to live in the shadow of a king's hate. I don't know why he hates me so. There is so much about me I don't know. Sometimes, I think the reason I fill my mind with knowledge is in hope that, someday, I'll stumble upon answers for my life."

Clarece bowed her head, exhausted. The answers, she was certain, she would never find. The slave regained her self-awareness. "I've never told this to anyone," she acknowledged quietly. She looked finally at the princess. "I don't know why I tell you now - except...." She could not finish.

The face she saw was broken with grief. Tears ran down her mistra's throat and into her blouse. Casica felt somewhat faint and then it occurred to her: she was not breathing, had not been for some time now. Josquin took a deep, sudden breath.

Clarece glanced away to the familiarity of her mittens. "They are my constant torment," she whispered in reference to the deadened things on her arm. "I sometimes consider having them cut off, but if I do that, I'll never find them. Or worse, what if my suffering does not leave with them?" The slave turned to her owner. She was wise. She might know. "Princess," she asked tentatively, presenting her hands, "you know God. Why does He hate me? Why did He do this to me?"

Casica gazed at the waiting woman. Her mind reeled with Clarece's story. She was still in the kitchen, in the livery. And now

Clarece was asking her a question she could not possibly answer. The princess' hands went to her face and then to her mouth. She felt numb. "God did not do this to you, Clarece," she whispered finally. "The evil one did, through evil people."

"But God could have stopped it. He could have protected me." Casica nodded in agreement. She had no defense to this. "Yes. He could have spared you. I don't know why He didn't. I can't know. But I do know He does not hate you, Clarece. From where I sit, I see His love for you." The princess glanced about the room. Looked at the questioning woman near her.

"Look at us, Clarece. We shouldn't be sitting here together. I should be in Cassica and you should be...." She couldn't say it. "As far as I know, The Edict's sole purpose was to bring us together. God moved five hundred years of time and space to bring into your life the only person in this world, perhaps, who can help you find your hands." "But I haven't them to find, my lady," the slave objected, tears rising again to her eyes. "I'm a monster," she said, honoring again that pretender to her heart's throne. "I am damned by God...."

"No. Goodness, no," Casica countered, tenderly. "You are *not* a monster, Clarece. You, you are perhaps the most human person I have ever known. What has happened to you, *that* is monstrous, but even so it has not been able to take from you your humanity. I think of what happened to your hands. No one should have survived that; yet here you are. Your very existence proves that God has not forsaken you. Your life, Clarece, it testifies of His love for you."

"You mean it testifies of His enjoyment of my prolonged suffering," Clarece observed wryly. "No," the princess objected. This lie was too deeply embedded to dispel with words but still.... "Are you in pain now?" she inquired. The slave felt for a moment. "No." "And your life... is it not richer than it has ever been?"

Clarece looked at her mistra. It was indeed. "Yes," she admitted. "But my life, though richer, it still makes *no sense*," she said frustrated.

Josquin sighed deeply. Meaning. It was not so much answers as it was meaning for which this woman so desperately fought.

Casica's hand went to the pocket which contained her pictures. She had no portraits to offer her friend. Her fingers caressed the soft camel's hide of her belt. Her karosh, she thought. That might help. She reached for her buckle, unfastened it, and lay the heavy belt before Clarece. "The markings on my belt," she asked. "What are they?"

Clarece looked closely, she had noticed them before. "I assume they are a Cassican design to ornament your belt." Casica smiled. "It looks that way to you because you don't read Cassican. This is my karosh, my belt of truth. If you had my eyes, you would see my whole life's story in this belt. It's written in layers, to be continued upon. But the bottom layer," she explained, passing her fingers over particular symbols, "it reads, 'Casica, beloved daughter of God.' It is *this* layer upon which all the rest are written." Casica turned her attention to Clarece.

"Clarece," she said gently, "I can't explain your story to you. To do so is for Someone else. But I do know that the bottom line of your life is the same as mine. You are beloved by God. And all that is written into you - no matter how horrific - has purpose. Your life may look like a series of meaningless chaos, but that's an illusion. Remember when you learned to read? Remember that moment when those strange markings came to life? The world opened to you, you said. It will again."

Clarece stared at her princess. All fatigue had left her. The senior slave felt invigorated with thought. New thought. Truth - perhaps. Once again, she found herself the served and, once again, wished so much for something to offer her kind lady. Clarece looked down at her mittened claws. "How I wish I had hands to give you, my lady," she said. "I wish I could serve you as I should, as you deserve."

Casica covered the leathered hands with her own. "You offer me something so much more precious than hands, Clarece; you've given your heart." Clarece glanced bashfully at her mistra. "A slave's heart, such as it is." "'Tis glorious," the Cassican observed earnestly, repeating one of her many dicta.

"Not so glorious my lady," replied Clarece, reminded of her fallen condition. "I've quite recently been consigned to hell. My spiritual state is highly suspect."

Casica nodded, fighting to repress her laughter. "Asla told me of your fight." "She did?" Clarece asked surprised. "Yes. She is heartbroken." "She is? I didn't think she concerned herself with spiritual matters." "Apparently she does. At least where you're concerned, she does..."

"She didn't mean it," Clarece defended her friend. "Still, the harm is done, and she can't undo it and I can't undo it."

Casica pondered Clarece. Already the slave's demeanor tottered towards despair. This matter of cursing would befog any movement towards truth, like smoke in a ballroom. The princess certainly didn't agree with her friend's beliefs, but how could she assist her within their confines?

"You may not be able to do anything, but might someone else?" she asked. "My lady?" "Well, I know you appreciate the power of a curse. But what of the power of blessing? What if someone whose 'eternal soul is secure,' as you say, covers an insulit's curse with a blessing? Would it not be expunged?"

Clarece considered the possibility. While she had never read of such a remedy, it seemed plausible. The word of the king, after all, overruled all lesser ones. It was worth a try. "I can't verify your theory, but it may work. Would you do this for me?" "Gladly," smiled Casica. "If you don't mind that I do so in Cassican; I speak more clearly to our Maker in Cassican." "Yes. That's acceptable - as long as He understands Cassican." *Is she serious?* the princess wondered. "Let us hope, for my sake, He does."

The slave stood and kneeled. She always kneeled before God, in case He *did* see her. Casica rose to join her. She prayed often for Clarece alone; what a gift it was to do so in her presence. Speaking in Cassican would afford her complete freedom.

The princess, whose soul was secure in ways neither woman understood, placed her hands upon her friend's head. And prayed. As Josquin spoke on her behalf, Clarece recognized the familiar warmth of her touch but, with it, came a new sensation. Something in the slave's heart stirred and, as word and spirit flowed against it, released its grip upon her.

By prayer's end, Clarece felt a full stone lighter. It worked! The princess' blessing had done its work, the slave thought, silently adding this new understanding to her spiritual repertoire. Clarece rose to her feet, freer than she had been in weeks.

"Thank you, mistra!" she smiled, bowing. "Success, I think. I'm not in heaven, surely, but I know I am not where I was." "I know

I'm not where I was either," Casica replied, feeling better herself. "Thank *you*."

The clock chimed, reminding the slave she had long missed her place in line for her mistra's dinner. "I must hurry, my lady," she said glancing at the face on the wall. She turned to leave and then remembered herself. Kneeling, she asked, "May I be excused from your presence?" Casica nodded and watched as Clarece stepped buoyantly below.

She  must hurry. She couldn't wait to tell her friend of their mutual release.

# XIX

Clarece lay in the cold, familiar comfort of her cot. Light from her tiny lamp bathed the ceiling above her with all manner of shadow. The dark movement flickered in and out of view like her thoughts. Across from her slept her dreamless friend, her breathing deep and steady. Asla had embraced her news with joy, more for her friend's release than any sense of her own.

How Clarece wished she could sleep, but in its place, something awful brewed within her: a panicked realization of having exposed herself to her mistra. *God, what have I done?* She had revealed before this woman all her shame. In doing so she had violated all boundaries of propriety and protection. What would become of her now? Would her mistra ever see her the same? Would she even look at her tomorrow?

And what of Casica? What would become of her? It was a strange experience of emotion in that, in addition to shame, Clarece could not deny feeling somewhat amazed and relieved: She had always believed that if she ever told anyone her dark secret, that person would be destroyed. Her darkness would consume them. Yet, Casica was whole. She didn't turn into a heap of ash; didn't flee in horror; didn't appear stricken in any way.

This truth confronted many, many lies imbedded in the slave's heart like so many living thorns. The princess' reaction challenged Clarece's view of herself as being dangerous or unclean. Before Clarece came below tonight, Casica had embraced and blessed her as was customary. She smiled into her eyes and told her, "Thank you, again, for your gift today. May you rest in peace."

Peace. The senior slave wondered if it were possible. Or rather, were it possible for her to accept? Deep peace did try to fill her; she sensed its presence in the midst of all her other emotions. This peace stemmed from the wondrous experience of having been known. Something for so long stored in darkness was shared. And what Clarece presented as a burden, in the presence of another, she experienced as rest. *Rest in peace tonight....*

Could it be the princess knew the backwash that could come from her sharing this day? Could it be that the young woman who appeared so spotless knew dark places in her own heart? Had she shared them with others? Clarece thought back at the time she first helped Casica dress after her flogging. The woman had lowered her head in shame of having her vicious scars exposed before another. Clarece's own body was covered with stripes, only her neck and face were spared. She felt no shame before other slaves, but before her owner? There was a reason she would not show Casica her hands. But she had revealed her heart; her story was told. What would become of it now? Become of her?

Peace. It beckoned her. *Rest, Clarece,* it invited. *Rest in the freedom that has come to you. The dark monster that has haunted your deepest sleep, you have brought into the light of telling. See how much he has disappeared, how less frightening he is in the light of day.* In opening the door of her past, Clarece had been given a key to release. She had shared her heart with a worthy keeper, she knew. Casica would store her story in her locket and safeguard it in her belt of truth.

Sleep. What her mind could not fully accomplish, Clarece's body did. One of the great graces of slavery was fatigue. She hadn't the energy to think anymore. Physical exhaustion came over her like a blanket of mercy. The senior slave did, indeed, rest and in peace.

Casica lay in bed, restless. So the injury was not burning as she had thought. It was boiling. Her mind skipped along memories of her culinary experiences which, granted, were few in attempt and dismal in effect. But she had boiled meat on several occasions. Chicken. The josquin watched as a chicken leg fell into a pot of boiling water. With time the skin gives way, then the sinews, meat and finally bone. But how long were Clarece's hands submerged? How far up her arms? - past her wrists certainly; her mittens' design revealed that.

Josquin's mind spun in an orderly fashion. Clarece's bones had survived; bone cannot live in the absence of sinew. Sinew cannot, in the absence of flesh. Clarece's hands were thin, horribly thin. This fact may have more to do with her sinews than with her flesh though. Her hands ached, in numbness Casica guessed; this hinted at nerve damage and even more, perhaps, blood flow. But her hands lived which meant enough blood reached them to nourish their tissue. Her pain worsened with time. This could stem from many causes.

But underlying all the healer's speculation was the maddening fact that none of this made sense. The damage Clarece had suffered was severe enough to disable her. Yet she had kept her life and even more confusingly, her hands. There were fingers in her flesh somewhere; Casica could feel their bones. But for the flesh to have melted enough to form a single mass (as she could only suspect), it should have sloughed off. Clarece should have developed gangrene; she should have lost her hands. She should have lost her life. Yet she hadn't, and her hands lived well enough to keep her alive to their painful presence.

Casica shook her head in the darkness. Who were the man and woman? she wondered. Were there male healers in this land? Were the stars she saw pobble stones glowing about the man's neck? Was the woman a healer? Were the tortured girl's memories all askew? No matter what the answers, nothing short of miraculous had happened.

The healer surrendered to sleep. Her mind drifted but in a wondrous manner. Casica loved the way sleep wove her fragmented thoughts into order. Her imagination formed the picture she needed. She watched as blood flowed through Clarece's arms into her hands, reaching the very fingertips which waited somewhere within. Blood. That was the key. Blood would wash away much of the damage and bring with it essential nourishment. Clarece would have sinews again; that was something Casica could give her. But blood was required for that healing to sustain.

Blood flow and sinew. *That's the starting point,* the healer decided. As for fingers, well, the mittens hid that vision from her, but she could do much without ever seeing what they sheathed. All that was necessary was an opened door. Clarece held the key.

# XX

Clarece awakened early, excited about her day. She enjoyed so much her tours of the palace, showing the Cassican princess the marvelous rooms and discussing their histories. Today would be the south wing, she decided, home of art and armor, and keeper of the guards' great room. The slave was certain Casica would appreciate the wing's many artistic offerings.

She rose in time to complete her pen chores and procure two breakfasts before the usual time. Asla had come in late last night, and Clarece hoped to give her stallmate a few more minutes of sleep by delivering Edsner's breakfast for her. Having delivered his and her mistra's, she returned to her stall. It was time for Asla to wake.

"Asla, wake up, you slothful g'Helderleit!" she teased, gently rousing her sleeping friend. "Cursed, Clarece, what are you doing waking me so early?" Asla grumbled, making no move to leave her bed. "Early? You mean late. It's half past six...." That got Asla's attention. "Scads! What are you doing waking me so late?!" Asla injected, startled. "Edsner would have his breakfast long ago - ." "Don't fret. I've fed him already; I thought you could use the extra sleep - you came in late last night."

Asla put her hand to her head. Last night. "You could say that. I was with Sgt. Pennel; where he got the gold for me I can't imagine. 'Must have won a huge bet or something. He was in a drinking mood and got me quite drunk. I had trouble finding my way back. Gods, what a night. I hate military men." Clarece glared at

Asla disapprovingly. Asla glanced up and realized her mistake. "I mean, all military men except for Sgt. Poul. Of course, he wouldn't have to get me drunk to make him look good," she declared, receiving Clarece's playful slap on the arm, as much a slap as she dared with her hand.

Asla leaned back. "You, chief slaveswoman," she observed, "you certainly are in a good mood. Were you having another dream about the aforementioned sergeant?" "Keep your mind off my dreams, insulit," Clarece warned jokingly. "No I wasn't, though I certainly would not have minded it," she confessed. "I'm excited because the princess and I are touring the south wing. I'm so enjoying showing off our palace, Asla. Tis a blessed change in activity for me."

"Well, when you find *my* palace, let me know," yawned Asla. "And stay clear of Baron Dower's chamber, unless you want to place your mistra in a compromising position. I'm servicing him this morning." "Stay clear of Dower's chamber. Check," Clarece nodded. "Could you braid my hair before I leave?" Asla sat up and reached for her hairbrush. As she combed Clarece's long sandy hair, the two women talked of the previous day, catching up on palace news. Asla had begun braiding her friend's locks when Clarece asked shyly, "*Have* you seen Poul recently?"

"Yes, as a matter of fact, I have. He was training in blades yesterday when I stopped by the gym. He was shirtless. Very nice chest, your sergeant has," Asla noted admiringly. She loved making the older woman blush.

"I've seen him train, thank you," Clarece replied. *And you're right,* she thought, *he does have a magnificent body.* "So he is well..." she ventured aloud. "I would say so - definitely," the insulit rejoined, grinning to herself. "There. You're all braided, senior slave."

"Thank you, Asla. Blessings upon you." "When horses dance, Rece. You and the Cassican enjoy your palace." Clarece glanced at Asla's schedule propped on the night stand. "So you'll be in tonight." "Yes, thank gods." "Well, then I'll see you this evening," said Clarece, rising from her friend's cot. Asla's good-bye accompanied her up the stairs as she stepped lightly to join the princess above.

Casica was just finishing her meal when Clarece appeared at her doorway. "Come in, come in!" she welcomed. Clarece offered her greeting kneel and approached the princess' table. The food smelled delicious. It looked delicious. Pony, how she longed for real food, she thought, swallowing. "You caught me sleeping this morning, Clarece," the princess said, inviting her charge to sit. "I came early, my lady. And how was your rest?" "Very well. I'm starting to sleep better here." "That is very good. And your meal?"

Casica glanced at her plate. "Excellent. I must say, Byzanthian fare is quite pleasing. It lacks Cassican spiciness but still, tis delectable." "I will relay your praise to the kitchen. They wonder what you think. My lady," she continued, "I thought I would leave clearing your dishes until lunch so we may visit the south wing this morning, if you wish."

"Fine," Casica replied admiring the elaborate braiding of Clarece's hair. The quiet slave seemed in a festive mood this morning. Could it be she was enjoying the tours so much? Perhaps. Clarece was a born teacher and the palace proved a rich classroom. Casica wiped her mouth. "I'm all yours, learned tour guide. Lead me to the south wing, or rather, keep me headed in the right direction," she added remembering that Clarece must walk behind her. "Don't worry, Mistra," the slave assured her. "I won't lose you."

The women exited through Bastien's darkened chamber. As she passed by his bed, Casica wondered if she would ever know what it was like to sleep there. At this rate, with Bastien gone for so long, she'd probably never feel him or his covers. *What are you thinking, Cass?* she berated herself. *You don't even know the man.* 'Must be that time of month.

The pair reached the south wing without incident. The palace still slept with very little traffic stirring. Only guards and servants met them along their way. Clarece grinned, knowingly, as they passed Baron Dower's chamber in route to the art that lined this hall. Her prediction proved correct. Casica thrilled at the paintings and listened to her tutor's historical and biographical data with keen interest.

It was an informative class: Clarece viewed the art with the eyes of a historian; Casica, through those of an artist. Among the many Byzanthian paintings, landscapes and portraits were scattered several Cassican works. Casica took great pleasure discussing these paintings from her uniquely Cassican perspective. Of particular interest to Clarece was Casica's explanation of the use of shading and shadow in painting. It amazed her to learn that all shadow, in art and life, was not truly darkness; it was, rather, a tinted shade of the color being shadowed. The quiet slave looked around, seeing this truth all about her. She reckoned aloud that this condition in art must exist in matters of the heart and the human condition. It was a concept she would work out later in her mind.

The students recessed from their hallway classroom to visit the great hall of the king's guardsmen. Clarece served in this hall every year of her life at the palace. She admired its dark wood and open floor. It reminded her of the king's hall where she and her fellow slaves celebrated every five years.

"Here is where the guardsmen have their annual dance and feast, my lady," she began. "As a prince, my Lord Bastien is a royal overseer of the king's guardsmen - and women, though not technically. As his slave, I serve at their yearly dance. Tis a festive occasion. Lots of drinking and eating and loud entertainment - truly a man's event," she concluded. "And with whom do all these guards dance?" inquired Casica. "With invited guests, such as I'm sure your lady will be - courtiers, noblewomen and with the female guard, of course."

Casica strolled into the center of the dance floor. The room was magnificent, paneled in red maple, carved with various flora design and, interestingly, lined above near the ceiling with shields of many coats of arms. "Who are the female guard, Clarece?" she asked, studying the crests above her. "They are the queen's guard," Clarece explained. "It is their responsibility to protect and accompany the queen. Since her death - may she rest - the guard is somewhat lost to itself."

*Tis a dangerous thing to have a group of armed soldiers with nothing to do,* thought Casica. "But what of Bastil's wife? She is the crowned princess. Do they not guard her?" "No, my lady. Only the queen. Until Princess Kalera ascends the throne, she is unguarded - by the female guards, I mean. The prince's guards keep her now." "I see. And, Clarece," the princess continued, still puzzling over the shields, "what of these shields? What do they represent?" Casica stood with her arms crossed, engrossed with the designs and colors of the armor above her, waiting for an answer. There was no reply. "Clarece?" She turned to where her charge had been and gasped, utterly undone by the scene that met her.

Clarece kneeled fully, her face touching the ground. Surrounding her stood eleven sullen women, dressed all in blue and blades. Gold chevrons graced their rich garments, vested with the royal seal of the queen. They were each of them armed, not only with steel, but with hate, openly unscabbard in their expressions. Not since that terrible night with Jonas had Casica sensed such pure loathing.

Josquin stood cautiously, assessing the situation, aware of her shallow quick breath. A dreadful woman, larger than she and decades older, emerged from the group. "Well, guards," she announced sarcastically, "it seems we have failed miserably in our mission to protect this room from vermin." The group laughed, knowingly. "How is it a Cassican slug has slimed her way into our hallowed hall? Was it you, Freak? Did you bring this Cassican filth here?" The captain addressed her words to the frightened slave but her gaze was on Casica.

"A thousand pardons, great guard," Clarece answered respectfully. "This is my doing." Slowly she lifted her head to look pleadingly at the princess. "*Go,*" she mouthed. "*Go now.*"

Casica glanced at Clarece. The lieutenant behind her pressed her foot upon the slave's back, forcing her head down. Casica took a full breath, anger spouting within her. Now was no time for indignation. "I apologize, captain?" "Captain Jamai." "Captain Jamai, for intruding. We were unaware of your presence." *Idiot,* Josquin thought. That was obvious; if they'd been aware, they'd have been nowhere near this place. The room reeked of violence. She and Clarece needed to escape, with or without her pride. "We will leave immediately. Clarece?" she addressed her charge, indicating for her to rise.

"You may leave, Cassican," the captain announced, "being as you are the wife of a prince. But your cur stays here. Don't worry," Jamai smiled ominously. "We'll send her home directly...." Clarece drew her hands more closely under her. *Leave me,* Casica, she begged, trying desperately to think the princess away. *Leave. They're only using me to bait you.* The guards had hurt her before -

Bastien's frequent absence rendered her easy prey - and she knew what they had in mind. But for the princess, they would kill her if she resisted, prince's wife or not. They were the queen's guard; their authority superseded the princess if she dared attack them.

Casica's throat tightened; she felt suddenly very, very cold. She was a healer, a josquin. Never had she physically confronted anyone in her life. She would wield the only weapon she knew for this situation. Words.

"I have need of her at this time, captain. We will both take our leave. Again," she added meekly, "I apologize for our intrusion." Casica addressed the kneeling woman. "Clarece. Come!" she ordered, and turned to walk away.

Clarece stood and carefully stepped towards the doorway, praying, silently, for the improbable. As with all her prayers, this one went unheeded. The guard at her back grabbed her collar, jerking her. Instinctively, Clarece reached behind and, reining herself too late, committed a cardinal offense. "You dare lift your hand against me, slave?!" the guard demanded.

Casica spun in time to see the lieutenant take Clarece's right hand and twist it, ever so slightly. Clarece gasped in pain. As the torment increased, her knees gave, and in that instant Casica saw her friend's bare midriff. Deep, ugly scars wrapped themselves around her waist. In horror, Casica watched as the guard twisted more. Groaning, Clarece closed her eyes and begged for what she knew would never be given: "Mercy, please, mercy...."

The guard gazed directly at the princess, daring her move. The two stood, frozen in the moment. Then deliberately, never releasing her eyes from the dumbfounded Cassican, the guard took both her hands and crushed them together upon the slave's. Clarece's screams filled the hall.

Josquin never knew how she gained the distance between her and the lieutenant. The guards could never determine how she swiped the lieutenant's sword from her side. Some swore the sword left of its own power to find its way into the Cassican's hand. In an instant, the livid woman held the lieutenant's sword to it owner's throat, pressing its tip until the guard kneeled before her. Released, Clarece collapsed to the floor, clasping her tortured hand to her chest.

Casica loomed over the lieutenant, wincing at her friend's cries. "Corporal," she said, addressing the woman standing to her right. "My lady?" the stunned guard choked out. "Help her up and take her from this place." The guard glanced at her lieutenant. "Do it," her superior said. Bending down, the guard lifted Clarece to her feet, keeping one eye on the princess. Clarece stood slowly, trembling.

"Princess," she whispered, begging her mistra to leave with her. Casica touched Clarece on the shoulder. Her pain subsided. "Tis well, Clarece," she said calmly. "Go." Clarece looked once more into her owner. Though she wanted to speak, she couldn't. She turned to the corporal and walked slowly towards the door.

Casica squatted before the pale lieutenant, keeping the tip of her sword firmly in place. "What is your name?" "Adara." "You hear me, Adara," she whispered. "Stand. Make one move without my word, and I swear, you will know *exactly* how it feels to go through life without hands." The terrified woman nodded.

Casica listened to herself, wondering all the while whose voice this was. Slowly she stood, letting the sword hang by her side. Though well-trained by K'net in blades, Casica had never fought a person with sharps. To do so was unimaginable. Her training was a requirement of a future defender of the throne, nothing more. She faced the captain. "I want no quarrel with you," she said flatly.

Jamai's response was immediate. "The Cassican is mine. No one interfere," she ordered her soldiers. Casica watched as the captain calmly drew her hip sword, first, then her hand sword. The sliding steel rang through the hall and into Casica's mind. This couldn't be happening.

For one awful moment, Josquin tasted metal in her mouth and thought, "I'm going to pass out." Then suddenly she sensed a rising from her shalonn, bringing with it a solid awareness of herself. Words could not save her now. She must fight. There was no other option. Casica studied her opponent. As she did so, she spun the sword in her hand. Stopped it. Spun. Stopped. One more spin. Stop. "God help me," she prayed in Cassican.

"I'll have that necklace of yours Cassican," Jamai smirked. "Your head won't be needing it...." "'Never fight in anger'," Casica could hear K'net say. "Hades with it," she mumbled. "I'm angry."

Casica broke into a dead run, and swinging the heavy sword over her head, brought it fully upon the startled Jamai. *Scads! - What is this?* The captain was caught totally off guard, responding purely by instinct. She easily blocked Casica's blow, but reeled at the strength of it. The two women circled each other now, each sizing the other.

Jamai attacked with deadly and expert skill. As in a dream, Casica's parried every strike - backing, spinning, dodging. None of this seemed real. Her response was automatic, like playing a piece of music from memory. Her body, drilled by countless hours of sparing with K'net, was fighting for her, without her, leaving her mind to wonder, absurdly, if this were a game.

A careless move exposed the inexperienced fighter to a blade at her face. Casica avoided being bloodied, but the near-miss stripped her of all illusion: This was no game. The woman across from her was determined to kill. Casica had always excelled defensively, irritating K'net until he goaded her with, "Attack! Attack!" Now she swung her mind offensively, drilling her sword again and again at the body of Jamai.

The captain parried, but did so completely oblivious to her advantage. In training, with K'net safely padded against dull blades, Casica went for the kill. But in this real battle, Josquin couldn't bring herself to harm. To kill Jamai was not in her. Casica must disarm her, instead. It soon became clear to Casica, however, that to do so without injuring her opponent was impossible; Jamai was both too expert and too intent upon the princess' death.

"Bide your time," K'net had taught his cousin. "Your enemy, no matter how skilled, will always make a mistake." Casica waited patiently, testing the captain with every move she knew. And then it happened. Jamai faltered, and before she could recover, Casica was upon her. Her blade glided into the guard's wrist, tearing the sword from her grasp. Jamai struck with her hand sword but too late. Casica swung her leg against Jamai's ankles.

The captain fell hard to the floor, her wind knocked from her. She rolled to her right. Casica's sword greeted her. The tip planted into Jamai's royal crest. And stopped.

Casica loomed over the panting, bleeding woman, her own breath coming in heavy draws. She looked into the stunned face of the captain. She didn't know who was more surprised....

"Will you yield," Casica asked between breaths, "or must I end this?" Jamai gaped at her wrist. Blood flowed from its wound. She had no desire to die. 'Never expected to die like this. "I yield," she surrendered, nodding. Casica closed her eyes, relieved.

The princess knelt next to the defeated woman. "If I weren't here, you would bleed to death." Josquin clasped her hand on the gaping wound. Jamai winced. An utterly foreign sense penetrated her being. What was this Cassican doing to her? The bleeding stopped and all pain left her body.

Casica searched the blue eyes of Jamai. "I don't want to be your enemy," she said quietly. "I have no need for hate. But if any harm comes to Clarece, I will come for you. If I am threatened by your women, I will come for you. Do you understand? This ends here. Now."

"I understand," the captain replied. Casica closed her eyes; hot tears wet her face. She reached for the captain's swords, then grasping her own, helped the woman stand.

"Your irons, captain," she spoke respectfully. She presented the captain her hip sword, hilt first, which the guard tentatively accepted. Then the hand sword. "Killing is easy," Josquin declared, shaking her head. "Living - now that's the real challenge." Slowly, Jamai nodded, wondering how she had possibly lost this fight.

Casica turned and walked towards the kneeling lieutenant. "Stand," she ordered. Adara stood, waiting for what, she did not know. "If you were my guard," Casica told her softly, "I'd have you jailed for this. Clarece belongs to the king - how *dare* you attack whom you have sworn to defend. Your abuse of authority is repugnant, a disgrace to your rank." Casica's eyes burned into the frightened guard. "This is what you do to save yourself, lieutenant. You will go to Clarece - unarmed - tomorrow night, during her supper. You have harmed her in the presence of your peers; you will beg her forgiveness in the presence of hers. If she grants it, I forgive you. If not, I will come for you. Do you understand?"

Adara was stunned. This wasn't what she'd expected. "Yes, my lady," she stammered. Casica took several steps from the guards before remembering the sword in her hand. She looked at it in astonishment. How on earth did this come into her possession? A swell of anger and repulsion overtook her. Grasping the weapon with both hands, Casica flung it, yelling, with the might of her shalonn.

The sword spun through the air. It impaled itself into the wall high above the shields. There it stayed, swaying with the distinct tone of metal in wood. The blade pulsed, still, as Josquin exited the hall, leaving the guard to gape at the permanent addition to their hall's armory display.

Clarece stood, as she had during the entire fight, propped in the doorway. Her eyes left the dancing sword in the ceiling and now focused on the woman approaching her. She knew this was her mistra, but after witnessing the past few minutes, she found herself somewhat afraid. The princess looked into Clarece's familiar eyes. "Please, take me from here." All fear vanished. "Yes, my lady. Come with me...."

Clarece guided Casica through a maze of slave passages, arriving finally to her empty pen. She led Casica to her own cot and sat across from her on Asla's bed. Casica bowed her head. "I'm going to be sick." Clarece grabbed the wash basin from her night stand and held it before the pale Cassican. Josquin purged her fear into the basin. Clarece comforted her brow and throat with a damp cloth. "Better?" she asked.

Casica nodded. "Much." She held her hand to her head. Thank goodness for self-healing. "How is your hand, Clarece?" "I'm alright, mistra." "Let me see." Casica felt the mittened hand carefully. No broken bones. They were stronger than she'd guessed.

"I'm sorry this happened, Clarece. Tis my fault...." "No, my lady," Clarece objected. "The female guards have hurt me before. They are cruel in their boredom." Casica shook her head, unconvinced. "Still, they wouldn't have hurt you today had I not been with you." "Respectfully, my lady? Don't bet on that. But I would wager that after today, they will never hurt me again." "Let us hope not. I can't stomach their kind of fight." Clarece sat wordlessly, waiting. After a few minutes she suggested, "Mistra, you need to rest."

"No, Clarece. You need to rest," Casica answered, looking at her friend. "I need to see the king." She sighed deeply. "God, what a mess. I won't be needing lunch today," she smiled wanly.

"Please eat it for me." Clarece nodded. "Thank you, my lady. I will see you this evening?" "God willing, yes."

Casica perused her surroundings: the tiny lamp, books on the night stand, a schedule of sorts; Asla's dagger, dried flowers on the wall, the scent of fragranced liniment. This was a pleasant nook. It felt like Clarece.

"You and Asla share a cozy sanctuary," she observed aloud. "Thank you, my lady." *"I mean thank you for defending me. And for defending yourself."* That's what Clarece wanted to say, but didn't know how. Words felt so empty at this moment.

"Thank you for your basin," Casica was saying, " - and for the tour. Tis a beautiful wing. I mean that. Let's go back and look further at the art."

Clarece stood with Casica. On impulse, she embraced her mistra, grateful for her life. Casica returned the embrace, relieved to rest in the comfort of this steady woman. "God's blessings upon you, mistra," the slave offered softly. "And upon you, Clarece."

As she watched the princess ascend the stairs, Clarece thought back to the fight, back to the spinning sword in her mistra's hand. She knew that gesture. She had seen another perform the same ritual as he prepared to spar in a training match. Poul...

# XXI

Casica must see the king at once. News traveled the speed of speech in a palace. Especially bad news. It was certain Ars already knew of her fight with Jamai, and she had no desire to be summoned. The princess paused in her room to wash her face and Jamai's blood from her hands. At the sight of it, Casica closed her eyes and wept. Here was proof. She had physically harmed someone. The fact that her action was one of self-defense mattered not. Casica was josquin and she had spilt another's life. With growing horror, the healer surveyed the terrible line she crossed today, one she had never imagined even approaching.

The troubled woman bowed, bringing her hands to her face. "Oh, God, what have I done?" she asked. "What am I becoming in this place?" Casica stood, a long while, willing her heart rest. Uncovering her face, she completed her task of washing. It was time to face the king. The princess exited through the empty chamber of Bastien, stopping at his table. Bourbon had made a fine chaser for prayer before; perhaps, it would again. "It can't hurt," she said taking a single swallow. Her stomach disagreed.

Judging from the guards' bored expressions, news had not yet attained the east wing. Upon entering the west wing, however, Casica experienced a very different reception. Guards glanced at each other as she passed, piercing her back with suspicion. *God help*, she thought. *If the entire guard is angry with me, I'm done for.* The princess finally arrived at the king's quarters. He was not in the throne room, the attendant informed her; he was in his study meeting with several officials.

"I have an inkling of what they're discussing, Lord Attendant. I wish to see His Majesty at once." The attendant excused himself. He returned and requested the princess to accompany him. When Casica entered the study, all eyes turned to her. She felt suddenly small. She ignored the officials; and focused her gaze upon Ars.

"So here is the one who would attack my throne," the king announced darkly. This was no time for subtlety, she determined. "Your, throne? Never, Majesty," Casica answered. "My father is a king; to attack you would be as to attack him. But to defend my head from a renegade sword? yes, I would fight." She took a deep breath. "The issue at hand is why I must. It was my understanding, Majesty, that The Edict allowed for only a single occasion to murder me. Is this not so?"

Ars examined the tall girl suspiciously. Indignation filled her eyes and now seeped into her voice. Who was she to define the issue? Who the devil did this wench think she was? "Leave us!" the king ordered. His tone scattered everyone from the room.

"Sit." Casica moved to the chair indicated by Ars. The king walked around her. His expression was the same as when he inspected a new horse. "You attempted to kill my captain, Cassican," he declared. "What have you to say for yourself?"

"Your captain drew me into the fight. I had no choice. But I didn't aim to kill her, Ars. Had I, she would be dead." Ars leaned against his desk, considering her reply. He had no reason to believe she lied. The injured captain, herself, reported that having disarmed her, the Cassican healed her wound. But why? Why attack and not kill? Cassicans were an exasperating lot. "That may be, but to wield a sword against my guard is no light thing, as it is to wield my name. What dare gives you liberty to address me so?"

Casica met his look with one of confusion. "You are my father in this land," she said simply. Ars smirked. Was she mocking him or telling the truth as she saw it? "If you believe that, you are the only princess in this house to imagine such a thing." "Is that what it is, my king, mere imagination, or are you not my father by law?"

Ars crossed his arms, restraining his sense of being played by this foreigner. Still there was something innocent about the young woman; she intrigued him. "Here, woman, 'father-in-law' is an empty phrase describing association in marriage, only. Are you Cassicans still practicing adoption?" he asked on a hunch. Surely they'd given up that practice years ago.

"Yes, your majesty," she defended. "No one in Cassica is without a father or mother. We believe it is our duty to place the lonely in families." The king shook his head. Stupid Cassicans. "So a father-in-law to you Cassicans is a true father - by law." "Yes, Ars. A father through birth or adoption, they are one and the same." "No wonder you're a defeated race," he observed disgustedly.

Casica swallowed the insult. Ars felt to her like he was investigating the contents of some jar Berea kept on her shelves. "What am I to do with you, Cassican?" The woman remained silent. "Tell me," he prodded. "What do you think?"

Casica measure her words carefully. "It seems you should do as my father would...." "Which would be?" he asked, his impatience growing. "May I speak frankly?" "For God's sake, yes."

"By depriving me of your son's presence, you have left me and all that is mine vulnerable. I have no cover here, Majesty. Except by 'association in marriage,' and it appears *that* is insufficient shielding in this land. *Your* command delivered me into your family. It was not my choice. I cannot cover myself, sir. Even if I could, to do so would be unseemly for a daughter of the king, living as I am under your roof."

The aging king (aging even at this moment, he felt) moved to sit near his last born's wife. Despite his irritation, he found it refreshing, being spoken to so freely by a woman. God, he missed feminine company even if it came in the form of a dark curiosity.

"I'm not sure I like the idea of siring a Cassican," he replied. "You are an unruly, ignorant people. And as for your being unequal to the task of self-protection, your actions of the morning, wench, would indicate otherwise. However ... I can't have you hacking your way through my house. It's too messy." Ars caressed the wood beneath his hand. "I will cover you as you ask," he decided aloud. "Only - sheath yourself, woman," he warned, pointing at her.

Casica looked into eyes that reflected so much his son's. "Thank you, your majesty," she bowed. The king leaned back into his chair. "Oh, I'm 'Majesty,' now, am I?" he said, almost smiling. "I would wager that you're a chess player, girl. Are you?" "Yes, my lord. Some." "Good. You will come here often...." "As you wish,

Ars," she nodded. "And princess: never address me by name in public." "Of course, Your Majesty," Casica replied seriously. Ars returned the jar to its shelf for now.

"You are excused, Princess of Cassica. I have some explaining to do to my officials." Casica bowed low before the king. Turning she exited the study, relishing the thought of her own chamber in the sunrise wing.

It was the smell of dinner that awakened her. Clarece was setting her place at the table. "You rested well, my lady?" the slave asked, concerned. "Yes. And you?" Clarece bowed in answer. "My lady, I have taken liberty of asking Asla to bathe and massage you this evening, if you don't object." Casica sat at her plate and breathed deeply of the aroma. "I would never object to that, Clarece. Thank you." She had no energy to speak further. *Unruly and ignorant.* What a description for her entire race. No. She shouldn't spend any energy on thought either. She ate in silence.

The next sound she made was laughter. It was evening, and the exhausted woman reclined in a tub of hot, scented water. Tension in her shoulders eased as Asla's bath plied its work of cleansing the day's stain. Asla washed the princess' hair. Her gentle hands massaged Josquin's scalp, bidding her rest.

The insulit had remained silent, until now. Under her breath she muttered in g'Helderleicht, "You do have balls, my lady." The lady's laughter filled the bath room, sounding all the world like an emotional stretch.

"Oh, God, Asla, don't tell me that! I've enough shock for the day." She looked up into the girl's smiling face. "But if I do have them, tis a mutation born of Byzanthian air." Asla shook her head. "I rather doubt that, Casica," she grinned. "I'm quite certain you came here fully equipped.... Captain Jamai. Scads, my lady. You *do* know how to make an impression." Casica had no rejoinder. She splashed the water. Would this judgment day never adjourn?

It would - and did - wonderfully so. Leaving Josquin in bed, the day slipped under a blanket of sleep, by Asla's hands woven, as the insulit massaged it all farewell.

# XXII

arjan was on a roll.... "So the milkmaid turns to the horse and asks, 'Did you do that?'" The entire table roared with laughter. Though every morsel of his humor he served tasteless, the truth was the old slave knew how to tell a joke. He was the wing's oldest slave, but even with his years, Marjan remained positively lusty. Though shorter than many men, nothing concerning his virility lacked stature. It was reputed that Marjan had sired several dozen slaves in this province. And if it were possible for words and leers to breed, every woman round the slaves' table would have borne his offspring many times over.

Clarece smiled, more at her contemplations than Marjan's jokes. How she loved this time of evening when all thirty slaves gathered in celebration of another day's end. She was quite certain it was their joined company that made their simple porridge so tasty. Tonight was especially blessed. No one was absent from the meal: no one gone to breeding; none held in chains or stocks; none ill or injured. What a rare occasion, more wondrous in its rarity.

Clarece turned to Asla on her left. Even she seemed happy at this table that treated her so inhospitably. The senior slave smiled at her laughing friend, then grinned at Raina a few women down. The small slave was telling Penelope, "I don't get it...."

Clarece had read once that it was better to be a poor man eating bread in the company of kindness than to be rich, feasting in a palace of strife. Truly this was their case. It would seem impossible for thirty people, living as they did under constant threat of death and harm, to enjoy each other's company. God knew they didn't all or always get along. Even now, several slaves were not speaking to each other. But there was something about gathering together for food, that great common dependency, which wove their lives together if only for this hour. Even Jonas sometimes smiled in this setting.

Tarrant served tonight. A huge, powerful man, he always brought more food to the slaves than other servers - for the simple fact he could transport a heavier tub. He served the men first, claiming their dominance. Clarece suspected, however, that it was his desire for the women to have their food warm. For no one ate until all were served and the slaves' blessing offered. Tarrant had begun serving the women when Marjan birthed another story, this one involving a moat and a cantaloupe. Suddenly, he stopped. He and the men on his side of the table looked up the palace stairway. The women joined their gaze. Who would possibly be entering their pen?

Several gasps rose from the women. "My God, tis a female guard," Clarece heard someone whisper. What was an officer doing here? Glances crossed the table as slavemen and women wondered who was being arrested and for what. Clarece recognized the lieutenant at once. The guard looked cautiously about the room, searching for her, Clarece knew. Slowly, the chief slaveswoman rose.

*Good, there she is,* Adara thought upon seeing the chief. She had begun fearing she'd come to the wrong pen. She'd never been anywhere below in the castle. Now she stood in a deadly silenced group. The lieutenant felt surrounded by hate - and disgust. She glanced at the faces. They reflected rage. There wasn't a slave at the table who had not experienced torment by a female guard. Now here was one of their number in their pen. This guard was unarmed each slave noticed. In his mind, Jonas saw himself snapping her uncollared neck.

The slave Clarece was coming. Adara had never noticed how tall she was. With her vest unfastened and shirt pulled out, she seemed securely relaxed, almost authoritative. The suspicious slave looked Adara in the eye, her companions' presence buttressing her courage.

"How may we help you, lieutenant?" Clarece asked, not un-kindly. She hadn't a clue why Adara was here. The shaken lieu-tenant glanced briefly at the table. Pony! she felt naked without her sword. She turned back to Clarece and delivered, carefully, the message she had rehearsed all day.

"Slave Clarece, I harmed you yesterday in a most cowardly fashion. I have come to ask - I have come to beg - your forgive-ness for my attack upon you." Clarece stood, stunned. No one in all her life, except Asla, had ever begged her forgiveness for any-thing. And now, here was this lieutenant standing before her and her fellow slaves doing that very thing.

A surge of indignation swelled within her. *How dare you?* You and your kind have harmed every person in this room, and yet you dare think any of us would forgive you? As if mere words could somehow right your many wrongs - your cruelty towards me and those I know. "Go to the devil, guard" - such was the re-sponse forming in Clarece's mouth. But then her mind served a scene from long ago - or so it felt.

She was changing a dressing on Casica's butchered flesh, winc-ing as the tortured woman wept. "You will never forgive my peo-ple for this injustice, will you?" she asked, certain the Cassican hated her – and all Byzanthians. Casica turned painfully to face her questioner.

"Forgiveness is not an option, Clarece, not for anyone. But for those with authority, this is especially true." She studied her hands. "The consequences of a bitter heart reach too far, too many people in the circle. I haven't the luxury of unforgiveness, no more than you."

Clarece had not asked for an explanation from the exhausted foreigner then. Now, she received it. Her circle surrounded her.

The lieutenant waited fearfully: "'If she does not, I will come for you,'" the Cassican had said. It seemed quite certain she was asking the impossible. Was this slave human after all? Had she pride and vengeance? Clarece strained against her rage and grasped for something better. She recognized that fear in Adara's eyes. Enough of this.

"I forgive you for harming me." Adara sighed in relief. She would not die. Now that she was cleared, however, she didn't know what to do. So she said, "Thank you, slave."

Clarece had a most remarkable idea. She extended her mitten to the startled guard. "I am Clarece d'Casica." She felt proud to have the princess' name attached to her own. The guard reached out tentatively to the clawed hand. "I am Adara d'Solce Nana." "Welcome, Adara, to our pen," Clarece wished. "We are about to sup. Would you join us?"

*Would she join them?* Clarece heard her colleagues' thoughts. What the devil was she doing, inviting this enemy to their table? Angry, astonished looks flashed from one face to another. The slaves' response was lost on neither Clarece nor Adara; but the senior slave paid them no mind, keeping, instead, her attention upon the lieutenant, inviting her to do the same. Adara's thoughts reeled. She couldn't imagine eating with slaves but if she didn't, might not the Cassican consider it a personal insult? Clarece was waiting. "Thank you for your invitation. I will."

The esteem with which the slaves held Clarece was proved in that none of the twenty-nine left their seats. They were upset, certainly. But as certainly they determined not to dishonor their leader's invitation to this unwanted guest. Clarece smiled genuinely as she led Adara to sit beside her on the right. She glanced at Tarrant who then continued serving the porridge. A thick tension, about the consistency of their meal, hung over the group. Clarece turned to Marjan. Her look challenged him. *I dare you,* it said. "So Marjan, continue with your joke," she invited. "The cantaloupe did what?"

Marjan cleared his throat. "Like I was saying, this cantaloupe...." Clarece sighed, grateful her fellows were at least trying to resume normalcy. The fruit completed a particularly distasteful course in time for the slaves to pray. It was Joslin's turn to lead. The slaves bowed their heads, with only Asla and Adara abstaining.

"God," Joslin began, "thank you for food. Thank you for keeping us this day. May You will us another to serve the king and to live well before You. Amen." "Amen," the table chorused. The slaves ate hungrily. The presence of food in their mouths worked to release their lips. Little by little, like wind passing through a field, conversation swept the table.

Adara ate slowly, studying her porridge. This might be the most bizarre experience of her life, she thought. In a few minutes, however, curiosity overcame her and she looked at the faces and surroundings about her. The large table was made of roughly hewn wood, yet it shone with polish and was graced with a vase filled with dried flowers. The room was neat, all about, with everything in its place. Only the cold seemed to wander where it shouldn't. The men and women around her talked, some of them laughing, most sharing news of the day - though surely censored in her presence. There were more jokes and teasing. This could be her own guards' table if it were not for the fact these people each wore the silver collar of bondage about their throats.

Clarece turned to her. "What part of Solce Nana are you from?" she asked interestedly. "The east." "Are your family there?" "Yes," Adara explained. "I was transferred from the garrison."

"I knew a slave from that garrison," someone noted. "Did you know the slave Catinsa?" "The one with the eye patch? Yes," Adara acknowledged. "I believe he's still there...." The exchange was short and superficial yet significant.

Supper, as always, ended much too quickly. The clock sounded the three-quarter hour. Time to dismiss for evening service. "We need to go now," Clarece explained to her guest as slaves left their seats. "Tis time for us to prepare our masters for bed. Please finish you meal, Adara. Leave your utensils; I'll take care of them. And thank you for gracing our table with your presence." Clarece stood. The guard rose with her. "Good night," the slave said, and, as an afterthought wished, "God's blessings upon you." "Good night, slave," Adara replied, "and thank you." Within minutes, the noisy pen had grown silent and empty, leaving Adara to wonder if all this had been a dream.

The lone diner returned to her bowl. She studied the flowers and thought what an extraordinarily courageous thing these slaves had done, inviting her to their table. No guard she knew would have risked that. She left her bowl as instructed and rose to leave.

On the second stair, Adara paused for one final look; she was certain this would be her only sight of a slave pen. Standing there, she asked herself which stall was Clarece's. She had no idea. Lt. Adara turned and continued on her way. As she stepped into the east wing, she wondered, somewhere within herself, if it might not be this world above that was the dream.

"We had the most extraordinary visitation at supper tonight, my lady," Clarece announced to her mistra. "Who was that?" the princess asked. Casica, already changed into her gown, nestled in her covers, writing. Clarece joined her on the edge of the bed to bask in the warmth of her lady's brazier. "Lt. Adara of yesterday, my lady." "And what did the lieutenant want?" Casica asked curiously.

"My forgiveness, of all things. She asked forgiveness for harming me. Strange. In all my years, I've never heard of a guard doing such a thing. I wonder what was her motivation?" She looked questioningly into Casica. The princess offered no answer. "Was this your doing, Princess?" she asked directly.

"'Sounds like God's doing to me, Clarece." *Only God knew the mind of a Cassican,* the slave thought, smiling. "What are you smiling at?" Casica asked. "Nothing, my lady. I invited the lieutenant to dine with us. You know she did?" "You didn't poison her food, did you?" Casica teased.

"No, my lady," Clarece laughed. "I remembered what you said about forgiveness, about how those with authority can't afford to withhold it because of their circles of influence. I am nothing, but, still, wouldn't a guard think twice before harming people with whom she has eaten?"

Casica nodded approvingly. "You are a wise queen, Clarece. Your people are blessed to have you lead their circle." "I don't know if they feel that way tonight," Clarece grinned. "Asla's accusing me of turning Cassican. But tis my people who are the blessing."

Clarece drew the heavy comforter closer to her owner. "Are you warm enough, mistra?" "Always," her mistra replied, beaming. Clarece reddened with the attention. "Well, good night, Princess. Rest well." She kneeled and moved to leave.

"Chief?" The slave turned. "Did you grant it?" Clarece nodded. "Forgiveness? Yes. I did." Casica nodded back. "Then good night, your highness," Josquin wished. "And blessings upon your people."

Clarece bowed her head and walked thoughtfully below.

# XXIII

The chief slaveswoman stepped quickly, spirited along by the notion that possessed her. It had been an exciting afternoon, one filled with deliveries. She smiled still, and even blushed if she could see her reflection, at the memory of tea.

Casica had accompanied their drink with refreshment. Spice cake, aptly named, judging from the aroma with which it filled the princess' chamber. Clarece stared at the cake, astonished. It had been years since she'd sat in cake's company, and even then, the memories joined with it were stale with sorrow. But now, the food seemed to beckon her with a kindness she did not know how to embrace. Could not embrace, she realized, shamed. One could not eat this delicacy with one's hands, even if one had them. Clarece panicked and considered, for a moment, feigning illness to escape the disgraceful predicament.

But then, Casica surprised her. Wordlessly, her mistra placed beside the cake silverware to match the silver plate that held it. A silver spoon. A silver knife. A silver fork, each fashioned with the ring necessary for Clarece's use. The slave sat, awed. "These are mine?" she asked, stupidly, as if they would be for anyone else. Her owner smiled, teasingly. "If you like them - and if they fit, though Apsterdan assured me they would."

"If I *like* them?!" Clarece laughed. "I've never seen such fine work in handless ware. 'Twill put my tin spoon to shame." She studied the fork. "You say Apsterdan made these?" "Yes. He's a fine craftsman, is he not?" The slave nodded. All the pen knew of Apster's skill but to have it grace her life was unimaginable. His hands served those of owners and royals; hers were unworthy of such extravagance. Clarece's mitten went unconsciously to her neck. Silver around her throat. Silver around her finger. It would be the nearest thing to a wedding band she would ever wear. She looked shyly at her owner. "I don't know what to say, mistra. They are beautiful and even more so thoughtful." Her lady did not respond except to smile broadly. *Hurry up and try them!* she was thinking.

The nervous woman carefully fit the silver fork upon her thumb. It was heavy, so much more heavy than her tin spoon. The weight was comforting. She glanced at Casica before lowering her eyes. "I've never held a fork in my life," she observed. "This may take time." "Take all the time you need," the princess replied, reaching for her own silver fork and cutting a bite from her cake.

Clarece adjusted the implement; Apsterdan had improved its design; unlike her tin spoon which fastened to the top of her thumb, this ring was angled so that the fork's handle rested under her thumb and on top her claw. The new design felt unnatural in its unfamiliarity but certainly made more sense in use. The slave carefully cut a piece from the soft cake. She easily gathered it onto the fork and slowly brought it to her lips. There. The spicy presentation in her mouth announced her success. Clarece turned to smile at her hostess, careful to keep her mouth closed as she did. She bowed her head.

"The cake is very good, mistra. Thank you. And for the silver, nai gode." Casica smiled with pleasure. This was such a simple thing, she thought. Once again was she reminded how little it took to encourage people - herself included. With this simple gift she felt queen of the world. It was always her favorite privilege of royalty: the power to bless.

Clarece warmed at this memory, now as she walked, and smiled to herself thinking of the afternoon's next delivery: Solange's child. Solange had been a member of her pen four years. During this time, she had produced three offspring for her mistra, Countess Dolca, the young wife of Sir Nahalt. Nahalt was a senior member of the king's knights, a brave man and just. Dolca had lived at the palace for seven years now.

Clarece remembered her arrival: there was talk of insult, placing such an esteemed member of the king's world in the east wing, but necessity ruled. Yet when a chamber in the west wing did become available, the countess declined. She preferred her east chamber, she said. Clarece liked to think that the spirit of her beloved wing was the reason. More than one person had commented on how the east wing felt warmer and more spacious than the other wings though certainly, it was not. It pleased the chief slaveswoman, this reputation of the world she slavishly ruled.

Clarece was happily relieved. Solange had bred well and delivered easily. The girl child she had birthed appeared healthy as did her mother. With joy of this sight arrived a tinge of sorrow. The east guild would be losing this valued member. Dolca had determined to transfer Solange to a town far north of Byzanthia. Transfers were not uncommon and Dolca had a sister who needed a fine slave.

What was uncommon (in fact, illegal) about the transfer was that it would include the babe. The sorrow Solange suffered with the transfer of each her children moved the compassionate owner. Her slave had suffered enough. "Mistra told me I have slaved her well," Solange confided to her chief. "She wants me to go to her sister with my babe - as though it were someone else's I wean. Think, Clarece, what this means. I will care for my own child - all her life. Have you ever heard of such a thing?"

Clarece smiled at the news. Dolca played a dangerous game, but she would not be found out. No one would question the explanation - it was common enough. The babe would be weaned by her mother, collared and kept in the house as an additional slave. The young woman's eyes glowed. "I won't lose this one," Solange continued. "I will miss mistra, but will keep her kindness all my life."

"When will you leave the palace?" Clarece asked quietly. No one else was bedded in the delivery keep; still, the words they spoke were criminal if heard. "I will leave in eight weeks, the time of transfer. The child will come to me outside the city." Clarece nodded approvingly. "'Tis a good plan, Solange. 'Tis good for you and the child both." The chief woman reached for Solange's offering. She held the warm life closely - carefully. "You are blessed little one," she whispered. "You will be known by the one who

loves you. Long life to you," she wished, kissing the pink brow
tenderly. She returned the infant to her mother and resumed her
role.

"Have you need of anything, Solange?" The slave shook her
head. "No. A servant is providing mistra's meals and she is sending portions to me. More warmth would be better, but we are
well-kept." Clarece nodded, pleased. Dolca was, indeed, a kind
mistra. "We'll miss you at our table, but you go to a far better one,
I think," she offered. "I will check on you in the weeks to come,
but if I can help you in anyway, send word."

The mother nodded, grateful. Her chief was another kind presence in her life. It was sad about her hands. Most likely they were
the reason this important woman had never bred. "Thank you,"
is what she said.

With a final touch to the unnamed child, Clarece made her way
quietly from the chamber. How many slaves had she seen transferred, sold or killed? she wondered absently, making her way to
her wing. She didn't truly want to know. The chief slaveswoman
avoided this line of thought; it only served to discourage her. She
may live many more years and likely would lose more friends.
She pushed against the image of Asla, but too late. Becoming a
sala of an insulit was a heart-foolish mistake. Insulit were destined to die young. Clarece fought the sorrow that nudged her;
she had been in this little world of hers for a very, very long time.

But it was in this world, a strange one indeed, made of silver
bonds and silver forks, that a truly inspired idea came to her. A
risky one. But she felt more open to risk these past few weeks. If
Dolca could hazard defying a law of slavery, so could she. Often
Clarece had considered the kindnesses Casica performed for her
and felt powerless to repay. But now she had a currency even
the princess did not possess. Regal access. Not the kind her mistra presently enjoyed, visiting with the king as she did – playing
chess and editing documents. But the kind she wished for and
could not initiate.

For months Casica resided in the palace, yet not a single woman had invited her to their chambers. Even the Cassican, who
seemed to live by rules of her own making, did not violate the
high law of propriety: she would not, could not, invite others
into her life without their doing so first. And no one had. Perhaps

had Bastien been present, this would have been different. But he wasn't and the lack of his person encouraged no one in the palace to venture hospitality to the strange, enemy woman who came into their midst beaten and humiliated. Clarece enjoyed her teas with Casica. She was a wonderful hostess and engaging conversationalist. And she no longer doubted her mistra's enjoyment of herself. Yet, she remained a lowly slave. Casica was a princess and needed the company of her peers, to bask in the light of women as she.

Was not Dolca as she? Was she not also of royal blood and, more importantly, of a kindred mind, at least regarding her kindness to slaves? And if with slaves, perhaps in other areas as well. Dolca would make a fitting companion, Clarece decided, winding her way through the north wing. She was intelligent and attentive - and younger than any other of the east wing's occupants. She might even become Casica's friend.

The senior slave skipped up a slave passage and emerged upon her wing. There was Dolca's door. The question now was, how to deliver this conceived idea in a productive manner? She reached up and knocked with her spoon. Inspiration overshadowed her. The door took its time opening, the reason of which became apparent. The countess, herself, answered.

"Clarece," Dolca acknowledged, surprised. The chief slave never came to her chamber. "Countess," Clarece replied, kneeling humbly before the royal. Taking a single step back, the slave bowed her head in labor. "Greetings, my lady," she wished. "Greetings. And to what do I owe thanks for bringing the chief slaveswoman to my door?" the royal asked, not unkindly. "Nothing to owe thanks, my lady, I am sure, seeing as I am certainly more a bother than a favor."

Dolca smiled. She liked this slave. Her own Solange spoke highly of the quiet, maimed woman. It was said the tall slave slept with a guard in the king's service. It was said also she could read anything with a glance. The countess stared at the mittened hands. She had difficulty believing either rumor; but, thought she, sensing the presence of authority in the collared form, she may yet do both.

"You favor me with your presence, Clarece," she replied. "What brings you today?" Clarece smiled. She liked this woman.

She was kind and respectful. "I come on behalf of the guild to congratulate you on your newest acquisition, my lady. Solange has produced a fine child for you. Both mother and infant seem healthy. We are thankful." "Yes," Dolca agreed. "I do believe they are well. Thank you for your wishes." Clarece bowed. "I also come to inquire of your needs, seeing that Solange is bedded and you have not employed another slave. Is there anything I may do to assist you at this time, my lady?"

The countess eyed the tall slave, appraisingly. It was worth a try. "There is something you may do for me, Clarece. Tell me: are you for sale?" Clarece started at the question. This wasn't what she had in mind. "To my knowledge, no, my lady. But I may be mistaken. My faults are legion; it could be my lady tires of me. You could inquire if you desire. Perhaps you could invite Mistra to your chamber, being as you are - it is commonly known - the most gracious hostess in the wing."

Dolca frowned skeptically. She was being played. This slave was playing her, she thought smiling. "I am, am I?" "It is commonly known, my lady. As it is known of your generous hospitality in serving newcomers to the palace." "It is, is it?" "Yes, my lady," the slave bowed. The countess was certain if she looked hard enough, she would see a smile gracing those hidden lips.

"So you think it would behoove me to invite the Cassican to my chambers for tea - or a meal, perhaps?" "Almost certainly, my lady," the slave agreed. "My mistra has a fine tongue to go with her appetite. Through her you may acquire a lowly slave but if not, you will most certainly gain a royal conversation."

Dolca crossed her arms. *Forget the owner - invite the slave,* she thought. Still she had considered doing this very thing, inviting the Cassican princess, but dismissed it. It seemed too far-fetched to hope a beaten girl from a foreign land would be fitting company. And the rumor she had heard about the fight with Jamai, well, that couldn't be true. However, what Clarece said *was* true - she did commonly invite new tenants to her table. And she regularly met with other royals for a meal and cards. This childless woman enjoyed filling her world with people.

"So what does your foreign mistra know of me, slave Clarece?" she asked, curious. Curious for the answer and curious to see how the slave would play the question. "Nothing, my lady. She has not yet gained the blessed knowledge of your person and certainly has no awareness of my speaking with you at this time." "Oh," observed Dolca, "I see." So this was Clarece's idea. "Well, Heaven forbid that I withhold from her the blessed knowledge of myself." Clarece smiled. This would most certainly be a live birth.

Dolca glanced at her life. A few days from now should work. "May I send with you, chief slaveswoman, an invitation to your mistra? I may yet have you in my service." The slave bowed low. "Of course, my lady," she replied. "We may see if the fates desire you the burdensome encumbrance of such as I." Dolca laughed. "One moment, chief."

Clarece waited patiently as the door closed in her face. It was most certain they would make a good pair. The door opened with time and a letter. "Here, chief slave. Please accompany this to your mistra." Clarece kneeled humbly. "As you wish, countess. I thank you for gracing me with your blessed person. I believe you will find the royal favor returned."

Dolca shook her head. This slave was a piece of work. "You are dismissed, slave Clarece." she announced. With a bow and kneel the burdensome encumbrance spun gracefully and continued her way, bearing with her the joy of an expectant delivery wrapped in the warmth of invitation.

# XXIV

Casica sat outside in the garden, a canvas and the familiar scent of oils before her. Heaven, it was good to be painting again! The thick growth of leaves above her cooled the unusually warm day. In front of her rose the east wing, her subject. During her art tours led by Clarece the princess had noticed several paintings forming a collection of differing perspectives of the Byzanthian palace. Surprisingly none displayed the east wing, a fact which befuddled the artist in her; the east wing possessed a lovely garden and a more encompassing view of the palace lawn than any of the other wings.

It was Clarece's opinion that the absence of pictorial record hinged upon historical use for the wing. The sunrise wing was the most recent of all the residential areas of the palace. As such, it housed the overflow of the king's keeping. In it you would find no direct descendants of royalty - with the exception of the last born prince and his wife. More peculiarly was the presence of slaves living, as they did, directly under the wing's former storage chamber. For every other wing, slaves were stored away from the owners they slaved; servants, instead, lived below. The short of it was that living in the east wing was the least honorable of any palace residence. It was as though history had sifted its tenants and only the lesser royals landed there.

*More's the pity,* thought the princess. She would not trade her morning view for any in the west wing. Even now the sun poured upon it light from above, and her position afforded the josquin views of parapets and towers, garden and fountain, lush grounds and a picturesque path leading to the guard house in the distance. The possibilities for presentation intrigued her; she was enjoying her task. For too long she had neglected this integral part of her gifting. *I just wish I had my painter's blade...,* she thought.

Next to her kneeled Clarece, engrossed in a small volume containing the history of aqueduct development in the western sphere. Casica glanced from her work to God's. Only God knew the mind of a slave and only He, certainly, could comprehend how a topic so exactingly boring could capture the attention of the chief slaveswoman. The princess smiled. Already Clarece was more than half finished with the tantalizing information. Despite her doubts, Casica looked forward to hearing the tutor's recitation of this knowledge. Somehow, she knew, Clarece would manage to present even this mundane subject so that Casica, too, would be carried away by the world of transported water.

The slave felt her mistra's gaze. She looked up and smiled, glancing into the canvas. Her owner was gifted, of that there was no doubt. Already, her mixture of light, color and darkness worked its craft conjuring the three-dimensioned scenery into a two-dimensional format. "What do you think?" the princess asked her charge. "I think you should have it hung with the others, my lady. You do it justice." The slave looked about herself. "'Tis a pity this view is so unknown by most of the castle's residents. What we lack in royal persons, we rule in beauty. Ours is the best wing," she announced, her voiced filled with pride.

Casica nodded, agreeing. She watched as Clarece's gaze turned from the canvas to her right, toward the guards' quarters. It was clear where and with whom were her thoughts. Josquin considered a moment then tore a page of her drawing pad. She reached for her paintbrush and sketched a short note. "Clarece," she asked, returning the slave's focus. "Would you please deliver this note to Sgt. Poul? Give it to him, personally, and wait for his response."

"Sgt. Poul?" the surprised slave asked, delighted. "Of course, my lady! I will go at once." Clarece rose to a half-kneeling position to receive her owner's message. Bowing, she turned and walked quickly towards her heart.

Casica stopped her work and watched with interest. On the horizon blew a blond wind. Asla was returning from the city by way of the west path and even now smiled at the approach of her senior friend. Whenever these two came together, the Cassican was learning, their combined affect upon each other rendered delightful skits rivaling any performances produced on stage. The two friends complemented each other almost too perfectly Clarece with her somber propriety and Asla with her passionate playfulness. If they weren't such dear friends, Casica thought, they would be irreconcilable enemies. She relaxed in her chair; the curtain rose....

Upon seeing her friend, Asla jogged lightly up the path. Clarece smiled at her approach. It was good to see her stallmate returning so early from her services in the city. She worried when she remained after dark. Asla stopped her jog and slid in the gravel up to her friend. With a flourish, she announced, not quietly, "Hail, Chief Slaveswoman! We lower forms pay homage to you!" With this, the blond woman knelt fully upon the ground, assuming the slave posture for meeting the king outside his throne room. Clarece glanced nervously about for witnesses.

"Scads, insulit, get up! You want I should lose my head?! Crispus, you'll be the death of me." The younger woman lifted her body and smiled winsomely. "As you wish, oh great one." From this resting kneel position, the gymnast in Asla leapt full into the air and executed a backward somersault, landing within inches of where she had sprung. The older slave jumped back, instinctively holding her hands before her in protection. "Scads, Asla!" she exclaimed. "You know I hate when you do that! You take my wits with your ways. You'll fall, someday, and break your frappin neck!"

Asla laughed good-naturedly at her friend. How she loved doing this kind of thing to her. Clarece made the perfect foil. "Clarece," she announced again, "I am so low in the eternal scheme of things that if I do fall, I can only go up! So where are you off to?" "I'm delivering a message from my mistra." "Oh?..." the insulit asked suspiciously, "and to whom do you deliver it?" "To Sgt. Poul of the royal guard," came the official reply. "Oh...." Asla repeated, her tone dripping with seduction. "Don't even think it," her friend warned.

"Too late! 'Already have. Well, what does your message say?" "I'm sure I wouldn't know," Clarece replied, indignant. "Sealed, yes?" "Sealed, no." "Honestly, Clarece, your honesty is as boring as...." She struggled with the image. "Boring as what?" the poet challenged. "Boring as... as bread crust?" Clarece shook her head; she was not impressed. "Lame, Asla," she declared, "very lame." "Not as lame as you," the g'Helderleit smiled, in blunt reference to the woman's deformity.

Clarece laughed. Only Asla could tease her about her hands without her feeling in anyway insulted or hurt. The g'Helderleit's inclusion of this painful fact of her life into the arena of comedy, warmed the woman. It made her feel not so much an outcast; in Asla's eyes, she looked like everyone else. The fact that no one had spent as much time caring for her weakness only made Asla's humor more precious. She had won the ruined hands' trust and had earned the right to tease them at will.

This privilege was mutual. Clarece, alone, could address Asla as "insulit" without provoking any wrath or humiliation in the vulnerable woman. Her particular use in slavery was for Asla what Clarece's hands were to her: a point of deepest shame, the type that could not hide, displayed as it was, so nakedly. For Asla, Clarece's references to her trade affected a similar result of bringing the outcast more closely within the realm of humanity.

It was a strange dance between these two, one perfected through years of partnering. Though neither woman would have put words to it, their enjoyment of each other, even in places most dark, proved that good reigned supreme in all courts, no matter how cruelly treated might the subjects be.

Clarece studied her friend. If she didn't stop Asla now, she'd pester her to no end. "So what are you so happy about?" she asked, cutting off anything else the insulit may plan. With a dazzling smile, Asla produced a paper from her vest pocket. "Look!" she ordered excitedly. Clarece glanced at Asla's service schedule. "So... you're laying the twins?" she asked, confused.

Asla poked indignantly at the paper. "Not that day. The next!" Clarece laughed at her friend's reaction. "I see it, I see it," she nodded. "You've the day off. Congratulations!" "Yes, a day off!" the insulit rejoiced. "I know it's a mistake, but I'm certain I'm not the one to bring it to Edsner's attention. A day free of men...." She looked to the sky, and, spreading her arms above her proclaimed: "There *are* gods in heaven!"

The insulit's eyes softened with genuine gratitude. A day of rest. She had not known one for so long. Her body needed it. Her heart, or whatever that place in her was, needed it also. Clarece noticed the change in her friend's demeanor. "I'm happy for you, As. You need a Sabbath," she observed seriously.

The insulit glanced at the ground and then found her friend's eyes. "Clarece, I wish a favor of you." The senior slave looked curiously. Asla rarely asked for anything. "What is it?" "I... I want you to ask for the day off, too. I want for us to spend that day together." Clarece was incredulous. "Ask the day off? From what? Living? Asla, I'm a slave, not a servant." "*I* know that," Asla rejoined, "but when was the last time you and I spent the day together?" "Asla, we've never spent the day together." "That's just my point, Rece. We've known each other what, four years? and we've never had a single day to share."

Clarece turned her eyes towards the gravel. "Such a day is for freewomen, Asla. Not ones as us." "But it could be, if we tried," her friend countered. "Clarece," Asla continued softly, saddened by the truth of her words, "I don't think we'll ever have another opportunity like this. Edsner won't make this mistake twice. And I feel my time is short." Clarece closed her eyes against her friend's prediction. Asla wasn't toying with her; she meant it.

"Please, Asla," she pled. "Please don't say that. You break my heart." "'Tis true, and you know it. Don't you want to see the city, Clarece? Wouldn't you want to share one day with me?" "More than I would the city...."

Asla shied from her friend's love. "Then would you at least think about asking Casica? She's human, Clarece. She'll understand. She would deny you nothing." Asla's observation rang true. Still.... "But I would not to presume upon her kindness," Clarece offered. "To the truly kind, there is no presumption," Asla observed. "Casica would consider it a gift to - bless you - as she says."

The senior slave brought a mitten to her lips. She was considering, teetering. Asla knew it was best to leave the matter where it was. "Promise me, you'll think about it. Whatever you decide, I accept that. Just promise you'll give it a thought." As if she could not give it or anything else thought. "I'll think about it," the older woman agreed. "But I'll not make any guarantees - ."

Asla smiled. "That's good enough for me. I should go now. I need a bath. Thank you, great lady," she concluded bowing and kissing the startled woman's mitten. Clarece rolled her eyes. Asla was positively insufferable this day. "You are dismissed, g'Helderleit," she replied, playing along. "As you wish, your highness." Her friend bowed and as a parting remark, gently took Clarece's hand and spun her gracefully in dance.

The Cassican sat smiling. Her paintbrush stuck out between her teeth, like a pipe, as was her custom. Kai, how she wished she'd been privy to that verbal exchange. What a piece of work were those two. The artist looked to her canvas. The beautiful landscape paled in comparison to what she had just witnessed. What she had concluded before, Josquin concluded again: in its truest form, people were the only art worth recording. In all the world, no beauty existed as that of people who love.

She took her pipebrush and dipped it carefully in paint. This would be her only landscape, at least for a season, she determined. The physical landscapes of Byzanthia simply could not compete with the human ones she was discovering about her. Fascinating people filled her world. Portraits. Yes. After this, she would begin recording human subjects. To the artist, this was a humbling proposition; for all the world would prove too small a canvas.

Clarece found Poul in the great room. The master swordsman was oiling his blades. The slave watched for several minutes, relishing the opportunity to embrace with her eyes the one she loved. Their time would be too short. Always.

The sandy-haired man with a ponytail - something he kept from his Cassican days, he said - studied his work. Tomorrow, he would be training a class of second year recruits in the use of two-handed sword play. They were an inexperienced group, having never fought in battle. It should be a challenging endeavor. An approaching figure interrupted his thoughts. *Clarece*, he thought excitedly, rising to meet her.

The tall slave kneeled fully before him, but not out of observance to protocol - a half-kneel, would do. For the slave who could not do otherwise, the gesture served as an embrace. "Clarece," the guard spoke softly. "Tis joy to see you." The woman rose, and bowed her head. No one was near. She looked into his face and smiled. "And you, Poul."

A guard entered the room. Clarece bowed her head and offered the princess' note. "From my mistra, my lord. I am to await your response." Poul glanced at the paper. His cousin must be painting again. "Feed Rigel. Speak with her," the note read in Cassican. That's all. Poul smiled. He owed her one.

"And how *is* your mistra?" he inquired. "Well. She is painting the east wing - a portrait of the east wing, that is," she clarified. "And Asla? How is she?" "Well." The slave grew painfully aware of a growing number of guardsmen coming into the room. Her continued presence was highly inappropriate. "And you, Clarece?" Poul asked quickly, sensing the woman's discomfort. "How are you?" "I am well, my lord," she said softly. "Your response?"

Poul sighed deeply, longing to keep her with him. "Tell her ... tell her I will, I did, and I thank her." Clarece nodded, and for a single second risked a glance into his eyes. "Good day, my lord," she wished. "With your permission...." He didn't want to give it. "Yes, Clarece. Good day." She kneeled and walked quickly from the room, whisking his response and heart away with her.

Asla stopped to visit with the artist. "You've sent your slave on her favorite path, I see," she said in her native tongue. "Yes. She looked like she needed the exercise," Casica replied in g'Helderleicht. "Indeed. It will help her sleep better," agreed the insulit, suggestively. "Gives her *deeply* satisfying dreams." Casica laughed, embarrassed. This seemed to be a good time to ask what she had wondered recently.

"Speaking of *paths*, Asla.... I've been wondering, when you return to the palace late, the doors must be locked. How do you gain entry to your quarters?" The insulit glanced at the oils. "By way of the southwest door." "Oh," replied the princess, noticing a sudden discomfort in the slave. She couldn't know Asla's thoughts, but she felt them.

Asla was seeing the men at the door. They were not guards as was the case in daylight. They were soldiers, with little connection to palace life. They knew her for one thing, and made her "pay" for the undesired privilege of returning so late, unaccompanied, to the palace. It was often not so much what transpired in the city that made her nighttime services so unpleasant as it was what she endured upon her return.

"That's a roundabout trek, I would think," the princess observed, "especially on a bitter night." The insulit made no response. "You know, my door is never locked," continued Casica. "It would be a shorter walk for you, here along the west path. I invite you: use my chamber as your entry - day or night. You can warm by my coals... and there is either mead or wine in the sitting area, whichever Clarece allows me."

Asla studied the princess. Was she serious? "I come and go at strange hours, Princess...." she said, feeling out her sincerity. "You won't disturb me, Asla. My offer is sincere." Asla weighed the proposal. She wasn't one to deny herself for the sake of propriety. "I accept," she said. "Thank you. I'll tell Rece to keep wine on hand."

Asla turned her attention to look admiringly at the construction coming to life on Casica's canvas. "I've never seen a painting of the east wing. Too filled with low-lives, I think." "Well, tis time we low-lives showed our true colors," the princess replied. "The world may think us the wrong side of the royal wing, but we know better, don't we?"

Josquin's words didn't escape the insulit. "I don't know, Casica. This afternoon...," Asla shook her head. "I feel like a sty," she concluded softly. "'Sleeping with pigs does not make one a sty,'" the princess offered, repeating a familiar g'Helderleit adage. "That may be. But sleeping with them certainly makes one stink...."

Casica stood. She looked into the young woman's face. The white hair of her mane and eye lashes reflected like sunbursts in the afternoon light. The princess took a deep breath. "You smell of beauty to me," she offered.

"That's because yours is a fragranced world, Princess," Asla replied. She lowered her head and stared at her feet. Gods, this woman felt so pure next to her. How could Casica bear to be near her? Josquin reached tenderly for the young woman's face, her familiar warmth filling her. Asla looked up into dark brown eyes. "If you only knew, Casica," she whispered.

"Tell me"

Clarece lay in her cot, restless. Scads! how she wished Asla never would have brought up this free day. Only that insulit would think of something like that. No normal slave would ever so much as imagine a day from service. Such a concept simply did not exist in their world. What on earth was she thinking? It was treasonous to even think about this, probably. Slaves did not have free days. Of course, Clarece thought wryly, neither did they have tea, or eye contact, or bread at the ocean or horse rides or - pony! It wasn't Asla's fault at all, Clarece concluded, frustrated. It was Casica's.

The possibility of considering Asla's proposal would never have existed in her previous life when her world was defined, solely, by Bastien. But with the Cassican, kai! everything in her world had changed. Her world wasn't made only of an owner, anymore. It had widened, widened so much it now included herself.

During these past months, much had awakened in the slave; things, she was certain, that if known in the freeworld, would condemn her to death. No slave had the right to think and feel what she did these days. If she weren't careful, she would outgrow her collar and strangle herself in the process. She should forget this entire issue. In fact, she should go upstairs and take back from the princess everything she had given. No more shared confidences; no more shared meals; no more shared thought. No more excursions into freedom. That was what she should do. That would be the wisest course.

But she couldn't. Living with Casica had awakened not only desire but knowledge. Not the kind of knowledge she gleaned for years from the library. But self-knowledge. Clarece was knowing herself in ways she'd never dreamed. She was seeing herself in a mirror that freedom fashioned in a land that had never known slavery. And she liked what she saw. She wanted to see more. It was as if the Cassican had captured her soul and preserved it in a locket of remembrance. The freewoman held that locket open as undeniable proof that she, though a slave bound and broken, bore the image of Something greater. She too dwelled in the family of God.

Crispus! even her theology was shaken, fretted the woman. She didn't know where she stood in the spiritual schema anymore. If it were true that she, like Casica, a queen, were the daughter of God... then her whole world must change. She must change. Clarece shook her head, exasperated. What was she saying? Her whole world already had changed. She had crossed into regions of desire and hope that refused denial. Even if she could return from whence she'd come, she didn't want to.

She tread on dangerous ground, Clarece knew; freedom could devour a slave. The mirror may very well fall upon her and crush her to death. She looked above to where the princess slept. But what if it didn't? What if, instead, she stepped into the reflection, and found on the other side what she had sought all her life? The woman she truly was.

Survival was as deeply bred into the woman as was slavery. But that, too, must be abandoned. There was no going back.

# XXV

The queen of Cassica sat stoically, awaiting the downfall of her faithful knight. He had served well these past weeks, but her kingdom's good must outweigh his own. The onyx horseman had kept her enemy's bishop and rook on the run for quite some time. She would miss him. She would sings songs about him, his liege thought, smiling within.

Without, Ars could tell nothing about this accursed Cassican woman. She wore a poker face to the wrong game, he thought, for the hundredth time. Their game was lasting weeks longer than he had anticipated. True, their meetings never lasted beyond a half-hour; even so, she was outlasting every move he made and, at times, seemed to be playing him for a fool. Women. That's what he got for playing the cunning sex.

*Look at her,* the king sat, thinking. The young woman was carelessly sipping some of his best scotch, studying a letter he'd written for an ambassador of R'Heina. She'd served in that court for a season as a representative from the Cassican counsel. Her role was peripheral, she explained, but she had become quite familiar with the R'Heina ambassadors' need for exact protocol concerning diplomatic correspondence. She now edited his throne's request for shipping rights into the western region of the distant land.

As for her, well, she loved this kind of work and enjoyed correcting the king's scribes' errors. Even now she smiled at an innocent mistake in transcription: with a single misplaced dot in the word "caldoord," the scribe had unwittingly rendered the shipping lanes as a brothel; the king was requesting use of R'Heina's whore houses....

"What the devil are you smiling at?" the frustrated king asked. "Nothing, Ars. Just doing my job." "Well, you wouldn't be smiling at all if you knew the fate of your knight. Kiss his ass, good-bye, Cassican." "'Tis not an ass, your majesty," the young girl replied, seriously, focused still on the letter. "'Tis a percheron he rides." "Well, kiss him good-bye, too. Your move, wench."

Casica placed the document on the table and imbibed further of Ars reserves. She studied the growing vacancies on the board. The king was leading her exactly where she wanted him to be. Ars studied his daughter-in-law, as he did regularly during their short visits. Today she wore a crimson blouse, no vest. Her body filled the cloth pleasingly. Beneath the crimson, he could see the pobble stones of her josquin's necklace glow. Her eyes, alert and bright, scanned the marble battlefield. She was keen, this one. Intelligent and elusive. And beautiful.

Again, Ars' eyes confirmed his mind's decision to keep his son in Valdera away from this woman. Bastien would lay her in a heartbeat. And Ars was unprepared to have his crown bed this enemy mystery. She seemed innocent enough. It could be that K'eran had not sent his daughter to spy and poison his land. Still... he could not chance it, not yet. A josquin could kill him, his sons and his whole house without anyone knowing it. She could not be trusted. Not only that, Ars' house was little prepared to have half-breeds roam the royal brood. But he *was* prepared to offer her a concession.

"Royal gilt," he began. The princess looked up expectantly. She had grown to appreciate Ars' strange choice of pet names. "Gilt" always proved a good omen. "I have been considering a gift for you, seeing how you have managed several days without hacking any of my people." "You are most gracious, majesty." "Always...," the king smiled pleasantly. "I give you leave to correspond with your family."

All humor fled the girl's face. *Good,* Ars thought. *She can be startled.* "My lord?" Casica asked, incredulous. "Yes. You may write your Cassican herd. Give your ramblings to me, personally. I'll see they are conveyed - both sides of the channel."

"Thank you, Father!" Josquin gushed. She had dreamt of this privilege but never truly expected it. "Thank you. I've some scratchings I could send now. Do you wish them sealed or no?" The king presented a shocked expression. "Sealed. Of course. I've no desire to read your mind."

Casica grinned. *Yes you do*, she thought. *You'd love to know why I'm making this next move*. What she said was, "I'll send my charge to your attendant today with my letters." "Do so. I will return her corpse to you by evening," Ars responded casually, sipping his wine. "*Your majesty*?" came her shocked reply.

The king of Byzanthia gazed ominously. Casica thought back to Clarece's references to Ars' hate; she had never truly believed it. Why would a king target a slave? "Why do you hate her so?" Ars studied his glass. "What do you know about that gimlet?" he asked. Casica fought back her initial response. "Only the little she's told and what I've observed. She is faithful and good." The king snorted. "She is devil's spawn." Anger laced Casica's fear. "Why do you say that? And if you believe it, why do you allow her life?"

Ars lowered his goblet. "I do not answer to you, Cassican," he replied darkly. "I give you warning: keep her from me or I will dis-allow her life." Casica swallowed her rejoinder; indeed it was not her place to question, especially when her friend's life hung so tenuously in a balance, made of what, she could not imagine. She nodded, humbly. "Yes, your majesty." The matter, she dropped. She looked at the playing field. She would remain patient and bide her time. Another, greater game was in play here.

Casica considered for a moment, then lifted a lowly pawn, one heretofore untouched. One space, only one. The king watched, astounded. With this single move, everything about his game had suddenly changed.

A knock came to the door. "Your Majesty?" asked his attendant, interrupting. "What?!" "Your counsel is being assembled." *Whose counsel?* he wondered. Ars glanced suspiciously at the woman before him. Innocence reigned in her eyes, but what ruled her heart?

"Your document, Majesty," she said softly, handing him his letter. "It is ready. Thank you for the pleasure of your company. The day after next?" Ars eased back into his chair, his momentary panic subsiding. "Yes." "I will bring my correspondence then. Again, I thank you," she offered, bowing her head low. The princess of Cassica finished her drink and departed calmly his presence.

"So how goes the battle, my lady?" Clarece asked, trying to mask her nervousness. She had practiced, the entire day, her request for time away next week. "Slow. Very slow. The king is a - cautious - player." Casica refrained from using the word "paranoid" which more aptly fit. "He doesn't know what to make of me, I think. You see," she explained pouring milk into her friend's tea, "His Majesty is accustom to playing men - not women. Men think and plot like this," she said, moving her hand from her nose, straight out. "Women, we do this," she smiled, moving her hand in a series of circles.

Clarece laughed. "So you think circles beat straight?" the slave asked. "Not always, but we'll see. Ars is *very* good. But I think within five weeks, he'll have me exactly where I want him." Clarece waited for her mistra to drink. Her nervousness returned. God, what was she doing? Asla's silence on the matter only increased her desire to ask the unimaginable. Fortunately, the princess was in a talkative mood, allowing her mental freedom to rehearse further. Clarece finished her tea without awareness. Every tick of the clock fed her panic.

"We have spiced cake and rum bread," Casica was saying. Clarece's heart pounded. Anxiety rose within her like a sneeze. It was now or never. "Which do you prefer?" her owner asked.

"Calsdaynextfree," Clarece blurt out. *Moron!* came her immediate thought. *You idiot! That's not what she asked and that's not how you rehearsed.* The slave's head dropped in humiliation. Casica's was up in confusion. Was Clarece experiencing another break, speaking Sladdish again? She hadn't a clue what she had just said.

"Well, this is unexpected," the princess voiced aloud. "I'm in hostess' hell. You've requested something I don't have. At least I don't *think* I have it. What was it you wanted?"

Clarece sighed. What a fool she was. This was a sign. She never should have asked. "Nothing, my lady," she mumbled defeated.

"No...," the princess prodded. "You want something, Clarece... what is it?" Clarece felt all the world as though her owner were calling her out. The slave took a deep breath. Looking into her mistra's face, she asked plainly: "I would like to have next Calsday free, my lady. Asla has the day and I wish spend it with her in the city." There. She had said it.

Casica smiled broadly. There. She had said it. "Of course you may have the day. Now would you like the spiced cake or rum bread?" Clarece sat confused. Was she serious? Was it this easy? "Rum bread, please," she said, dumbly. Surely, this couldn't be the matter's end. There must be a catch.

Clarece watched as her mistra served a slice of rum bread on her silver plate. She put spiced cake upon her own and began to eat. Clarece was still watching her when the princess stopped and looked up. "Is something wrong?" she asked. The question jerked the slave back into the present. "No, mistra," she answered quickly and began to fit her thumb into the silver fork's ring.

Casica glanced aside toward her charge, a grin brushing her lips. Only God knew the mind of a slave, she thought. And only God knew the mind of a king. A pang of worry pricked the woman's heart. Ars' hate for Clarece was frightening. What could she possibly have done to provoke such loathing? It must be more than her deformity, certainly. But what?

"The bread is very good," Clarece noted, fighting the distaste of sustained nervousness. The women ate in silence, each lost in their own frettings. Casica broke the verbal fast. "What will you do in the city, Clarece?" The slave swallowed before answering. "I don't know, mistra. I've never been to the city." "Really? You've lived here fourteen years and have never seen the royal city?" Clarece shook her head. "I've never seen any city. Asla knows all the city, though. I'm sure she has a full day planned." "Well, I haven't seen the city either. You must take me on tour." "Yes, lady." Clarece still sounded uncomfortable. Casica frowned.

"Is there something else you wanted to ask me?" The senior slave slowly lowered her fork. She hated how her owner could see her. "Well, yes, Princess. I am wondering, what must I do to earn this day? Surely you would not simply give it me." "I see.... How many days have you had free these past years?" "None." "There. It seems you already have earned one," Josquin smiled.

"I'll give you... one free day every fourteen years. How's that, chief slaveswoman?"

Clarece smiled in return. "More than generous, my lady. But you must not mention this to anyone, please. This is an errand you send me for." "I understand," her owner nodded. And she did. "I will prepare you an official pass." "Thank you," her charge replied, beaming.

There. It was settled. A day in the city with Asla. Already her nervousness turned to excitement - like water into wine. She would share a cup with her sala tonight.

# XXVI

Clarece heard the coughing from where she was, crouched before her mistra's brazier. Kai, it was cold already. She looked wretchedly towards the large windows of Casica's chamber. Wind buffeted the glass, rattling against the peel of thunder in the distance. *You're distant now*, thought the shivering slave, but soon you'll be upon us, ravaging our bones with your cold and wet. Another cough came from her pen.

The chief slave glanced down at her claws; already her maimed flesh ached with the changing weather. She looked to her mistra. Casica nestled in bed, lost in thought and writing, trying desperately to complete this last letter for the morrow. She wished to include all she could in this, the first, correspondence to her family. It was all she did today: write.

Clarece smiled, despite herself; her owner was nothing if not focused. When she wrote, it was as if the whole world ceased existence. Asla had made the same observation about Clarece's reading. The aching woman placed two additional shovels of coal in the brazier. An orange glow warmed her face as she blew steadily into the fire. A stoked fire filled a cold room with blessing; through years of practice, she had become expert in her technique. Consistency was the key, consistency in coal distribution and in breath.

Clarece coughed once, quietly. She lifted her hands towards the heat, placed them into the hood itself. Nothing. No feeling at all. God, this was going to be a bad night. Once more she glanced at her mistra, oblivious to her slave's presence. No, this wasn't the time to intrude, clearly. An offer was one thing; to interrupt her mistra's mission, another.

She stood silently, waiting for her owner's acknowledgment. It wasn't forthcoming. "My lady?" she asked softly. Nothing. "My lady?" she repeated, somewhat less softly. The healer glanced up from her work. "Are you warm, my lady?" Casica seemed to look around her. "Yes, Clarece, thank you." Her owner had already resumed her writing. Clarece looked again to her throbbing hands. She would try. "My lady?" This time the look of irritation was unmistakable. "Yes, Clarece?" "I... I will leave you. Good night, mistra." "Goodnight, Clarece." The slave took one step back and turned on her heel. How she hated leaving the warm room. She glanced back at the inviting glow of her fire; it lit her way a full five steps before deserting her to the cold darkness of her pen.

Asla was pulling on her boots as Clarece stepped into their stall. "You're not going out in this, are you?" "No. I'm in the north wing," Asla replied, " - all night, thank gods. Scads, it's cold. I'm happy I don't sleep here tonight. I probably won't sleep much where I'm going but at least I'll be warm," she concluded lacing her left boot.

"Well, be safe too. Better cold than sorry," offered Clarece. "I will, chief slaveswoman," the insulit grinned. "The baron's a bore, but he's a safe lay." The younger woman finished her lace and studied her stallmate. Clarece wore an expression she knew well. "Tis bad tonight," she stated more than questioned. Her stallmate nodded wearily. Pain always exhausted her. "Would you have time?" Clarece asked. Asla took a mental look at her schedule. The baron wouldn't notice a few late minutes. "Of course, if I hurry. Let me get the ointment."

Clarece began unfastening her mittens as Asla reached up and pulled the curtain across their stall. She shook the heating liniment in one hand and helped her friend with her mittens with the other. The older slave glanced at the curtain before presenting her destroyed body to her friend. "Scads, Rece, they're little blocks of ice. Have you been working them today?" "No," was the answer. "They're just in a bad way." Asla shook her head. "This isn't going to help," she mumbled, rubbing the ointment into her friend's thin flesh. Clarece winced when she tried to uncurl the melted fingers.

"I'm sorry," Asla whispered, seeing tears creep down the tortured woman's face. Clarece rarely let on her pain; she must be hurting terribly. The gymnast massaged as best she could the deadened hands, thinking of the woman sleeping directly above. "Rece, this is no good. Why not ask her for help. She told you to, you said you would." "I was - I tried. Truly. But the king takes her letters tomorrow; they're all that exist for her tonight." "What do you mean?" the insulit asked, slightly frustrated - more at her inadequacy than at her friend. "You exist more for her than any letter."

"No," Clarece shook her head. "Those letters are her lifeline. They're all she has between her and her home." "You discount yourself, too easily," Asla observed, taking the woman's left wrist. Her bones came out of her forearm like sticks from a snowman. "Someday, you'll be placed in a position where you'll have to take yourself as seriously as those around you do." "Well, until that day, I'm not interrupting my mistra when she's writing home," declared Clarece, irritated at her own blatant inadequacies. Crispus, how she despised her body.

The clock chimed the quarter hour. Asla glanced over her shoulder. She needed to leave. "I've gotta go, Rece, I'm sorry. Look, get your warm mittens - the wool ones. I'll put them on for you. It'll help." Clarece nodded gratefully. There was no way she could place those on her hands tonight.

Asla quickly threaded the cloth over the stiffening claws that served as her friend's hands, wondering as she did, what sort of night awaited the hurting woman. "I won't be back till morning," she explained, addressing the attentive hands. "Until then, you be good," she ordered the left hand, kissing it. "You hear me?" she asked the right one, kissing it also.

Clarece smiled; it amused her, the way Asla related to her hands as though they were separate entities. Her stallmate stood, this time addressing the keeper of the hands. "If they're not good, you let me know. There'll be hell to pay," she finished glaring mockingly at the silent cloth. "And I'm the one to pay it," Clarece replied, smiling despite her pain. She wished she could unscrew her hands and tuck them in the night stand this evening.

As an afterthought, Asla dropped to her knees. She quickly unlaced her friend's boots and slipped them off her feet. "Gotta go!

Rest to you," she said quickly, sliding back the curtain. "And Rece, use my cloaks." "Thank you, As. Goodnight." Clarece listened as the steps of her friend raced through the pen. She looked down at the plotting mutineers. "You heard what she said," she reminded them, hoping against hope they would obey. "Be good...."

The rebellion occurred at half of eleven, precisely. The rest of Clarece's body slept soundly, comforted and warmed by the weight of three cloaks upon it. Her mind recognized the battle cries of insurrection, distant at first, but approaching rapidly. Valiantly, her cognizant troops fought to ignore them. *Ignore the tormentors, sleep through them,* they ordered. *Rest in the remainder of your body.* For a long three minutes she kept the rebels at bay, then suddenly, one ripped through her thin veil of oblivion.

Clarece bolted up with a short cry, jarred into consciousness by the molten lead that scoured her wrists and hands. She fought her instinct to groan. It would not do to wake the pen with her private hell. She released her agony instead by taking Asla's cloak and clinching her teeth on it. She pounded her hands against her chest, enraged at the dead things that mocked her with their numbness. They would not yield.

The slave switched to the more familiar stance of kneeling. Releasing the cloak, she took her right wrist into her jaws and bit - hard, gnawing up her forearm and returning to bite her hand. Nothing. She tried the other arm, but still, no relief. She glanced at her stallmate's cot. Asla wasn't there; of course, she wasn't there.

Clarece begged, "*Oh, God. Help me! Please,*" as fire rolled down, surging into what would have been hands. Her voice steamed the chilled air. The kindly light of her lamp mocked her in her lonely struggle. Her eyes fought to focus on something - anything - to take her from this place. And then she saw it. The tiny brass bell hanging between two others: her mistra's bell. She looked up above to where a healer slept. Torment and propriety challenged each other. A slave did not - ever - wake an owner. To do so was to breach a sacred boundary. A blunt knife seared through her right forearm.

*Mercy,* she heard something say. *Go obtain mercy!* Before she knew what it was she did, Clarece d'Casica stepped from her cot unto the icy floor of her pen. She had taken four steps up her mistra's stairs before even questioning herself. Agony drove her forward.

Casica, in a dead sleep, never even sensed Clarece's approach. The first hint of her presence was a pained cry, *"Mistra?"* The healer waked, startled. Turning, she saw Clarece standing next to her bed. The tortured woman fell to her knees and begged, *"Help me, please!"*

Josquin was fully awake now and sitting up, reached for the outstretched arms. As she touched them, both women gasped - one in the release of pain, the other in receiving it. Casica winced at the onslaught. "My God, Clarece!" she breathed, stunned. "You're on fire."

*No, I'm not,* thought Clarece somewhere within herself; not any more. Someone had plunged her arms into ice water. She dropped her head upon her mistra's bed with relief. *"Thank you,"* she breathed into the warm covers, *"oh, God, thank you."* And then they came; sobs of release flowed from the tortured body. She was warm. She was safe. The mutineers were vanquished.

Casica massaged the arms and wrists of the exhausted woman, concentrating, as she did, on flow. She coaxed, gently but persistently, blood from the fertile regions of the upper arm, past the delicate elbow, into the constricted netherworld of the forearm. Her aim was intent and true. Clarece's body surrendered to her touch. "Good arm," Josquin comforted, in Cassican, as she caressed the mittened subjects, "that's a good arm. Tis well."

Clarece looked up into the shimmering blue eyes of Casica. She was too tired to be unnerved. "Forgive me for waking you. I... I was hurting." "That's an understatement," her owner replied gently. "How do you bear it?" "Not well. And worse with the years," the slave confessed. "My hands will be the death of me." Casica grinned wryly. It would take much more than this to be the death of this woman. How much she had borne, only God knew.

"It's not your hands, you know," she offered aloud. Clarece looked up with weary interest. "What do you mean?" "Tis your wrists, truly. Your forearms." A warm hand ran along the slave's arm. "Your blood's not flowing as it should. It's not reaching your hands. That's a root of your problem."

The worn woman thought silently, free of the noise of pain. "Can you help me?" she asked finally. Had she known them well enough, she would have noticed the shining eyes smile. "Of course - if you wish." The slave did not hesitate. "I wish. What must I do?" "Give me some of your time. A couple hours everyday - more if you can." Clarece debated but for a moment. This was a simple request. "All a slave has is time," she answered. "And all of mine is yours. If you loan me some, I'll give it back to you." Casica nodded in the darkness. "You've a deal, chief slaveswoman. It will be my pleasure to slave you."

Clarece wondered if all this were a dream. Surely, it must be a dream. The warmth of the brazier embraced her, slipping between the threads of her thin gown. Inside it was met by the warmth of her mistra's power. The clock on the wall comforted her with its familiar ticking. Safety and warmth mingled, rendering an irresistible lullaby. The blond head nodded slowly upon the bed. Casica smiled at the blessed sound of her friend's deep, steady breathing.

Josquin placed her hands on Clarece's head, and brought them down her neck to rest upon her shoulders. These shoulders stored so much, the healer thought, like a lair of Clarece's anxiety. Fear reached out to her: Asla, her safety and... burial? she didn't understand. Raina. Cold. Her people's health this winter. Her own name arose as did Poul's.

Casica shut her mind's ears as a dozen worries surfaced from the woman's body. It wasn't necessary for her to hear them to help them. The josquin massaged her hands deep into the steely muscles. How Clarece bore the weight of her world. A unique healing flowed fervently into this region of her friend's body, touching both flesh and mind - and spirit. For hours, the healer plied her trade - powerfully. Clarece had given her the key to this door and now that she had stepped through it, she would not waste a moment. The clock chimed two before her friend woke, sleepily. The wonder of it all, to the princess, was that the kneeling legs were not asleep. Only God knew the body of a slave - but of this one, He was revealing a glimpse.

"I seemed to have fallen asleep...," Clarece observed, embarrassed. "You still have some sleeping to do, I think," her owner replied kindly. "Yes." The slave rose easily to her feet. "Thank you, mistra," she whispered, still dreaming. She recognized the warmth pulsating inside her. She would not feel cold tonight. She rested against it. "Goodnight, dear Clarece," her healer beckoned, as from a distance. "Sleep well."

Clarece would not remember going to bed. She not wake until Asla, returned from her service, roused her, concerned. The day had begun without her, but the effect of the night remained. The slave greeted her mistra with an energy and peace alien to her. Another door had been opened. And from within it, flowed a wellspring of life.

# XXVII

Casica strolled leisurely down the west wing, nodding to the guards as she passed, noting the cloudy weather through a procession of windows. Each revealed a new piece of the day, a cloud here, a partial cloud there, but all derived the same conclusion: the day was cold and dark.

The princess stopped and viewed the weather with interest. It looked like home. The same clouds, same gray horizon, same feel of cold upon the panes. She placed a hand against the glass. It steamed with her touch. Casica smiled at the trick, one she'd discovered when she was only three. She remembered thinking how strange it was that other children couldn't do this, couldn't warm objects at their will.

In her young mind, it never occurred that she was different from others; the shalonn that hung on her neck was, for her, part of her body - she couldn't remember a time without it. It was during this season that she and the necklace were coming into knowledge of each other. Certainly the pobble stones knew her first, having been placed, as they were, upon countless throats before hers. But for the girl, only now were she and the ancient jewelry becoming separate identities. Now as she embarked on this odyssey of learning to control herself and its power. Steaming a cold glass was one of her favorite games. With practice Casica could turn the steam on and off in step with her breathing. It was the first of many exercises she would master in the development of her unique gifting, like practicing scales for the hammerschord.

A clock in the hall struck the tenth hour. Fifteen minutes to meet the king. The princess scraped a web from the glass. The king of Byzanthia was an enigma to her. On the one hand, he disdained her openly. These chessly meetings served as much to give him opportunity to ridicule her as it did to provide him other entertainment. He didn't trust her, Casica felt, and she could do nothing to prove her loyalty. On the other hand, Ars allowed her access to her country and family through letters. What sense did that make?

She imagined the small parcel of letters she had entrusted to the king. Had Ars delivered them or were they, even now, sitting on a desk somewhere or added to the ash in some fireplace? Was Ars toying with her? Sometimes it did feel as she sat across from the older king, that he wished to humble her. It seemed the chess game may embody more meaning than the girl wished. *Perhaps I should intentionally lose*, she thought to herself, turning to continue her trek west. Perhaps it was wisest to capitulate to the crown. Perhaps if she did, her prince would be returned to her.

The princess pushed the last thought away. Surely, Ars would not hold hostage his son over a meaningless game. Then again (she rolled her eyes at the insanity of this memory), had he not sacrificed two powerful pieces in a desperate attempt to capture her pawn? That tiny onyx piece that she had moved as an afterthought tormented His Majesty. It was as if his goal were not to capture her royals at all but to snuff out this insignificant broad foot. What kind of reasoning was that? For that matter, what kind of rationale propelled anything this man did - except for the relentless tyranny of paranoia.

The attendant ushered Casica into the king's antechamber. His majesty was not yet prepared for her visit, she was informed. Would her highness like something to drink - her usual, perhaps scotch? Casica thanked the servant and tasted the liquid. Her father preferred scotch; she had seen him nurse it countless evenings. It was his tutor, he said, accompanying him in thought. The princess studied the heavy glass in her hand. Within seconds, the drink had warmed to a pleasant level. She used to warm her baba's drink, too. Another trick.

As she sat waiting, the young woman compared the two kings. Certainly her father knew anxiety, but she had never seen him live in what she would call paranoia. Of course, all royalty lived with the specter of assassination and betrayal. No kingdom was assured security. But her parents bore this dark possibility with grace - or if not, they never let on their fears.

Baba had taught her there was a reason crowns weren't fastened to the head that wore them. They fall quickly, he said, and changed owners easily. It is best to remember Whose crown it truly is, K'eran reflected. Best to remain humble, to see the gold as a honored loan and not a deserved property. The princess' line enjoyed generations of unquestioned reign, and, though it was impossible for all to support the ruling family of Cassica, certainly they lived under the protection of most of their subjects' loyalty.

Casica caressed the pobble stones about her neck. Often she had wondered if the presence of josquins in her family served to reinforce their throne's foundation. Every queen in her line had served as a josquin, caring for the many needs of her people. This normal contact of queen with subject flavored the royal relationship with a commonness. Casica smiled at Clarece's reference to royals being divine. No Cassican would think that. It would be impossible to witness a healing, to see the queen sweat and cry and fight for life and think her anything but human.

Royalty for the princess was a mundane inheritance: gold framed in wood. She couldn't leave a healing, her hands and royal garments covered with a peasant's blood, and think herself anything other than like them. Surely, the princess reasoned, surely this earthy eminence of healer/royal helped to balance and secure the crown. Casica took a deep sip. At home, her people addressed her as "Josquin" much more often than "Highness." She missed this intimate association.

"Your Highness." The servant roused her attention. "His majesty regrets to inform you that he is unable to accommodate your presence this day. He asked me to convey - and these are his words, your highness, not my own: 'Tell the royal gilt that I haven't space for her to root in my day. She may swill my drink and return next week.'" The servant bowed. "Such were his words...." Now he offered his own. "Please, finish your refreshment, Princess. May I attend you?"

The Cassican woman smiled, shaking her head. "No. The quality of his majesty's scotch is worth the journey. Send His Majesty my regards and tell him I look forward to boaring him at a later date." The servant looked askance. Was the woman making a jest? He wasn't certain so he settled with a humble bow and excused himself.

Casica returned to her drink. 'Royal gilt.' Now there's esteem for you. The princess glanced out a window. Clouds had given way to a solid bank of gray. Cold. It would be cold tonight. Her mind wandered to Clarece and the slaves below her chamber. How often she felt cold air fleeing the basement for her warm room. "'Blankets are for horses....'" Casica studied the royal appointments surrounding her. She had an idea. The woman gulped the remainder of her drink and walked quickly from the room. A royal service was at hand. Surely, Silian was in need of a healing touch in this weather.

"My Lord Steward!" the princess greeted, happy to find the industrious Silian busy at his desk. "Princess," he welcomed, rising to meet her hand. The kindly man bowed but with difficulty. "Just as I thought, my lord," she observed. "This frigid weather wreaks havoc upon your hip." "Indeed, it does, my lady," Silian agreed looking fitfully at his side. "I have considered approaching your highness about this condition but have found myself too involved with other movements about the palace." "I'm not surprised, Silian," Casica replied, nodding acknowledgment. "A man as yourself, with responsibilities beyond number, does not hold a vast store of personal time. May I?" she asked. "Please," was the man's grateful response.

Joints were an easy thing for the healer. A mere touch to his shoulder restored Silian's hip immediately. The relieved man smiled broadly. Already his day was improving. "I thank you, your highness. I must avail myself of your care more often." The healer smiled in turn. "I hope you will. Tis a small thing to do in return for your many acts of accommodation. I enjoy my tea set immensely. Your kindness is a daily attendant." Silian smiled again, pleased at the woman's acknowledgment of his service. Rarely did anyone mentioned it unless something was awry. Such was the nature of a steward's world.

"And how are you now, my lady?" he asked. "Is there anything of which you find yourself in need?" Casica looked away, feigning thought. She shook her head. "No. Nothing for me - but now that you mention it, there *is* a problem." Silian's brows raised attentively.

"As you are well aware, I'm sure, Lord Steward, my chamber lays directly above the slaves' quarters." Silian glanced at the palace. "Yes. It would be located above the women's pen," he agreed. "Exactly. And that is the problem: winter has come and with it the sounds of cold. These slaves spend their nights - and mine - in fits of coughing and sneezing - and worse. In their sleeplessness, they wander about their pen, making all manner of noise. I find it difficult - on some nights impossible - to sleep a'tall. I am told that the slaves own no blankets - is that true?"

The steward nodded. "Yes. Tis true. Slaves are allotted one set of linens consisting of a bed sheet and cover sheet. Such is the proper provision for slaves - according to their class." Casica nodded. "Tis a generous allotment, to be sure. However, it is allotted to me to sleep above this class, and my allotment is not nearly so generous as theirs. My sleep lessens by degrees, Lord Steward. I hold no grudge against my neighbors, per se, but find myself at war with their noise. Is it possible to provide these basement dwellers cover?"

The Lord Steward mused for a minute. True, the Cassican princess was the only tenant of his wing living above a slave quarter. In fact, the east wing was the only one housing slaves at all. However, he could not fathom providing blankets for this class. Even if desire banked his heart, there wasn't enough money in his treasury. "I 'm afraid I'm at a loss to serve you, Princess," he decided. "I haven't the means to provide blankets for so many slaves."

Casica sighed. "I understand. Of course. Blankets are better provided for horses." The steward smiled. She understood. "Exactly," he agreed, placing his hands deep in his vest pockets and rocking on his healthy hip.

Casica brought her fingers to her lips. "However," she continued, recapturing his attention, "what of rags?" Silian squinted. "*Rags,* lady?" "Yes," Casica nodded, looking into her mind. "The palace of Byzanthia is matchless in its station and appointments. I would think the store closets filled with many useless, discarded comforters, being as linens are often replaced with finer ones - ."

This last part, Casica concocted completely. She had no idea how old was the comforter on Bastien's bed, though, certainly her own was new. Silian stood silent, mentally rummaging through the east's stores. There might be a dozen - perhaps more - comforters in keeping. "I may find enough covers for half the slaves, Princess, but certainly not all." "Half?"

"Yes, half." "Comforters sized for beds such as my husband's?" "Yes." "Perfect, Lord Steward! You are a magician," the woman announced. Silian wasn't convinced. "Slave cots are not a third of a royal's bed," she explained. "Tell me, could you arrange for the coverings to be halved? By halving them, I may fully gain my sleep."

The Lord Steward Silian stood, gauging the situation. It would require an investment in time, having the laundry servants alter the old comforters, but would expend nothing from his treasury. This was a strange request to be sure; never did any royal ask anything for a slave. But this royal was different. Silian smiled to himself. *No, perhaps not so different,* he thought. Her petition, certainly, was bedded in her own comfort more than any regard for slaves. It was a small favor. The steward felt his hip. She offered him something of much greater value than old covers.

"Yes, Princess," he voiced finally. "I can arrange this. It will take some time - ." "I understand perfectly, Lord Steward. A man as yourself is busied with the truly significant. That you would even entertain my weakness for comfort is a favor. I'm certain whenever your lordship is able to conjure this magic will serve all parties well."

Silian liked this woman. Royal but respectful. His desire to help the Cassican grew with the moment. "And again, Silian," she continued, playing her highest card, "please, feel free to come to me anytime with your hip or other health needs as they may arise, though surely, I hope none will."

With this, the princess excused herself. She had not yet reached the door, however, when she spun around. "Oh, Lord Steward...." Silian looked attentively "I would thank you for not mentioning this to anyone. You know how slaves are. One word of my involvement and I'll have a queue at my door." The steward smirked. Yes, he knew how slaves were. "Of course, my lady. It will be my decision - to better use our majesty's resources." "Thank you," Casica smiled. She turned then spun again.

"One, last thing, Lord Steward." "Yes?" (What more could she want?) "If there is purple among the covers, could you see that one be placed on my own slave's cot? She slaves well." Silian bowed to the request. Clarece *was* a good slave. "Of course, my lady." Casica offered her most winning smile and departed. She had not missed her game day, after all.

## XXVIII

W hy do you think she's inviting me?" The princess of Cassica was nearing the end of her lacing. Her newly oiled boots shone from Clarece's enthusiastic labor. Today was the big day, the day her mistra would convene council with a royal peer.

"As I have explained, my lady," the senior slave explained, again, "the countess is known for her custom of inviting new residents of the palace to her chambers. She's our unofficial hostess."

Casica wasn't convinced. "It doesn't feel right," she argued, again, shaking her head and stamping her foot to set her high boot. "If that's true, why the delay? I've been here months and no one, his majesty excepting, has so much as given me a word much less an invitation." "But mistra, the countess Dolca, she is a very busy royal. Most likely she'd only now found time in her full schedule."

The tall, dark woman stood, receiving the vest her charge offered. The chief slaveswoman bowed and half-knelt with the transfer. "I don't know, Clarece," Casica confessed, placing the garment upon herself. "Maybe tis only pride. I've felt slighted. Insulted by the ruling class. If it weren't for horses and your people, I'd have no social life a'tall."

Casica finished buttoning her vest and turned her gaze from the floor to her confessor. "I'm not used to being unwanted. I guess that's the heart of the matter." Josquin buttoned her collar to hide her shalonn; Clarece noticed a moist sheen about her owner's eyes.

She saddened at her lady's hurt. *Pity a kingdom that won't welcome such a treasure as this woman,* thought Clarece. What she said was, "I believe you'll find the countess a fine hostess, and I know she'll find you a delightful guest." Casica offered a wan smile. "You think?" The slave nodded confidently. "Yes, my lady." "I don't know... what if she doesn't like me? If she's the door of society you make her, to have her closed would shut me out forever."

Clarece cocked her head quizzically. Her lady was always surprising her. Never would she have thought Casica to be nervous about the opinion of others; she certainly didn't present herself in such a manner. She always exuded an air of self-acceptance that seemed impervious to outside critique. But here she was, a princess, generations in rank above the lady Dolca, yet concerned about making a favorable impression. Perhaps she had overestimated her owner's degree of confidence or, more likely, underestimated her loneliness.

Casica ceased her fretting to present herself to her living mirror. "Well, chief slaveswoman: how do I look?" she asked, somewhat coy. The senior slave appraised her mistra approvingly. High boots, blue trousers, deep green vest - with the crimson karosh peeping from underneath - wine silk blouse - all freshly ironed and creased, compliments of herself. "You are beautifully Cassican, my lady," she declared bowing her head.

"'Beautifully Cassican,'" the princess repeated. What the pony did that mean? she wondered, irritated. *Kai! Why was she so short with life today?* "Are you suggesting I change? Am I unfit for a Byzanthian?"

The slave blinked, confused. "No, my lady, not at all. I'm saying you look very much yourself - beautiful. Tis you just don't dress like a Byzanthian - ." "You mean not blueonblue, brownonbrown, redonred...." Clarece paused, uncertain of her owner's tone. Sarcasm wasn't Casica's normal flavor. "I only say you dress with your artist's taste, Mistra, choosing many colors from your palate - all of which flow beautifully upon you."

The princess dropped her head, sighing. "This isn't the artist in me," she explained, her words falling over a cliff of thought. "This is how *all* Cassicans dress. My people love color...." *My people....* God, how she missed her people. How exhausted she was of living on this alien stage with so little of the set reflecting home. Sometimes she thought if it weren't for the clouds and sky - and Rigel - there would be no familiar mooring at all. A wave of home-sickness washed over, threatening to sever Casica from her fragile buoy of hope. The truth was, she didn't want to feel hopeful today. She didn't want to meet this royal today. She wanted to go home today. To just go home. Home to where her life had been so filled, time alone must be scheduled.

Clarece watched the storm from shore, unsure of what she could do to help her foundering lady. For once, she decided to ask. "My lady? How may I help you?" Casica looked up at the lighthouse, feeling a strong urge to tell herself 'grow up.' Acting was an essential oil in the royal rub. She hated playing any part, but she could. Could do it with the best of them, do it as well as, doubtless, this countess was preparing herself to do at this moment. She dropped her hands in defeat.

"You can pray for a surge of maturity, chief slaveswoman. I'm just homesick and want to whine like a three-year-old. Any advice for my maiden voyage into the uncharted waters of Byzanthian feminine royalty?" The slave thought quickly. "You ask one who's never sailed that sea, but may I suggest you wear you cloak?" "My cloak?" Casica asked, confused. "What? And conceal all this Cassican beauty?"

"No, my lady," Clarece began, buffeted against a seawall of emotion. "I only mean - the countess is a master seamstress - like your mother. You're concerned about an entry. Perhaps the garment may serve as a carpet to conversation - in the event you find yourself treading water - or worse: wanting to abandon ship altogether."

Casica's laughter was genuine. No wonder courts employed jesters: royalty would drown in its own self-importance, otherwise. "That's a wonderful idea, Clarece," she admitted, succumbing to hope, despite herself. "Fetch me my float." "Aye, aye, my lady," her mate smiled. The princess adorned herself with a flourish.

The cloak; that was another familiar prop. "There. Where do I find this countess?" Clarece bowed, humbly. "If it pleases you, mistra. Tis customary for a royal's slave to escort her to a visit and for her hostess' slave to accompany her return." "It pleases me," the princess declared. "Otherwise, I might drift."

Clarece offered her half-kneel and preceded her owner to Bastien's door, opening the heavy oak for the princess to exit. From here, the women embarked. The countess' chamber was easily gained. The slave glanced at her owner for permission, knocked on the door with her spoon then stepped back behind her whispering, "Good voyage," as she did so. Casica was about to voice her rejoinder when the door opened, unexpectedly. She stepped back, surprised; the countess must have waited at the helm.

Casica wasn't the only surprised party. Dolca, looking low for a young girl, started at the tall woman meeting her raised eyes. This was no beaten child. "Your highness," she greeted, adding a graceful kneel. "I am the Countess Dolca, wife of Sir Nahalt, knight of our majesty." She stood now to face her superior. "Welcome to my home," she wished, smiling.

The fretting princess was undone, all frustration and suspicion erased by the young hostess' warmth. "Thank you, countess," she replied, her own voice warmed with genuine gratitude. "Tis my honor to meet you." She turned to her waiting escort. "Thank you, Clarece," she said, dismissing her, adding in thought, *Thank you for many things.*

The slave's hidden lips formed a smile as she raised from her kneel to turn, as a slave does, from her owner. Now that her mistra cleared the harbor, it should be smoother sailing, she thought, walking happily to her pen. Surely this would prove a successful venture.

The countess ushered her honored guest into the spacious chamber. Casica studied it with delight. Dolca appointed her rooms elegantly but not at the expense of coziness. This truly was a home. "What an inviting sanctuary you've made, Dolca," she offered. The hostess bowed. "Thank you, your highness," she replied, pleased at the princess' observation. The tall royal turned to the watching royal.

"If you would indulge me, please," Josquin asked, extending her hand, "I am Casica...." "As you wish, Casica." Dolca received the hand with a slight gasp. Warmth and a sensation she could not identify flowed from the dark woman into herself. She glanced up. No surprise showed in the foreign features; the princess seemed utterly oblivious to her effect. She held the hand a breath longer before releasing it with a surprising reluctance. "May I take your cloak?" the hostess inquired, still savoring the strange feeling.

"Yes, please," the princess replied, unfastening the cape. "Clarece says you're a master seamstress. She suggested I wear it as a conversation piece." Dolca looked again into the dark eyes, thinking, *"You are conversation piece enough...."* Never had she seen a woman like the Cassican. Every part of her showing was dark, like the color of desert - everything except her hair, which shone with the black of ink, and her lips, which flowed with a slight pink complexion. Underlining all this alien hue was a profound sense of presence, at once regal and familiar.

The countess smiled at Casica's reference to "master seamstress." "I don't know about my being master; it would be more truthful to say that sewing masters me. I am a slave to its passion." Casica nodded, understanding. "Then you should meet my mother; it is she who made my cloak. She always said that if it weren't for the crown, she'd happily spend her days subject to a loom."

The seamstress studied the garment as long as she dared, but not as long as she wished. The cloth and handiwork were as strange to her as the garment's owner. "Feel free to put it on," the owner offered.

Dolca glanced up suspiciously, feeling the woman out. It could be a test, such a question. To wear another's cape was an intimate indulgence; it could be this royal were trying her degree of propriety. Often was the case in the royal class of Byzanthia. Women made a game of judging each other. "Here," the princess took the cloak and without so much as waiting for her inferior to bow, wrapped the heavy garment around her.

Instantly, the cloth did its work. Warmth stirred within the woman and the sense of another - or rather others - brushed against her personal fabric. The sensations astounded the countess and would have somewhat frightened her were it not for her spinning curiosity. She brought her arms through the cloak and found to her delight they came out sleeved. "There are sleeves hidden here!" she laughed.

"They're for additional warmth during occasions of having your arms out - as in riding. But you don't have to use them." The princess opened the cloak and showed her mother's trick. "See? They're sewn so that you can bypass them entirely and place your arms outside as a normal cape." The seamstress was smitten. "And these tassels?" "Pull them...."

Dolca pulled the little cords. Obediently, the hem rose. Again she laughed. "You say your mother made this?" Casica nodded. "You mother is a queen," Dolca stated. Perhaps royalty was as queerly sired as it was shown in Cassica, thought she. The princess laughed. That statement rivaled Clarece's "your brother is a boy."

"Yes. It is the case in my land. A princess' mother generally serves as queen." "Forgive me, your highness," the countess bowed, though certainly she felt no need to ask it. This royal girl brimmed with good-naturedness. "Tis only that I find it difficult to comprehend. This cloth: tis unknown to me. Tis her own weaving, I'm sure." "Yes." "Well, to make such a garment would require a king's ransom in timely investment." "It does. It took Maman months to fashion it." Dolca nodded. Indeed. "Only months? Well, I'm not accustom to any woman of your mother's rank devoting such time to the work of her hands." Casica smiled, touched by the compliment. "On my island, mother's cloaks are legendary. She makes only several a year and gives them as gifts."

Dolca hesitated. She should surrender the garment but had no desire to do so. Like most of the palace's residents, the woman lived in a state of chill for much of the year. The warmth and comfort exuded by the queen's gift tempted her to dismiss royal etiquette. "There is more to this garment than meets the eye," she began, "or is it my imagination, what I'm feeling?" "That depends on what you're feeling," answered Casica playfully.

"I feel the cloak *makes* heat - not merely preserves it." Dolca's surmising was met with a nod. "And..." she was reluctant to share this. Surely it must be her imagination. "And it seems the cloak bears about it another feeling, one I can't articulate." "Several feelings, I would venture," offered her guest. "And how does your mother do this?" Casica shook her head. "I truly don't know. Mother is a josquin - a healer - and has in her giftings a way with cloth beyond my ken."

The countess caressed the garment admiringly, certain there was much about this foreign woman's world beyond her ken. With reluctance she removed the cape to hang it, realizing only then her hostessing error. Scads! This entire time, she'd neglected even to invite her guest sit. "Forgive, me, Casica," she apologized. "I forget myself. Please...."

She ushered the royal to her living area's dining table. It was the table's size Casica noticed first. Evidently, this woman hosted large gatherings. She'd learned her trade well. A huge flowered tapestry served as the table's cover. At its end was placed utensils for tea and refreshment. An emerald doily graced a lovely vase filled with greenery. The flora set off the rest of the table, creating a cozy nook, as it was, for a mere twosome.

Casica sat at the head where she was directed and smiled: Dolca chose the same seating arrangement as herself. She smiled even more happily at the sight that now met her eyes. The cup at her place sported fleurs d'lis, her homeland's beloved symbol. The princess lifted the china, gingerly admiring it - it and her hostess' thoughtfulness. "How did you know?" she asked. The moist pool in the girl's eyes wasn't lost on Dolca. "I've seen Cassican ships," she divulged, "and... I interrogated a Cassican priest. The intern."

Casica shook her head, overcome with the simple act of kindness. "Tis very kind of you, Dolca." The tears now escaped their harbor. "I... I've been homesick. I thank you." "You're welcome," the countess of Byzanthia replied softly. "It must be lonely, being so far from everything you know," she offered, modestly avoiding the royal's tears. *So much for acting,* thought Casica. "It is... I am...."

Dolca poured into her cup the freshly steeped drink. It filled the chamber with a unique, striking aroma. The princess wiped her nose with a royal blue kerchief. "No intern could know this is my favorite blend." The countess had brewed the royal blend, the one Casica shared so often with Clarece. Dolca grinned. "No. This secret I learned from your slave." "Of course," the princess nodded. "She's filled with secrets, that one. Only God knows the mind of a slave."

Dolca smiled in agreement as she lifted her cup to her guest. "A toast, Princess. To your arrival to this land. May it blossom in ways the seed could never suggest." Casica bowed humbly, moved by the loveliness of the toast and by the hint of acknowl-edgment that wrapped it. She sipped the drink contentedly and looked about the surroundings.

All around were the signs of industrious femininity. Tapestries both small and large hung on the walls. A tapestried runner ran above the fireplace. Next to the hearth were several baskets filled with yarns and string. Needles for knitting and ones for crochet-ing laid about like words on a poet's tongue. And towards the far end of the chamber near the wide solitary window stood the larger tools of their mistress' trade: a quilting frame and tapestry looms - two looms, in fact, dominated by one that looked more a machine than it did a lady's pastime. The tapestry in process bristled with bobbins.

The princess grinned within. It almost was like taking tea in a workshop. All the trappings reminded her of the music room in the library. Clearly, Dolca was an artist. Conspicuous in its ab-sence was the lack of childish disorder. The countess must send her progeny to boarding school.

"You are a busy woman, countess. How ever do you find time to play all these instruments?" Dolca warmed at the analogy. Perhaps the princess was a musician. "Well, my slave, Solange, helped me a great deal, and I've long ago given up weaving my own cloth. I use the market now - except for special occasions. I've concentrated on tapestries over the past few years. Tis very challenging work."

"I should say," replied her guest. "I see you weave on both low and high warp. Which do you prefer?" Dolca beamed. "Do you work with tapestries, Princess?" "Goodness, no!" Casica smiled. "I haven't the patience. But I did have the exquisite privilege of serving as ambassador to the royal court at Kieta - ."

"Kieta?! Have you seen 'The Glory of Creation?'" Casica nod-ded mid-sip. "Twice. *Twelve* weavers working such a loom as is difficult to imagine. They faced the image and wove in a single piece." "They faced the image?" Dolca questioned. "Are you sure?" "Yes." "You mean they wove with the warp?" "Yes."

The seamstress frowned. The venture of weaving a piece of such magnitude was ambitious, but to weave with the warp was madness. "Why did they weave with the warp?" Her guest glanced into her memory. "I believe it had to do with the artist's insistence upon a single piece." The seamstress shook her head, considering. "How sad. The weight of so much thread will cause the weft to slip on the warp eventually. With time the piece will sag." The princess frowned. About such things she didn't know. "Well, I saw it finished. It truly does justice to its subject." "I can imagine," Dolca nodded. She should speak again with Nahalt about making the trip to Kieta. She wished to do more than imagine the piece.

"So you were an ambassador?" she asked now. The dark woman took a sip. "Yes, in several courts. But I'm certain it doesn't require the mental dexterity of your work." The seamstress caressed her table cloth. "I do enjoy tapestries, but I don't know. Looking at your mother's cloak makes me wonder if I should return to clothing. Your clothing, Princess. Is it from her hand?"

Casica glanced down at her palate. "Yes it is, now that you mention it." "Such striking colors...." The princess smiled into her tea. "So I've been told. What think you, Dolca? If I dressed more in similar shades, could I blend into the Byzanthian race?" Dolca studied the dark woman intently. "No. You need also cut your hair. Then, no one could tell the difference." The women laughed. It would take much more than that to weave this Cassican curiosity into the fabric of Byzanthia life.

"Do all Cassican women wear their hair long?" (Casica's hair was striking but not in color only. In Dolca's country, only slaves grew their hair long. Her own stayed at shoulder length. Loose hair was a sign of freedom.) "Yes." "Then how do you differentiate between the slave and free?" The guest restrained her offended look in time. Could it be this woman was so ignorant of her land? "We have no slaves in Cassica," she answered.

"None? I mean I know slavery is reputedly not practiced in your land, but you truly have none - not even the royalty?" "*Especially* not the royalty. We would die to keep it from our land." The implication of the statement was clear.

"But how do you function without them, without class?" Dolca asked. "I can't say we don't have class," Casica explained. "We do, very similarly as is known here in Byzanthia. But it hasn't the feeling as Byzanthia. Labor is shared by many. There are servants for those who choose and can afford them. There are guilds and apprentices. Land owners - but most are not of royal blood. Most are commoners who own their land." "Commoners owning land?" Dolca injected. "How queer. How do you keep the commoners from usurping your authority?" Casica shook her head slowly. "I guess we can't, truly. But why would they wish?"

"Why?" Dolca smiled patronizingly. "So as to cast off your dominance." Casica shook her head. "We haven't dominance, Dolca. Not as you think. Perhaps, centuries of living under the domination of Byzanthia has evened the playing field of subject and king." Dolca sipped thoughtfully. Such a strange land Cassica must be. "But to have no slaves. Who builds your cities?" "Builders...." "But who pays them?" "The residents of the cities." "Through taxes?" "As is needed, yes."

"*No slaves,*" Dolca repeated to herself. The prospect was unimaginable. And yet the princess clearly said her throne would die to prevent slavery in her land. "So how does it feel - if I may ask - having been the princess of a slaveless land, to now *own* a slave? You've become something, you seem... strongly to dislike." *Touché,* thought Casica.

"Indeed, I have. How does it feel? As queerly in my heart as my dress feels to your eyes. Tis alien. Utterly bewildering to me." Her expression was a mix of puzzlement, distaste and sadness, leaving the hostess feeling somewhat defensive.

"You know, Princess, God Himself doesn't forbid the owning of slaves or is your isle's interpretation of the Holy Book different?" "No. It isn't. And His lack of a definitive discourse on the matter perplexes me. I plan to hear an explanation some day." Dolca smiled. She'd no doubt the woman before her would dare question God. Casica continued. "But God does not explicitly condemn many things that we, his children, view as obviously wrong. But that's no answer. I still find it incomprehensible."

In her mind she saw the slave she knew best. Her eyes teared. Sorrow ruled her heart now, not anger. "You know Clarece, Dolca, or at least know of her." The countess nodded. "How could anyone burn a piece of metal about her throat and consign to her a life of unquestioning servitude and bondage? Hers is by far the most knowledgeable mind - male or female - I have ever known, as are she and her friends some of the most human of humans." Casica rubbed the table thoughtfully. "Clarece is a daughter of God, yet she lives bound by laws of hellish origins."

"But she's *happy*, Casica," Dolca countered. "I'm certain you've never heard her complain about her class. Tis as much a part of her as her skin." "Her not complaining means nothing, Dolca. Has anyone in this country ever given slaves a choice? A choice about anything? What do you think Solange would choose, if she could: a life of freedom or one enslaved?"

Dolca frowned. The question never occurred to her. It felt positively unnatural, such a thought, like changing one's religion. "I don't know. I don't think *she* would know. Slaves can't think on such levels of theoretical concept." Casica smiled at the assertion. As if Clarece could think anywhere else.

"Besides," continued Dolca, "tis a moot issue. Slaves are slaves. They're born slaves. By God's will they are bred slaves; they should live in that will. They are the not-human. To place them in the position of freedom would be cruelty. They haven't the mental or spiritual resources for it - like releasing a caged parrot to the outside world. It would die."

"How many houseslaves have you owned, Dolca?" Casica asked, kindly. This was a kind woman to whom she spoke. Dolca raised her brows. "I don't know. Fifteen... maybe more." "And what became of them?" "Some I bred and sold. Some I transferred. I gave two as gifts. Several died of fever." The princess nodded. "Clarece says you've the reputation of being a kind mistra." "I try." "Why? Why be kind to something not human?" The countess squinted. She saw where this was going.

"I try to be kind to everything, Casica, if that's what you mean. Slaves are property. A unique property, like owning a prized dog. I'd be kind to that, too." She looked down at her waist. "I'll answer someday for the steward I've been. The Book makes that clear." Dolca spoke definitively, but something in the countess was amiss. In all her life, she'd never considered anything Casica had raised. Never spoken to anyone who questioned the institution that existed in her world like color. The entire conversation, she found disrupting.

The Countess of Helan sat back into her chair and looked her guest in the eye. She could play a part when she must. "I've positively no qualms concerning the ownership of slaves, Princess. Tis clear, however, that you do and bear this moral conundrum of ownership uncomfortably. I can relieve you of this burden and

would do so gladly. I offer now to buy your slave. I will pay you...
500 pounds for her at this hour and, for your assurance, promise
her lifetime enslavance. She will not leave my house."

*Five hundred...?* Clarece *far underestimates her self-value,*
thought Casica. She smiled. "Your offer is generous and very kind,
Dolca. If I were selling her, Clarece would come to you. But I've
already assured her lifetime enslavance *(so that's what you call it).*
However," here she smiled to herself. "Even if I had not, I would
never sell Clarece. To do so would be to be to deprive myself of
a priceless gift. She's my friend. If I could release her, now *that* I
would do. I would gladly sacrifice our friendship to see her free. I
would do almost anything to see her free."

Dolca watched the thoughtful tears that formed silently in the
princess' eyes. She had heard of the foreigner's affection for her
slave. It glistened clearly. Even more clearly showed this truth:
Casica loved the woman Clarece. Not a slave.

The princess startled her musing. "Clarece tells me you're losing Solange." "I am," Dolca answered carefully. "I'm sending her
to my sister. She needs help with her children. Solange will slave
excellently in that capacity." "And what of your own children?"
Josquin asked. "Where are they?"

At once, the healer regretted her question. Like a knife, it
cut into her hostess' heart. Red flooded Dolca's graceful throat.
"I haven't any children," she answered softly. God, how she despised this question. It hung over her like a sword. She never
knew when it might fall. "Nahalt and I... I am barren." The confession came determinedly, like self-flagellation. It was penance
to confess her fruitlessness. Penance for whatever sin dwelled in
her that blocked her fertility. It wasn't for nothing God closed her
womb, she knew. But for what, she hadn't a clue, and no amount
of confessing and pleading could release her.

"Please, forgive my question, Dolca. It was forward. I... it's just...
well, you're so clearly made for motherhood." Dolca smirked.
Motherhood. "Apparently not," she answered bitterly. Bitterness:
perhaps that was her sin. She hadn't submitted to God's will for
her to be childless.

Casica's heart beat with compassion. She had sat with such
women before. With rare exception, she had found childlessness
to be so very unnecessary. When next the healer spoke, it was

only after removing the shoes from her words. This was a most holy ground of conversation.

"May I ask, who told you you were barren?" Dolca stared. Who told her? "Well, I've been married seven years and have never conceived. Life has told me. The *physicians* have told me, if that is what you ask." Dolca's tone and expression turned hard, as was Casica's observation anytime reference was made to the court physicians. How resentfully the healers here were regarded. What must they be like?

"Dolca, I don't know you. And you've no reason to trust me. But I am a healer. And it has been my experience that for a woman to be truly incapable of conception is rare indeed. You are young and in obvious health. I would greatly wonder at your being barren." She reached for the countess' arm. Her hand rested safely and warmly there. Dolca looked up at her, pained. "I offer you my services. I am no physician. It would cost you nothing. Would require of you no pain or humiliation." Dolca closed her eyes. The physicians had cost her much. They had required her pain. Their examinations and treatments mortified her with shame.

The hand left her but the warmth remained. "Please," Josquin ended gently. "Consider my offer. God is not angry. I can help you." *God is not angry,* thought Dolca. How could this woman possibly know her fear?

The countess couldn't answer but looked instead at Casica's shirt. Underneath her blouse she could see it, see the strange light burning. She'd heard from someone in the crowd the day the princess came stripped and beaten to her country. The witness said the woman wore a necklace made of light. The town caller said the necklace proved she was the Queen of Cassica's daughter. It proved she was the one to fulfill the edict. Did it also prove she was a healer? Was it true that healers existed on the island across the sea? Did one sit with her now and could she help Nahalt's lineage continue?

"I thank you, Princess," was what she said. "And I thank you for your company this day." The warmth spread from her arm and now touched her heart. Dolca contemplated the effect. She'd misjudged the princess of Cassica in many ways. "I've a confession to make," she said. Casica grinned. "I'm only a healer, Dolca. Not a priest." Dolca smiled back. "Still. It would do me good to confess. I should have invited you long ago. I did think of it but dismissed the idea. I couldn't imagine a captive girl from Cassica to be worth the trouble. I greatly erred in this uncharitable prejudice and would have remained in my sin had not your slave spurred me to repentance."

Casica frowned. "You mean Clarece put you up to this?" "Yes." She shook her head in disbelief. Only God knew the mind of a - . "That slave. You see why I won't part with her? She does me good at every turn." The josquin warmed her cup. Dolca wasn't the only prejudiced person present.

"I, too, have a confession," she began. The countess grinned. "I came very reluctantly this day. My heart, also, was quite uncharitable. Will you forgive my prejudice?" "If you'll forgive mine." Casica wasn't used to bartering for forgiveness but happily paid the price; she nodded. "Then we receive mutual absolution," declared Dolca.

"Am I correct in thinking," Casica asked, "that I'm free to return your hospitality in my own home?" "Yes." The prospect pleased the countess. While clearly Clarece lied in implying her mistra may be open to selling her, it was as clearly true she hadn't exaggerated her owner's gift for conversation. "I look forward to it. Your honesty is refreshing." Casica glanced about the workshop. She could easily become this woman's friend. "So, Countess," she asked, "on what day does your loom enjoy its Sabbath?"

It was with a changed and happy heart the princess sailed toward her eastern wing. Once again the land of her dread surprised her. Not all that was good in the world dwelled on the other side of the channel. Pearls of great value were to be found everywhere, if she had eyes to see them.

She burst into Bastien's chamber and stopped. Casica surveyed his bed and wondered what it would be like to dive into him. Blushing, she abandoned the imaginative adventure. If she were to blend *that* fully into Byzanthia - well, living as she was on a unmanned ship, it was best not to drop anchor on that fantasy. She chose, rather, the harbor of her chamber where, with her first mate, she would share wine and tales of the Byzanthian sea.

# XXIX

The women woke, joyously. Their day of freedom had come to them during the night, and now they laughed and giggled in its presence. They roused earlier than usual and, having decided the best course of action, dressed before completing their morning tasks.

Asla chose her yellow silk blouse covered with the blue velvet vest given her by Tartan. Clarece donned her nicest white blouse and placed over it the royal blue vest of her mastra. They parted ways then, determining the quickest route to the day was for Asla to perform Clarece's pen chores and the senior slave to procure breakfasts for both their owners. Asla's hands made short work of the senior slave's morning duties; she had already begun braiding her hair when her friend came below, bearing her mistra's meal.

"I caught Edsner sleeping," Clarece shared. "I left his meal for him on his night stand." Asla nodded, approvingly. "Excellent. He was gambling last night; he probably won't even notice its presence - or my absence - until noon." She grinned at her stallmate. "I can't believe we're actually doing this, Rece. It should be a beautiful day." "Yes!" her friend agreed excitedly. The sun was showing itself in the halls above, always a good sign for this time of morning.

Having completed her own, Asla reached for her friend's locks. Clarece's long hair was thick. It always challenged the g'Helderleit with new ways of plaiting. Clarece smiled at her friend's touch, wishing, as she had a thousand times, for fingers that worked like hers - weaving as a loom, quick and precise. The women stood and examined each other, pleased with their reflections - except for one thing.

The insulit reached for Clarece's collar. "Let me fasten your blouse completely, Rece," she explained. "We can't pass for free if our collars show." The senior slave nodded. Asla was right. The finest dress in the kingdom was rendered rags by metal welded about one's neck.

"You know this is forbidden," Clarece reminded her friend, not that legality moved Asla in any way. She referred to the law requiring slaves to display their collars at all times. "Tis only forbidden if it's witnessed," was Asla's reply. "And we'll be out of sight before anyone can know. We'll unbutton on our way home." Clarece nodded. She didn't care. The law may do as it like upon her, she decided, only please, God, let her live this day as free.

Asla slung her satchel over her shoulder and wrapped herself in her red cape. She took her stallmate's cloak and examined it. She shook her head, disapprovingly. "Your cloak will be a dead giveaway, Rece. No lady wears a brown woolen cape. It's like a sign: 'Slave on the loose.'" Clarece nodded, wistfully. She had always admired fine cloaks. "I know, As, but it's all I have." Asla frowned. "Well, tis unfit wrapping for the treasure it holds but - you'll fool them anyway." Clarece smiled at her friend's encouragement. "Well, junior slave, I'm at your disposal. Let's deliver Casica's meal and lead me where you will."

With this, the women bowed to one another, and, with breakfast in one pair of hands and a brown woolen cloak in the other, ascended the stairs, fifteen steps closer to freedom. Halfway up, Asla remembered herself. Racing down to her stall, she stripped her left ear of its gold ring. She debated for only a moment before hiding the sign of her trade in her writing pad. Her steps caught Clarece easily, and they arrived at the princess' doorway together.

The princess met them with curtains open and a smile on her face. She had been up early, herself. Clarece offered her greeting kneel and awaited her invitation. "Good morning, ladies!" the princess wished in Cassican. "Up early this day, I see." "Yes, my lady. The occasion won't wait," Clarece replied, moving to set her mistra's meal upon her table. "

"Asla, I trust you will take good care of yourselves," Casica offered in g'Helderleicht. "Yes, your highness," the insulit replied. "I must watch her closely. She would be a strumpet, this one, given half the chance. I rather fear loosing her upon the unsuspecting city. But I will keep a tight moral reign on her and deliver her back to you chaste as she leaves you, the degree of which is highly suspect." The princess laughed, shaking her head.

"I can't understand what you say about me, insulit," came the senior slave's voice, "but I'm certain tis of the most flattering nature." "Always, dear Clarece," came the sincere response. "Are you not yet done, slave?" Asla was positively jumping in place. She didn't want a moment wasted, so precious was this day. It was as though she had awakened with a certain amount of food served on this day's plate and wished not a morsel left untasted by its end. "There. Your meal, my lady," Clarece announced putting a filled glass in its proper place. She joined her friend and took her cloak.

The two women presented themselves before the princess. Asla asked, "Can you see them or will we pass as free ladies?" "Oh... I see," observed Casica. "Your collars - you've hidden them. Going incognito, are we? I can't see a thing." She looked closely at her friends. They were absolutely radiant. "You're the perfect ladies... except for one thing." Casica went to the door and gathered her cloak. "Here, Clarece, let's exchange capes, you and I." Asla offered her friend a look that said, "I told you so."

With a bow, the slave received her mistra's offering. She wrapped the garment around her, immediately registering its affect. She always felt a queen in this beautiful piece. Clarece smiled at the warmth that already stirred within it and relaxed in the sense of its owner that now embraced her. "Well, what do you think now?" she asked, shyly.

Casica stepped back, appraising the art before her. "I think... I think I was wrong." The slaves glanced anxiously at one another. "Tis your slave garments that are the disguise. This..." she announced, extending her arms, "this is your true selves." The women smiled, pleased with the compliment.

"Two more things," continued Casica. "One: your pass, my lady," she said handing Clarece an unsealed document. The slave glanced at her permission. Her lady knew how to prepare a fine letter. "Thank you, mistra. This will serve well." "Good. And second, I have neglected dashing you these past months, senior slave. This is for your day." She handed a heavy gold coin to the outstretched mitten.

Clarece stared in disbelief. A crown. Her mistra was giving her a crown. "You know a fine inn, I'm sure," Casica was saying to Asla. "Several." "Excellent. Dinner is on me." Clarece couldn't contain her guilt. "My lady," she began, objecting, "this is too - ." "Generous - ," interrupted her blond friend. "You are too kind my lady; we thank you. Here, Rece," she continued, taking the gold. "I'll hold this for you."

Clarece was still glaring at her friend when the princess took Asla into her arms. "God's blessings upon you, His Beauty," she wished in her native tongue. "When horses dance, but thank you," was the light reply. Casica turned and embraced her charge warmly. "God's blessings, Clarece. Have a wonderful day," she said softly. The cloak responded with a heightened warmth at her touch. "Thank you, lady. Thank you so much for this day." "God gave the day," Josquin grinned. "Enjoy it...."

The princess walked to her door and with a flourish, invited them away. "Ladies," she announced, officially, "the day awaits you with wonder." She bowed low before them. The two slaves grinned and returned her bow. Without looking back they skipped down the stone stairs, scraping their boots against the pavement just for the pleasure of the sound.

Casica stood on the landing and watched. At the bottom, the pair turned and waved; then, taking each other by the arm began jogging playfully in dance towards the west gate, the sun warming their backs and the sky covering them with grace.

Casica returned to her empty chamber. The door closed behind her. She felt strangely alone. She sat at her table and offered a prayer for the safety of her friends. The cooling meal she enjoyed in silence. No Clarece to sit with her and talk of whatever was on her bountiful mind. No sense of another's presence. It occurred to the woman that this was the first time in months she kept her own company. She too, had the day to herself, she realized. How would she spend it?

Casica looked out the full windows Bastien had installed. She thought of him and smiled sadly. How could she miss someone she didn't know? Had never spent time with? She couldn't answer her question but accepted the reality of missing him.

She glanced back into the dark room that was his. If she had eyes, she was certain, she would see him everywhere. This entire chamber, after all, was his making: he made the table she sat at, the bed she slept in, the dresser which held her clothing. Only now did the young woman consider what this meant. Clarece had said her owner began renovation of his storage room two years before her arrival. It was an ambitious project, being as her chamber was, a solid stone structure resting above a supporting room of the palace.

Casica ran her hand over the table. Clarece's attentiveness rendered it a warm mirror. Quarter sawn work. The king's last born must be a gifted and accomplished woodsmith, a diligent worker, she thought, admiring the panel and stone design of her walls. And he must have cared. What kind of man puts such labor and time into the quarters of a woman he has never met? What kind of man would prepare such a place at all when this woman would come to him as his wife. He could rightfully have taken her into his own chamber, forced her into his own bed.

But he hadn't. Bastien had given this beautiful room for her own, waiting for - she wasn't sure what. Friendship? Trust? Love? Casica bowed her head again. Though she didn't know for what nor how, she offered a prayer for this kind man and felt, for the first time, a loneliness for him that surprised her. And for the first time, also, asked that God would return him - quickly.

Asla and Clarece reached the portcullis. A guard familiar to the insulit greeted them. "Both to the city today?" he inquired. "Yes, good Stoane. My companion and I are on an errand of royal apportions," Asla replied, handing him her senior's pass. The guard read it carefully. He recognized the name but not the handwriting. "So the Cassican is your owner?" he asked. "Yes, great guard," Clarece replied, half-kneeling. God, she felt nervous. Surely, they would be caught, caught as what, she didn't know, but there must be something punishably wrong with what they did. Stoane returned the parchment to Asla. "Success upon your mission," he wished and ushered them free of the grounds.

The women passed through a stone corridor that led them to the world beyond. Clarece absorbed every detail: the cold, damp air that surrounded them; the musty smell of stone; the double, spiked, gates that hung at ready in front and behind them; feet and voices echoing though the small passageway. Twenty steps took them into the light of day.

Clarece stepped from the passage into her first glimpse of the city of Byzanthia. And laughed in wonder. It was as though she had never seen color in her life. Color, a kaleidoscope of it, swirled about her, the color of life and human activity coming upon her as that first sight of the ocean. There was no fear here, however; only amazement. People, hundreds of them, moved freely about her, each on a mission of his or her own. The awe-struck woman stopped in her tracks and stared, feeling all the world as though she had stepped into a symphony.

"Well, what do you think?" her friend asked loudly, smiling at the pleasure and joy cascading from Clarece's face. "Heaven, Asla! I don't know if I can bear it! Look at all these people! I'd no idea Byzanthia housed so many people!" Asla laughed. "Amazing, isn't it? Aren't you happy you serve only one?" "Yes. The prospect, otherwise, is overwhelming. I wonder how many are slaves as us?" "Many. We'll see more at the market. They say three thousand slaves live in the royal city. But today they're less two! Come. There's much to see. I thought we would tour some buildings, spend some money and then visit the ocean at foot level - if you'd like."

Clarece turned to her friend. "Whatever you want is what I'd like. This is your day, Asla. Have your way with me!" The g'Helderleit smiled broadly. She had rarely seen Clarece so exuberant.

The first building on their tour would be the armoury. Clarece had a long love affair with armour. She had read that history could be found in differing styles and metals of knightly suits and had voiced, once, a desire to see this history in sight. The women entered a famous armory guild, the "Maud Catou." It was the first time in her life that Clarece had seen a store of any kind. The entry room smelled of oil, and in it were displayed shiny new suits of armour for every occasion.

The scholar recognized, at once, the differences between armor for battle and armor for show. The weight and composition of metal distinguished the two. Metal that preserved life was of a much sturdier grade than that preserving reputation. Helmets, breastplates, leggings, coats of mail - it was all here, she saw excitedly. But the guild's true treasure awaited them. Behind the entry store, stood a museum. In it was displayed five hundred years of defensive wear.

"Oh, Asla!" Clarece exclaimed. "Look! Tis King Handsin's progression of suits!" Of this, too, she had read. Apparently this monarch, who reigned nine generations earlier, required sixteen different sizes of suits, growing, as he did, into his throne gradually. With excitement, the teacher described historical events accompanying each size. Coming from another mouth, this recitation would utterly have bored the gymnast. Metal was cold and unyielding. But in her friend's words, Asla found the room and its contents a fascinating banquet of iron.

The women spent quite some time here. They left by the back way and entered an alley familiar to the insulit. "The man I call 'Noll'? This is where he lives," she said, pointing to a room three floors above the street. Clarece registered the location with interest. Asla often serviced this man. "What does he do?" she asked. "He works in the armoury. We won't stop to say 'hello', if you don't mind." *So that's why Asla smells like polish when she returns from Noll's,* realized her friend.

The next building on their tour was the day's glory hole. Asla had purposely scheduled their day around this gem. The women walked a maze of alleys and streets before they reached the prized destination: the city's largest bookstore. Clarece stopped in her tracks. "This can't be what I think it is," she ventured. Surely the world could not write so many books. "Come and see," her friend invited.

The women stepped into the building. It had the smell of the king's library, but that was its only point of reference for the scholar. Her steps rang hollow on the wooden floor as she walked. Clarece stepped into the middle of the room and gasped, raptured at the sight that welcomed her. Every wall was lined to the ceiling with books. "Blessing! So many...." "How long do you think it'd take to read all these?" the voice beside her asked. "Three eternities - and a day." "Well, you'd best get started." "I don't know where to begin," Clarece confessed. "The poetry section is over there...," suggested Asla.

The friends walked to a large section displaying new and ancient volumes. Clarece chose a book sporting a blue leather cover. She opened its stiff pages and sniffed. Oh, how she loved that smell. *Songs of the Wind* read the title. With a glance at her companion, she absorbed five poems before replacing the book for another. From poetry, she grazed history, from history, literature, and from there to religious works. Asla did not accompany Clarece to religion, choosing instead to linger in the company of poets. Clergymen made her nervous.

The women spent much of their morning here in this cathedral of knowledge. Of books, Clarece could not have her fill, but this store satisfied her, nonetheless. Simply knowing such a place existed pleased her. Surely it must mean her passion of words was shared by many others; so often she felt embarrassingly alone in her love for reading. Here was proof she was not.

As the pair proceeded from the bookstore, the elder could not express, enough, her gratitude at Asla's forcing her to experience this day. As she dodged people and animals, carts and horsemen, Clarece exuded excitement and gratitude. Asla surrendered, finally, trying to contain her friend's outpourings; let Rece speak to her heart's desire, she decided. This was a poet's paradise.

Asla lead her delirious comrade to her favorite section of the city: the market. Now this was *her* element. Their first stop was to a favorite vendor of hot food. Clarece watched, admiringly, as her friend bargained - and flirted - with the older man. She successfully procured two sticks, strangely wrapped about with roasted pork. "Here, Rece," Asla offered. "Try this. Tis shenit, a g'Helderleit food." Clarece bit into the warm flesh. Spicy, surprising tastes filled her mouth. She'd no idea such richness existed in meat. "It's all the spices," her friend explained.

From here, the women visited another vendor, this time purchasing sweet ale. They sat with their culinary treasures and watched as much of the city roamed about them. "I feel as though I'm in a hive of life," Clarece observed. "Tis truly overwhelming.

No wonder slaves are kept inside." Obviously, however, many weren't.

All around her worked men and women with heavy iron collars about their throats. Laborer slaves most likely; that, and houseslaves selling from their masters' fields. Clarece considered the silver band about her neck. By these standards, her ring of bondage was a light one, a precious burden. Though she no desire to be enslaved, fate had sired her as such, destined her by seed and womb. Still, she decided, watching her weather-beaten fellows, hers was an easy lot compared to theirs.

As she sat, Clarece wondered if those who had bred her were slaves such as these. Did they walk in this city at this moment? Her eyes were unique in both shade and form, with the dark ring that framed them. For years, Clarece looked into the eyes of other slaves, hoping to glance herself in one of them. She had discarded the practice long ago, but something about the day made her wish to do so again.

The companions ate and drank until a powerful bell peeled loudly that their day quickly passed. "The cathedral," Asla answered to Clarece's questioning look. "Our next stop." The two rose and wound their way through the cornucopia of scent and activity, stopping only long enough for Asla to purchase three apples. One they shared along the way. Two she kept for later.

Byzanthia's royal cathedral had required several hundred years to construct. The blood of countless slaves poured its mortar. The women paused at two great gates, Clarece lost in the beauty of its architecture. "Look!" she exclaimed. "Horianian flying buttresses, common among the western sphere of the Colegian dynasty. And over there! See the gargoyles? There are the Kanion spirits and Quitu demons and there...." She laughed delightedly, "and there is the legacy of a sacrilegious, drunken mind. Some mason made that gargoyle to have water flow from his - ."

Asla laughed aloud. She had often studied the holy site but never, ever noticed the man with his bum facing the yard. She stopped laughing and looked about nervously. This place both frightened and intrigued the young woman. She had witnessed hundreds of people enter its doors for worship and confession. Burial and marriage. And the mysterious rites of christening and mass. The insulit could only imagine what drew them into this place. But she did know that the key of entry was a soul, and that, no vendor could provide.

"The cathedral contains many works of art and sculpture, Rece," Asla explained. "I've heard there's even a burial section for poets, kings and queens. It's a living museum, the cathedral is. You'll enjoy it. Take your time. I'll wait here for you." "What do you mean, Asla? You aren't coming?" The insulit shook her head solemnly. "No. Such is not a place for me." "But no one will know you are insulit," Clarece prodded. "Come. You'll enjoy it too."

The young woman shook her head emphatically. Someone would know, she thought, glancing up into the sky. She had heard that holy ground would burn the feet of insulit.

Clarece studied the grand structure before her. The wonder and knowledge it held beckoned. She struggled with desire then dismissed it. She would not feast upon a meal unavailable to her sala. "If you can't enter, neither will I," she said finally.

"Don't be tete dur," her friend countered. "Tis your right to enter there. I'll wait. I'll be fine." Clarece smiled happily. "No," she declared. "Another day," she ventured, absurdly. There would be no another day. "I've come to spend time with you - not with stone and glass." Asla looked to her boots, frustrated at her friend's stubbornness yet warmed with her kindness. "Then let us go to another cathedral," she suggested. "Gods do not forbid my feet sand."

Casica perched on the ledge that beckoned her so long ago. It was impossible to sit here and not think of that day nor of the one she first shared with Clarece. Fog obscured her anticipated view of the lighthouse. No Cassica in sight today. The healer looked above her. These clouds passed her home before coming here. Somewhere beyond the water that seemed to span forever, lived, at this moment, her parents, brother, Berea and many, many others she loved. Their faces filled her mind and their love, her heart. Was she really here? she wondered. Did she truly sit on the shores of Byzanthia?

As if to answer, Rigel walked behind her and nudged her bare back. His back was bare, too. The sun laughed upon her naked torso. Often she would lay in the sun's warmth along the shores of

Cassica. Her family owned a private beach, one she visited along her circuit to Ser Hosanna, the city of refuge assigned her. Casica lay back into the grass, soaking in its life-filled scent. DeLeah would be caring for Ser Hosanna now.

Her thoughts visited Erin and Jakob, the clergy who flocked that fortified city. How often she had slept in their guest room and eaten Erin's delicious vegetable stew. She wondered how they were, they and the many others who dwelled safely there. God, how she missed those rides in her circuit; missed the people who made up her world. Missed the healing that flowed so often through her body, into her hands - and beyond.

Her shalonn aroused to life. It brimmed with power and light, begging her for release. Josquin hopped to her feet and faced her beloved land. Raising her hands, she leaned back into the sun and wished the sea christen her more. She felt it rise, the power that dwelled so mightily within her; it flooded her chest and over-flowed into the pobble stones that embraced her throat. It was coming; she could feel it. The girl relaxed and surrendered to the sensation. It was no longer her now; it was a separate life.

Casica closed her eyes as a pleasure and joy and power she could not contain surged through and out of her. She cried out as sun and stones met. Rigel jumped at the sight: light burst from his keeper into the air around her. The stones about her burned with a pure white. The girl fell to her knees, overcome. Then, lay back in ecstasy, basking in the life that consumed her.

Asla and Clarece continued their colorful trek to the ocean. Along the way, they came upon an artist, furnishing his canvas with the world. It was the market he painted today, capturing the color and life that flowed, like so many streams, along the streets. The two women glanced, knowingly, at each other. They had money. She would enjoy a gift.

The artist paused to study the works before him. The blond woman was a ray of sun. "My lady," he declared, smiling at the pleasing form, "I must ask you to step away; your beauty shames my feeble attempts." Asla smiled winsomely.

Clarece stood beside her, invisible, and wondered as she had before, what it would be like to elicit such response wherever you went. She felt no jealousy - it would be like being jealous of a star or other heavenly body; Asla was in a class of beauty all by herself. She did wonder, however, if her friend ever felt lonely in that place. But for now, no loneliness touched her; Asla's beauty only blossomed in the light of this man's attention.

"Your attempts aren't feeble," she replied. "They are lovely; you capture the life of the market - though you do seem to lose some of its romance." The man looked to his canvas, puzzled. She was correct, this lady. She must a student of art; perhaps a model, even. "I fear I have no romance fit for this scene. May I borrow some of yours?" The girl bowed charmingly. "But of course, great artist. I have *much* to spare...."

Clarece contemplated where this interlude might lead had her presence not curtailed it. "Excuse me, sir," she interrupted. "We have a friend who is an accomplished artist. She is newly arrived, however, and hasn't many implements of her own. Could you suggest something she might desire but would likely not own?" The artist turned reluctantly to the taller woman. Though not entirely unpleasant, she certainly had not fallen from the other's tree. "So, she is accomplished...," he thought aloud. He reached for a brush that was no brush at all, but a knife of sorts. Fine as a human hair.

"I would suggest this, a painter's blade. Only a trained artist would know its use, but not many have one. 'Too costly." "And where may we find such an implement?" Asla asked, drawing the man's eyes to where they wished. "Do you know St. Khol's?" "Yes," she replied, "I know it." "There's an art shop on the west side. They have everything you may want."

"Not everything...," Asla replied, suggestively. The man beamed. "We thank you for your help." "Will I see you again?" the artist asked, hoping, though surely no lady as this would grace him again with her presence. "Perhaps," she smiled; "There is much more to see, I'm sure." With this the women bowed gracefully and walked towards the art store.

"Scads, As," Clarece commented beyond the artist's hearing. "Do you never tire of flirting?" Asla smiled teasingly. "Professional development, Rece. I mustn't lose my form." "You've no danger of that," her companion replied. "You stir men like water." "Not all men," her friend observed. "Poul's eyes are for you, alone."

The comment warmed Clarece. She glanced gratefully to her beautiful friend and continued her walk happily.

Their quest at St. Khol's was quickly accomplished. Painter's blade in tow, the ladies sailed for shore. Trees in the form of masts, and wings, disguised as sails, hailed them from afar. Clarece thought how the port looked like an alien forest. The women reached the boardwalks that crisscrossed the port like so many spider webs. Asla jumped with excitement.

"Look, Rece! See that sail over there? The one with the green osprey? Tis a g'Helderleit ship! It would take me home - if I could bear the presence of the sailors... and over there, the ship flying the crimson fleur d'lis? - tis a Cassican vessel. You always know them by the crimson. That's a royal ship. I wonder what it brings? And those over there, the tall ones? They are all Byzanthian." The young woman hopped to a pier. "Come on - you'll see better!" she ordered.

Clarece gauged the jump. Her legs could execute it but not her hands. She ran along another pier until she gained her friend's side. From here, she better understood Asla's excitement. There was something awesome about the huge vessels, rocking dizzily upon the approaching swells. Creaking surrounded her as did male voices. Burly and wiry men walked all manner of wood and clung precariously to ropes and masts. What would it be like to board a ship, she wondered? Certainly, her body would never know, but, still, her imagination could. Gulls hung everywhere, feasting near fishing ships and perching on boat and pier. They were fascinating creatures, these birds. Clarece saw them often outside, flying high over the palace, leaving where, she did not know. But surely, this must be their destination. She would know where they traveled, next time they passed over her head.

The women walked along the pier until it ended in a sandy lane. Asla sat and quickly freed her feet from their leather bonds. "Here, Rece," she offered, removing her boots. She tied their laces and walked easily; her friend joined her, not so easily. Clarece, who had never felt sand before, laughed at the sensation, at once cool and warm. "Scads, Asla! This isn't easy. It's like walking in... in... sand!"

Asla joined her laughter. "It gets easier as you near the ocean." The ocean. Even now, Clarece didn't want to walk; she wanted to wait, to lose herself, again, in the power and motion of the sea. It was so different here, standing level with the pounding surf. She looked to her left. Asla had shed her vest and even now ran along the water, jumping and somersaulting with joy.

Clarece shook her head at her friend's exploits. No one she knew enjoyed being herself as much as Asla did in dance. She eyes returned to the waves. They were not nearly so frightening at foot level. She walked up to them. A train of foam swept over her feet. "Yow! Scads, that's cold!" she yelled to the world at large. Her feet stung with the icy wet. Asla was running to her in the surf, water up to her shins. "How can you bear that?!" asked Clarece. "Bear what?" "The cold!" "You get used to it - like this...."

Before Clarece knew it, the powerful g'Helderleit grabbed her about the waist and spun her full into an approaching swell. "Kai!" Clarece yelled, laughing and cursing at once. As the waters receded she laughed at the queer sensation of sand slipping from under her feet. Seaweed slithered across her bare skin and little fish nipped at her toes. Asla laughed uncontrollably. "Isn't it fun?!" Clarece nodded, joyfully. The ocean - she was *in* the ocean and it embraced her, now, not so coldly as before.

"I'm going to run aways," Asla friend said. "I'll be back." She stopped herself and asked, "Do you know how to swim?" Clarece shook her head. "Well, stay close to shore. Don't let the current take you out. If you drown, Casica will kill me." "Thank you for your concern," Clarece called after, watching as Asla raced the wind.

Clarece looked at her hands. Taking their clasps in her mouth, she removed her two mittens. She must at least try, she decided. She reached into the frothing wonder and gasped. She could feel it! she could feel the cold wet! - either that or her mind was playing a delicious trick. The woman brought a deformed hand to her lips. Salty. Wonderful sea salt. Here she was, Clarece d'Casica, standing in the source of all the world's salt, the staple of life. Something of this realization overcame her and before she knew it, her own salt joined that of the ocean.

"Oh, Great Mastra," she whispered to the waves. "Thank you." She looked out onto the horizon. A ship was there, waxing and waning, in time with the swells that bore it. Above and to her right were seven gulls, mysteriously gliding left to the oncoming wind. How could they do that? She walked slowly along the surf and studied rocks, worn smooth with their endless travel. She picked one up. The dark, striking color on its surface disappeared with its drying. She replaced it into its watery foil. It was prettier there... that must be where it belongs.

A school of minnows startled her as she startled them. She watched as flashes of silver sprung into the air like a fleshy hatch of gnats. Crispus! what a classroom this was! Everywhere she looked was life. Even, here, in a shell she now discovered. Little legs pulled back at her touch. This must be a crab. There were many shells along this area of the shore. She stooped and examined several. She found one, smooth as marble, unoccupied. This one she placed in her vest.

Another few steps and there, half-buried in the sand, was the ridge of a pointy crest. Clarece removed it cautiously from the sand. A conk. It had to be. She lifted the bluish shell to her ear. She had read that the ocean resided in conks. It did! she laughed, listening as a rush of sound met her ears. This treasure she would keep. It would offer her the ocean in the midst of her dark pen. But the shell, she would give to her mistra as a first fruits offering from her first visit to the beach.

Asla came running lightly to her, boots, vest, cape and satchel all in tow. "What do you think?" she asked happily. "Tis beyond my capacity of thought." "Now *that's* saying something," her friend jested. "I'm sure the almighty is impressed with himself, finally." They walked in silence, deeply content. It *was* a perfect day. Asla spotted a grotto she knew well. She loved to rest inside it to hear the roar of the sea amplified, as it was, within the rocky walls of her fortress.

"Come, Rece," she invited, taking her friend to her secret place. She spread her cloak on the sand and motioned for Clarece to sit. "This is one of my favorite places, Rece. I'm happy you can share it with me." Asla took her satchel and unbuckled it. Usually it contained extra clothing and oils - soap. It was her insulit's bag. But today it served a sacred task. From it the young woman produced a flask, a cup, and a small loaf of bread.

Clarece smiled, recognizing the elements of the sala'd. Asla had never taken the leading role in this ritual. She watched as her young friend broke the bread, self-consciously. The insulit wasn't accustomed to handling something holy. She broke several pieces of bread and laid them on her cloak. The women kneeled before each other. Asla smiled, shyly, into her friend's eyes.

"You are my sala, Clarece... my cherished, eternal friend," she announced softly. "May you be filled with life and never know hunger." She was left-handed but offered the gift of friendship with her right. She placed a piece of bread into her friend's mouth and waited as her sala ate. Then Clarece reverently reciprocated the act. The bread of life eaten, they waited a time for the next course.

Asla looked out at the ocean, trying to bolster the resolve she had determined to show this day. This was the day she would do it. The day she would defy her hollow state and offer from somewhere something she had never voiced. She took the flask and timidly poured a cupful of wine. It was real wine, not mead, she had taken from Casica's decanter. She had asked permission, though, wanting to keep this offering pure.

Asla looked down at the glass and spoke into it. "You are my sala, my dear friend. With this, I remember you as my heart re-members the blood that flows from it." She took the cup into her hands, feeling the heart she mentioned, pounding. She stopped and swallowed hard. Looking directly into her friend's sea eyes, she declared, openly, something she had wanted to say for years but never had. "I love you, Clarece." Clarece blinked, surprised. Her face broke into a radiant smile. "And I, you."

Asla grinned shyly and glanced at her cloak. She lifted the cup to her sala's mouth and gently poured wine into it. Clarece drank slowly, savoring the moment as much as the wine. She took the cup from her friend and waited. This she could not do without help. Four hands poured wine into the beautiful mouth.

Asla finished the cup. She placed it on her cloak then reached out to her friend. The two held the other's face for a time, then ca-ressed their hands along cheeks, until, palms meeting, claws and fingers folded as in prayer. There, the women bowed their heads as, quietly, Clarece prayed for them both. The sala'd performed, the friends knelt in silence, listening as the ocean serenaded them, embracing their holy meal with ethereal song.

Casica woke to the bristly hairs of Rigel's nose. He was sniffing his lady, telling her the day was ending. The young woman opened her eyes and stretched luxuriously. *God, how I love being a josquin,* she thought, feeling wonderfully exhilarated and satisfied - and filled. Then she had the strangest memory: She was with Berea visiting a new mother. They were having tea when Rachel's baby began to cry. Before Rachel could bring the infant to her breasts, milk began squirting out! The babe squinted at the white washing his face. Berea howled! For herself, Casica was stupefied; she was only four at the time and had never witnessed such a sight.

"That's how I feel now," she spoke. Filled with life and longing to release it. She must settle for song on her journey home - that and maybe a long run beside Rigel. And perhaps, she hoped, Clarece would wish some treatment for her hands tonight. Casica stroked her companion. Time to go. She rose and gathered her shirt and vest. Best not to arrive at the royal city half-clothed. Having dressed, she walked to the ledge one final time.

Fog was rolling in from the ocean. Her home would be cooling now. Hansel would stoke the sitting room's fire and mother and father would drink, smoke, and talk until bedtime. As for K'ardan... no telling where he was or what he did, that one. She would give a day of her life to be with them now.

But not this day. This had been a perfect day. A "keeper," Clarece would say. The princess bid goodnight to her land and saddled her steed. She would let him run first. With a kick to his flanks, she flew, wondering as she did, how her friends enjoyed their time.

The women sat on Casica's cloak, reluctant to leave their ocean sanctuary. They watched as waves fell upon themselves at the shore. "What would it be like to spend everyday at the sea, Asla?" "Heaven," came the longing answer. Asla had grown up on the ocean and missed it like innocence. Of course, she would come here again, but her friend could not - not unless Casica brought her which, of course, she would if Clarece asked. Still the two of them could not come together.... She clung to the sadness of this thought only a moment; life was motion for the g'Helderleit. It was dangerous to think much at all.

The two returned to the pier. Asla shod their feet with socks and boots. They enjoyed a final view of the sea. *Always changing,* thought Clarece; *always the same.* She looked into her friend's sunburned face and smiled. The sun hit Asla's white hair, whiter from having spent the afternoon in light, and seemed to reflect off it like sparks from an anvil. Wind blew her white mane and caressed her mouth into a smile. This was a moment captured, the poet realized. She would never forget the way her friend looked now; it was a portrait locked eternally in her heart, one to which she would look often in the days ahead. No words joined them now; none were needed.

The sun hung low upon the horizon. It would set in an hour. Asla turned to her friend. "Hungry?" she asked quietly. What a silly question for a slave. "Always...." "Let's go see the bear."

The Bear, it turned out, was the finest shoreline inn in the royal city, boasting a kingly heritage to compliment its name. The women preceded the evening crowd. The waiter met them optimistically. Two ladies out to enjoy the sea, obviously. The possibility for a fair dash invigorated him with a renewed desire to please. The fact that the younger of the ladies was a goddess did nothing to dim his focus. Clarece let Asla lead; this was her element.

"May I seat you, ladies?" he asked officially. "You may," Asla answered, offering to him an advance on his dash, in money and attention. The man bowed and kissed her outstretched hand. "The window room off your back porch would suit perfectly." "My lady knows our inn?" "I've the pleasure before, yes," she replied, thinking to herself the day she spent with Tartan. That day had held many, many pleasures....

"Come with me," the eager man invited. The women walked through the large dining area. Clarece, as she had done much of the day, stared in wonder. Such appointments she had never seen. Perhaps the king's throne room was so furnished, she did not know, but surely no home in the city could boast this setting. Silver and velvet, mahogany and maple greeted her everywhere. Fine crystal and china awaited service on every table. There was carpet on the floor; mirrors framed a large bar. And everywhere, everything was fragranced with the smell of food, glorious food. Her mouth watered, like a dog's, she observed, embarrassed. *If they only knew who we were,* she thought, *they'd have us flogged.* But they didn't and they weren't.

The window room was fittingly named. A row of three wide windows graced them with a view of the sunset over the sea. It appeared the room was built over the ocean. Asla confirmed that it was. The waiter began describing the evening's selections. With a slight panic, Clarece thought of the crown. Surely a crown would be enough. Wouldn't it? The truth was, she didn't know, knew nothing of the value of money beyond her tiny world of the guild's necessities. What she did know was that Asla knew, and judging by her friend's careless behavior gauged that, yes, they could afford to eat in such a place.

Clarece surrendered her fear and remained silent, hiding her hands safely in her vest. She watched as the breakers foamed and fell away on the evening tide. She half-listened as Asla selected a bottle of some sort of wine, pausing to ask politely, "May I order for us?"

Clarece nodded. For some reason, she was speechless - a rarity in itself. It must be the overwhelming affect of the day, she determined, smiling kindly to herself. But it didn't matter. She relished this experience of not having to make a single decision.

The waiter returned quickly with their wine. He opened the bottle in their presence, something, in all her life, Clarece had never witnessed. The wine she knew came in skins. She watched, curiously, as he offered a small portion for Asla's approval. The slave sniffed and tasted. Clarece grinned. Scads, she was a bumpkin compared to her cultured friend. Having poured their drinks, the waiter disappeared, closing a heavy door behind him. Only now did the Clarece speak.

"How did you know about this room? The view is matchless...."

"Tartan and I come here when he visits. I like the privacy." Worry usurped her friend's faith. "Can we afford this?" Clarece asked. "We've already spent some of our crown on Casica's gift. I don't want to have my neck rung."

Asla smiled good-humoredly. "Rece, we've more money than we possibly could spend. Your mistra dashed you well. A toast to her?" Clarece, very carefully, lifted her goblet with both hands. Crystal. She was never fond of it. "To Casica," announced Asla. "May she know much pleasure at the hands - and other bodily members - of her husband and," she continued, more seriously, "may she know much joy in return for the measure she has granted us this day." Clarece bowed and toasted her goblet. "And to friendship. May our hearts be free in ways no collar can bind." "Huzzah!" Asla smiled. The women toasted and drank, relaxed. Both were somewhat fatigued; it had been a full day.

The waiter knocked before entering. Asla waited until her friend had safely hidden her un-mittened hands before answering. With him he bore a tray, upon which sat a rather large congregation of utensils. Clarece's wrists winced at the sight: a cast-iron pot, a smaller iron pot, bread, humus, a small bottle of port accompanied by two smaller glasses. On the side was balanced a delicate dish containing two dark pieces of something Clarece did not recognize.

With a flourish, the waiter revealed the pots' contents. From the smaller, he ladled an unfamiliar soup which steamed with a thick richness in her china bowl. The other pot, oh, she recognized that smell: venison. Potatoes, greens and carrots garnished it. Clarece prayed it was not drool she felt on her mouth. Their waiter served them both generously; asked if there were more he could do (as if anything more could possibly be done for mere mortals, thought Clarece), then excused himself.

Clarece stared in disbelief. "We should pray," she said reverently. Asla rolled her eyes. Clarece really should get out more. "Of course," is what she said. "God," the awed woman began, "I never knew such food existed this side of heaven. Thank you!" Clarece reached for an appropriate ending. "Amen," was all she could conjure. "Amen," Asla echoed. Clarece brought out her claws and waited patiently for her friend's hands. Asla dipped a large silver spoon into the soup bowl.

"Here, Rece, try this," she said. "Tis an offering from the sea." Clarece chewed the offering slowly. The soup contained a strange food, very fleshy and rich. The taste was unlike any to which she could compare. "What is this?" she asked, intrigued. "Scallops. Do you like it?" "I've never even read of scallops. Sea food is so different from land's." She took another spoonful; now that her mouth adjusted to the texture of the mollusks, her tongue was won to its taste. "I like it," she decided.

Asla now cut her venison. She placed a single piece upon her friend's tongue. As Clarece digested this decidedly exotic culinary experience, Asla cut some meat for herself. "What do you think?" she asked between bites. "Oh, Asla. I am spoiled for life, I fear." "Good, isn't it?" "I have not the words in my vocabulary to express the delectable possession of this moment."

The women ate thus, Asla serving her friend soup and meat, vegetables and bread and then herself. Clarece now understood her thoughtfulness in procuring this private room. Otherwise she would not have been able to eat. What a proper change in roles from Asla's experiences at the guild's table, thought the maimed woman. The women ate their fill, careful to leave room for their dessert. "What is that?" Clarece asked curiously.

"Chocolate. From Hathen. Tartan has positively ruined me with this." Clarece tasted her piece and understood, immediately, Asla's devotion. The candy was sweet and somewhat bitter, only enough to cleanse the palate with pure delight. As they sipped their port, the friends watched as stars ascended their thrones above the ocean. Fog would soon hide them, but for now they glistened with joy.

The sea was now lost to their sight, but not to their hearing nor smell. It seemed to Clarece the ocean had been their guardian this side of the city. Asla took out the painter's blade to study it more closely. It was a beautiful work of craftsmanship with its cherry handle and silver blade. "Do you think Casica will know how to use this?" she asked. "Most certainly," replied Clarece. "There is little she doesn't know concerning things she loves."

She reached for the instrument. She stroked the wooden handle. Asla watched intently. "Can you feel that?" she asked finally. Clarece turned to her, a tentative grin on her mouth. "I think so. I'm not sure - I haven't felt in so long - but I do *think* I feel it. It may be my mind is feeling for me, though." Asla considered for a moment.

"Close your eyes," she instructed. She took her dinner knife and held it briefly over the candles that lit their meal. She touched the metal to make sure it wouldn't hurt her friend, then placed the blade against a shapeless finger. Clarece flinched!

"You *do* feel it!" her friend smiled. "You see? Even the little time the healer has spent with you is helping." Clarece poked the blade at her palm. It was true. Casica's ministration *was* helping her. She wondered if the princess would be available tonight.

"She can heal you, Rece, if you'd let her," Asla ventured, interrupting her thoughts. The maimed woman looked quietly at her deformity. The thought almost frightened her. What would it be like - truly - to have hands after so many years of living without them? It seemed that the state of living painlessly should satisfy her. To want more would be to want too much.

The women sat for a long time. A knock broke their reverie. It was the waiter, asking if more could be done, if they enjoyed their meal, if they were ready to leave. Asla handed him part of their crown. He bowed and returned shortly with their change. Asla took one coin and handed the rest to the smiling man. He was right; this was a profitable pair. Rarely was anyone so generous. Bowing low, he thanked them and invited them to his table again. The women sighed at one another. Time for the day to end.

Asla poured the remaining port. "To the perfect day," she offered. "To the perfect day," she was answered. The friends toasted a final time and bid their meal farewell. The ocean escorted them along their way. As she walked, Clarece listened for it as she did a key on the hammerschord, seeing how long she could hold to the sound of a slowly fading note. Their watery chaperone departed them as they topped a hill separating the port from the market area.

The city held a night market now, explained Asla; in a night market, you might find different wares than you would in daylight. Clarece smiled at the sight. All around her were little lanterns; from her lofty perspective, they looked like little earth stars. The smell of oil paved their trek towards the palace as the two women took a different route, a shorter more direct one, home. The cathedral sounded eleven.

"I hope my pass works," mumbled Clarece, "or I'll end this perfect day in irons." Asla slipped her arm around her friend. "It'll work, don't worry." The friends walked silently now, each relishing the day in her own thoughts, each regretting its end.

But regret would not rob this day, Clarece decided. Part of her had feared that enjoying a taste of freedom might ruin any capacity she had to enjoy life in bondage. It had not. Though there was no hope she could ever live free upon this earth, it seemed to her this day served to offer her a glimpse into eternal freedom. She now had tasted some of what awaited her beyond death, if she managed to arrive to that Royal city. She wondered who there would take Asla's place as guide.

The castle walls loomed before them. Asla stopped to look once more at Clarece outside those walls. "Rece, this has been the best day of my life. Thank you for making it so." "Thank *you*, Asla," her sala replied. "You've given so much. I could never repay you. We make fine free women, don't we?"

Asla crossed her arms. "Yes, we do. Pity the kingdom that doesn't let women as us live freely within it. You would be a greater asset to Ars as a freewoman than you ever will be enslaved, Clarece. I mean that."

Clarece looked down at the compliment. She was feeling the weight of her collar now; she had lost it during the day. "Well, we can live freely in God's kingdom," she offered. "When horses dance," Asla grinned. "You must enjoy that place for me." She embraced her friend warmly and whispered in g'Helderleicht, "I love you." Clarece exchanged the gift with her own. "Of all that happened today," she said softly, "this has been your greatest gift, Asla. Thank you."

The insulit glanced away, shyly. Not knowing how to reply, not knowing how to end, she concentrated on the west gate. "Well, shall we?" She took her blouse and unfastened four buttons. Silver glowed in the torch light. She reached to Clarece's throat and unbuttoned her blouse - only twice.

The slaves presented Casica's pass to the guard at the gate. He read it and smiled. "Mission accomplished, ladies?" He appreciated a quest. "Yes," they replied. The heavy, spiked gate lifted before them. Clarece heard it close behind her as she made her way through the stone corridor. She had returned to her world. Heaven must wait.

Casica sat cozy in bed, writing. Her body still warmed from the hot bath she had taken. Kai. She couldn't remember the last time she had drawn her own water and bathed her own body.

The privacy felt wonderful as did the sense of freedom with time. She had shared a book with her bath and read for a long while. Now she wrote of her life at the palace: her days, her friends, her observations. To share this information with her family filled the princess with a pleasure strangely tinged in sorrow.

Her eyes glistened as her fingers caressed the parchment. Her mother would touch this. Perhaps she could learn to do with paper what her Maman did with cloth; seal herself in it somehow. She thought for a moment and wrote, "Touch these words. See if you can feel me." She then placed her fingers over the Cassican letters and concentrated. Light from her shalonn shown under her gown as her fingertips warmed the parchment. For several minutes she held the flow. Perhaps it would work.

She turned towards her door. They were coming. They should reach the landing about - now. The handle of her door moved quietly as a red figure entered, followed closely by a blue one. "Good evening, ladies!" Casica greeted. "Welcome home." The women grinned at each other; she *had* awaited them.

Asla bowed to Clarece's kneel. "I have returned her safely, as promised," smiled the g'Helderleit in her tongue. "But is she still chaste?" came the question. "Mostly - except for a few excursions of the tongue." Casica coughed. She addressed herself to the tall slave busied with folding her mistra's cloak. "Asla says you had a wonderful time, Clarece." "I'm certain that's not all she says," she commented dryly, casting a disapproving glance to her friend.

The two walked to the princess' bed and spoke happily. "This has been the best day of my life - again!" Clarece beamed, excitedly. Casica looked to Asla. "Mine too," she smiled. She opened her satchel and handed the conk and shell to Clarece. Next she revealed a wrapped object. "We've something for you, Casica." She handed the gift to the surprised woman.

"Well, nai gode, ladies. This is unexpected," Casica observed, unwrapping the paper. "A painter's blade!" she exclaimed, astonished. "Where on earth did you get this? How did you know to get this? I've been wanting this." The slaves smiled. "We spoke to an artist in the city. He suggested it as a gift for an accomplished artist," explained Clarece. "Well, tis beautiful," her owner replied, admiring the knife's craftsmanship. "And it will do beautiful things. I'll put it to good use. Thank you," she smiled, embracing them both with her eyes. Asla took her leave. "If you will excuse me, ladies," she said with a nod. "I have a service, soon and I need some sleep. This was a big day. Rece, could you wake me at three?" Her friend nodded. "And, Princess, your change. Dinner was exquisite. Thank you. And thank you for letting your slave run free today. You've given me a priceless gift."

Casica watched the young woman's eyes. She had never seen them shine with such softness. "I... I am indebted to you," Asla added softly. "Goodnight." Clarece embraced her friend warmly and wished her rest. She waited until Asla disappeared into the darkness of the stairwell then returned to sit on her lady's bed.

"You are positively radiant, Clarece." "I believe it, my lady," she replied happily. "I have never experienced so many things for the first time as I did today. The city, the market, the bookstore, the armoury, venison, scallops, shenit, chocolate - the ocean. I touched it, mistra, I touched the sea and was not consumed." She reached for the smooth shell. "Here. This is my first shell. I want you to have it - as a tithe for giving me this day."

Casica studied the shell, reverently. "Tis a beautiful gift, Clarece. I will treasure it. Nai gode." The slave smiled, pleased. "The conk - it will let me keep some of the ocean," Clarece observed, fondly rubbing its smooth, worn shell. She looked up and announced, shyly, "I could feel today, you know. The ocean, heat. Another first...." Casica leaned against her pillow and nodded, pleased. "I was wondering," her charge continued, "if you are not too tired - if you would josquin my hands tonight."

"Are you hurting?" Casica wondered, concerned. "No, my lady, I... I'm encouraged," she explained tentatively. The healer reached for her friend's mittened hands. This was going to feel so good, she thought, the image of Rachel teasing her. Clarece took a deep breath. This was going to feel so good.

Warmth and healing flowed into the slave's ruined hands with an intensity she had not experienced before. She closed her eyes and sighed. How does she do this? she wondered. She opened her eyes and began to tell of her day. If she could write, she would record it in a book, she said happily. This day was worthy of its own book. If she could write.

The woman studied her hands. *If I could write.* Clarece thought back to the vast world she had known today. Could it be that the greatest release, she might know here? Here in her small world of stone and slavery? She looked up and continued her tale. She described the seagulls, gliding across from the ocean's wind.

There were so many things she did not know. So many mysteries. The fullness of her story was one of them.

# XXX

Casica laughed aloud. Her friend was in fine form this morning. Once again, Clarece's dry wit came at her like a bandit, stalking her from behind as the two made their way to the library. The chief slave's reservoir of literature had run dry. Time for fresh pools of knowledge to quench her mind.

For Casica, the library wing held another refreshment: music. She smiled in anticipation of dining upon the hammerschord. The Byzanthian kingdom held a treasure trove of musical instruments, all of them housed in the end-chamber of the library. Though rarely used, each instrument was kept tuned and polished, awaiting their discovery. The Cassican princess often visited the coffer and spent its notes extravagantly.

The women were rounding a corner as the voice behind Casica's right shoulder ventured another witty truism. Casica turned to proffer a fitting reply when, suddenly, a presence before her accosted her thoughts.

There, standing not fifteen cubits from her, loomed the king of Byzanthia, accompanied by three of his counsel. "Your majesty," the princess stammered, kneeling upon the marble floor. Panic christened her bowed head: Clarece and Ars. T'was a deadly mix. Even now she sensed a rising rage within the monarch. *Dear God,* she thought, aghast. What will he do? What will *I* do if he moves to kill her? Fear surged over the woman, followed by the familiar voice of her chess opponent. "Stand, Wench." Ars looked past the rising woman to the one farther behind her, kneeled fully upon the ground. He could not hear the prayers she offered.

Casica watched, desperately, as the angry man glared beyond her shoulder, his arms folded, his right hand caressing the hilt of a large sword hanging on his hip. What the king thought, she could not know, but she recognized the paranoia that scented him like a deadly cologne. *He's going to kill her*, she realized in horror.

"Woman," he ordered quietly, dangerously. The king's eyes pierced her own. A dark smile crossed his lips. "Call you gimlet here." Casica looked for a single breath into her father-in-law's eyes. *Obey him at once*, a voice from within ordered.

The princess glanced over her shoulder to where Clarece kneeled. She wasn't there. Casica turned farther. There she was, a good ten cubits distant. She had seen the king sooner than did her owner.

"Clarece," Casica commanded, trying to sound calm. "Come here." Terror seized the kneeling slave. *Run!* she thought, *for the love of life - run!* She couldn't. Surely there was no place she could flee, but it was not this knowledge that held her. It was her breeding. She was the chief slaveswoman. Obedience was not a choice. It was instinct. She would not disgrace her mistra, nor her fellows, with cowardice. Clarece lingered only long enough to end to her prayer: "Receive me, please. Comfort them." For twelve years she had eluded this moment. Today she would die. Rising she walked, resolved, to her executioner.

The senior slave stopped a step from her owner and kneeled. It was a mercy, being forced to bow, to not look into her mistra's eyes. The strangest thought crossed her mind; she had forgotten to refill Casica's decanter.

The princess turned away from her friend to gaze questioningly into the king's eyes. The look that met hers oozed malice - malice and something else. What on earth was he thinking? Ars remained silent, relishing the fear in his daughter-in-law. No smugness now, thought he. No confidence. She was at his mercy as greatly as the cringing form at her feet. *"So. What will you do in this game, Cassican?"* he thought. *"To whom will you ally yourself? The moral, self-righteous upbringing of your native land? Or to me, captivity's king?"* Ars glanced down at the doomed figure. She had grown. Much taller than - . He looked back at the cringing princess. A smile relaxed his face as her ordered her, simply: "Strike her."

Casica blinked. Strike Clarece? That's what he wanted? What on earth for? she asked herself. She had never struck anyone in her life. And now to do so to her friend? To the observing men, there was no hesitation. They watched as the alien woman turned to face her slave. "Clarece," she ordered authoritatively. "Look at me."

Slowly the slave presented her face to her owner. Casica winced at the trust that brimmed in those sea-blue eyes. Their day at the ocean flooded her mind. She could not speak. Could not explain. Could not wait. The princess of Cassica drew back her right arm and backhanded her friend, brutally, across her right cheek.

Clarece reeled at the force of the blow. Something within her shattered; her mind could not reconcile violence and her healer's hand. Clarece caught her breath, then returned her gaze to her mistra. Tears welled in the pained eyes that met hers.

Casica lifted her left hand and aimed. This blow felled the slavewoman. Clarece crouched on the cool marble, stunned and gasping. Blood filled her mouth and ran from her nose. She coughed at the presence of it and struggled to right herself. The slave regained her kneel and looked up at her owner. Casica stood above her, fighting for her own breath, fighting for composure. She must play this game to its end. She looked into the face that she had broken and watched as her friend's blood crept down her neck onto her silver collar. The eyes still held their trust. A wave of nausea threatened to undo the healer. She forced it away. *Forgive me, Clarece,* she begged silently. *Oh, God forgive me....*

Her right fist all but knocked the slave unconscious. Even Ars winced at its force. Clarece lay on the floor, gasping and grappling with the blackness that sought to pin her. *Stay down! Stay down!* the princess plead silently. But even now, the senior slave fought to rise.

The king, his counsel and the guard who witnessed this vicious contest watched, incredulous. All knew the reputation of this owner's affection for her slave; yet, here she was beating her senseless even as the slave determined to receive more of her mistra's punishment.

Clarece coughed. Her blood sprinkled the floor. She swallowed and managed to find her knees. Once again, she looked up, forcing her eyes to focus on the woman who loved her. *Blast your stubbornness,* Casica thought, drawing back her left hand. This time the slave closed her eyes against the strike. She could not withstand this one, she knew.

A voice caught Casica's arm. "Enough." Casica closed her eyes and took several deep breaths. "Send her away," Ars ordered quietly. "You may leave me," the broken woman whispered to her friend. *"You may leave me and never trust me again,"* she thought to herself. She had violated Clarece beyond repair, she knew. She may have saved her life, but lost it in the process.

Casica watched, chagrined, as the slave lowered her head, humiliated. She reached out her maimed hands and wrapped them around her mistra's ankles. Then carefully, kissed her feet. Clarece's head touched the floor before her owner. Ars drew back, astounded. What kind of woman commands such a response? The slave returned to her kneeling posture. "My sovereign," she said, acknowledging her king, with a humble bow of her head.

The men stared as the bleeding woman regained her balance, somehow, to rise unsteadily to her feet. The slave stood, took three steps back, turned on her heel, as a slave does, and walked slowly away.

Casica's eyes accompanied the form until she disappeared into a slave passage. She turned to face her challenger. Tears flowed unheeded down her face. "What now, Great King?" she asked steadily.

Ars studied the young woman. In her eyes was not anger; it was sorrow he saw. Deep sorrow. Ars nodded despite himself; she had won this hand. She would keep her pawn. "You are excused, Princess Casica," he announced. The princess kneeled. Rising, she continued her way to the library.

The startled guard watched as the Cassican walked past him into the library. She was weeping. And she was alone. Usually her slave accompanied her. Soon the hammerschord filled the hall, penetrating the heavy door that hid it. The guard listened attentively. He enjoyed the impromptu concerts furnished by the foreign princess. Rarely did anyone use the musical instruments of the library. Today the music she chose sounded of angry turmoil.

It was a technically challenging piece, one the princess had never fully mastered. It was the master now, buffeting her into passion.

Casica played until her fingers ached with the absurd intervals demanded by the composer. He was a Cassican prisoner of war; a former professor at the university, returned to his homeland, tortured and enraged. Casica had never embraced his works, finding them brutal, in technique and emotion, but today, he was her muse.

Spent, the woman sat quietly on the bench. She lowered her head against the oiled wood and rested, the familiar smell of polish comforting her. Tears fell silently upon ivory. How long she wept, Casica didn't know, but she stood finally, weary and sickened. How could she face Clarece?

The princess made her way to the door then stopped to study the rows of books surrounding her. She walked to a particular place on the seventh row from the bottom. She removed five books then exited to go home, home where the morning light awaited her.

Clarece sat on her cot, watching little drops of blood fall into her basin and dissolve, losing themselves in the water. Her mistra packed a blow, she thought, smiling wanly. She would hate to think what she might do if she were angry. The slave closed her eyes and replaced the cloth to her nose. What intrigued her most in this moment was the conspicuous absence of pain. Nothing hurt. Not at all. She was disoriented certainly, both emotionally and cognitively, but not from hurting. A healer must be the only person in the world who could beat someone senseless without leaving a trace of pain. The bleeding stopped.

Clarece cleaned her face and leaned back against the wall. Where was Casica? She had been gone a long time now. No sound came from her chamber above. Fatigue had begun to overtake the slave when a familiar presence filled her stall. She opened her eyes to find her mistra. The princess placed the library books on Asla's cot.

"Clarece," she began, "I'm so sorry. I... I...." She never finished. Clarece stood quickly as she could and now wrapped the sobbing woman in a tight embrace. A maimed hand caressed the dark hair.

"Tis well, mistra," she comforted. "I know... I know." Casica lifted her gaze. "Clarece, I had to - ."

Clarece cut her short. "I know, mistra. You saved my life." The slave offered a kind smile. "It is said that the blows of a friend are better than the kisses of an enemy. I would rather your blows than the king's. You bloodied my face - but spared my head, I think."

Casica looked at the woman before her. "Can you forgive me?" she asked quietly. Clarece nodded. "All I ask is, please, never strike me in anger. You hit royally." The princess lowered her head. "I thought it safest to obey in earnest." "Your sincerity leaves a most lasting impression, mistra."

Clarece regretted her words immediately. This was not a slave to whom she spoke. Casica saw no humor in her comment; she turned away in shame. "Please," Clarece implored. "Do not burden yourself, Princess. I'm alright." "Are you sure? I might have broken your nose." Casica lifted her hand toward Clarece's face then stopped. "May I?" she asked cautiously.

A mitten brought her hand to its owner's face. Warmth flooded Clarece as healing ministered to the cuts in her mouth and opened the passageways of her air. Her thoughts cleared. She smiled. Even the ringing in her ears disappeared. "Asla says my head is an impenetrable fortress. If I must be beaten, it was the kindest target. Your heart is not nearly so fortified," she offered gently. "Do not fret."

Josquin was unconvinced. "I am breaking, one by one, every vow I have ever made as a healer," the princess observed, her head dropping in defeat. Clarece sighed. "You made those vows in Cassica where they could be kept, my lady. Here you live on a different playing field. Do not torment yourself with things you can't control. All I know is twelve years ago the king made a vow that, today, he did not keep. If you have fulfilled it for him, I am indebted to you."

Casica shook her head, wearily. "You must rest, my lady," Clarece said softly. The young woman stood, numbly. "Come," Clarece ordered and began to lead her owner to the stairs. She followed silently as Casica made her way up to her chamber. In its familiar warmth, Clarece pulled back the bed covers and helped the princess in, not bothering with her boots or vest.

The exhausted woman closed her eyes against the day. Clarece drew the heavy comforter around her owner's shoulders and tucked her in. She sat quietly on the edge of the princess' bed, smiling gently. "Sleep, Princess," she invited. "I will wake you for dinner." Casica nodded wearily.

The slave leaned down and kissed her owner's brow. "God's blessings upon you," she whispered in Cassican. The recipient of her offering did not respond, having already received the blessedness of sleep.

Asla opened Casica's door quietly, chiding the wind for its noisy entry. Scads, it was cold tonight. What a relief it was to come into a warm, safe place. The insulit removed her chilled cloak and began her soft tread to the brazier. A noise in the dark room arrested her. She could not see the form but knew it was Casica. She had, several times now, returned to the east wing to find the princess kneeling on her floor, praying. On those occasions, Asla had ignored the josquin and continued to her cot below; one does not interrupt communion with the Almighty - even an insulit knew that.

But tonight was different. Asla had never heard Casica weep in prayer before. The insulit stood uncomfortably, wondering within herself the proper response. If God weren't involved, she decided finally, if she had found Casica crying by herself, she would inquire upon her. So why should she let some Sovereign who didn't know her existence stop her now? The blond woman followed the sobs and sat beside their creator.

"Casica, what's wrong?" she asked gently, laying her hand upon the princess' shoulder. Casica looked up. For some reason, her eyes never frightened Asla. Little of darkness startled the insulit. "Nothing's wrong. I'm praying." "I've never heard you weep in prayer," the younger woman noted. "My heart is broken." "Oh... I see," said Asla, stroking her cloak. "Do you want some help?" she asked tentatively.

Casica smiled despite herself. "I thought insulit couldn't speak to God." "We can't. But I can speak to people. I help men pray, all the time. When I'm with them they say things like 'Dear *God*',

'Oh, my *God*' and 'Oh, *yes! God....*' I'm quite gifted at facilitating the transcendent."

Casica bowed her head and smiled. Asla's playfulness mocked her despair - in a wonderfully healthy manner. The insulit leaned closer. "What happened today that has broken your heart so?" she inquired, seriously. Casica looked into the face that could not see hers. "I struck Clarece." "Clarece who?" Asla asked, never thinking Casica could mean her friend. "The only Clarece I know."

"*My* Clarece?!" Asla rejoined stunned. "Yes." "My God, Casica! What in blazes for?" "The king commanded me." Asla's mind raced in horror. "You mean Rece and Ars met? Does she live?!" "Yes - yes, she's alive. Alive but beaten. By me." Asla sighed in relief. "Ars met us on our way to the library. He commanded me to strike her. And I did. Brutally. I feared if I refused, he would kill her."

Asla nodded. She couldn't imagine the scenario but she could imagine Ars' rage. The king was paranoid about Clarece's existence. "You were right to beat her, Casica. Ars is the king - Rece understands that. And she adores you." Casica closed her eyes in shame. How could anyone adore someone like her? The image of Clarece groveling at her feet tore at her soul. "As you have said, it is Clarece's way to forgive. But if you had seen what I did to her. I shamed her so deeply," she confessed to her friend's sala, "she kissed my feet. I can't forgive myself for violating her honor like that."

Asla sat back on her hands. "Is that what bothers you?" she asked, curious, "that she kissed your feet?" "Yes. I utterly broke her." The insulit thought for a moment, watching as her eyes adjusted to the soft light. "Let me guess. Clarece took your ankles into her hands, kissed your boots and bowed her head to the floor, yes?" "Yes. How could you know?" the princess questioned, surprised. The slave smiled gently. She could see the princess' face now. She spoke in g'Helderleicht.

"You flog yourself with ignorance, Casica. You misconstrue Clarece's behavior because you don't understand a slave's language. If *you* kissed another's feet, that would be an act of defeat and shame. That's because you are free and live life on your feet. Slaves live life on their knees. Kneeling - bowing heads to the floor - these are not humiliating for slaves. Tis their language. As for the public beating, now that was disgraceful," she explained gently. "And because you're her cover, it *was* a violation - Ars knew this when he commanded you. He wanted to shame you both. But as for Clarece's response, she wasn't groveling. She was offering you the deepest expression of devotion allowed a slave - in public. You know slaves are forbidden to touch the free, but she could do this because it is a slave's ritual. It is her right." Asla shook her head at her next realization.

"What Rece was telling old man Ars was, 'You can force this woman to do anything upon me - beat me to death if you command - but you still won't win. I love her and will continue to devote my life to her.'" The younger woman smiled to herself. "That pigheaded slave - what she did, basically, was thumb her nose at her supreme owner - most respectfully, of course."

Casica shook her head. "She would never do that. The king hates her, Asla. If he sensed any disrespect from her, he would have killed her."

"Not necessarily. I'm not saying it wasn't a risk, but Clarece has lived under his death sentence for years now. And he didn't kill her - for whatever reason. This feels like it was a contest of sorts, not only between you and Ars, but between her and Ars. He was testing her. You see, we slaves, ours is a peculiar bond to the king. Like the slaves' dance. The king sponsors this affair himself, from his personal coffers. Pays for everything. Of course slaves are the guests, so who serves?" Casica shook her head.

"Free ones do," Asla explained. "Royals, owners, guards, even clergy. But it is the slaves' right to choose whom they want as servers. Tis considered a great honor to be invited to serve at this royally slavish night. But. Guess who's never invited...." "The king?" "Yes - and not because it would be unseemly for a sovereign to serve slaves. He's not invited because the slaves don't want him."

Casica's fingers went to her lips. Despite everything, Asla's information intrigued her.

"Now you'd think an arrogant ass like Ars would send his troops to render that dance a festival of dismembered slave body parts, but he doesn't. He sends three vats of his finest wine, instead. Ars understands the slaves resent him, their ultimate owner."

Casica shook her head in confusion. None of this made sense. Perhaps the unnaturalness of owned and owner permeated the institution after all. Slavery could not exist sanely.

"Ars inquires about you, you know," the insulit continued. "He doesn't trust you, Casica. Doesn't know whose allegiance you hold. My guess is, he wanted to test you to see if you would obey him - even if it meant harming someone the whole palace knows you love. If you hadn't obeyed as you did, he probably would have killed her." Casica frowned. "I still am not convinced I haven't dishonored Clarece irreparably," she argued.

"That's the Cassican in you," Asla countered. "You honored her enough to do what you must. You knew she could bear your beating. That's a great compliment to a slave. Our reputation is that we can't bear life as the free do. Remember her gesture to you." She grinned mischievously. "Remember her gesture to the king." Scads, she wished she could have seen that. "I haven't a twelfth of her courage - or class," Asla observed to herself. The insulit turned her attention to the princess. "Clarece walked away on her feet, Casica. Don't forget that. My guess is she feels quite good about the day's events."

The weary woman took a deep breath, pushing against the fatigue that encroached upon her. "I have a service in three hours. I need sleep." "Thank you for praying with me, Asla," the princess said. "Your presence answered my prayers."

The insulit laughed, wryly. "I know naught of the Almighty, my lady, but it seems to me He needs flesh more often than not. Rece tells a story of when He spoke through a pigeon or muskrat - something like that. I guess your God can use an insulit when He must."

The women stood. "Asla," the princess asked, "why do you think Ars hates Clarece so?" Asla shook her head. She had wondered it, herself. "Her deformity, I guess." "But that's not rational." Asla smirked. "No one would ever accuse Ars of ruling the realm of rationality, Princess. By the way, you madden him, you know. He speaks quite unflattering of you, but he's also intrigued. " She grinned impishly. "I hope you win that accursed chess game."

Casica looked questioningly at her friend. "How do you know all this about Ars? You don't... service him, do you?" The insulit smiled disarmingly. "Now, Princess, you know I couldn't answer that. Let's just say I have received the royal seal of approval."

*Good Heaven*, thought Casica, rejecting the images forming in her mind. Instead she pulled the young woman to herself. Asla relaxed in the warmth and refreshment that flowed into her. "You will sleep long in a short time," Casica whispered. "Thank you again, God's Beauty. You've made my chamber a chapel tonight."

The insulit did not know how to respond to words such as these. So she bowed. "Good night, Princess. Rest in peace." It was something she hoped for herself. Casica watched as her kind minister went below in preparation for the service to come.

# XXXI

"Ocean still there, Rece?" The senior slave was listening to her conk happily. "Still there," she smiled to her stallmate. "Want to hear?" She handed the shell to Asla. The blond woman listened intently. It *did* sound like the ocean. What a fun game to play this evening. Evening. Finally. No more services until the early morning; until then, the night was all her own. Asla even looked forward to the boring prospect of porridge. Already, Penelope was dishing it into the slaves' bowls, she could hear and smell. A small form, the smallest in the wing, walked furtively to their stall.

"Raina!" Clarece welcomed, "come in." "Hi, Scamp!" greeted Asla. "And how is the donkey tonight?" The tiny slave kneeled humbly before answering. "Mistress Clarece... Asla - ." With Asla's name she smiled shyly. "I've not read his story today. I don't know how he is." Her face, Raina hid, an unusual posture for the bright girl. The women glanced at each other.

Clarece rose from her cot and kneeled before the standing child. From here she could see Raina's swollen face. Her mistra had been beating her again. "She's been hard on you today," ventured Clarece, caressing the smooth left cheek. The little slave nodded and began to weep.

"I'm a stupid slave," she whispered, repeating what she had heard all day. "No, you're not, Raina," Clarece gently countered. "You're a fine slave. Remember what I've told you: being a houseslave is a two-part invention. It can't be played with one hand only. Tis your mistra who doesn't know her part." The girl nodded, but she didn't believe. She was stupid and now here was this new chore and she hadn't a clue how to do it.

"I'm sorry to bother you, mistress, but I've a worry." "You did right to disturb me. What is it?" The little slave wiped her nose on her too-long sleeve. Her blue-green eyes were filled with confusion. "My mistra told me today she will be gone tonight and her cousin is coming instead. She says I am to serve him tonight. I told her I've never served a man before, that I've never even been with men, much. My last mistra didn't even have a husband in her house – only her three cats and two dogs that I fed and walked."

Two small hands fought with each other as the girl tried to explain. "I said I didn't know what to do. She told me that he would show me what to do and that for me to shut up. I asked Penelope what to do and she got mad." Raina's sobs were small, like her body. She looked up pleadingly, "Please tell me what to do so I won't be lashed."

Clarece closed her eyes, stunned into silence. What on earth was Muriel thinking? Raina was the only female slave Clarece had ever known who had not been taken by this age. Her former mistra was an old woman who had bought the girl to care for her pets. Clarece's mind reeled with the memories of another child; the woman in her shoved them away. The chief slaveswoman looked the small, frightened moppet in the eyes and did the only kind thing she could think of: she lied.

"Raina, listen to me." The girl looked attentively. "You needn't worry about this now. You've done right to tell me. Don't speak to anyone else about it. Look, supper is at hand. Are you hungry?" Raina nodded enthusiastically. She was always hungry. "So am I," her leader smiled. "What time are you to attend this cousin?" "Half past ten – I've never stayed up that late."

"Half past ten is late to be sure," Clarece concurred. "Well, let's do this. Eat supper and go check on your mistra as you always do. Then come straight here. I'll come talk with you before your time comes. Do you understand?" "Yes, mistress," the slave replied, relieved. Clarece was not afraid. She was not angry. This must not be as bad as it felt.

"Alright, then," the chief said, rising. She drew the girl to her and kissed her head. "You're a good girl, Raina. A very good girl. I'm happy you're in my pen." The slave smiled, warmed by the compliment of this important woman. She kneeled to her superior and then smiled shyly at Asla who perched stoically in her cot. "Thank you, mistress," Raina said to Clarece's nod and, with a half-kneel and graceful turn, walked lightly to assume her place at the table.

Asla sat, awaiting the eruption which would surely come. Clarece paced their stall until she could contain her rage no longer. *"No!"* she yelled, quietly. She kicked her cot viciously. "Blast, that witch!" she screamed softly, pounding her fist into the air. Even an explosion must be controlled in quarters such as hers.

The furious woman slumped heavily on her cot, burying her face in her mittens. "No!" she whispered, weeping. *God, no!* She must wait for her anger to dispel so that she could think. She must think clearly. She looked finally into her friend's moist eyes. "What is Muriel doing?" she asked. Asla looked away. "She's a wicked woman, Rece." "But she's a *woman*, Asla. She has grandchildren." The insulit shrugged her shoulders. "Women can be evil, too."

Clarece leaned back into her cot, her hands rising to comfort her mouth. "God, Asla. Raina is innocent. How can I explain this to her? I can't just send her in there – not knowing." "Explain what?" Asla countered. "That something she doesn't even know she has is going to be stripped from her? How do you explain innocence to a five-year-old?" Clarece nodded. Her friend was right. "What would you tell her?"

Asla glanced at the floor. "I'd tell her to run like hell. Any man who does this – ." She shook her head. "But what if she can't run from hell?" asked Clarece. The blond woman thumbed her palm. "Then I'd tell her to make herself at home," she replied softly. Gods knew, she had. Hell was her habitat. But Raina – simple beatings threatened to destroy her. This... the insulit didn't want to think what this would do to such an innocent soul. That was the awful part; Raina had a soul.

Penelope was ringing the dinner bell. "Come, Rece," Asla invited her friend. "Follow your own advice and eat. You'll think clearer afterwards." Clarece nodded. Asla was right. There was noting she could do now. During supper, she listened below the gushing voices in silence, wanting to hear the smallest voice. Raina's spirits had improved already. Even now, she was telling

Joslin, excitedly, about a red bird she had once seen eating snow. It amazed Clarece, how resilient were children. But Raina was a tender shoot. She wondered how far she could bend before her spirit was irreparably splintered.

Supper ended. Clarece departed with the other slaves, each to their owner's chambers to prepare their beds. She needed desperately to talk to her mistra.

Casica felt the heaviness preceding Clarece's greeting kneel. "What's wrong?" she asked. The chief slaveswoman didn't even attempt to contain her tears. "Something awful, my lady," she wept. She sat beside her owner at the table and explained all. "The worst of it, is she trusts me," she concluded. "If I were another woman - ." The idea halted at the image of the scars that riddled her body like webs. "But I am a despicably unacceptable substitute." The princess sat, silenced by horror and rage. Her mind convulsed at the situation. She looked at the weary woman beside her. No queen she knew carried more burden than did this simple woman.

"What would you do?" Clarece asked, interrupting Casica's thoughts. Josquin glanced from her friend's tortured eyes. "I daren't voice what I *want* to do, Clarece. But if it is as you say, there is nothing to be done. Except perhaps to tell Raina to do whatever he asks – and to come to me afterwards. I'll see what I can do then for her," – *her body* Josquin's thoughts continued, but as for the girl's mind... her heart. "But first we will pray for God's intervention and mercy."

The senior slave smiled weakly. "You'll need do that, my lady. God... He doesn't hear me very well." Josquin took a mittened hand into her own. "Then let's pray together now. And I will pray this night for her – and for you." Clarece nodded gratefully. The night would come too soon.

Asla slipped into the stall, a worn book in her hand. A little form knelt on the floor by her cot, waiting patiently for her chief. "Waiting for Rece?" a kind voice asked. Raina smiled at the sight of the beautiful woman. "Yes," she nodded. "My mistra wasn't in so I came here. But I can leave if I bother you."

"Bother me?" smiled Asla. "I *like* having you. Here, sit on my cot." The little girl rose excitedly, happy to visit as a big slave. "I've brought something for you," Asla began, handing the reading book to the little girl. "I think the donkey is missing you. He's jealous for you to read about him this evening." "I will – if I have time," Raina promised.

Asla squatted in front of her. Raina was so very, very young. This night she looked particularly fragile. The woman gazed into the blue-green eyes.

"Raina," she asked softly, "do you trust me?" Raina blinked. Of course she trusted Asla. "Yes," she replied simply. "Then there is something I want you to do, but you must trust me. Understand?" The girl nodded. She didn't understand.

"I'm going to take your place tonight. Let me explain," she hastened at Raina's worried look. "You are a very good slave, Raina, but this serving a man... you're not old enough for this. Your mistra should know better – that's why Penelope was angry. Not at you, but at your mistra. I... I think I might know this man. I'll slave him for you."

Raina frowned. "But my mistra, if she finds out - ." "That's why I need you to trust me. I want you to lie, Raina. I don't think anyone will ask, but if they do, you tell them this: you tell them you were so nervous you got sick, so another woman in the guild covered you. You don't know who. Clarece took care of it."

"But you're not *in* the guild," the girl observed. Asla smiled despite herself. Why did it irk a woman like her so much, the fact she wasn't included in their group? "Well, I can cover you anyway. That's what friends do. But you must tell no one anything of this, Raina – especially not your mistra. Will you do this?"

"Does Mistress Clarece want me to?" Raina asked, concerned. She didn't want to disappoint the senior woman. "She will. I'll tell her. Now do you understand?" The little child nodded. She understood. She was not old enough, but somehow, Asla would make it right.

"Good," Asla smiled. This wasn't as difficult as she had anticipated. "Now the best part is, you can sleep in my cot the whole night. And in the morning, don't deliver breakfast. You stay here and let Clarece do that for you." "But this is *your* cot," Raina worried. "Where will you sleep?" "I'll be fine. This is your cot tonight.

Here," Asla continued, slipping worn boots from little green-clad feet. "I'll tuck you in."

Raina complied. She *was* getting sleepy. Asla tucked her sheet around thin shoulders then draped her red cape over the girl. Raina loved the garment, she knew. "Now, why don't you visit with donkey before Clarece comes down," she suggested. She stopped short to look suspiciously around the stall. Raina looked with her. "But hear," Asla confided, "I must warn you: the chief snores." Raina laughed. "Good night, scamp," the beautiful woman whispered. "Good night, Asla. I hope you sleep good." The insulit sighed at the kind wish. "I will," she answered softly and taking her dark cloak, slipped silently from the stall, closing its curtain behind her.

Clarece wandered wearily down the stairs. The curtain was drawn. Just as well, she thought, numbly. There were many curtains she would draw this night if she could. She stepped into her stall and blinked. There was Raina, sound asleep in Asla's cot; a familiar red cape covering her, a familiar worn book under tiny hands. She glanced about. A note lay on her pillow.

Clarece looked again at the sleeping child before reading it. Asla's distinct hand met her eyes. "Gone to take her place. I think I can make this work. You deliver his breakfast and don't fret. A."

The chief slaveswoman bowed her head and wept.

# XXXII

The night never lasted so long. Clarece lay in her bed listening to her young stallmate. The little girl slept soundly, barely even stirring in the cot. The chief slaveswoman watched as shadows danced on the ceiling. Her heart was torn in two. Part of it beat with relief at the sound of her young keep's safety; the other bled openly at the thought of what her friend must be doing at this moment. *God, keep her safe,* she plead, repeatedly, noticing, eventually, that she offered her prayer in time with Raina's breathing. What an evil world she lived in, thought the tortured woman. Bred in evil. Ruled by evil. Devoured by evil, only to breed again. What a hopeless kingdom.

She turned to watch the little form. Raina had pulled Asla's cape up to her head, burying her face in its comforting warmth and scent. It smelled like its owner, clean and fragranced. *How ironic* thought the senior slave. Asla used perfumes to hide the stench that clung to her from services, covering evil with beautiful scent. Even now, evil was prevented, but only by another being performed. Asla, herself, was the fragrance. Clarece's thoughts frightened their thinker, growing more and more dark as they did with the passing night.

In the midst of all this dark rumination, glowed two beacons of warmth and light. Clarece studied her hands. They seemed like barristers silently disputing her dark judgments. From within, they pulsated, enlivened by her mistra's touch. These dead things that had tortured her endlessly were warm tonight and at peace with their world.

The exhausted woman smiled, despite herself, in memory of the ocean, of feeling. At this moment she could feel the leather that covered her hands. How could that be? she wondered, rubbing her mittened flesh together. How was this happening? It required something outside herself, she reasoned, someone more powerful than the previous harm inflicted. Healing required something wonderfully good to move into death and impart life.

She looked again to Raina. Her future was bleak. Any mistra who would do this.... Clarece closed her eyes at the thought. Still, for this night, the little girl was safe. Goodness, in the most remarkable form of an insulit, had infiltrated Raina's world and protected her from irreparable harm. Perhaps – and this possibility offended Clarece's dark mood - perhaps even this minute, Goodness worked on behalf of her friend. But Clarece did not know. There was so much she did not know.

The clock struck twelve. The chief slaveswoman glanced at her oil lamp and wondered what Casica did. She struggled with a desire to be with her. That was impossible of course. She could not interrupt the princess. Probably her owner had been sleeping for a long time now. Clarece looked up at her mistra's floor. Yes, she surely slept.

The barristers beckoned her attention. The slave studied them again. What a crazy world, she determined. What an insane world. Here she was writhing with sorrow and anger over the darkness of life while all the while relishing the exquisite sensation of painlessness. There must be something wicked in her to enjoy her hands while her friend gave her body to a faceless man.

The conflicting feelings whirled within the woman's heart but in the end, it was her hands that won out. Clarece entered their blessed peace, slipping from the darkness to embrace a deep, refreshing sleep.

Casica stood at her window. It had been a long night. She had not slept at all, yet felt fully rested this morning as though she had. She leaned her head against the cool glass and watched as the sun began his ascension, assuming his rightful place in the dark sky. Her breath clouded the vision, fogging the glass as it did, but nothing could fully obscure the scene. It was coming. Morning was truly coming. And nothing could stop it.

Josquin took a deep breath. She glanced down at her shalonn. Raina had not come. Some time during the night, the healer concluded that the little slave's absence indicated either a miraculous event or an utterly tragic one. But now, now in the coming light, Casica felt certain it was the former. The little girl she had never met was well. In fact, after the night she had spent, the princess felt certain that - somehow - all was well with everyone, everywhere - including herself.

It had been months since she'd spent an entire night in prayer. The last time was the week before leaving her home when she had stayed the night in the palace chapel, begging God to intervene, to somehow undo destiny and time and to rescue her from the awful fate awaiting.

The woman smiled. Her knees were out of practice but her soul remembered quickly enough, turning as it did away from the distressing needs, away from the awful situations. Turning away so that she may lose herself in the glorious presence of Something much greater, so much more beautiful and fearful than anything threatening to devour her. What a grace, thought Casica, to know, again, that she did not rule the world. Pain did not rule the world. Neither did darkness, she thought, watching the sun rise; it was overcome, everyday, by light. Another reigned on a heavenly throne and offered her the extravagant freedom of surrender to His care.

Casica placed her hand on the glass. As she watched the air steam, she contemplated the two memories night had delivered her. The first came as she stood looking at the stars that peeped through the trees of the garden; they reminded her of a particularly magical night not so long ago.

She and Rigel were returning from a healing. It had been such a long, grueling day. The healing went well, finally, but she was exhausted and gave Rigel his reins to find to their way home. She dozed in her saddle until something woke her and turned her attention to the night sky. She stopped at the  remarkable sight. Stars were falling all around. Three, four at a time.

She hopped off Rigel to gaze more fully. Casica had heard of such a thing but had never witnessed it. The night was silent as death but around her lived a symphony of light. Stars lit with different colors as they blazed through the sky - yellow, orange, green - even red at times.

As she watched, the young healer was struck with the metaphor that they were falling down in worship, the stars, burning themselves out in a crescendo of joy. It seemed fitting that they left in their wake a foggy path in the cold night sky. *Life goes on,* they seemed to tell her. Life is the final word in this passing world.

Later, the night brought the second memory, one reminding her how it felt to be with Baba. No matter how busy, her kingly father never seemed irritated when she came to rest in his arms. How often she would fall asleep there in that place of perfect care. Casica caressed the royal seal on her karosh. It revived her, last night, to rest in the arms of the One enthroned. His company cleansed her mind and with the cleansing brought a renewed perspective, properly aligned.

Casica wiped her breath from the glass, smiling. The morning light was coming into her room – in more ways than one. She sensed the presence of Clarece, now, walking up her stairs.

Clarece stepped up to her mistra's chamber, a warm breakfast in her hands. At the doorway, she stopped, surprised. There was her mistra, awake, leaning against the window, the morning light bathing her countenance. The princess stood dressed in what she'd worn the day before, fully vested and booted. Clarece glanced at the bed to her right. It was untouched. Casica had not slept, she realized. She was looking at her feet, still pondering this sight, when the puzzled woman heard her name.

"Clarece," her owner beckoned, softly. The slave looked up and, startled, offered a greeting kneel. She entered the room, feeling a prick of guilt over what, she didn't know. Quietly, she placed her mistra's meal on the table. The dark woman turned to face her. "How is she?" Casica asked gently. Clarece bowed. "She is well, mistra. God answered your prayers. Raina spent the night sleeping in Asla's cot." Casica blinked. *Asla.*

"Asla took her place," Clarece explained, weakly. "I went down last night to find Raina in our stall and a note on my bed. I brought the cousin food this morning but he had already gone.

I don't know how Asla is, but Raina is unharmed and...." She couldn't finish. From deep within the chief slave came a wave of sorrow and confusion. "I don't know," was all she could say, lowering her head.

A warm presence embraced her. The exhausted woman disregarded all propriety and rested shamelessly in her owner's arms. It was as that night, a thousand days ago, with Berea. Her mistra held her in silence, watching as the sunlight slowly filled the chamber.

Clarece finally looked up. "I'm sorry, mistra," she apologized. Casica shook her head. "Don't be. You've had a long night." "Not as long as you," her charge observed. "I slept; you didn't." "Good," the princess nodded. "You need rest."

The princess looked outside. A great darkness encompassed Clarece. Her friend needed to leave this place, needed the company of sunlight. "Is there anything you must do for Raina?" she asked. "No," Clarece replied. "She's returned to her mistra's chamber to clean."

Casica glanced again out her window. It was a lovely morning. "Then let's you and I go for a ride," she suggested. Clarece did not feel like riding. She felt like hiding in her dark stall all day, but her mistra wanted to ride so she would ride.

"Yes, mistra," she obeyed. "I'll fetch my cover." "That's not necessary," the princess replied. "You can wear mine." She gathered her cloak. Clarece loved the garment, Casica knew. And little fortified a discouraged woman as wearing beautiful clothing did. Clarece resisted. "You won't get cold?" she asked, knowing the answer. "No," Casica smiled. "I'm always cold," the slave observed standing as her owner placed the cloak around her. *But not in this,* she thought gratefully, feeling its warmth stir. She loved this garment.

The slave stood as her mistra opened her chamber door. Cool air flowed into the room and brought with it the smells of the garden. Even though nothing bloomed this time of year, the garden teemed with life. The scents caressed Clarece's mind as the women walked silently through the crisp air. The gravel crunched beneath their feet and the sun cast their shadows away from them. It was, indeed, a beautiful morning, the kind that invited you to live.

At the livery the women were met with disappointment: Poul was not present. They waited in silence as a stable hand saddled Rigel and Leharen. Clarece noticed as the man bridled her mount that her horse seemed anxious to see the day. The ladies mounted and rode with Casica leading their way down a path Clarece did not know. They rode for almost two hours and almost in complete silence, breaking it only occasionally to comment on some plant or bird.

The peaceful journey led them to a place new for both, a tender meadow surrounded by wood. All around them, trees stood like sentinels, reinforced by a small company of mossy rock. This seemed a good place to rest, decided the healer. She dismounted and let Rigel walk free. Her charge took her horse and carefully tied its reins to a branch. A fallen tree made a comfortable bench.

Clarece sat heavily beside her owner. Casica looked around. She took a piece of grass and chewed thoughtfully on it. "So, Clarece," she asked finally, "how are you?" The slave glanced at her lady and then to the ground. "I don't know, my lady," she replied, wearily. "I am darkened by many thoughts." The princess leaned down and nodded slightly. "What kind of thoughts?"

Clarece sighed, sitting back on the solid log. "I'm afraid for Raina," she began softly, shaking her head. "She won't live." "What do you mean?" Casica asked. "Her mistra. Her mistra cares nothing for her, cares nothing for her life. Muriel hasn't invested anything in her. No clothing, nothing. And now with what she did with this cousin...." The woman shook her head. "She hates her slave - anyone can see that. A young slave like Raina, she has no value. Her loss would be nothing to a woman like Muriel." On the log beside her was a piece of bark curled up with age. The slave picked it off with her mitten. "She's going to kill her," she announced simply. "I know it. And I'm powerless to stop it."

Angry tears crept silently down her face. There were so many things she knew and hated and was powerless to stop. People called her "the queen of the slaves." What a pitiful queen she was. All responsibility; no authority. She stared at the dewy boots of the woman next to her. There sat a true queen. But for herself, she was nothing. A queen of slaves was still a slave and slaves were less than nothing.

"And I look at Asla," Clarece continued. "Edsner's making her a whore. Tis only a matter of time." She paused to look at her mistra, reminded of something she needed to do. She had no authority but Casica did. "Princess," she began, awkward. "I made a promise to Asla years ago. She's... terrified at the thought of being burned. She made me swear I would find some way to keep that from happening to her body. I have no power. I only promised to quiet her. But my encounter with the king has reminded me I may not outlive her. If I don't, will you...?" She looked away before returning her eyes. "Would you see to it that my sala is buried and not burned? Will you do this for me?"

Casica swallowed her breath, horrified at the prospect. She studied her friend. The despair that shrouded Clarece was palatable, encroaching, even now, upon her own spirit. She resisted it with truth. "I will," Josquin answered, assuring the distress woman. "I promise." Clarece was visibly relieved. Casica waited a moment, then voiced the conviction in her heart. "But I do not expect you to die anytime soon, Clarece. Nor Asla. Nor Raina. You are all destined for long life, I think."

"I doubt that," her friend said simply. "Life is dark and evil. And those born into it as we have little hope of anything better." The woman looked at the world around her. A soft breeze played the trees, filling the air with a music all their own. Sunlight warmed her face and lit the grasses with an ethereal glow. A fleet of large, white clouds sailed the sky above her. Twas a lovely day and nothing about her heart could change that. Her heart could keep her from enjoying the day but could not change the day itself.

Clarece glanced internally at her hands. They were enjoying the day, certainly. Enjoyed grasping Leharen's reins and now enjoyed each other's company in a quiet banquet of warmth. Clarece shook her head.

"The insanity is that last night while I was thinking all this? what truly captured my attention? was my hands. I can't tell you how good I feel, not to be in pain." The slave glanced away in shame. "My soul is utterly bankrupt. What kind of woman enjoys anything while her friends suffer?"

Casica looked about at the beauty of the day as she considered the question. "A queen," she answered simply. The slave looked at her owner, confused. "What do you mean?" Clarece asked.

Casica munched her grass. Only DeLeah knew this story. "When my sister died, I thought my mother would die with her, so great was her sorrow." She looked at her companion. "I do not say she hurt more deeply than would any other woman who had lost her child, but a josquin, we're intertwined with life, it breeds in us. And for her womb to deliver death...," she shook her head, unable to comprehend her mother's agony.

"I was very young, and didn't understand all that was happening, but even so, I saw Maman's pain. My father, he was devastated." She smiled, sadly. "Mother is the heart of our home and without her joy, the whole palace became a tomb."

Casica looked down at her feet, stroking the memories which now flooded her. "We Cassicans mourn thirty days. My sister's burial was short of three weeks before my birthday. It was raining. It was awful. We all wore black. But in my childish way, what I truly mourned was knowing I wouldn't have birthday cake."

Casica dropped her grass, smiling softly at the unfolding memory. "The morning of my birthday, my mother woke me - tickling my nose with a carnation - I love carnations - ," she glanced at her companion, shyly. "I looked up and there Maman was, beaming at me, dressed full in her royal gowns - the ones she wore for celebrations. You should see my mother when she dresses as queen, Clarece. She rules.

"Anyway..." Josquin continued, "I was so surprised. The time of mourning hadn't ended, yet here was Maman, dressed for a party. And she was happy. She was truly happy. And since Maman was happy, Baba was happy, the whole palace was happy. I had a wonderful day...." The princess smiled brightly now, her eyes aglow with joy. "I received gifts - helped Berea with a healing - that was fun - played outside and in - went riding - took a nap and at the end of it all, had my favorite cake that Maman baked." The woman grew silent. Her eyes glistened with memory.

"It wasn't until the end of the day that I saw what it was truly like for my mother. She came into my room to kiss me goodnight. She had unbuttoned her vest and loosened her blouse, and it was then that I saw it." A hand went to her chest. "She was wearing a black camisole. Under all her festive dress, Maman mourned her dead daughter, my dead sister."

Casica closed her eyes and allowed a sorrow she felt at the most peculiar times. She still mourned this sister she never knew. She would have been Asla's age. Her heart ached. What would it have been like, she wondered for the countless time - to have shared life with Anasis? Would she recognize her in Heaven?

Clarece watched her mistra's tears. She was far away. "When I was older," Casica continued, softly, "I asked her about that day. I asked if she was really happy or if it were all an act. She said no, it wasn't an act. She truly had had a wonderful day with me. Maman said it was proper that she mourn the death of her daughter; but that it also, equally fitting she celebrate the life of her other." Casica harvested another blade of grass. She shook her head at what she next thought.

"My mother told me something I hope to never forget. She said, 'God is supreme and supremely good. And that gives us permission to dance on the way to a funeral and to eat cake in a house of mourning.'" The princess looked at her attentive friend. "My mother believes this is a friendly universe, truly. I've seen it so many times, the way she lives this. She might spend days healing someone only to have them die. And yet there'll be a smile in her tears. Nothing is ever despairing to her - sorrow, yes - but not despair." Casica smiled again. "Maman's heart is always moving forward. Like it's propelled by hope. I want to live like that," she concluded to herself.

The slave sat quietly, picturing the story, picturing her owner's mother. What a queen she must be. "I wish I could meet your mother," is what she said. Casica turned and looked strangely at her.

"You will someday," she said softly, picturing what only she could see. Clarece stared. There was an intensity about her mistra's words that made her uncomfortable. She pushed the statement away with a jest.

"What, are you a prophetess too, mistra?" she asked, teasing. "No," Casica smiled, shaking her head. "Just a healer. But I see things sometimes." Clarece glanced away from the look she saw. "Your Cassicanness obscures your vision, I think," she countered. "This is Byzanthia."

"So? Tis still part of God's kingdom," the young woman grinned at her companion. Clarece wore the expression that said she was teetering. "This is a hopeful world for you, Clarece d'Casica. You wait and see. Life will surprise you yet."

Clarece hated to acknowledge what she felt. Just hearing her mistra's words stirred something within her, uplifting the darkness in her heart. What Casica said felt like truth. But that was ridiculous, Clarece argued within herself. This was not a friendly place; she held a lifetime of evidence to disprove any other claim. "You make it sound as though God has friendly thoughts towards me," she sparred, ignoring the flutter of hope in her heart.

"He does, chief slaveswoman," came the expected reply. Clarece shook her head; this foreign woman would not be dissuaded. The slave of Byzanthia glared at her mistra with a mocking challenge: "When horses dance, my lady."

Casica looked away, rolling her eyes. *There goes that phrase again.* All right, she thought, nodding her head. The princess of Cassica snatched a handful of grass and tossed it playfully into the wind. Rising, she removed her vest and, as her curious friend watched, stretched luxuriously. She placed her hands on her hips. The friendly grin she flashed Clarece accepted her challenge, positively oozing good-natured defiance. *You're on!* It said.

The slave watched as her owner stepped into the meadow. Casica wondered if he would remember. They hadn't done this in a long time. Josquin clapped her hands twice. "Rigel!" she yelled.

The white horse stopped his grazing. His head jerked up expectantly. Was this what he thought it was? "Ki hasa ma hel! Mau kot'et k'nasa!" It *was* what he thought! The horse pranced, excited, to his owner. Casica addressed her friend. "We'll do this in Byzanthian - for your benefit."

Rigel stood before his mistress, expectantly. There she went. Casica stomped her left foot four times. Rigel bobbed his head as she did so. She followed her feet with four claps of her hands. At this, Rigel answered, pawing four times on the ground with his right hoof then bobbing his snowy mane four times. He reared fully, pawing the air as his lady began her song....

"Who's this mighty horse? His name is Rigel, great Rigel! He's the kingly horse who rides in majesty! Bowwww, low, yes, now, we bowwww low, we bow to Rigel! the rider of the nighttime sky...."

Clarece gaped. At Casica's "bowwww low," she bowed low, and as she did, the white horse stood on his back feet, and nodded his head royally. Her song continued.

"Dance to the left!" she called, stepping in a leftward circle in time with her music. Her partner joined her, prancing to his right. "Now prance to the right..." she laughed, producing a mirrored image of their steps. "Sash shay up," step, step, step. "Promenade home," step, step, step.

At her steps, the equestrian partner followed the princess, looking fully the part he played. He was a graceful dancer, Rigel.

"Who rides this royal steed?" Casica asked, raising her hands above her. The horse bowed, low... low. "I, the Queen of Life!" Bow... bow. The princess jigged playfully. "All the fillies get the thrillies at the sight of your white mane!"

The horse danced in kind, hopping, if it were possible, in place. The girl spun and announced, "You're the mighty horse! If you had balls, you would be in the halls. of. Stud. ly. fame!"

At this announcement, the mighty horse jumped, full into the air. He landed in perfect time for the song's conclusion. "Hail, Rigel!!!" The partners stood, panting. Then curtseyed and bowed to one another.

Clarece didn't realize she stood until now, now as she offered muffled applause to the pair. Casica turned and curtseyed again, her horsy partner bowing with her. The laughing girl embraced the sweaty neck of her Rigel. Clarece shook her head, astonished. Not only did horses dance, she now knew: they smiled. The image of her mistra dancing with her horse would never leave the slave, reminding her often of the woman after life had taken her away....

Casica approached, mischievously. "There, Queen Clarece," she bowed. "You see? You slaves have another phrase, I think," she smiled, catching her breath. "'It's not over, till the spoon hits wood.' Well, tis not nearly over for you. Just wait and see. There's still much you haven't tasted."

Clarece beamed with joy. The crushing darkness had left her, retreating sometime during Rigel's dance. How or where it went, she cared not. "I kneel corrected, my lady," she laughed, humbled. "I will yet give life time and dare to hope."

As she spoke the words, something deep within the woman moved. And in that moment, the slave allowed herself a risky grace: to question whether all the evidence in her life might be false. Her mind went to a massive orchestral score in the king's library. She was surprised to see that during the silence of some instruments, others played. A symphony could not be read in a single staff. Perhaps, thought Clarece, perhaps it was the gaps between the darkness she needed most intently to behold. Who knows what other music played?

On impulse, she embraced her laughing mistra. Casica stepped back. "I've soiled you with Rigel, I'm afraid," she apologized. "It matters not, lady," Clarece smiled. "I wash tomorrow."

Tomorrow. The grim realities of life would still be there tomorrow. Would be waiting for her what she returned to the palace today. But what she had experienced would not be denied. The healer reflected the tall slave's smile. "Come, my friend," Josquin invited. "Let's care for your hands."

The two queens approached their wooden throne, ascending, as they did, futures only The Edict could imagine. The past was coming.

# About the Author

Life is made of people. As an educator, I've been blessed to know many extraordinary people. In classrooms of Africa, factories in South Carolina, drug rehabilitation centers, and a private counseling practice in Colorado, I have witnessed the transformative power of love and hope. In this new series, it is my desire to explore contemporary issues in a fantasy setting. I know, personally, what it is like to be freed from bondage and death. It is my hope that as you enter the world of Casica Elespoir, you will be inspired to pursue greater freedom and Life for yourself.

I am a graduate of Louisiana State University (B.M.E.) and Colorado Christian University (M.A.). Currently, I serve as schoolmarm for Nathanael and AnnaMarie, my children. Along with my husband, Kyle, we live on a small farm in beautiful rural Virginia.

Please let me hear from you at Martha@cassicanpress.com.

Thank you for reading and remember: horses dance....

*Martha J. Vaught*

Next in the *Cassican Chronicles* Series: *Clarece d'Casica, Queen of Slaves*

www.ingramcontent.com/pod-product-compliance
Lightning Source LLC
Chambersburg PA
CBHW020251200626

46816CB00001BA/245